A GUITAR NAMED SWAMPY

A NOVEL

U-NAM

Swampy Tales

A Guitar Named Swampy

Published by Swampy Tales Publishing

an imprint of *Swampy Tales Entertainment*

From Paris to Texas: Songs from A Guitar Named Swampy—An Original Soundtrack

© 2025 Skytown Records, a division of Swampy Tales Entertainment

All songs (lyrics & music) © 2024 Emmanuel "U-Nam" Abiteboul

Published by Music by Skytown Publishing (BMI), a division of Swampy Tales Entertainment

Used by permission of Music by Skytown Publishing

For more information, visit: u-nam.com and swampytales.com

First Edition: 2025

ISBN: 979-8-9990036-0-7 (Paperback edition)

Cover Design, Book Design & Artwork Concept: U-Nam

Printed in the United States of America

DISCLAIMER

This story is a work of fiction. Characters, incidents, and
dialogues portrayed are products of the author's imagination.
Although inspired by real-life experiences,
any resemblance to real people, alive or dead, or actual events is
purely coincidental.

And if by any chance you think you recognize yourself or
something—
well, shit happens.

DEDICATION

To my two sons, the greatest notes in my song.

To everyone who ever believed — and to those who didn't.

You all made this possible.

And to all the survivors.

PROLOGUE

We were—I was—on top of the world, living the dream. Music, success, family, love, and happiness —a life's purpose.

Until it all collapsed, and everything was taken from me.

This is how it happened. The beginning of the end—and the start of something I never *expected*.

ACT 1

1

THE DISCOVERY

T*hanksgiving.* It's just another day when you're on
your own.

The morning sun crawled its way across the
cracked horizon, painting the dry Texas earth in shades of
orange and gold. The kind of beauty you appreciate when you
don't have much else to hold on to. I'd fed the horses, fixed a
busted fence by the north pasture, and made myself a pot of
black coffee so bitter it could scrape the rust off a truck.

The silence of this place never used to bother me. Out here,
it's just you, the land, and the wind. *No traffic, no noise—no people.*
Some days, that's a blessing. But today... well, today it feels like a
curse.

Thanksgiving used to mean something. Family around the
table, friends dropping by, laughter that filled up the house.
These days, it's just me and the ghosts of all I've lost.

So, I saddled up Buck—my old roan who's seen better days
but still has some spirit left—and decided to ride. If I wasn't

going to sit around feeling sorry for myself, I might as well let the land remind me why I chose this lonely life.

We headed south past the ridge where the mesquites grow thick, and the desert opens up wide like a canvas waiting for something to happen. The air was crisp, cooler than usual, and smelled faintly of sagebrush and dust. Buck's hooves crunched against the dry earth, a steady rhythm that matched the beat of my own thoughts. It wasn't until we'd gone farther than usual that I noticed something off.

At the start, it was the smell—*wet, earthy, and rich,* like rain-soaked soil. Out here in the desert, that scent is as rare as a kind word from an old, *lonesome cowboy.*

Then I saw it—a thin haze curling low over the ground, softening the edges of the desert like a mirage come to life.

I heard it next: a whispering trickle of water, calling me to come closer.

I pulled back on the reins, and Buck snorted, his ears flicking toward the sound.

"Easy, boy," I muttered, scanning the horizon.

Sure enough, there it was—a patch of green in the distance, shimmering in the heat.

It didn't make any sense. I've ridden this land for years. There ain't no swamp out here.

Curiosity got the better of me and we wandered closer. The humidity thickened as we got closer, wrapping around me like a heavy shroud. Even the air itself had changed—the kind that sticks to your skin and makes you feel like you've stepped into another world. Cattails swayed lazily in the breeze, and patches of moss clung to gnarled trees that twisted toward the sky.

And there it was, half-submerged in the murky water.

At first, I thought it was an alligator—motionless, green, and covered in moss. But the shape was wrong. Too angular, too deliberate.

—A guitar.

It looked like a Telecaster. But that didn't make any damn sense.

My breath caught as I took another step, the swampy earth sucking at my boots. My heart began to race—not fear, not excitement, but something deeper. *Recognition.*

And then, like a crack in a dam, the memories came flooding back.

The spotlight was hot and blinding, the crowd a roaring ocean of faces I could barely make out. My fingers danced across the strings of my Tele, the one that had paved the way, from dive bars and backroad gigs to the kind of stardom I never saw coming.

I could still feel the hum of the amp, the weight of the guitar against my body, and the way the music seemed to flow through me like a river.

And then I saw *her.*

She wasn't cheering like the others. No, she was just... *watching.* Quiet, focused, with a half-smile that felt like it could see through every wall I'd ever built.

Marie.

Of course, I didn't know her name back then. Didn't know who she was or why that look stayed with me long after the show ended. Hell, I wouldn't even meet her until a year later at some diner halfway across the country. But in that moment, on that stage, it felt like the world had shifted just enough for her to slip into view.

"You remember every face you've ever played for, don't you?" she'd tease me, years later, when I told her about that night.

"No," I said, brushing a strand of her hair behind her ear.

"Just yours."

Buck shifted and tugged at the reins, impatient, snapping me out of it—before I drifted too far.

And here I was, standing rooted in the middle of the swamp, staring down at a moss-covered guitar like it was a ghost. I swallowed hard, my throat dry as the desert beyond this impossible patch of water. It couldn't be the same guitar. That was impossible. My beloved Telecaster had been smashed to pieces on a night I couldn't bring myself to think about.

But this... this guitar wasn't a ghost.

It was *real*.

And somehow, it felt like a buried treasure—waiting for me all this time, just to be *found*.

2

BRINGING THE GUITAR HOME

Right by the time I got back to the ranch, the sky was painted with deep shades of orange and pink, the kind of sunset that almost made the loneliness feel worth it. Almost.

Buck snorted as we reached the yard, his breath fogging in the cool evening air. I slid off the saddle, the weight of the guitar slung over my shoulder like it might slip away if I didn't keep hold of it.

The old ranch loomed ahead, its paint peeling and shutters creaking in the breeze. It wasn't much, but it was mine—a sanctuary from the world I'd left behind.

I stepped into the workshop, the familiar scent of sawdust and oil greeting me like an old friend. The place hadn't seen much use lately. A few projects abandoned mid-way, tools scattered on the bench. And now, there it was—sitting on the workbench under the dim light, waiting for me to decide what to do next.

I laid it down carefully, brushing off some of the dried moss that clung stubbornly to its body. Yep, it was a *Telecaster*—or at least, it used to be.

I could see the faint outline of its iconic shape beneath the wear and grime. The few strings left were rusted and frayed—curling like dead vines, stretched and twisted like old barbed wire across the warped bridge—but the neck still held its curve, like it hadn't given up just yet.

As I scrubbed away the last of the moss and grime, the wood of the body started to show through, bare and raw. The paint and polish were mostly gone, stripped away by water damage and time, leaving behind the naked grain of the wood.

Well... got me wondering how crazy it is, living in a world where you might have to sell your house to buy a brand-new *"heavy relic."* Anyway. Go figure.

Just then, I froze, staring at it, my breath catching in surprise.

"Well, I'll be damned," I muttered.

"Swamp ash."

The texture of the grain, the way it shimmered faintly under the light—it brought me back to another time, another place.

Back then, I wasn't even in the States. I was still in France, working as a rookie door-to-door salesman to scrape by while I chased a dream most people didn't believe in. I'd been lugging my feet through cobblestone streets all day, the kind of day where the sun beats down just enough to make you sweat but not enough to make it worth complaining.

It was a small village tucked in the countryside, the kind of place where time moves slower and everyone knows your name, except for me, the outsider with a bag of useless things to sell.

I'd knocked on door after door, the rhythm of rejection becoming almost routine. Most folks weren't interested—a few polite *non, merci* here and there, but mostly doors slammed in my face.

I was just about ready to call it quits when I came to this old house a little outside the main village. The garden was over-grown, the shutters weathered, but the place had a *charm* to it—like it had seen years of stories.

An older woman answered the door, her eyes bright and kind, though lined with the weight of time.

"Come in," she said, smiling.

"I'd love to hear what you're selling. And besides, I could use a coffee."

It was clear she didn't really care about what I had to offer, but I wasn't about to turn down a bit of kindness—or the chance to make a few bucks.

Inside, the house smelled of lavender and old wood, and she poured us both cups of coffee as we sat down across from each other.

We talked about my job, the people I'd met, the villages I'd seen. But when she asked why I was doing this work, I told her the truth: I was just paying the bills.

"What I really want," I said,

"is to make a living as an artist. A musician. A guitar player. I want to tour the world someday and move to America."

She smiled at that, a wistful sort of smile, like she was thinking about something far away.

"Wait here," she said, standing up.

"I'll be right back."

The stairs creaked softly as she ascended, the wood worn smooth from years of use. I sat there, sipping my coffee, as the minutes stretched on. The silence began to feel heavier, and to distract myself, I let my eyes wander.

A crocheted runner lined the steps, its edges fraying, and on the wall beside it hung a collection of old black-and-white photographs—smiling faces frozen in time. The living room itself was cluttered but cozy. A small table near the window held a lamp with a fringed shade, its light casting a soft glow over a pile of dog-eared books. A china cabinet stood in the corner, its glass doors smudged but still offering a glimpse of delicate teacups and plates with intricate floral patterns.

As my eyes roamed, they landed on a big painting across the room—something I hadn't noticed at first. It dominated the far wall, framed in ornate, gilded wood. The painting showed a woman standing against a soft, undefined backdrop, her white dress glowing softly as if lit from within. Her long dark hair framed a face that was calm, serene, and strangely haunting. There was a lightness to her expression, a kind of quiet knowing that felt both comforting and unsettling.

I leaned forward, my cup forgotten in my hand, and stared at it. There was something about her that held me in place, like she was watching over the room, over everything, in a way that felt *almost alive*—almost ethereal.

The sound of footsteps on the stairs broke my trance, and I quickly straightened as the old woman reappeared, carrying a worn black case. She set it on the table and flipped the latches.

Inside was the most beautiful Telecaster I'd ever seen. Pristine, with a body of golden swamp ash that shimmered in the light.

I was speechless.

"Is this... yours?"

"No," she said, her voice soft.

"It was my husband's. I gave it to him for our anniversary. But... he passed away before he could really play it. It's too hard for me to keep it, and I don't see many people out here, let alone musicians."

She pushed the case toward me.

"I want you to have it."

I shook my head, my heart racing.

"I... I can't. I can't afford this."

She smiled with soft insistence.

"It's not about money. I see something in you, young man. You

have a dream, and this was my husband's dream too. Let this be my contribution to it, my way of honoring his memory."

Her words hit me like a freight train. I wanted to argue, to tell her I wasn't worthy, but she wouldn't take *no* for an answer. She closed the case and placed it in my hands.

Even then, I couldn't take it for free. I reached into my pocket, pulling out all the cash I had on me—it wasn't much, just enough for a meal or two—and handed it to her.

"Please," I said.

"Let me give you something. I need to feel like I earned this. For my own peace of mind."

She hesitated for a moment, then took the money with a small nod.

"Alright," she said.

"But promise me you'll use it to chase your dream."

"I will," I said, my voice barely above a whisper.

That Telecaster became my world after that. Every note I played felt like a promise to her and her husband. It was more than just a guitar—it was a piece of someone's story, entrusted to me to carry forward.

The memory faded, but the feeling stayed with me. That Telecaster had been my world for years, the thing that carried me through every stage, every song.

But this one, was it really a *Fender?*

There was only one way to know for sure.

Grabbing a screwdriver, I loosened the bolts and pried the neck free, lifting it carefully.

The entire stamp was worn, the ink barely hanging on, almost completely erased. But still, I could make out a few things.

And there it was.

Fender. Made in USA.

Wow. Definitely a workhorse. Built to last.

Now, as I ran my hand over the bare wood of this new guitar, it felt like a piece of that old life had found its way back to me.

"Hi, Swampy," I said aloud.

The sound of my own voice startled me, and I chuckled under my breath.

"Swampy? That's... childish," I said with a laugh, shaking my head.

Maybe it was. Maybe it was just one of those things you start doing when you're old and alone—talking to objects, giving names to things that can't talk back.

I'd never named a guitar in my life.

Hell, I'd owned dozens—some of the finest instruments a player could dream of—but not one of them had ever felt like it needed a name.

Until now.

And somehow, it felt right. Like it was meant to be.

Swampy.

3

HEADING TO TOWN

U ntil now, I hadn't realized just how much the ranch had started to feel more like a cage than home, like the walls were closing in on me. The endless expanse of the Chihuahuan Desert just outside my door should've made it feel the opposite, but lately, even the wide-open spaces felt stifling.

So when I needed to pick up a few supplies in town, I figured it wouldn't hurt to make a day of it—stretch my legs, get out of my own head for a while.

The drive was uneventful, the desert sprawling out for miles in every direction. Low scrub mesquite and creosote bushes dotted the land, while the occasional yucca stood like a sentinel against the horizon. The sun blazed overhead, casting scorching heatwaves on the distant two-lane highway. This was the kind of land that tested you, made you earn your right to stay. Some days, I felt like I was just barely passing.

The town wasn't much to look at—a tiny, rural western place with one main street, where the hardware store shares a

building with the post office, and everybody knows your name...
even if you wish they didn't.

After picking up the replacement parts I'd ordered for the
tractor and a week's worth of canned goods, I decided to stop by
Joe's for a beer and maybe a bite to eat.

The bar was quiet, the smell of fried food and stale beer
hanging in the air. A few regulars sat at the counter, swapping
stories that probably weren't half as interesting as they thought.
I found a seat at the end of the bar, ordered a Bud and a burger,
and let the background noise wash over me.

That's when I saw it: a poster tacked up on the corkboard by
the jukebox.

OPEN MIC NIGHT – ALL WELCOME
Friday 6:30 PM

The words jumped out at me like they were lit up in neon.
Beneath them was a drawing of a guitar, scrawled in bold black
marker, and a tagline that read:

Got a song in your heart? Bring it and share it.

I stared at the poster, the words swimming in my head.
An open mic night.
"First time hearing about it?"
I turned to see Joe, the owner, a guy in his fifties with a
graying ponytail and a face that had probably seen more fights
than birthdays. He nodded toward the poster as he slid my beer
across the counter.
"Yeah," I said, taking a sip.
"Didn't know this place had live music."
"We didn't, not until recently," Joe said, leaning on the bar.
"Town's been growing, you know. More folks moving in, more

ideas floating around. Somebody suggested we try live music—get people together, give 'em something to look forward to. Once in a while, we get a local band, maybe someone from out of town, but this open mic thing? That's new. Figured it'd be a good way to get folks out of their houses. A lot of people around here got guitars, banjos, fiddles, or even mandolins collecting dust, or songs they've been too shy to share. Thought it'd be fun."

"*Sounds... ambitious,*" I said, my voice half-lost in my drink.

Joe chuckled.

"*Maybe. But you'd be surprised. Folks around here, they got stories, songs. They just need a reason to share 'em.*"

"Mm. Yeah, I guess so," I said, drifting my eyes back to the poster.

A reason to share.

The thought stuck with me as I finished my beer and my burger, sitting there in the quiet hum of the bar. I hadn't played in front of anyone in ages.

Hell, I'd picked up the guitar again recently—nothing serious, just enough to kill time when the boredom got too heavy, and maybe remind me what it used to feel like.

But something about this—the open mic, the idea of sharing again—was pulling at me, almost against my will.

Like something inside me was waking up, even though I'd sworn I was done with it all.

I didn't know if I was ready.

But maybe I didn't need to be.

4

THE RIDE BACK

Though I wasn't in a rush to get back, I loaded the supplies into the truck and headed back home. Desert sunsets had a way of making you lose track of time, the sky already on fire, stretching long shadows across the dirt road.

The drive was slow, the kind of pace you keep when you don't really want to get anywhere too fast.

And that damn poster tacked up by the jukebox? I couldn't get it out of my head.

An open mic night.

I'd never been much for open mics, even back in the day. I preferred a stage, a setlist, a crowd that knew what they'd paid for. But there was something about the idea, something about the way Joe talked about bringing people together.

And then there was *Swampy*.

Ever since I'd pulled that guitar out of the swamp and brought it back to life, I'd been playing again. Not much—just bits and pieces when the mood struck—but enough to remind me of what it felt like. My fingers were a little rusty, sure, but it was still there, that spark, that connection.

Swampy felt *alive* in my hands, like it had been waiting all these years for someone to wake it up.

Every time I played, it was like a piece of me I thought was lost was coming back, note by note.

The thought of standing up there at that open mic, playing in front of a crowd again... it was equal parts terrifying and thrilling.

By the time I pulled into the driveway, the sky was streaked with purples and golds, and the first stars were starting to show. I turned off the engine and sat there for a moment, staring out at the fading light.

The last time I played in front of a *crowd...*

5

NO ENCORE

eat me like hell.

Blinding lights. Hotter than I'd remembered. Deafening noise as the crowd roared, a wall of sound that drowned out my own thoughts. I stood there on the stage, my Telecaster hanging heavy against my hip, its neck slippery in my trembling hands. I'd played hundreds of shows, thousands of songs, but tonight felt different.

Not better. Not worse.

Just... *wrong.*

Marie wasn't by my side.

Hell, she wasn't *anywhere.*

The plan had been for her to join me, like always. She'd said she wasn't feeling well, that she just needed to rest a bit and would catch up later. She told me to go ahead, take care of soundcheck, and she'd be there in time for the show. I had gotten used to having her on stage—even though she wasn't officially part of the *Sweet Bandits*, she had found her way in.

At first, she'd just tagged along, traveling with me as my girlfriend. Then, without me even noticing, she started slipping onto the stage beside me—smiling sweetly, as if she'd been invited. She began singing background vocals here and there, just enough to blend in. But before long, she was pushing for more—more lead parts, more spotlight. And before I knew it, she had made herself a part of every gig, every appearance—insisting gently at first, then more firmly. It wasn't long before she implied that things between us would suffer if she wasn't there, that we were inseparable.

I never wanted the *drama,* so I let it happen. And I was fine with it.

I was so *blindly in love.*

But this time, she wasn't there—only, she never showed.

Right before we took the stage. I'd called. I'd texted. No response. I asked around, and someone from the crew said, *"I heard she left the hotel in a cab earlier."*

The hotel was just a few blocks away—no sirens, no emergency calls.

Nothing. So...

Still, somehow, the music didn't feel the same without her there.

It wasn't just her voice, or the way she lit up the stage—maybe it was just the damn habit of having her with me.

And now, with no real lead singer up there, the whole set was fucked.

Fuck. I never should've fired Kota.

That regret hit me like a punch to the gut. Damn fool, that's what I was.

At least then, we wouldn't be drowning in this fucking mess.

We were winging it—shuffling the set list on the fly, stretching solos, trying to make it look like it was all part of the show.

But it wasn't.

It was *damage control.*

The crowd cheered as we launched into the next number, their energy pressing against me like a wall. My fingers moved automatically, hitting the chords I'd played a thousand times before, but my heart wasn't in it.

The band was tight, sure, but I could feel their eyes on me, their unspoken questions hanging in the air.

What's wrong with him?

What was wrong with me?

The last chord rang out, and the crowd roared, but it didn't touch me.

There would be *no encore* tonight.

I turned my back on them, walking off the stage without a word.

Backstage was chaos—roadies rushing around, bandmates packing up, the hum of voices and equipment filling the air. But all I could hear was my own voice, echoing in my head.

You're not losing the music.

You're losing *yourself.*

And you're *losing her.*

My Tele was still strapped across my shoulder, its weight pulling me down like an anchor. I ripped it off and threw it onto the couch, its body landing with a dull thud. The sound reverberated in my chest—a cruel reminder of everything I'd built and destroyed.

Then I snapped.

I grabbed the guitar by its neck and swung it against the edge of the table. The crash was deafening, the wood splintering under the force. I swung again, and again, until the body was nothing but shards and fragments on the floor.

No one said a *word.*

I didn't stick around.

The after-show chaos, the looks, the tension—I didn't care. I grabbed my jacket, downed one last drink, and left.

By the time I got back to the hotel, I was exhausted. Everything felt heavy—my body, my head, my goddamn soul. All I wanted was to crash, to let sleep dull the edges of everything that had gone wrong tonight.

But as soon as I stepped inside, I knew something was off.

The room was *cold.*

Too *clean.*

Too *empty.*

I called her name.

No *answer.*

I checked the bathroom. The closet. Her suitcase.

Gone.

Marie was gone.

6

ON THE PORCH

With my coffee cold and my nerves shot, I set the mug down. My thoughts had been running in circles all morning, chasing the same questions, the same doubts.

The open mic night felt like a challenge I wasn't ready for—but maybe that was the point.

Swampy leaned against the wall, catching the sunlight. It almost seemed to glow, the bare wood reflecting shades of warmth I hadn't noticed before.

Before I could overthink it, I grabbed the guitar and headed out to the porch.

The chair creaked under me as I settled in, Swampy resting across my lap. The breeze brought the earthy drift of sagebrush, cool and steady, while the heat of the sun warmed the weathered boards beneath my feet.

My fingers hovered over the strings, hesitating before plucking out a few notes. The new ones I'd strung up still felt a little stiff, but the sound was there—clear and warm, like the guitar was waking up alongside me.

I hadn't planned to play, *not really*. I'd picked Swampy up just to check the tuning—or maybe just to feel a presence—but one chord turned into two, then into a tune I hadn't touched in years.

Each note felt unfamiliar at first, rusty, like I was trying to remember a language I used to speak fluently.

Music had a way of sneaking up on you like that.

I leaned back, letting the notes drift out into the quiet morning. It wasn't much—a simple blues riff, the kind of thing I could've played in my sleep back in the day. My hands stumbled here and there, but as it took shape, I started to feel it again.

That passion, that vibe—subtle but *unmistakable*.

The memory of the last show tugged at the edges of my mind, sharp and painful like an old scar.

But this... this was different. It didn't feel like trying to recapture something lost. It was more like discovering something *new*.

I stopped playing for a moment, staring down at the guitar. The wood caught the light just right, its grain swirling like waves frozen in time.

"*Swampy,*" I murmured, brushing the neck with a slow touch.

The name still felt strange, almost silly. But as I sat there, the guitar in my hands and the music still buzzing in my veins, it felt right. Like the guitar and I were rebuilding each other, piece by piece.

The thought of the open mic crossed my mind again, and my chest tightened. The idea of standing in front of people—of sharing music again—was terrifying.

But it also felt like a *challenge*.

Like the universe was daring me to take that first step.

I looked out at the horizon, where the fields stretched endlessly, the sun slowly burning through the morning haze.

My fingers paused there, resting gently on the wood.

The way I used to rest my hand on her belly, without a word —just *listening.*

7

FEELING THE FIRST KICK

As the tour had wrapped up and our last shows were behind us, we were at home, just the *two of us*.

The quiet of the house felt strange after so many months on the road. Marie was sitting on the well-loved couch, her belly just starting to show beneath the loose fabric of her dress.

I had my guitar in hand, strumming softly as we worked through the melody of a new song.

It wasn't much yet—just an idea, a spark, something we thought might become beautiful.

She was humming along, her voice soft but sure, finding the harmonies like she always did.

"Hold that note," I said, my fingers dancing across the fretboard.

"Right there. That's the one."

She laughed, her eyes lighting up as she leaned closer.

"You think this is going to be the one?"

"I know it is," I said, smiling back at her.

We sang together, the words coming easier with each pass.

The music filled the room, wrapping around us like a warm blanket. It felt good, effortless. Like the kind of moment you don't realize is special until it's already gone.

And then she stopped.

"Wait."

Her hand suddenly on her belly.

I paused mid-strum, the sound cutting off abruptly.

"What? What's wrong?"

Her face softened, her lips parting in a quiet gasp.

"I felt something," she said, her voice barely above a whisper.

"What do you mean?"

Her eyes met mine, wide and *shining.*

"Here," she said, grabbing my hand and placing it gently on her belly.

"Do you feel it?"

I held my breath, my fingers splayed across the curve of her stomach.

And then I felt it—soft but *undeniable*, like a tiny knock from the inside.

"He's moving," she said, her voice trembling with wonder.

"Do you feel it? He's moving."

For a moment, everything else faded away. The song, the guitar, the weight of the world outside that room—it all disappeared.

It was just the *three of us.*

The memory shattered like glass, snapping me back into the present so hard I almost knocked over the damn chair. My hands gripped the edges like I was holding on for dear life, my breath coming in sharp, uneven bursts.

Tears were already there—hot, uninvited, unstoppable.

I didn't even try to wipe them away.

The weight of it all—the *joy*, the *loss*, the unbearable ache of everything that came after—slammed into me like a wrecking ball. I buried my face in my hands, letting the sobs wrack through me.

The breeze stirred, bringing a wisp of sage and a stillness that felt older than the land itself.

When I finally blinked through the tears, my gaze fell to Swampy, resting across my lap.

A single drop slid from my cheek, landing on the wood, catching the light like a tiny crystal.

My hand drifted to the neck, gripping it gently—and for a moment, it felt like the guitar was holding something deeper, something just beneath the surface, waiting to rise.

Something stirred inside me. Not loud or clear—just a flicker, like a spark catching in dry tinder.

Warm and fleeting, like something I wasn't ready to name.

I froze, my fingers tightening around the neck. The feeling lingered, faint but steady, threading through me like a whisper.

It was subtle, but it coursed through my veins, quiet but powerful, like the first notes of a song you didn't realize you needed to hear.

The intensity swelled, the music and memories colliding in my chest, and before I could stop myself, the words slipped out.

"Not maybe," I said, my voice trembling but resolute.

I looked at Swampy, its grain glowing softly in the morning light.

"I'll give it a try. For you. For us."

The air around me seemed to still, thick with unspoken meaning, as if even the world was holding its breath.

It wasn't a promise, not yet.

But it was enough to pull me out of the past and back into the present, one small step closer to the person I used to be—and the person I'd hoped to become *again.*

8

LIFE AT THE RANCH

Since out here, days passed slow as molasses, one bleeding into the next until I couldn't tell you what day it was if I tried. Not that it mattered much anyway.

Most of my time was spent with the horses. Folks came from all over for training or breeding, and I made decent money from it. Enough to keep the ranch running, take care of my booze, and keep a bottle of Good Ol' Jack on the shelf for when I needed a stronger kick. Horses were honest, predictable creatures—much easier to handle than people.

That morning, I stood by the paddock, leaning on the old fence while a young colt pranced around, its legs too long for its own good. His mama followed close behind, her movements smooth as butter.

"Easy now," I murmured, not that they needed to hear it.

They had their own rhythm, their own way of making sense of the world.

By the time I finished up my work in the paddock and the barn, the sun was hanging low in the sky, casting long shadows across the yard. The horses were settled, and my body ached in that familiar way, a dull reminder of the years.

I headed back toward the house, brushing the dust off my jeans. Swampy was propped up in the corner of my bedroom, where I'd left it earlier. Lately, I'd started keeping it close, almost like I didn't trust it to sit too far away.

After washing up, I cracked open a beer in the kitchen—the cool bite hitting just right after a day like that. I leaned against the counter, took a long sip, and stared out the window into the quiet.

Some evenings, the beer was enough. But not *tonight*.

Nights like this, when the quiet felt heavier than usual and the loneliness crept in no matter how much I tried to ignore it, *Good Ol' Jack* was my go-to. I grabbed the bottle from the shelf above the sink, setting it down with a thunk.

"*Yep,*" I muttered, turning the bottle in my hands,

"*Good Ol' Jack, always there for me with his Good Ol' stories.*"

Stories I made up half the time—funny ones, strange ones, anything to fill the silence. The kind of stories that kept me warm when the hours dragged on, slow and *lonesome*.

I wandered to the porch, the whiskey in one hand and Swampy in the other. The breeze had cooled, crisp against my skin, and the stars above looked sharp enough to cut.

I sat down on my old wooden rocking chair, the guitar resting across my lap.

As my hands brushed over the strings and the worn wood, I felt it again—that soothing vibration, like Swampy was humming its own tune even before I started playing.

It felt good, right, like it wanted me to keep playing, to find whatever was buried in there.

Or maybe it was just the *booze*.

I let out a dry laugh, shaking my head.

Whatever it was, I wasn't about to question it *tonight*.

9

THE OPEN MIC DAY

H*ere we go.* The big day had arrived.

Yeah, *big day*—right. Just a small open mic in a middle-of-nowhere desert town bar, but somehow it loomed over me like it was the damn Goldies.

I'd spent the whole week getting ready.

Not for the music, no. The ranch.

I'd worked sunup to sundown, making sure every chore, every loose end, was tied up tight. The horses were fed, stalls cleaned, fences mended. There wasn't a thing left that needed doing.

You'd think I was heading out on a month-long trip the way I was running around. But the truth was, staying busy was the only way to keep the nerves at bay.

And as the clock ticked closer to evening, I kept finding new reasons to bail.

"Too tired," I muttered, rubbing the back of my neck as I stood in the kitchen.

"What's the point? No one cares about me, let alone wants to hear some old washed-up musician. I'd rather share some good stories with Ol' Jack."

The excuses came easy—too easy.

I sat down, staring at the counter. The thought of getting in that truck, driving to town, walking into a room full of people, and pulling out Swampy... It all felt too big.

That's when I heard it. A soft *thud.*

I looked up and saw Swampy lying on the floor, just beneath where it had been propped against the wall. The guitar hadn't hit hard—more like she had just tipped over, sliding down like she was trying to get my attention.

And there it was, lying on top of a picture frame. A picture I hadn't seen in years. I walked over and picked it up, brushing the dust off the glass. The boy in the photo stared back at me, his blond curls catching the sunlight, a tiny toy guitar clutched in his little hands.

I swallowed hard, my throat tightening as I held the frame. A single tear rolled down my cheek, hitting the glass with a soft plink.

"I know," I whispered, the sound catching in my throat.

"I made a promise. For you. For us."

I set the picture down and reached for Swampy, my fingers brushing over the worn wood. The vibrations hummed faintly, just like they always did, but tonight, something felt different—stronger, clearer, like a pulse I couldn't ignore.

It was like Swampy knew. Like she was calling me, reminding me that some words are meant to be kept, even the ones you wish you could forget.

Something in me steadied, the doubts fading just enough to push me forward.

I didn't think about it after that. I grabbed the case, slid Swampy inside, and headed for the truck.

By the time I pulled out onto the road, the sun was setting low, casting the sky in gold and purple. Town wasn't far, but the drive felt longer than usual, the weight of what I was about to do pressing down on me.

But I'd made a promise. And tonight, I was going to *keep it.*

10

AT JOE'S

I almost turned around when I pulled into Joe's parking lot, gravel crunching under the truck's tires.

It was *damn full.* Packed like a sardine can!

For a moment, I just sat there, staring at the glowing neon sign above the door. It gave off a faint buzz in the cool night air, the sound almost lost beneath the distant murmur of conversation and the occasional laugh spilling out from inside.

I wasn't expecting this many cars.

My hand hovered over the key in the ignition, temptation tugging at me to just turn around and head home.

But I'd made a *promise.*

Pushing the door open, I grabbed Swampy, snug in its case, and climbed out, my boots grinding against the gravel. The hum of voices grew louder as I stepped inside, and I froze for a second, taking in the scene.

The place was packed. Tables were full, groups of people standing wherever they could find space. Glasses clinked, bursts of chatter rising and falling under the low crackle of a PA system coming to life.

The air reeked of the usual funk—cheap beer, grease, and the ghost of a thousand cigarettes. My boots creaked across the warped wooden floor as I made my way to the bar.

Joe was behind the counter, his graying ponytail catching the light as he wiped down a glass. He looked up when I approached, his sharp eyes narrowing slightly in recognition.

"Evening, Joe," I said, setting Swampy's case gently down against the bar.

"How's this work?"

Joe gestured toward the far end of the counter.

"Sign-up sheet's over there. Just write your name down, and when your turn comes, they'll call you up."

I followed his nod to a sheet of paper clipped to a clipboard, already half-filled with scrawled names.

I hesitated.

"It's, uh, more crowded than I expected."

Joe let out a low chuckle, leaning on the bar.

"Yeah, it's been picking up. Used to be just the locals, but now we're getting folks from all over. Word gets around, I guess. People like having something to come together for."

I drew a slow breath, gripping the worn handle of Swampy's case as I took in the crowd. The thought of standing in front of them made my chest tighten, but there was something about the energy in the room—electric, expectant—that pulled at me.

"Better get on that list," Joe said, a small grin tugging at the corner of his mouth.

"Won't be long before it fills up."

11

WAITING FOR MY TURN

Damn right. Guess word got out fast. Joe wasn't just blowing smoke after all.

I scribbled **Jesse L.** on the sign-up sheet, my hand hovering for a second before I set the pen down. The list was already half-full, names scrawled in all sorts of handwriting. A quick glance told me there were plenty of folks ahead of me.

I exhaled slowly, stepping back toward the bar.

"Bud," I said to Joe, sliding a crumpled bill across the counter.

He slid the cold Bud over with practiced ease, giving me a quick nod before turning back to the next customer. Swampy's case dangled from my hand as I scanned the place. I wasn't much for crowds, and this one didn't make it easy to find a spot out of the way.

Eventually, I found a dim corner near the edge of the room, as far from the main stage as I could manage. It wasn't completely out of sight, but it would do.

I settled into the shadows, keeping my head down and my drink close.

As the open mic got underway, it didn't take long for the characters to start crawling out of the woodwork.

The house band was decent—better than I'd expected for a setup like this. They played a tight groove, trying to follow each performer, but some folks made it a challenge.

There was a young girl, maybe twenty, with a sweet face and a voice that couldn't find the right key if it had a map. She smiled through it, though, blissfully unaware of the train wreck happening behind her.

Then there were the attention seekers. A guy in a flashy shirt trying to work the crowd more than the mic, gesturing wildly as he butchered a classic tune. The musicians did their best to keep up, exchanging amused glances as they covered his mistakes.

And then, there was this old dude with a harmonica. He shuffled to the mic, his hands shaking slightly, but the moment he started playing, the room fell silent. He howled out bluesy, soulful licks that felt like they came from somewhere deep, someplace most people couldn't reach—something raw and anchored in the land, like old roots twisting through plowed dirt, holding tight.

Laying down a soft rhythm that let his harp shine, the band followed him with reverence. I couldn't help but nod along, tapping my finger against the neck of my bottle. That man had lived through some things—you could hear it in every note.

But the quiet didn't last long. The next performer jumped on stage with more energy than skill, and the poor guys behind him scrambled to hold things together again.

I drained the last of my beer, the cold condensation lingering on my fingers.

"*Next on the list,*" the bandleader called out, glancing at the clipboard in his hand.

"*Jesse L.? Is Jesse L. here?*"

My chest tightened as the room fell still, like the world around me had hit the pause button.

I took a deep breath, grabbed Swampy's case, and stepped out of the dark corner.

"Yeah," I said, my voice carrying just enough to be heard.

The bandleader nodded, gesturing toward the small stage.

I could feel the eyes on me as I walked, my boots dragging like they were moving through sand. Each step brought me closer to the end of the tunnel, and the spotlight ahead seemed brighter than I remembered.

This was it.

12

SMALL STAGE, BIG FRIGHTS

Don't they say—*eyes don't lie?*

Yeah, right! Eyes do lie after all!

I swear the stage shrunk the second I stepped on it—looked a hell of a lot bigger from the other side. Just enough room for the band and a single mic.

Cold feet, stage fright—turns out, even the stage itself wasn't immune.

The bright light overhead cast long shadows, making it hard to see past the first few rows of tables.

I set Swampy's case down and flicked the latches open. As I pulled the guitar out, I caught a few looks from the guys and some of the folks closest to the stage.

A couple of smirks.

One guy leaned over to whisper to his buddy, his eyes fixed on Swampy's worn, bare wood—weathered and raw, a far cry from those shiny, polished showroom queens everyone loves to flash around.

The bandleader stepped closer, giving the guitar a quick once-over before clearing his throat.

"What are we playing tonight?"

I adjusted the strap on my shoulder, letting Swampy rest against my side.

"You guys know this old tune From Paris to Texas? It was a big hit back in the day. By that Frenchy guy."

He frowned for a second, then glanced back at the others. The bass player shrugged, and the drummer gave a little shake of his head, clicking his sticks together even without thinking.

Shit. *Great.*

Step one of public humiliation: choose the one song that screams *has-been.*

And then—boom—surprise. The guitarist perked up.

"Wait, you mean the one from Frenchy and The Sweet Bandits? Yeah, I know it!"

"Yep, that one," I replied, a bit relieved.

He turned to the bass player.

"Just look at me for the changes—it's easy stuff, you'll see."

Then, glancing at the drummer, he added,

"Just follow us."

The bandleader raised an eyebrow but gave a small nod.

"Alright then, let's give it a shot."

13

WHEN YESTERDAY RETURNS

Experience had taught me one thing—some players talk, others just play. Head down, fingers flying—the guitarist jumped on the riff like it owed him money.

The drummer caught on quickly, tapping out a rhythm, and the bass slid in smooth, holding down the groove.

Didn't give myself time to overthink—I just stepped up to the mic, my hands steadying themselves on Swampy's neck as I joined in with the riff. My voice broke through, raw but deliberate, riding the flow of the rhythm, the words rolling out in time with the beat.

The first verse unfolded naturally, each line falling into place like it had always been there. The guys followed close, locking in tight, the rhythm steady yet fluid, alive with energy. The chorus hit strong, lifting just enough to pull the audience in, and by the second verse, we'd found our stride.

By the time the second chorus faded, I could feel the shift— the moment when the music takes over, when it becomes something more than just melody and words.

And then came the *solo*.

I closed my eyes, letting my fingers glide over Swampy's fretboard, the notes spilling out like they'd been waiting there all along.

The people faded, the bar dissolved, and suddenly I wasn't at Joe's anymore.

I was back in the arena.

The stage lights blazed hot and bright, the roar of the crowd thundering around me like a living thing. Thousands of faces stretched out into the darkness, their cheers crashing against the stage like waves.

Marie was there, just to my right, holding her mic with that confident ease she always had. She caught my eye and smiled, her whole face lighting up like it always did when she was truly happy.

My heart swelled. God, *I loved her.*

I'd never felt anything so sure in my life.

She was the love of my life, the one who made everything make sense, even in the chaos of nights like this.

I couldn't help but smile back, the kind of grin that only came when everything felt right.

The Bandits behind me were on fire, the groove locked in tight—right in the pocket, as we say.

This was our biggest hit, the song that had taken us from smoky clubs to sold-out arenas.

And tonight, it felt like the peak, like nothing could touch us.

The cheers grew louder as my solo reached its climax, their energy feeding mine, my Tele screaming and soaring higher and higher.

Then it was *over.*

I was back at Joe's—the small stage, that thick barroom blend of hops, grease, smoke and sweat pressing in around me.

My fingers still danced on the strings, about to end this totally improvised solo.

I opened my eyes and saw the band staring at me. The guitarist's mouth was slightly open, his pick hovering mid-strum. The bass player looked frozen, stunned stiff like he wasn't sure what he'd just witnessed.

And the *faces*.

The faces I could see were slack, their expressions somewhere between awe and disbelief.

It wasn't the kind of reaction I'd expected—no clapping, no cheering.

Just silence, heavy and thick, like the air itself was holding its *breath*.

The final chord faded into nothing, and still, they didn't move.

The bandleader stepped forward, taking the mic.

"Y'all, give a big round of applause to Jesse L.," he said, his voice cutting through the stillness like a jolt.

And then, all of a sudden, just like a volcano finally fed up with holding back, the room erupted.

Now it was clapping, shouting, hollering—like pressure releasing all at once. People shot up, pounding their hands together, shouting my name. It hit me hard, a wave of noise crashing through me, wild and hot and overwhelming.

I stepped back from the mic, Swampy still in my hands, my chest tight with something I couldn't name.

I didn't understand it.

Not yet.

But as I stood there, taking it all in, I knew I'd reached them.

Somehow, *I did.*

And that *feeling*—damn, I hadn't had it in years.

But right now, it was like yesterday had *returned.*

14

THE FAN

No freaking way.

I felt like I'd just cheated death and won a jackpot all at once. I bent down to put Swampy back in its case, the applause still ringing in my ears. My hands were steady, but inside, I might as well have been walking on clouds.

Jeez, it had been ages since I've been onstage and faced a crowd, and the response... it was more than I'd ever dared to hope for.

As I latched it shut and straightened up, a voice stopped me.

"Excuse me, sir."

I turned to see a young man standing near the edge of the stage, his expression a mix of awe and excitement. He looked to be in his twenties, though there was something about the way he carried himself with confidence that made him seem older—well-dressed but not flashy.

"That was... amazing. Moving. It's one of my favorite tunes, and..." He hesitated, his eyes narrowing slightly as he studied me.

"Your voice, your style—even the way you play guitar. It sounded

just like him. Everything, just like 'Frenchy.' It was like hearing him live again. Would it be by any chance him? I mean... you? I mean, is that you? The one and only Jesse 'Frenchy' Lawrence?"

My heart skipped a beat.

For a moment, I considered brushing it off, pretending he was mistaken. But the way he looked at me, like he'd just seen a ghost, made it impossible to lie.

"Well, that might be him you're talking to then," I said, my voice a little quieter than usual.

He leaned forward, his excitement growing.

"No way. I mean, the sound, the flow, the guitar—" He paused, shaking his head in disbelief.

"It's like you're still channeling the same magic from back then. I grew up listening to your records. Your music was everywhere, man. It was part of my life before I even understood it. And now, here you are. I thought you were gone for good."

I glanced at him, unsure of how to respond. My past felt so distant, like a life I wasn't sure I belonged to anymore.

"Well, thank you, appreciate it. But that version of me belongs to the past, so why even bother now?" I said, trying to keep my cool, though part of me wished I could take it back.

"Why?" His jaw dropped slightly.

"Because I've spent my whole life idolizing you, man. You were more than a musician—you were a voice, an inspiration. And hearing you play again, it's like I'm hearing it for the first time."

He paused for a moment, as if to catch his breath, before continuing,

"My name is Ryan Brooks, by the way. And yeah, I'm your biggest fan. I was just a little kid back then, but you're the one who inspired me to get into music, into this business. You're the reason I'm here."

I didn't know what to say, so I just nodded, feeling more embarrassed by the second.

"I mean it," he continued, reaching into his pocket and pulling out a business card.

"I'm a manager and promoter now. I work with some big national acts, and I'd love to help you. The world deserves to know that the one and only Jesse 'Frenchy' Lawrence is alive and well—and still sounds incredible."

He pressed the card into my hand, his grip firm but warm.

"Please, stay in touch. I mean it. Whatever you need, I want to help."

I looked down at the card, his name and contact details printed in bold, glossy, professional lettering.

"Thanks," I said, slipping it into my pocket.

"I'll think about it."

But even as I said the words, something flickered inside me.

Maybe all it takes is one die-hard *fan* to stir the embers and relight an extinguished *fire.*

Like a phoenix rising from the ashes... *a new old version of me.*

15

THE AFTERSHOCK

R ippled down like a shockwave, the impact hit deep—
like a full-blown earthquake shaking my core.

It had been only a couple of days since the open
mic, and I'd barely left the bed. Only to refuel—some bread,
some beers—and to at least feed the horses.

The night had been great. Better than great, really. But the
aftershock was bigger.

Standing on that stage again—it broke through a wall I
didn't even know I'd built.

It had brought it all rushing back—the memories, the pain,
the dreams I'd buried so deep I thought they'd never surface
again.

Swampy leaned against the wall in the corner of my
bedroom, her bare body catching the faint light that slipped
through the curtains. Just looking at her lit a slow burn in my
chest—a tangled mix of pride and unease. I wanted to play her
again, to chase that feeling of connection I'd felt on stage.

But I couldn't. *Not yet.*

Music used to be everything to me. It was where I found my purpose, my voice.

But now? Now, it felt like a weight I couldn't carry anymore. Because every note I played, every chord I strummed, brought me back to them.

To her.

To him.

The music wasn't just music anymore. It was a tether to everything I'd lost. The sound of my own guitar felt like a reminder that I'd failed—not just on stage, but in the parts of life that mattered more.

As a husband.

As a father.

But it hadn't always been like this.

When I started as a kid, there was no "her" or "him." It was just me, wrapped in my own little world—a place to escape, where nothing else mattered. Each moment felt limitless, full of freedom, a spark of hope.

Back then, it was simple—go all in, let it flow, and never look back.

I thought about that old woman in that small village in France, the way her hands trembled as she handed me the case.

"Go chase your dream," she'd said.

"Do it for him. Do it for you."

Back then, it felt like a mission—something I had to carry forward, for her, her husband, and for *myself.*

And *now?* Now I couldn't shake the feeling that somewhere along the way, I'd strayed from it.

I rubbed a hand over my face, trying to push the thoughts away. But they always came back, *stronger* and *louder.*

Marie's laugh echoed in my mind, the way she used to hum along to my songs, her voice blending with mine like they were made for each other.

And then the image of him—my little boy—tiny hands clutching a toy guitar, the way his face lit up when I showed him a new chord.

They were *gone.*

And the music was all I had left of *them.*

16

TAKEOUT MENU

I hadn't set foot back at Joe's since. Done. I was done!

So why keep fooling myself?

For weeks since the open mic, I'd done a damn fine job avoiding that bar.

Hell, I hadn't even picked up Swampy—or barely touched her.

Ryan Brooks' card sat on the counter, curling at the edges, untouched, like it was waiting for me to make a decision I wasn't ready for.

The days blended into one another, filled with the same routine: feed the horses, handle clients, fix what needed fixing, and drink enough to blur the edges. I kept busy enough to ignore the pull of the music, the itch to pick up Swampy again.

That's why, when I heard the sound of tires crunching on the gravel outside, I tensed. Clients usually called ahead. Unexpected visits didn't happen out here. My hand instinctively brushed against the shotgun leaning by the door. Out here, you couldn't be too careful—unexpected visitors were rarely the friendly kind.

I stepped onto the porch, squinting at the car pulling up. It wasn't anyone I recognized—a small, clean sedan that looked more at home in a city than out here in the middle of nowhere.

The driver got out, brushing dust off his jacket, and for a moment, I didn't know who he was.

"Mr. Lawrence?" he called, shading his eyes against the sun.

I tilted my head, stepping fully into the light, resting one shoulder against the doorframe.

"Who's asking?"

He smiled, stepping closer, and something about him tugged at the edges of my memory.

"Wait... Ryan... something, right?"

His grin widened.

"Ryan Brooks. You do remember! Good, I was worried I'd have to reintroduce myself."

I crossed my arms, still unsure how I felt about him showing up unannounced.

"What are you doing all the way out here, Kid?"

Brooks' face turned sheepish as he approached the porch.

"Well, I was hoping to hear from you after the open mic. When I didn't, I went back to Joe's to see if you'd been around. No luck. Took me a while to track you down."

I raised an eyebrow.

"How'd you find me? Clients don't even come out here without calling first."

He chuckled nervously.

"I've got some connections. Let's just say, when you admire someone as much as I admire you, you figure out ways to connect the dots."

I huffed, still wary.

"So, what do you want, Kid?"

He stepped up to the edge of the porch, his hands out like he didn't want to spook me.

"I mean what I said that night, Mr. Lawrence. You were incredible. You're still incredible. I think the world needs to hear you again."

I shook my head, already regretting stepping outside.

"Look Kid, I've been out of that world a long time. I'm not interested."

"Please, just hear me out," Brooks' said quickly, unzipping a scuffed-up leather bag—the kind that looked like it had seen more coffee shops than boardrooms—and pulled out a folder.

"I've been working on some ideas—venues, connections, people who would kill to see you back on stage."

I stared at the folder like it was a takeout menu I didn't ask for.

"I'm not asking for a decision right now," he said, his voice softening.

"Just... take a look. Think about it."

I hesitated, but eventually, I took it. My fingers lingered on the edges. It felt heavier than it should.

A relieved smile spread across his face.

"Thank you. That's all I'm asking."

He turned back to his car, giving me a small wave as he got in.

I stood there on the porch long after the dust from his tires had settled, the folder in one hand, the other drifting to my beard, fingers tracing the patch under my chin—a habit I'd had for years when I was thinking.

Yeah, well, much more than just paper. It really felt like one of those late-night menus.

You say you're not *hungry*.

But you *are*.

17

THE INVITATION

Give or take. *Best case?* This kid had some real chops and knew his business. *Worst case?* Just an annoying hustler—the kind of stubborn pain in the ass who could sell ice to an Eskimo.

Still planted there, rolling that thought around in my head, I heard the sound of a car door pop open and slam shut again.

I looked up, and there he was—Ryan Brooks—standing by the open driver's side door, hesitation written all over his face. He rubbed the back of his neck, then took a few steps toward me.

"*Look,*" he started, his voice softer now, less polished.

"*I know I showed up out of the blue, and I probably crossed a line finding you out here.*"

I stayed silent, just watching him.

"*But I meant every word I said,*" he continued.

"*Your music? It wasn't just something I listened to—it was something I felt. I don't know why, but something in it pulled me in. The* soul of it, the depth... it was like it spoke to me in a way nothing else ever did. I felt like it belonged—like I belonged."

That caught me off guard. My fingers tightened around the folder, and for a moment, I didn't know what to say.

Brooks took a step closer, emboldened by my silence.

"Look, I know you've got no reason to trust me. But I really believe you've got something left to give the world. Even if it's just one more song. One more show."

I let out a dry laugh, shaking my head.

"Look, Kid... I already told you. I've been out of that world for a long time. And honestly? I'm not sure it ever wanted me back."

His eyes lit up, his grin returning, though it was softer this time.

"That's where you're wrong. People don't forget music like yours. And even if they did, I wouldn't let them."

He reached into his pocket and pulled out a folded piece of paper.

"Look, I'm organizing this showcase next week—just something local, small crowd. A couple of really great new artists I'm working with. Thought you might want to check it out."

I hesitated but finally took the paper. It was a flyer for a small showcase event nearby—an intimate venue, the kind of place that didn't promise much but could lead to something bigger.

"I mean... if you've got time. Just—see how it feels," he said.

Brooks backed away toward his car, hands up like he didn't want to push his luck.

"Take care, Mr. Lawrence," he said, his tone lighter now.

"And... thanks. For everything."

I nodded, still holding the folder and now the flyer, my mind spinning as his car disappeared down the dirt road.

I stayed on the porch for a while, absently scratching my

beard, eyes wandering toward the pasture. The horses shifted in the distance, one of them letting out a soft snort.

As the quiet settled in, familiar and steady, I shook my head and let out a low chuckle.

"Damn, that kid is good. Stubborn, but good. He could probably really sell ice to an Eskimo."

18

TOO BIG TO DREAM?

How did that happen? How did I end up there?

I was in the back of a van, heading to the festival venue, the early afternoon sun still shining brightly through the windows. The nerves were kicking in, but so was the excitement.

My first big show in the US—it felt *unreal.*

The driver, a guy who'd been to more than a few gigs, was singing along to the radio, the quiet hum of the engine almost making it easy to forget where I was.

Then, out of nowhere, I heard something familiar.

My *song.*

I froze for a second, my ears immediately locking onto the melody.

Yes. It was my tune playing on the radio. I couldn't believe it.

I leaned forward.

"Wait—wow, that's my tune," I blurted out without thinking.

The driver glanced at me in the rearview mirror, a half-smile on his face.

"Oh really? Well, I love that tune. They play it all the time around here—big hit. That's my favorite right now."

I blinked, heart kicking hard. Damn. The reality of it all started to sink in. I hadn't realized that my song was being played all over America, especially with me still living in Europe.

I had spent years trying to get noticed—sending demos to labels in the States, some directly, others through my publisher—always hoping someone would listen, someone would care.

Finally, a small label signed me, and just like that, I was on my way—booked for a festival tour across the country.

The reality was that I was now living the goal I'd worked for.

This wasn't just a track on a record—it was reaching people.

And now, I was about to play my first show on American soil, where it was a hit. I was actually starting to make it. It was *happening.*

But back in France? The story was different.

Most people thought I was *crazy*. They'd laugh, say things like,

"The States? Pfff, in your dreams. They don't need you over there."

Or worse,

"You'll never make it. America is a different world. You're aiming too high."

It was like hearing the same line over and over, like they were determined to make sure I understood how far I was from being good enough.

And those words didn't just sting—they cut *deep.*

It felt like I was being told that I wasn't worth it, that I didn't belong in the world I had always dreamed of.

People tried to bring me down, tried to make me feel small.

Sometimes it felt like *pure bullying.* And actually, it *was.*

Those looks, those words—they were like weights on my

shoulders, dragging me down, making me question if I was even capable of achieving what I wanted.

What hurt even more was when the few people who were supposed to support me—pushed me down, too.

They'd come back to me later, defeated, almost apologizing for having tried to believe in me.

It was *crushing*.

Was it *jealousy*?

Envy?

Or just *cruelty*?

I don't know. But the impact was the same.

It was really hard not to believe them. It made me feel like maybe they were right.

Maybe I was just clinging to an illusion, something too far out of my reach.

But I didn't give up. I kept pushing forward, even when it felt like the entire universe was trying to shut me out.

But here I was, hearing my tune on the radio in the States—the place I had only fantasized about, and the place people told me I'd never get to.

The moment I heard that song, I knew things were different. Folks back home never believed it could happen. They thought I was chasing some pipe dream. But this was real. I was actually making it.

We got to the venue, and my nerves hit me again. The sun was high in the sky, the crowd was buzzing, waiting for the headliners later in the day, but I was up first.

My first gig here, in front of a crowd I didn't know, with a band I didn't know. I had no idea how they would play, or how I would feel, but I was about to find out.

The set started okay—definitely some tension, some off moments. The sound was off a bit, and the band wasn't exactly in sync.

There were times I wondered if the audience even cared—they were all waiting for the bigger acts—but then something shifted when I kicked off the riff of *From Paris to Texas*.

It was like the whole energy of the place changed. The crowd started singing along, shouting the words they knew, and I felt it —the energy that only a crowd like that can give you.

The cheers, the claps, the stomping—it all came together, and in that moment, I felt like I was where I was meant to be.

After the show ended, and I was rushed off stage to an auto-graph session. Fans were lined up, holding albums, programs, and posters for me to sign. There was no time to catch my breath. I was still processing the energy of the show, but the fans were already waiting. They were telling me how much they loved my tune, how amazing the show was, and asking for pictures.

I didn't even get to see the other acts. The audience stuck around, wanting more autographs, more photos—anything they could get their hands on. It felt like hours, my hand cramping from all the signatures, my mind racing. I tried to talk to every-one, to remember faces, but it all felt like a blur. I was green. I didn't know how to handle the attention, but at the same time, I couldn't believe it was happening.

I hadn't planned for this moment. But here I was, trying to soak it all in, still unsure what to do with it all.

All I knew was that this was just the beginning, and for the first time, I was starting to understand what it meant to truly touch people with my music.

But in France, no one *cared*.

I was just another musician trying to make it, trying to achieve something that seemed impossible.

I used to hear people talk about the States as if it was some far-off land where ambitions went to die, not to be realized.

But here, I was starting to see that maybe they were *wrong*.

And their doubts had been my biggest enemy all along.

Because maybe I was exactly where I was meant to be—living my *American dream.*

Such a long way to go... for sure.

But somehow, I might have found my *sweet home.*

19

HOPE ON THE LINE

Truth was, I'd been dragging my feet for days, staring at Brooks' card and that damn folder, finding every excuse in the book.

Each time I thought about calling, something held me back. I kept wrestling with myself, the weight of the decision heavier than it should have been. I knew what The Kid wanted—what he was offering—but I wasn't sure I was ready to step back into that world.

Today, though, I made up my mind. After days of hesitation, I finally decided to make the call. I owed him at least that much —a thank you, some acknowledgment of The Kid's passion and persistence.

But the limelight, the music—it was all part of my past. It was over. The ranch, the horses, the clients—my life was here now. Not on some stage in front of strangers.

I grabbed the phone, my fingers trembling slightly as I dialed the number. The phone rang twice before he picked up.

"Ryan Brooks speaking, how can I help you?"

I cleared my throat, keeping my voice low but steady.

"Hey, Kid."

There was a brief pause on the other end, then his voice brightened instantly.

"Jesse? I mean Mr Lawrence. Is that really you?"

"Yeah, it's me," I replied, leaning back in my chair, still unsure of what I'd say next.

"I just wanted to give you a call and thank you. You know... for everything. Your drive, the passion you've got... I can see it. I really can. Not everyone would go to all this trouble just for an old guy like me, and I really appreciate that."

The Kid chuckled, but his tone held a mix of eagerness and confidence.

"Well, I'm glad it means something to you. You've meant a lot to me...so. And I just know you've still got it in you."

I rubbed my temple.

"Alright, look, Kid, I respect that—I really do. But like I told you, too many times now. This game is over. There's no rematch."

His voice wavered slightly, but he pressed on.

"Mr. Lawrence, I really think you've still got so much to offer. We could set something up—a gig, a new band—did you, uh, have a chance to look at th—"

I cut him off, keeping my tone firm.

"No, Kid. Are you hearing me? I'm not doing it. Sorry, I can't do it. I can't do this anymore. I wish you the best of luck, Kid. Take care."

Before I could hang up, he rushed in, cutting me off.

"Wait, wait." His voice softened immediately.

"Look, I knew you would say that, and I know how much you care about your new life, all the things you've built. But hear me out..."

I felt the tension building. I really wanted to hang up, but he wasn't backing down.

When does he? That kid is so stubborn. Reminds me of someone. Maybe that's why I like him.

"I figured that'd be your first concern," he said quickly, his tone confident.

"So I already planned ahead. I found someone to help with the ranch—solid, experienced. Just to take that weight off your shoulders... so you can breathe a little. So you can just be 'Frenchy' again."

He paused.

"So you won't have to worry about a thing. Just focus on being an artist. And here's the thing..."

His voice picked up, eager.

"I've got this club in Austin. I do a lot of booking for that place. I've got a few of my artists lined up, and I'd love to have you there, just to test things out. It's not huge, but it's a nice-sized venue. The crowd's great, and I've got a band lined up for you. I'll take care of everything —logistics, promotion, all of it. The only thing you'd have to do is show up."

The pressure mounted, but before I could speak, he pressed on.

"How about I come by the ranch in a couple of days?" The Kid continued.

"I'll introduce you to the person I've found to help you with the ranch, and we can get things moving from there. What do you say?"

I sat in silence for a moment, trying to brush off his offer— but damn, it wasn't that easy. I hadn't expected this—he had thought of everything. The ranch was no longer an excuse—I'd made my peace with that life.

But why the hell couldn't I turn down the chance to perform again?

And how long will I be lying to myself since I found Swampy?

Well, maybe just because this time... I didn't have to.

I took a deep breath and, after a pause, finally said,

"Alright, Kid. Let's see what you got."

His voice lit up immediately.

"I knew you'd come around! This is going to be great, Jesse. I'll be seeing you soon. You won't regret this. Trust me."

I finally hung up the phone, the decision made. I wasn't sure what was coming next, and I was anxious.

I'd said there was no *rematch.*

Well, even the legends—Tyson, Ali—they all found a reason to step back in the ring.

Not for the fame.

Not for the money.

No.

For the *thrill.* For the *fight.*

Just to feel alive again.

And maybe it was time for me to lace up and get back in there.

One more round. One more swing. One last time.

And look, even when you're in the rope—there is *hope.*

20

THE INTRODUCTION

The past had left its mark, and trust wasn't something I handed out lightly. But here I was, about to put my faith in a stranger.

A few days later, after ironing out the details, Ryan showed up at the ranch—just like he said he would.

I spent the morning pacing around, trying to shake the buzz of anticipation in my head.

I gave my green light, already laced up—and now it just felt like I was standing in the corner, waiting for the *bell.*

This wasn't just about a gig anymore. More like a fight, with doubts and fears.

And this was round one.

But there was still one question that lingered: Who the hell is this person Ryan has found to help with the ranch? I don't trust *anyone.*

The sun was high when I heard the crunch of tires on gravel.

Ryan's car pulled up first, kicking up dust as he parked.

Another car followed, rolling to a stop beside him.

I stepped forward, expecting some ranch hand, some guy who'd talk too much and know too little.

Then the door opened.

A *woman.*

She stood next to Ryan, casually leaning against the car as they both looked over at me. I squinted, trying to make out her features from this distance. Ryan waved and nodded toward me, but that woman got all my attention. I couldn't take my eyes off her.

She was taller than I expected, with a quiet confidence in her stance. Her hair was pulled back in a no-nonsense ponytail, her jeans and boots worn but practical.

She had that easy way about her that someone who's spent years in the field has, like she wasn't worried about anything except what was in front of her.

And when she smiled, there was something warm but determined in it.

"*Jesse,*" Ryan called out.

"*This is Emma. She's the one I was telling you about.*"

I gave a nod, walking toward them, but I couldn't shake the feeling that there was more to her than just her presence. I gave a nod, walking toward them. The way she held her ground—calm, steady—made me wonder if she knew exactly what she was walking into.

Ryan shot me a knowing look, sensing my hesitation.

"*Don't worry, Jesse. Emma's the real deal. You can trust her.*"

She extended her hand to me, her grip firm, sure.

"*Emma Angelle,*" she said, her voice warm but respectful.

"*Nice to meet you, Mr. Lawrence. Ryan's told me a lot about you.*"

I shook her hand, still trying to piece together why she was here, why she was the one Ryan picked. She didn't look like someone who needed work—or anyone's approval.

And that bothered me a little, as much as it made me curious.

"Well, I guess we'll see how this all works out," I said, my voice carrying more uncertainty than I intended.

She gave me a small smile, her eyes meeting mine with an almost unspoken understanding.

"You've got a lot on your plate. But I think we'll figure it out. I'm here for as long as you need me."

Before I could say anything more, Ryan stepped in, his tone brisk and matter-of-fact.

"I've already taken care of it, Jesse. Everything's been figured out —business, logistics, all of it. You don't need to worry about how Emma will be taken care of. She's got what she needs to get started."

"You're not making it easy for me to say no, are you, Kid?" I said with a wink, feeling a bit of the weight lift off my shoulders.

It was clear Ryan had everything lined up, and that meant I didn't have to focus on the details right now.

"Alright then—relax. Just messing with you, Kid. Let's give it a shot."

There was a moment of silence as Ryan clapped his hands together, eager to keep things moving.

"Great!" he said, with that usual energy of his.

"I'll leave you two to get acquainted. Jesse, I'll catch up with you later about the gig. I know you've got a lot on your mind."

As Ryan headed back to his car, I stood there, unsure of what to say next.

Emma didn't seem in a rush. She glanced at me, taking in the ranch, the horses grazing in the distance.

"So," she said, breaking the silence,

"you've got a beautiful place here."

"Thanks," I muttered, still unsure of how to approach her.

"I've had it for a while now."

She nodded, her gaze shifting to the horses again.

"They're good animals. They've got a real connection to you."

I didn't know how to respond to that. Maybe she was right. Horses had always been my escape, my silent partners when the world was too loud.

I looked at Emma again, trying to figure out what kind of person she was, what kind of help she was really offering.

"We'll make it work," she said, reading my thoughts like she'd done it for years.

"And you'll get back to what you need to do."

It wasn't a promise. It was a *fact.*

Still, there was something about her—an *aura* I couldn't quite put my finger on. Comforting. Peaceful. Trustworthy.

And hell, I'd just handed my music—my career—over to some kid I barely knew.

So maybe... giving her a *shot* wasn't the craziest thing after all.

What do I really have to lose *this time?*

21

HUSBAND AND WIFE

Happiness? *A lifetime promise?* I was way too head over heels to let that chance slip away.

It was September, and I was on stage, the lights a blur around me, the crowd alive and electric. The show was going fine, though the tension between Marie and the band had started to rise over the past few months.

But tonight felt different. I don't know what it was—maybe it was the way the crowd responded, or the way the music felt tonight—but I knew.

Tonight was the *night.*

Marie had been away for months overseas, for her work and studies—there had been space between us, but I knew it was time.

As one of the songs finished, I turned to the crowd with a smile, throwing my thanks to them for their energy.

"And now," I said, looking at the Bandits,

"Here's a new tune that I've just finished writing, it's our first time playing it. It's called 'Husbands and Wives.'"

As I turned back to the band to start, I caught Marie's eyes.

They were wide, surprised—like, *"What the heck? What's this song?"*

Without saying a word, I just gave her a big smile and nodded.

We kicked in and played the song—a short, sweet tune. It wasn't much, but it felt like everything right then. As it came to an end, I glanced over at the guys and gave them the cue for a clean, abrupt stop.

The silence hit hard—loud, awkward even.

The audience wasn't sure if it was finished or if something went wrong. Then the room fell still, *waiting.*

I reached into my pocket, turned my head towards Marie, and, without missing a beat, said into the mic,

"Will you marry me?"

I dropped to one knee, opening the box—the perfect ring I'd picked for her, sparkling under the lights.

A few weeks later, it felt surreal. I was standing there, in front of the most beautiful girl in the world to me—her long blonde hair flowing, wearing that white, gorgeous wedding dress.

She looked like an *angel.*

And in that moment, I swear, I was the luckiest guy in the world.

Right out of my thoughts, I heard it:

"Yes, I do."

The Marshall, his voice steady, smiled and looked at us.

"You may kiss the bride. I declare you husband and wife."

22

THE WEEKEND TRIAL

Effortless. That's how she made it look.

The morning started early—another busy one, just like the last. Emma was already up before sunrise, moving from task to task like she'd been running this place her whole life. Horses, clients, the little details—I watched her handle it all without breaking a sweat.

I stuck to my usual routine, keeping an eye on things from the sidelines. I wasn't sure how I felt about someone else stepping into a role I'd carried alone for so long.

She was good, though. Too good.

By mid-afternoon, I couldn't deny it—Emma wasn't just stepping in. She was taking over. And hell, she was doing it better than I cared to admit.

By the time the sun started dipping low in the sky, the day had already slipped by in a blur. I hadn't said much, and neither had she, but there was a quiet understanding between us.

That was one thing I appreciated about Emma—she didn't need to fill the silence.

She stopped near the old cattle pens, brushing her hand over the weathered wood like she was trying to read the years etched into it.

"*What's this area for?*" she asked, her voice breaking the stillness. "*Looks like it hasn't been used in a while.*"

I leaned against the post, tilting my hat back to shield from the glare of the sun.

"*It's from before my time here. This ranch used to run cattle, back when that made sense in this part of the desert.*"

She turned, raising an eyebrow.

"*So how'd you end up with it?*"

I hesitated, my eyes drifting over the rusted chute and the branding station overtaken by weeds. It wasn't a story I told often. Hell, I wasn't even sure how much of it was true anymore.

"*The guy who owned it before me was looking to get out. I was looking for somewhere off the grid. Figured this place fit the bill.*"

Emma didn't say anything for a moment, just looked back at the abandoned pens like she could see the ghosts of what used to be. Finally, she gave a small nod.

"*And it works for you?*" I shrugged.

"*Most days. It's quiet. It keeps me busy.*"

I gestured toward the horses in the distance.

"*They don't ask much, just that you show up.*"

Her lips quirked in a small smile.

"*Sounds like you and this place were a good match.*"

I laughed it off, but as we walked back toward the house, something about that line stuck with me.

The old cattle pens faded into the dusk behind us, but they felt closer than ever. The past might not have been mine, but it was still here, woven into every plank and post.

Back then, years ago, in the aftermath of the storm, I was just sailing wherever the wind pushed me—no map, no compass, no destination. Then out of the blue, in the middle of nowhere, this place appeared. Like Columbus, I thought I'd found the land. But for some reason, as fate has it, maybe the land *found me.*

23

CALL ME JESSE

Resting my boots on the porch railing after another busy day, I let out a slow breath, watching rabbits dart off into the sagebrush, vanishing like ghosts in the dusk.

The evening air was cool against my face, and the ranch had fallen quiet, save for the wind rustling through the trees.

Emma joined me a few minutes later, stepping out with the same calm presence she'd carried throughout.

"You fancy a drink?" I asked, jerking my chin toward the cooler beside me.

"Sure... Mr. Lawrence," she replied, taking a seat next to me.

"No need to call me Mr. Lawrence, just Jesse," I said, giving her a small smile.

I grabbed a Bud, cracked it open, and handed it to her.

"Well, I only have whisky or beer. But Good Ol' Jack needs a refill. So?"

She laughed softly.

"A beer will be fine, thanks... Mis... huh, Jesse," she said, giving me a small smile back.

I took a long sip from my bottle, still watching her as she took hers. She'd earned it, no doubt. The way she handled things this weekend, how effortlessly she slipped into the role... I was impressed, even though I wouldn't admit it out loud.

"So," she said after a moment, breaking the comfortable silence,

"what do you think? Did I do okay?"

I quirked an eyebrow, a little surprised at her straightforwardness.

"Well, better than I was expecting," I said, settling into my chair, meeting her gaze.

She gave a quick grin, lifting her drink to her lips.

"Better than expected, huh? I'll take that as a compliment."

I nodded, a bit of a chuckle escaping me.

"You've been solid—the whole weekend, really. Handled everything like you've been doing it your whole life. I can't argue with that."

She shrugged, her eyes meeting mine with a steady, knowing look.

"I'm here for the long haul, Jesse. Whatever you need."

I paused for a moment, thinking over her words. I'd seen a lot of people come and go over the years, but something about Emma felt... different.

"So," she continued, reclining slightly,

"Ryan mentioned you used to be pretty famous back in the day. And that you're from Europe, right? France, I think?"

Her words hit me like a splash of cold water.

Of course The Kid talked. He always talks too much. Probably said more than he should've.

"Yeah," I said slowly, trying to keep my tone neutral.

"A long time ago. But that's... that's not really important anymore."

She nodded, but there was a softness in her gaze.

"*I get it. Europe, the music, the fame... it's a lot to carry, isn't it? People probably saw the spotlight, but not everything that came with it.*"

I hesitated, unsure of how to respond. She was reading me in a way I hadn't expected, but her understanding was almost comforting.

"*I don't know if I'm ready to go back to that,*" I admitted, my voice lower now.

"*Things aren't like they were.*"

She didn't push me, just gave a warm, reassuring smile.

"*You don't have to go back to anything, Jesse. You're here now. And sometimes, that's all that matters.*"

For the first time in ages, I felt like I was talking to someone who didn't need me to explain everything, who understood without me having to say much.

Her words kept spinning in my head, carrying something unspoken beneath them. I was trying to decipher the code, the puzzle, the whole meaning of it.

I wasn't close yet. Only bits and pieces. But maybe this time, I won't have to solve it *alone.*

24

SWAMPY TALES

E ach town has its *stories*—buried treasure, ghostly brides, cursed mines, outlaw gold, or just some drunk talking to the imaginary monkey on his shoulder, swearing he saw the devil at the bottom of his whiskey.

Joe's bar was no exception. This place wasn't much to look at —dim lights, scratched-up tables, and the kind of quiet that came from regulars too tired to talk.

Perfect. I liked it that way.

I slid onto a stool at the far end of the bar, nodding at Joe as he shuffled over with a towel draped over one shoulder.

"Hey, Jesse. Bud as usual? Draft or bottle?"

"Draft today," I said, leaning on the counter.

"Let's be crazy for a change. Kinda fits the mood today."

Joe grabbed a glass and filling it from the tap before setting it in front of me.

"Gotta say—you killed it the other night at the open mic. That guitar of yours... well... uh. Hell, it was like the room stood still. Mesmerized everyone."

"*Thanks, Joe.*" I wrapped my hands around the cold drink, letting the coolness soak into my palms.

"*Yep, I call that guitar Swampy. Found it in a swamp by my place. And, well... it's just weird.*"

"*Weird how?*" Joe said, raising an eyebrow.

I shrugged, taking a sip.

"*When I touch the strings, it's like Swampy knows me better than I know myself—every note feels like raw, jagged truth. Funny thing is, I found it on Thanksgiving. Was out riding Buck, clearing my head. I've lived on that ranch for years, but I swear, I didn't even know that swamp was there. It just appeared—out of nowhere.*"

Joe frowned, his hand pausing mid-wipe on a glass.

"*Thanksgiving, huh? And a swamp shows up? That's one hell of a holiday surprise.*"

"*Yep.*" I nodded.

"*Fog was low, thick. Could barely see ahead. Buck stopped, snorting like he knew something I didn't. Then I saw it—dark water surrounded by mesquites and sagebrush, with cattails poking out like they didn't belong. The kind of place that makes you feel like you shouldn't be there. And there it was—a guitar, just sitting there like it'd been waiting. Felt like a gift, you know? And maybe not the kind you're supposed to take.*"

I hesitated for a second. Strange how I never noticed it before. Maybe it was the haze of too many hangovers back then, or maybe I just never rode that way before.

Or maybe... *who cares.*

Some things show up when they're *meant to.*

Joe opened his mouth to say something, but a voice from the corner of the bar cut in.

"*Swamp, huh?*"

I turned to see a guy hunched over a table, a cigarette hanging loose between his fingers. His face was rough, lined with stories he probably didn't want to tell.

"That swamp's got its own rules," he said, standing and making his way over.

"Ain't many folks around here like to talk about it, but yeah, people know. Old place, older than any of us. You're sure you just 'found' that guitar?"

I set my draft down, narrowing my eyes.

"What do you mean?"

He took a drag off his cigarette, the smoke curling around his words as he exhaled.

"Depends who you ask. Some say it's cursed, others say it's where deals get made. The kinda deals you don't walk away from clean. Some even say it's got... supernatural ties."

He leaned in slightly, closer, his gaze sharp and unsettling.

"You sure that swamp didn't find you?"

Joe cut in, laughing nervously.

"Don't listen to him, Jesse. That swamp's just swamp. Superstitious nonsense, that's all."

The guy took another drag off his cigarette.

"Believe what you want," he said, responding to Joe's nervous laugh. *"Never heard of the Swampy Tales? Whole bunch of them floating around. Ghosts, curses, deals gone bad. Depends on who you ask."*

His eyes locked on me again, more curious than accusing.

"Maybe you're part of one now."

I didn't say anything, just took another sip of my beer. The bar felt quieter now, the kind of quiet that sinks into your bones. I could feel all their stares on me—Joe's friendly, the other guy's knowing, like he saw something in me I hadn't figured out yet.

Swampy was sitting at home, waiting. And for the first time, I wondered if I'd brought more out of that place than just a guitar.

The truck rattled as I drove back toward the ranch, the old suspension creaking over every bump in the road. The cab smelled faintly of oil and dust, a scent that felt like it had soaked into the seats for decades. The headlights barely cut through the night, but I didn't mind. The drive gave me a lot of time to think.

Emma had gone to bed, and I was still out here with my thoughts, feeling like the projectionist had fallen asleep, letting the same reel run over and over.

So funny how it crept back in, right now. Or maybe *not.*

It was just a few days ago—before she showed up, before that weekend trial.

I'd gone into town to pick up some supplies and other stuff.

Nerves buzzing over whoever Ryan was bringing to the ranch.

Jeez, I hadn't set foot in Joe's in a long, long while, but somehow, I needed to stop by. Maybe to prepare myself for having guests over.

Hell, if I know. I'm not exactly used to have some—'less you count coyotes and the ghosts I drink with.

Though, I couldn't stop thinking about what that guy had said at Joe's. Stories about the swamp, deals, and curses—it was the kind of nonsense you hear in small towns, the stuff people whisper about to make life feel a little less ordinary.

I wasn't a believer. Never had been.

Fairytales and folklore weren't my thing.

But *tonight?* I wasn't so sure.

It wasn't just his words. It was *Swampy* itself.

Even now, I could picture it back at the ranch, propped up against the wall where I'd left it. The way the light caught its worn finish, the way the strings seemed to hum with something alive every time I touched them.

It wasn't just a guitar—it felt like something else entirely.

A *soul* of its own, maybe. Or maybe I'd just lost my *mind.*

But if it was magic, who was I to argue?

It wasn't like I had much else to hang on to. The losses had piled up—Marie, my little boy, the career. The loneliness sat heavy most days, like a shadow that wouldn't budge.

If *Swampy* was the one thing in my life that still felt real, still felt like it mattered, then maybe it didn't matter where it came from.

I gripped the wheel tighter as the truck rattled over another pothole. The swamp, the legends, *Swampy*—none of it made sense.

But damn if it didn't feel like the first good thing in a long while.

And then it hit me, like a *punchline* I didn't see coming.

If the *devil* wanted my soul,

he was about *twenty-two years* too late.

ACT 2A

25

TAKING THE PLUNGE

Back he was—punctual as a school bell on a Monday morning. Ryan arrived at the ranch, his confident stride matching his usual energy. Proud as a first grader on his first day of class. Dust kicked up under his boots as he approached the porch, where I was nursing a cup of black coffee, its bitter warmth doing little to ease the tension sitting heavy in my chest.

"Morning, Jesse," he said with a smirk, his eyes bright with excitement.

"How'd it go? You ready to take the plunge?"

I eased back against the wooden railing, taking a long look at the land stretching out before us. The sun was still low, casting a golden glow over the dry Texas earth.

It felt peaceful, serene—a stark contrast to the whirlwind I knew was waiting on the other side of Ryan's offer.

I took my time. Didn't need to rush a good silence.

"Well, I have to admit, Kid, you did a great job. Found someone

solid, someone I can trust with the ranch. You've impressed me, and not many people do that anymore."

Ryan's grin widened, like he'd been waiting his whole life to hear those words.

Before he could say anything, the front door creaked open, and Emma stepped outside. She had that same *je ne sais quoi*, a steady presence she carried everywhere, like nothing could rattle her.

"Good Morning," she said, giving me a look before turning to Ryan.

"Nice to see you again."

"Good to see you too, Emma. Hope Jesse hasn't been too hard on you," he replied, giving her a friendly smile.

Emma chuckled softly.

"No complaints so far. He's been... fair."

I lifted a brow, but didn't comment. Truth was, she'd handled everything better than I expected. She was solid, reliable—and for once, the ranch didn't feel like it would collapse if I blinked.

"Alright, let's do this," I said, setting my coffee cup down on the porch railing.

"You won, Kid. Let's see what this next chapter looks like."

Ryan practically bounced on his heels, his excitement infectious.

"You won't regret this, Jesse. Trust me, it's going to be great."

"You sure you're ready for this? It's a lot to handle," I said, looking at Emma.

Her expression didn't waver.

"I wouldn't be here if I wasn't. You can count on me, Jesse."

I studied her for a moment longer, then said,

"Alright. I'll hold you to that," with a small tilt of my head.

Ryan clapped his hands together, his enthusiasm damn near contagious—classic Kid, almost impossible to ignore.

"Perfect. We've got a lot to do, but first things first—I need to take

care of the musicians and get things rolling. Jesse, I'll see you in Austin next week."

I nodded.

"See you then, Kid. I'll be there."

"Emma, if you need anything while Jesse's away, you've got my number. And thanks again for your help." He added.

"Thanks, Ryan. You're welcome—and no worries. I've got everything under control," she said, her tone smooth and confident.

"Okay then. You guys take care," he said, waving as he headed to his car. He drove off, leaving me and Emma standing in the quiet.

I stepped off the front steps, exhaling as I took in the fresh morning air.

"Well then," I said, glancing at Emma.

"How 'bout we get the day started?"

26

AMERICA'S MOST WANTED

Austin. The drive was long—several hours that gave me time to think. Or overthink, really.

As I got closer, the landscape shifted, the wide-open ranch land giving way to the city's sprawl. Austin was alive with its own kind of rhythm—a mix of college kids, artists, tech folks, and tourists all blending into something unique. The streets were lined with music bars and food trucks, their scents and sounds mingling in the cool afternoon air.

I drove past murals splashed across aged brick buildings, those seemed to tell a hundred stories without a single word. Neon signs already flickering above small clubs, advertising tonight's lineups—names I didn't recognize, but I was familiar with.

This was Austin, after all. A city built on music, dreams, and a little chaos. It had its own pulse, a beat I once knew by heart but now seemed strangely distant from.

The noise, the rush, the constant movement—I wasn't used to any of it anymore. I felt irritation rising, and before I knew it, my anxiety kicked in, putting me on edge. It wasn't just the uproar or the unfamiliarity—it was that old weight creeping back in, the one I'd thought I'd left behind. The tension had never quite vanished since everything fell apart.

When I finally pulled up to the venue, a wave of uncertainty hit me. I had no recollection of it—probably a new spot, or maybe I'd just forgotten. It had been forever since I last played in Austin. The place looked smaller than I expected, but the buzz of anticipation in the air was the same.

I grabbed Swampy's case from the backseat, feeling its weight in my hands. Or maybe just the weight of it all.

Was I really ready to step back on stage? For real?

Then I spotted Ryan out front, scanning the parking lot like a kid on Christmas morning. When he finally saw me, his face lit up, and he waved me over.

"Jesse! You made it! How was the drive?"

he asked, his voice full of energy as usual.

"Long, Kid," I muttered, shaking off the knot in my stomach.

"But I'm here. Let's see if I still remember how to do this."

Ryan gave me a confident tap on the back.

"You'll be fine. Oh, and by the way, I have a little... surprise waiting for you inside."

I stopped mid-step, narrowing my gaze.

"Surprise? What are you talking about?"

A mischievous grin spread across Ryan's face as he shrugged.

"You'll see. Think of it like one of those old TV shows—like America's Most Wanted... but not for criminals."

"You digging up skeletons or something?" I said, raising an eyebrow.

"Not quite," he chuckled.

"More like The Dating Game—but it's not a date. It's about reconnecting with something you didn't expect."

I groaned, rubbing my temple.

"Stop with the childish games, Kid."

Ryan waved me off, still grinning.

"Relax, Jesse. It's fun. I think you'll love it."

He winked, clearly enjoying the suspense.

"You'll see."

We entered the building, and Ryan led me toward the stage.

And there, standing in a loose circle, were a few figures I hadn't seen in decades. I've never been good with faces—but those... familiar shapes, familiar posture... I could never forget them.

My heart raced as the past *resurfaced.*

"Ta-da! Looks like a Frenchy and The Sweet Bandits reunion!"

Ryan said, spreading his arms wide, his smile as big as ever.

I blinked hard, taking them in.

Steve Franklin—my trusted music director and right-hand man—was front and center, his posture straight and controlled. He wasn't just the one running the show; he was the one who had the knowledge, the proper training, and the discipline to make sure everything ran smoothly. He was the one who kept everything in check, the one I always relied on.

Danny "Sticks" Taylor was fidgeting with his drumsticks, tapping them against his palms, against his legs, against anything that moved—or anything at all, really.

A rebel by nature, he had the spirit of a kid who never quite grew out of his troublemaking phase. He had this restless drive, always seeking the next challenge, always pushing the limits. His hands were constantly moving, even when he wasn't behind his kit, but when he did hit the drums, it was like everything in the room came alive. He was the fire, the one who kept the energy high.

And Billy Ray.

Billy Ray McCoy, standing with his bass slung low, arms crossed, looking like a hippie cowboy who'd strolled in from another era. He didn't say much, but his laid-back attitude spoke volumes. When he did speak, it was always worth listening to, but his real power came from the way he played—effortless, like the music was flowing through him from some timeless place.

Despite their different personalities—Steve's methodical precision, Danny's restless energy, and Billy Ray's free-spirited calm—they all had one thing in common: their pure, unfiltered love for music.

And beneath it all, they were some of the kindest, most genuine people I'd ever known. They were true to themselves, and in that honesty, they had formed something *rare*.

The Sweet Bandits wasn't just a name—it was a testament to who they were.

A band of misfits, but a family bound by music and *heart*.

The memories came rushing back, and for a moment, I couldn't speak.

"*Steve,*" I finally managed, walking up and pulling him into a brief hug before shaking his hand.

"*Man, it's been ages.*"

"*Hi, Frenchy. It's good to have you back,*" he said warmly.

"*Sticks,*" I said with a grin. He launched at me like a bar fight —hugged me like a long-lost brother, drumsticks still in hand.

"*Still banging away, huh?*"

"*You know it,*" Sticks replied a playful glint in his eyes.

"*Thought I'd never see this day.*"

"*Billy Ray,*" I said, giving him a nod and a firm handshake.

"*Still holding it down, cowboy?*"

He laughed softly.

"*Somebody has to.*"

I tilted my head toward Ryan.

"*And who's this?*"

Ryan stepped forward, his smirk growing wider.

"Oh, and by the way, we found someone very talented to fill Dakota's shoes. Jesse, meet C.C.—Cassidy Chase."

The young woman moved forward, her guitar slung over her shoulder. A nervous yet eager expression crossed her face as she extended a hand.

"It's such an honor to be here, Mr. Lawrence. I've always been a huge fan of your music... and the band."

Her enthusiasm caught me off guard, but I shook it.

"Nice to meet you, C.C. Big shoes to fill."

"I'll do my best," she said, her tone earnest.

Ryan clapped, cutting through the moment.

"Alright, let's run through the soundcheck, guys—shake the rust off a little. Bandits' style. And Jesse, I know you're gonna kill it."

Turned out the guys had already dialed everything in before I got there—sound, levels, gear, the whole setup. It was just me now.

I plugged in, checked my amp, my mic, made sure the monitors were right. Took a second to roll my shoulders and breathe.

The others stood quiet, ready to go—but nonetheless, all eyes on me. Some looked tense, some just uncertain. I couldn't blame them—we hadn't played together in what felt like another life. I was the one still catching up.

"Alright, Jesse. You all good now?" Steve asked, giving me a quick nod.

"We've got a setlist prepped—figured we'd start with the classics and feel it out from there. That work for you?"

"Yep. All good," I said simply.

"Let's roll."

As we jumped into the first song, it struck me. I wasn't hitting the right notes. I was missing parts, struggling to find my rhythm. I'd spent time going back over the tunes, doing my homework, trying to get my hands to remember what my heart hadn't forgotten—but still, my fingers kept slipping. Everyone exchanged glances. They were polite enough to keep playing, but I could tell—this wasn't going as smoothly as they'd hoped.

Ryan stood off to the side, watching me, throwing me thumbs-ups. Always confident, always optimistic—non-stop on the up and up—*but was he right?*

Was I really ready for this?

"Keep it together, Jesse," I whispered under my breath, trying to shake off the nerves.

But I wasn't convinced. It was *terrible.*

We started the second song, and it was worse. My timing was off, the music felt disjointed. The band stopped, and there was an awkward silence hanging in the air. I could sense their judgment without even looking at them.

Ryan walked over to me and rested a grip on my shoulder.

"You sound great, Jesse. You just need a minute to get back in the saddle. It's okay—I know it's gonna be awesome. Trust me."

I wiped the sweat from my forehead, still unsure.

"You sure? I feel like I'm not hitting it."

"You've got this," he said, his ever-present enthusiasm lighting up the moment.

"Just trust me. It'll be fine. I believe in you."

I took a deep breath. I had no choice. If I was going to do this, I needed to believe in myself, too.

"Alright," I said, straightening up—buckled in, finally ready for the ride.

"C'mon, Frenchy. The Bandits are waiting. Time to rob the damn bank now. Okay, guys—shoot it."

27

THE SWEET BANDITS

Doubt crept in, uninvited. As I sat in the green room, the cold Bud in my hand doing little to calm the knot in my stomach. The can was almost empty, but I didn't seem to care. My fingers kept tapping nervously on it, as if the rhythm could shake off the unease.

The dull chatter of the venue outside only seemed to make the whole thing worse. The buzz of the crowd—it was already there, waiting for something, waiting for me. But the tightness within me hadn't loosened.

The door creaked open, and Ryan stepped in, looking fresh and confident as ever. His smirk was easy, but there was something in his expression—a hint of concern, maybe, though it mostly carried trust.

"Everything alright?" he asked, his tone light, the kind that made everything seem under control—even if it didn't feel that way in my gut.

"Need anything?"

I took a long sip, the beer cooling my throat, but it did little for the tension coiling in my chest.

"*I'm good,*" I muttered, forcing out the words like they weighed more than they should. The half-hearted grin I attempted didn't help; I wasn't fooling anyone.

Not even *myself.*

"*You sure?*" he said, lingering near the doorway, his words spilling out like he couldn't stop himself.

"*It's gonna be great, Jesse. I believe in you, man.*" He paused, his voice taking on that familiar tone, carrying reassurance and belief—even if I didn't feel it yet.

"*And look, it's amazing. Full house tonight. How's that for a come-back? Word got around fast. People haven't forgotten, Jesse—just like I told you. See, they came here to see Frenchy. Once you step out there, let him take over. You're not just Jesse Lawrence anymore. You're Frenchy, the artist. You've got this. Just step out there and own it.*"

I raised my chin slightly, the words bouncing off my brain like they meant nothing. It was easy for him to say. He hadn't felt the weight of the past few years like I had, hadn't been there in the dark corners, stuck in the chaos of the things that had torn me down.

Before I could say anything else, there was a knock.

A voice from the hallway called,

"*Showtime!*"

Ryan gave me a final, knowing look; his smile reassured me, but his expression hinted at doubt, as if he wasn't fully convinced yet was willing to let me find my own way.

"*This is your moment, Frenchy,*" he said.

I grabbed the last of my drink, threw it back in one quick gulp, and tossed it aside. I pushed myself up from the chair, legs stiff and body heavier than it should've been—like it knew what was coming and wasn't sure it wanted to go.

"*Alright,*" I said, trying to say it like it was nothing, but it wasn't.

"*Let's do this.*"

As I stood, ready to face the crowd, I couldn't help but think back to the old days—before the struggle, before all hell broke loose. Back when it wasn't about the pressure, the constant pull of everything I couldn't quite hold together.

Billy Ray's words from earlier echoed in my head.

"*Yep, it was fun back then. Even though we always had to babysit Sticks, like that time in Tucson...*"

The memory flooded back. I could almost hear the distant sound of the jukebox, the clinking of glasses, and the rise and fall of conversations blending with the noise of another small, nameless town we'd rolled into for a show.

It was one of those nights that started as any other—nothing special, just a show, a few rounds, and the usual mix of road fatigue and excitement. We were in some dive bar in the middle of nowhere, a spot with no real vibe but plenty of character, the kind of spot where we'd settle in like we owned the joint, just to feel like we had a purpose.

But then Sticks, with his uncanny ability to find trouble even when he wasn't looking for it, ended up tangled in something none of us saw coming.

Some guy spilled his drink on him as he walked past the bar, and before we knew it, the man was shouting, getting in his face.

Nothing major at first, just a stupid misunderstanding—but the guy kept pushing, egged on by his buddies, and things escalated fast.

One minute, Sticks was trying to walk away. The next, he was on the floor, fists flying.

It didn't even feel like a real fight—nothing personal.

Just bad timing, wrong place.

Sticks wanted out, but the guy wouldn't let it go. And then, just like that, the cops showed up.

"Man, you gotta be kidding me," Sticks said under his breath, rubbing his jaw as the police dragged him outside.

It wasn't even his fault—he was just trying to defend himself, but the story they had was a different one. They were not listening. They were seeing the mess, the chaos, and that's how they treated him.

I stepped outside after the officers, trying to smooth things over, to make sense of it all. Steve, always the calm one, was already on the phone, working his magic.

"You're not going to throw him in jail for something that wasn't his fault," he said, the steadiness in his words cutting through the night air.

He wasn't raising his voice—he was making it clear that Sticks was getting out of this, no matter what.

Billy Ray stood by the van, arms crossed, his eyes scanning the scene like he was trying to understand what had happened.

"This is a damn mess," he grumbled.

"Sticks didn't do anything wrong, but of course, the cops just see the disaster."

I tried to hold my tone steady when I walked up to them.

"Look, he didn't start this. It's just a misunderstanding."

One of the officers raised an eyebrow.

"Your guy was the one throwing punches."

I shook my head, trying to keep composed.

"No, he wasn't. He was defending himself. The other guy started it. Ask anyone in the bar."

Sticks stood there, angry, embarrassed, and unsure how to handle what had unfolded.

"It's not like I wanted to get into this," he mumbled, glancing down. *"This dude started running his mouth, and I was just trying to get away. You know how it is..."*

That was Sticks' way—trouble found him, even when he wasn't looking for it. It was as if the universe just threw him into these situations, and we were there to pick up the pieces. But this time, it wasn't his fault. And we weren't about to let him deal with it alone.

After hours of talking with the police and Steve working his connections, the charges were dropped. Sticks was free to go, but the mood didn't lift immediately.

We didn't just get him out of a jam—we had his back, like we always did. No one got left *behind.*

Back at the bus, Sticks had that sheepish look on his face, the kind he wore when he knew he'd done something stupid, but also trusted we weren't going to leave him hanging.

He clapped Steve on the back.

"I owe you a drink, man. You got me out of that mess."

Steve just shook his head with a small smile.

"Don't make a habit of it."

Billy Ray, never one to get too caught up in the drama, just looked at Sticks.

"Man, you really know how to stir up trouble, don't you?"

Sticks shrugged with a hint of amusement.

"Hey, it's not my fault. But you know how it is. Always something."

Standing in the green room, I felt the memories wash over me, pressing down on my chest, reminding me of the bond we'd built over years of chaos and camaraderie.

No matter the case, we'd always had each other's *backs.*

And now, I was walking out there, not just as Jesse, but as part of something bigger.

As part of *The Sweet Bandits.*

28

OFF KEY, ON TRACK

W hile we got on stage, Sticks slid behind his drums, his usual energy taking over. I heard him mutter a few words to Billy Ray as he settled in.

"Hey, by the way, what happened to Kota?" Sticks asked, tapping his drumsticks against the kit, his voice low but carrying.

Billy Ray just shrugged, twisting some knobs on his amp, not even looking up.

"I don't know, man. Haven't heard anything."

The question briefly hung, then vanished within the crowd's clamor and harsh glare. The bright lights were almost blinding, and the chatter was deafening. I could feel the pressure of all their eyes on me, but none of it felt familiar—not the spotlight, not the sound of the audience, and certainly not the music. My hands were clammy, and I gripped the neck of my guitar as if it might slip away from me.

I stepped up to the mic, took a breath.

"Hi Austin," I said, doing my best to sound steady.

"It's great to be back."

The Bandits kicked off the first song, and I followed, but everything felt wrong. My timing was off, my fingers felt stiff, and the notes didn't come out right. My head raced, trying to find the groove—the old flow, the cruise control, the speed I used to ride so easy.

The guys kept glancing at each other, their faces polite but unsure. They were waiting for me to find my footing, but I wasn't sure I still had it.

But the audience, bless them, seemed patient—nodding along, tapping their feet—but I knew they did not feel what I wanted them to. They weren't with me. I could hear the hesitation in the music, the awkwardness in my playing. I was clinging to every note, and it wasn't working.

My chops were rusty as hell. That open mic? Just a one-off, incognito—a few minutes, spur of the moment, no real pressure. But this... this was the real thing. My show. My name on the bill.

What would people think? If any even showed up, that is— and my last show with The Bandits? Let's just say it didn't end with an encore.

Ryan watched me from the side, arms crossed. I caught his eye, and he gave me that nod—like he knew this would happen. That wasn't the look of disappointment. It was the look of someone who had seen me do this a thousand times before, someone who believed in me even when I didn't.

"Come on, Jesse," I said to myself, striving to push through the fog of doubt.

We jumped into the second song, and it felt worse. The band tried to follow, but it was like I was dragging them behind me, struggling to keep up. The clumsiness hung in the air, thick and uncomfortable. I couldn't face the crowd. I was afraid they'd see how badly I was choking.

But then, without warning, as the guitar solo kicked in.

I launched into some licks I didn't even know I could still play—signature licks that had once been the core of everything. They just poured out of me, like muscle memory with a soul.

It felt like Swampy remembered what I couldn't.

And as my fingers started noodling on the strings, something *shifted.*

With Swampy's takeover, all else faded. The stiffness in my hands melted away. Just like it used to, the music started to flow. The Bandits found their groove, and so did I.

The rhythm was there. It was all there—and *magical.*

The audience's energy shifted, too. I could feel them leaning forward, the tension breaking as the sound flowed with ease. Each note fell perfectly into place—natural, effortless. It was as though I was infusing life back into the performance, rediscovering a deeper connection than just music—a connection that had always existed within me.

As the tune played out, I closed my eyes, letting it all carry me.

This is where I belonged.

This is where *Frenchy* belonged.

Except now, with a new sidekick—*Swampy.*

As the show went on, the Bandits and I were locked in. We were in sync with every note, every rhythm, every little cue.

It wasn't a fight or a car chase anymore—finally, I wasn't chasing the music. It was a part of *me.*

A silent moment punctuated the end of the last song.

Then the crowd erupted.

I opened my eyes to see them on their feet, clapping and cheering. It wasn't just polite applause anymore—it was real.

They were with me.

With *us.*

I looked at Ryan—he looked like he was about to jump

onstage, wound up like a jack-in-the-box, all thumbs up and a smile as wide as Texas.

He was damn right all along.

The night might've started off key, but I was *back—on track.*

29

THE RECORD DEAL

Ryan, I had to admit, was starting to really impress me —or at least wear me down. At first, I figured he was just another loudmouthed kid, talking himself up, trying to sound more connected and skilled than he really was.

But damn if he hadn't pulled off a few things. Got the *Sweet Bandits* back together, lined up some gigs—hell, maybe *The Kid* actually had some real chops after all.

We've played a few small gigs since the comeback show. That night in Austin had been packed—a full house, standing room only.

But the ones that followed? Nothing *flashy.*

Just rooms where the floors creaked and the lights hummed.

They weren't bad though—always a great turnout, even if the club owners were a little frisky about it.

But it was enough to shake off the rust and feel like *Frenchy* again—at least on a good night.

On the bad ones, it was harder to tell who was finding their way back—me or the crowd. But a start's a *start.*

Ryan had called yesterday, said we needed to talk—something important to discuss, but not over the phone. He mentioned he'd be in the area today, and with the way he sounded, I figured sooner was better. So I told him to meet me at Joe's, since I'd be in town and not at the ranch.

I got there early. Or so I thought. The place was almost empty and so quiet, you could've heard a pin drop—or maybe even a fly flap its wings.

Then the door creaked open, loud enough to make me flinch. Ryan shuffled in, all hurried steps and restless energy, like the world couldn't move fast enough for him. His voice broke the stillness.

"Hey, Jesse!" he called, already halfway over.

"You're already here?"

I raised my bottle, greeting him.

"Hi, Kid. Yes, I'm here, not going anywhere. So slow down and take a breath."

I watched as he slid onto the stool next to me, a folder tucked under one arm.

"Yeah, yeah," he said between gasps, drumming his fingers on the counter. Classic Kid—always fidgeting when he had something to say.

"Go on," I urged, waving my beer.

"Spit it out. You look like you're about to explode."

Sheepishly grinning, he then took a deep breath.

"Okay, so I've got some news. Big news."

"Big news, huh? Let's hear it."

"You've been killing it at the clubs, you know? The small venues, reconnecting with the audience—it's been great. But Jesse, you need a new album. Something fresh to really get back out there."

I settled into my seat.

"A new album? Just like that, huh? You got a magic wand I don't know about?"

He laughed nervously.

"Not exactly. But I've been making calls, talking to my contacts. Got them to remember who you are—Jesse 'Frenchy' Lawrence. The legend."

"Yeah, yeah," I said, deadpan.

"And?"

He rubbed the back of his neck.

"Well... a lot of them were glad to hear you're still alive."

"Glad I'm still alive. That's touching, Kid."

"They are! But, uh, most of them don't want to take the risk. The music scene has changed, Jesse. It's all new artists, new sounds. They're not sure where you fit. And some of them... well, they're not sure you've still got it."

Although it stung more than I'd admit, I tried to stay stoic.

"So, they're not interested. Is that the big news?"

"No," Ryan said quickly.

"I pushed harder. And I found a label willing to bite."

"Willing to bite, huh? What's the catch, Kid?"

He opened the folder and slid a paper toward me.

"They'll back you if you record an album with re-recordings of your old hits and maybe a few new tracks—but they have to fit the vibe. Nothing experimental. They want safe, familiar."

I stared at him.

"So, a greatest hits album? Slap a sticker on it that says, 'Best of Frenchy and The Sweet Bandits,' and call it a day?"

Ryan shook his head, leaning closer.

"No, Jesse. This is a chance to show them you're not just some old legend collecting dust. You're still here, and you've still got it. It's a foot in the door."

Swirling the beer in my bottle, I felt grounded by its usual weight. Then I squinted at him.

"By the way, tell me, Kid—how do you know all these people? All those contacts? You're very young. What are you, twenty-something?"

Ryan straightened up a little, almost like he'd been waiting for the question.

"I'm twenty-two, to be exact."

"Twenty-two," I said, turning the number over in my head.

"All right, go on."

Bending forward, he spoke in a steady tone, yet a deeper emotion was detectable.

"Let's just say... I've been around. My whole life, I was raised in the industry. My parents were always connected—there were always producers, managers, and agents around. I spent more time at label meetings than at school, learning the ropes, how to negotiate, how the business side works. I guess you could say... I got a crash course in the game."

My fingers brushed over my beard as I mulled it over—skeptical, yet intrigued.

"So, you're telling me you're some kind of industry wunderkind? You're like... the Wunderkind!" I said, smirking.

He let out a dry chuckle, barely a smile.

"Not exactly. But I know how this works, Jesse. I get it—what you're trying to do with your music, your comeback. I know it's not just about the notes—it's about staying alive in this industry. You need someone who knows how to make it work."

I exhaled, sinking into my seat.

"Well, not quite right—but close enough. Okay, if we're doing this, we're doing it my way."

Beaming, Ryan's face lit up.

"Deal."

I raised my drink in a small salute.

"To Wunderkid! The new superhero to save the day—rescuing the damsel and the orphan." I paused, the smirk fading just a little.

"Or, in this case, the old geezer and his beat-up guitar." I let out a soft laugh.

"Guess Swampy and I better bring our A-game if we want to join the League."

30

US AGAINST THE WORLD

I had walked away from all this once, figured I was done for good. But some things have a way of calling you back.

And now here I was—back in the industry game, standing inside the *Skytown Records* office in downtown Austin, with Ryan, having just agreed to sign a deal for a new album—some kind of greatest hits revisited project.

He was the one who got us here—pulled the strings, knocked on doors, wouldn't take no for an answer.

It felt surreal, though—like stepping into the middle of *Main Street* after years in the hills, called out of retirement for one last showdown.

Me, a worn-out gunslinger, a dusty old outlaw. And by my side, Ryan *"The Kid"*—a fast-talking wunderkid with a twitchy trigger finger who dragged me back into the fight. Too quick on the draw, too green to wait, but sharp enough to land the shot when it mattered.

Then, the door swung open, and there she was—Aurora Miles, or simply *Rory,* as we called her.

"Jesse Goddamn Lawrence!"

Before I could react, she pulled me into a firm, warm hug, squeezing my shoulder before stepping back to get a good look at me.

"It's been forever. Thought you'd disappeared off the face of the earth."

I smirked.

"Hi, Rory. Great to see you too. You haven't changed a bit."

She arched an eyebrow.

"Sweet talk, as always. You haven't changed either, Frenchy." She winked, shaking her head.

"Still got that smooth charm." Then, with a teasing smile, she added,

"Oh là là... always the Frenchman."

Despite all that had happened, seeing Rory again after all these years felt like a spark of familiarity. She hadn't changed much—the same strong, fierce woman I remembered.

Rory, around my age or perhaps slightly older, possessed an unparalleled, seasoned perspective on the music industry. She was known for making the tough calls—the ones no one else wanted to make. And when it came to advocating for her artists, she fought for them, no backing down, no matter what. Charismatic and insightful, she had a way of reading people and situations that made her a force to be reckoned with. Once a musician herself, she knew the grind and the passion it took to stay in the game, and that earned her respect from everyone who worked with her.

She carried herself with the same calm confidence that effortlessly commanded attention, her stylish yet practical attire a reflection of someone who had nothing to prove. Seeing her again brought back memories of the early days, when our paths first crossed in this chaotic world of music. She'd always believed in me, even when I didn't believe in myself.

To celebrate the signing, Rory treated us to lunch at her favorite spot. It was a cozy, rustic place with wood-paneled walls, and a jukebox in the back spinning old rock and country classics, running through its playlist without a second thought.

As we settled into a corner booth with a round of drinks between us, the air felt lighter, like maybe this was the start of something good.

Rory rocked back, her eyes gleaming with triumph, like she'd just hit the jackpot.

"Well, boys, here we are," she announced, her glass raised.

"Who would've thought, huh? Frenchy and The Sweet Bandits, back in action."

Ryan lifted his glass, smirking.

"Cheers to that."

I managed a half-smile and clinked mine with theirs, though my mind was somewhere else entirely. The deal was done, the future looked bright, but all I could think about was the past.

"You must have some wild war stories from back in the day," Ryan said, turning to Rory.

"What was Jesse like? Y'know, before all this."

Setting down her drink, Rory chuckled.

"Oh, boy. Where do I even start?" She shot me a look—not just playful, but with a flicker of something else—and I braced myself for whatever memory she was about to dredge up.

"You know, Jesse and I go way back," she said.

"I used to help out with logistics, admin, a little marketing—whatever needed doing, really. Mostly behind the scenes. But I saw a lot."

"So, anyway... There was this one time, during the second tour... sold-out show, crazy crowd... Jesse and Marie were on fire. You should've seen them—completely in sync, like they were made to play together. The crowd was eating it up, and I remember thinking, 'Man, they're unstoppable.'"

She paused, a mischievous glint in her eyes.

"*And, well, there are some other stories that I can't share. Anyway, that was a long time ago.*"

She winked at me before taking another sip, leaving Ryan with a raised eyebrow and more questions than answers.

A knot formed in my stomach.

Yeah. *Unstoppable.* We were. Until we weren't.

"*Unstoppable,*" she repeated softly, her smile fading.

"*It was like magic back then.*"

The knot tightened, and what I'd been trying to avoid came rushing in, uninvited.

The lights were blinding, the audience a sea of faces lost in shadows beyond the stage. The heat from the overheads was intense, but I barely noticed it. All I could see was *Marie.*

She stood next to me, microphone in hand, her voice blending perfectly with mine as we finished the last chorus.

The roar of the crowd was deafening, their applause echoing through the massive arena like a thunderstorm. The energy was electric, and for a fleeting moment, I felt untouchable. *Invincible.*

Marie turned to me, a smile playing on her lips. She leaned in close, her breath warm against my ear.

"*It's just us, Jesse. Us against the world. They'll try to tear us down, but they can't as long as we stick together. We're unstoppable.*"

At the time, her words felt like a promise—a bond only we shared. But now, looking back, they felt more like a chain. Ensuring I remained blindly loyal and faithful, never questioning her or looking further than her.

"*Earth to Jesse,*" Rory said, her fingers snapping in front of my face.

With a blink, the flashback evaporated like smoke. My chest felt tight, and I realized I'd been holding my breath.

"*You okay, Jesse?*" Rory, concerned, asked.

"*Yeah,*" I muttered, as I forced myself to breathe.

"Just thinking." I took a sip of my drink, hoping it would steady me.

"I used to have it, Rory. That... magic. Now I'm just an old guy with a beat-up guitar."

She shook her head, a knowing smile playing at her lips.

"Nah, you're still that guy. More scars, more soul. And don't forget —real songs don't get old. They just wait for the right moment to come back around."

Ryan's eyes lit up with curiosity.

"Wait, wait. What did Marie say to you back then? During those shows?"

I hesitated, the words still echoing in my mind.

"She used to say... 'It's us against the world.' Made it sound like we were invincible together. Like nothing could touch us."

Rory's smile faded slightly. For a moment, she studied me before speaking.

"Y'know, looking back now, that kind of talk wasn't just about the music, was it?"

"No," I said quietly.

"It wasn't."

There was a pause. No one said a word, and for a second, the restaurant's noise faded into the background, like the world had stepped aside to let this moment breathe.

I glanced down, fingers tracing the worn edge of the table, Rory's words still echoing in my head.

Maybe I didn't need to be who I was back then. Maybe it was enough to be who I was now—scars and all.

Breaking the silence, Rory raised her glass again.

"To the future. Whatever it brings."

Alongside Ryan, I cheered as well. The tightness in my chest eased—just a little.

Maybe I wasn't invincible anymore.

Maybe it wasn't *us against the world* after all.

But at least today, I was living in a *free world.*

31

WELCOME TO THE ECHO PONDS STUDIOS

LEGENDS, GREMLINS, AND GHOST COWS

The ink had barely dried on the contract before Ryan was already making calls, setting things in motion.

"I've got the perfect place," he had said, eyes gleaming.

"Not just any studio—this one's legendary. Magic in the walls, man. Some of the greatest albums ever recorded, right there. It's got soul, history—artists say the music gods are looking after it."

I wasn't sure if I believed in all that, but something about the way he said it made me want to.

A few days later, Ryan picked me up at the ranch just before dawn, the truck's headlights slicing through the quiet. The air was sharp, dry, the kind of cold that settled deep in your bones before the sun had a chance to burn it off.

I stepped onto the porch, exhaling a cloud of breath, stretching off the weight of too little sleep.

He had insisted we go together—said it'd be part of the experience. Figured I might as well leave my truck at the ranch in case Emma needed it for work.

Ryan rolled down the window, looking just as tired.

"Morning, Jesse."

"You look like hell," I muttered.

"Yeah, well. Crashed at that shitty motel in town for a few hours. Not exactly the Ritz." He smirked.

I tossed my bag and Swampy into the truck bed, eyeing the oversized ride.

"So, Kid playing in the big boys' league now?"

"What?" Ryan squinted.

I gestured at the truck.

"Oh, this? My car needed service, so I figured I'd rent a big truck for our road trip. Didn't want you feeling out of place." He chuckled.

"Alright, then, so you sure you're awake enough to drive?"

Ryan rubbed his jaw, stifling a yawn.

"I'll live. Anyway, we gotta hit the road if we wanna make it by late afternoon."

I huffed, pulling open the door.

"Long-ass drive for some studio. You better not have oversold this place."

His smirk widened.

"You'll see soon enough."

So here we were, chasing that magic all the way west.

The drive stretched long, taking us through endless open landscapes. We left behind the burnt-orange sands and jagged cliffs of West Texas, the Mars-like terrain of the *Chihuahuan* Desert fading in the rearview.

Sun sat heavy in the sky, baking the land into something almost surreal, like a mirage that never quite vanished.

We passed through Marfa, then farther east toward Abilene, where the land spread flat and unbroken, dust swirling in the wake of passing semis.

The towns along the way felt like they were barely holding on—gas stations with flickering neon signs, diners with sun-bleached menus, weathered billboards promising cheap motels and the best barbecue for miles.

By the time we hit Dallas, the sky was cut through with high-rises, and the roads swelled with traffic, the endless stillness of the desert replaced by the hum of a city that never really slept.

But we didn't stay long. We pushed on, the skyline shrinking behind us, highways thinning into backroads, then backroads stretching into rolling fields fading toward the horizon.

Another few hours east, and we were deep in pine country, skirting the outskirts of Texarkana. The flatlands gave way to thick woods, the atmosphere growing thicker and darker. It felt like we were leaving Texas behind and entering the Sherwood Forest.

As we drove deeper, the road to the Echo Ponds curved through dense, leaning trees, the canopy growing heavier with every mile. Ryan was getting antsy, his knuckles whitening on the wheel as he pushed through the final stretch. The GPS had given up five minutes ago, and the only sign we were on the right path was the faded wooden sign ahead:

THE ECHO PONDS — Legendary Sound Awaits

"Legendary sound," Ryan grumbled.
"More like a legendary pain to find."

I didn't reply. Because I was too busy staring at the sign, I didn't notice it was half-hidden by vines. It felt like we were stepping into history—or maybe a ghost story.

Nestled in a clearing, a sprawling, weathered set of buildings came into view—part barn, part cabin, part time machine. The paint was peeling in patches, and the roofs looked like they hadn't been touched since the seventies. But it had a presence. There was something about the way it stood, surrounded by silence except for the faint chirping of crickets, that made you stop and take it in.

Ryan parked, and we climbed out, the gravel crackling like dry leaves beneath our boots. He took one look at the building, then back at me.

"This is it?"

"Yup, looks like it" I said, grabbing Swampy's case from the truck.

"The Echo Ponds."

I glanced at him—Ryan's expression had twisted in doubt.

"How the hell did you even find this place?"

Ryan scratched the back of his neck.

"Some guys recommended it. Said it had 'history'—you know, real magic in the walls."

I gave him a look.

"Some guys?"

"Well, they seemed legit." He shrugged.

"Besides, you know what they say—don't judge a book by its cover."

I let out a short breath, sizing up the property.

"Yeah, except this book looks like it used to hold hay bales."

Ryan dropped his arms, staring in disbelief.

"You've got to be kidding me."

"Relax, Kid. I've been told legendary albums came out of here." I smirked.

The Echo Ponds was less of a state-of-the-art studio and more of a once-functional barn turned into a recording space— long wooden beams, faded red paint, and rusted hinges that had seen better days. A few timeworn outbuildings leaned nearby, like the place had been stitched together from forgotten scraps. If you listened close enough, you could almost hear the ghosts of cows judging us.

Who knows?

We might just need *more cowbell.*

As we finally found our way inside, the studio smelled like old vinyl and something faintly metallic. Gold and platinum plaques, dulled but gleaming with age and history, lined the walls. Names like *Elvis Presley, Aretha Franklin,* and *Otis Redding* stared back at us, a reminder of the legends who'd recorded here.

Ryan paused in front of one, his fingers brushing the glass.

"Do you think they had to deal with duct tape and broken gear, too?"

"Nah, maybe not," I said.

"But that's okay—'cause Swampy's a damn fixer."

32

GETTING DOWN TO BUSINESS

I n the control room, there was a mix of charm and chaos. The hardwood floors creaked, the console gave off a low hum, and one of the overhead lights flickered intermittently. But there was a warmth to the space, a feeling like the walls themselves had soaked in decades of music.

We'd had just enough time to stretch, caffeinate, and shake the road off before getting to it.

The Bandits had already been here for over a week, working on the basics, and the weariness showed. While Billy Ray idly plucked his bass on a worn leather couch, Steve muttered about cables as he tinkered with his keyboards.

"Bout time," Steve said as I walked in.

"Thought you were gonna leave us stranded."

"Had to get The Kid acquainted with history," I said, dropping my bag in the corner and setting Swampy's case on the floor.

Before I could say more, a familiar voice rang out—

"Hey, look who finally decided to show up!" Sticks called with a grin, twirling a drumstick between his fingers.

"Thought y'all got lost in those legendary woods outside."

"Good to see you too, Sticks." I smirked.

Then, turning to Steve,

"Alright, maestro. how's everything shaping up so far?"

Steve straightened up, rubbing his temples like he'd had one too many long nights.

"We're moving along. It's been an... eventful ten days. Some good takes, some minor catastrophes, but hey, nothing's on fire, so that's a win."

Ryan raised an eyebrow.

"'Eventful?' That's not exactly a confidence booster."

Steve smirked, adjusting a few knobs on the console.

"Relax. We had a few hiccups—some wiring issues, a mic preamp that decided to give up on life, and, uh... let's just say the AC has a personality. But we worked through it. This place has its quirks, but it's got a sound, Jesse. Feels like the walls are still holding onto something."

Ryan crossed his arms, skeptical.

"Holding onto what, exactly?"

Billy Ray chuckled from the couch, his Texan drawl easygoing as ever.

"Call it spirit, call it history—some places just bring out the best in you."

I nudged Ryan with my elbow.

"You heard him, Kid. Let's see if the barn's tales are real."

Steve cleared his throat, steering the conversation back.

"So, we've locked in the rhythm tracks. Now we need to focus on the vocals and your guitar parts. Time to start bringing the songs to life."

I exhaled, rolling my shoulders as I looked throughout the room. The air smelled of warm wood and old amps, the faintest hum of electricity buzzing from the console.

The studio wasn't perfect—hell, it was far from it—but there was something about it—like it had a heartbeat of its own. One I could feel.

I ran a hand over Swampy's case before flipping the latches open. The lid creaked slightly as I lifted it, revealing the well-worn ash beneath. She came to life under the studio lights, like she'd been waiting for this moment. I wrapped my fingers around the neck, feeling the grooves, the years of music pressed into the fretboard.

"Alright, maestro," I said to Steve, lifting her free.

"Let's get to it."

Sticks leaned back, twirling a drumstick between his fingers.

"No pressure, boss, but Swampy's been killing it so far. Let's see if you can keep up."

I shook my head, laughing despite myself.

"Guess we'll find out."

33

FALLING OUT OF RHYTHM

Never had I felt so out of place in a studio before. The worst part? I'd come in motivated—thought maybe I still had some fire left. But the moment I plugged in, it was like someone had cut the wires.

The following couple of days were a frustrating and self-doubting haze for me. What once felt like an extension of my soul now seemed foreign and unyielding. The hum of the recording equipment, the faint scent of wood and metal, and even the comforting click of buttons on the console felt offbeat —as if the space itself knew I didn't belong here anymore.

Day one proved to be the most challenging. I stood in the middle of the live room, Swampy slung over my shoulder, staring blankly at the microphones set up around me.

Steve, ever the optimist, tried to coax me into the groove.

"Just play what you feel, man," Steve said, his voice crackling through the studio monitors from behind the glass.

But that was the problem. I didn't know what I felt. Although my hands hovered over the strings, the music refused to come.

Every strum, every note, felt mechanical, lifeless. I cursed under my breath and yanked off my headphones, muttering something about needing a break. Steve exchanged a worried glance with Sticks, who was tapping idly on his drumsticks.

By the second day, I had settled into a routine of avoidance. I arrived late, lingered too long over coffee, and found excuses to tweak my guitar's tuning or recheck the lyrics of old songs that didn't need revisiting. Sensing a storm brewing inside me, the band gave me space.

"*You know,*" Billy Ray finally said during a smoke break,

"*it's like riding a horse, Jesse. You've been thrown off, but you've gotta get back in the saddle. Nobody expects you to gallop on day one.*"

I nodded, yet my jaw clenched. I appreciated Billy Ray's cowboy metaphors, but the truth was, this wasn't just falling off a horse. It felt like forgetting how to ride entirely.

What a fool I was—thinking a few gigs would get me back in the saddle, just like Billy Ray said.

Like some cocky rookie who thought playing a dive bar prepped him for studio red lights. Performing and recording? Two different battles.

And right now, I was on the *front line.*

That night, after everyone else had left, I sat alone in the control room. The dim glow from the console cut through the dark, shadows pooling in the corners like secrets waiting to be heard.

I put down Swampy in her case, almost about to kiss her goodnight—like a bedtime routine after years of marriage.

But that can't be—we're still in the honeymoon phase. And still...

That unique sensual connection—the way my hands slid across her curves, the caress of the strings under my intense, craving pressure.

The way I used to solve the puzzle when my fingers danced

along the fretboard, like we were speaking a secret language only we understood.

But that vibe—that electric energy when her and I made one —it was gone. Disappeared.

I started to wonder if it was the Echo Ponds. Maybe the place, with all its ghosts and mystique, had sucked the soul right out of Swampy.

Maybe she was just waiting for something I couldn't give her.

Or maybe... I just didn't deserve her anymore.

I looked at her, still resting in the case—quiet, untouched.

"No. It can't be—not this time. I won't let it happen again. We have to work it out."

I picked her up, holding her close.

"We have to try again"

I began to play, the notes hesitant at first, then growing steadier. Memories surfaced with each chord—long nights on the road, the thrill of a crowd's roar, the solace of creating some-thing from nothing. Slowly trying to relight the spark, that dying flame, reconnecting with something *deeper*.

By the time I stopped for a second, the clock read way past midnight. I was exhausted, but I was starting to feel it again.

"Alright, time to go sleep and get some rest now," I murmured to Swampy.

Tomorrow, I thought.

Tomorrow, I'll try again.

We'll try again.

34

THE SLOW BURN

G oing through the motions wasn't cutting it. The next day, the studio felt heavier—its walls almost closing in on me, pressing my frustration back on me.

I pushed through the recordings, take after take, but nothing clicked. Every note sounded like I was chasing something just out of reach. By the afternoon, I couldn't take it anymore.

I set Swampy down, yanked off my headphones.

"I need a break. I need some fresh air."

Yesterday's spark had flickered back to life, but today, it barely smoldered. Whatever had stirred in me the night before didn't carry over—it got lost somewhere between the studio walls and the weight I woke up with.

Inside, the atmosphere felt charged—thick with unspoken tension and unresolved emotions. I couldn't stay in that space any longer. I needed to breathe.

Stepping outside, the door clicked shut behind me, the sound sharper than it should've been—final, like a line had been drawn.

That's when the air hit me—damp and cool, clinging to my skin like a second thought. A welcome breeze. It didn't bring peace, not exactly, but it cut through the fog in my head.

I drifted across the gravel driveway, letting my boots find their own path. The soft rustle of leaves was the only sound—a far cry from the chaos I'd just walked away from.

The late-afternoon sun slipped through the trees, revealing the shadows of silent guardian figures—tall, imposing, watching —slightly leaning, like sentinels listening in. It felt eerie, almost magical, like the place had its own pulse, its own rhythm that I couldn't quite catch.

Zoning out, I took a sip from the flask I'd brought with me, the whiskey burning a path down my throat. *Good Ol' Jack* was never far—always traveling with me, just in case I needed the company. The warmth spread through my chest, dulling the edges of my thoughts.

"Jesse?"

Steve's voice broke through the quiet. I turned to see him stepping out of the building, his silhouette outlined by the soft glow from inside. He hesitated for a moment, then walked over, his footsteps crunching against the gravel.

"Been looking for you."

"Didn't go far," I said, raising the flask slightly in a mock toast. *"Just needed some air."*

Steve came to stand beside me, crossing his arms.

"Figured. You've been quiet all day."

I shrugged, staring out at the woods.

"Just... trying to get my head straight. It's not coming as easy as it used to."

Steve exhaled, nodding.

"Yeah... I get that."

"Doesn't feel like it," I muttered.

"This place, this whole process... it's supposed to feel like home, but it doesn't. Feels like a cage instead."

"It's not the place that's the problem, Jesse." Steve's voice was steady, but there was an edge of concern.

"It's you."

I turned to look at him, my jaw tightening.

"What's that supposed to mean?"

"It means you've been running for years. From the music, from the people who care about you, from yourself." He studied me for a moment, then added,

"It's not about getting back to where you were. It's about finding out where you're supposed to be now."

I swallowed hard, glancing toward the studio door. The walls inside held more than just sound—they held history, memories, ghosts I wasn't sure I was ready to face.

Steve shifted his stance, lowering his voice.

"She's still in there, right?"

I frowned, confused.

"Swampy?"

He shook his head slowly.

"No. Her."

I looked away, jaw tight.

"You left the stage, the spotlight, your friends, the whole damn world... but not her. You didn't, Jesse. She did."

He glanced toward the studio.

"So maybe it's time to reclaim your own—and stop leaving pieces of yourself behind because of her."

Steve's words hit hard. Not because they surprised me, but because they were true.

I didn't say anything, just stood there.

He gave my shoulder a quick pat, let out a breath, and turned back toward the studio.

For a long moment, I stayed frozen, eyes locked on the dark tree line.

By now, the silent guardians had started to fade—no longer watching. Their sentinel duty complete, their purpose *fulfilled.*

I took a last sip from the flask, then turned on my heel, heading back in without a second thought.

Swampy was waiting, beautiful, and ready for me.

I ran a hand across her curves, feeling the grooves, the weight, the balance—it was all the same.

But I wasn't.

I picked her up, settled her on my lap, and let out a slow breath.

Then, without thinking, I started playing. The sound rang out, loud and clear.

And tonight, I won't leave anything behind anymore.

Because *Swampy*—she didn't *leave me.*

35

NEVER LET GO

Once upon a time, everything felt *so right,* like it was always going to stay that way.

But then.

It had been years since I last set foot in a recording studio. The last time, Marie and I were putting the final touches on what was supposed to be our second baby—a *duet album.*

From time to time during the recordings, we brought in lil' Jesse Jr. He was always so happy—dancing, moving, laughing. It wasn't always easy to focus, sure, but those were beautiful moments, the kind that stick with you.

A happy family, full of *joy* and *love.*

Even though the sessions weren't always flawless—the tension, the arguing, the push and pull of being married—we had something real.

Or at least, I thought we did.

I was in *heaven.*

Until I went to *hell.*

And that *"second baby"* never saw the light of day.

The flash faded as quickly as it came. Stillness reigned in the Echo Ponds; it was the quiet after a storm. The live room felt less like a cage now and more like a sanctuary. Tension from the past few weeks had begun to lift, but the weight of everything I'd poured into this project was still heavy on my chest.

Tonight, I was the last one left. Steve had insisted I take a break, but I couldn't leave. Not yet.

My vocals and guitar parts were done, every note, every line recorded. It was all complete—but something still lingered, a pull I couldn't ignore.

From the control booth, a faint murmur of sound filled the room—the engineer was laying down rough mixes, dialing in levels, adjusting the balance.

Then, through the big monitors, the familiar opening riff of "Never Let Go" rolled out, rich and full, filling the space like an echo of everything we'd built.

I leaned forward, resting my elbows on my knees as the track unfolded. My voice, my guitar—it was all there, layered and alive, yet it felt distant, like hearing a memory play back in real time.

Swampy was resting on my lap, her wood smooth and warm under my hands. She had carried me through this whole process, guiding me in ways I couldn't explain.

And then, without thinking, I reached for my headphones and slipped them on.

As the first chorus swelled, my fingers found their place on the strings. I started playing along, weaving into the mix as if the song was pulling me in, demanding something more.

The song wasn't new—it was one of our hits, an anthem that had carried us through countless tours. But today, it felt different. It wasn't just a performance or a recording session. It was a message.

"Take my hand, into the night
As we dance with the stars, we can touch
   the sky...
Close your eyes and let it go."

The words resonated deeper than they ever had before. Each line felt alive, infused with something beyond me.

Swampy's tone was rich and vibrant, the notes soaring and weaving through the room like they had a life of their own. It was like the guitar was singing with me, amplifying the emotions I couldn't put into words.

As the chorus hit, I closed my eyes and let the music take over.

"Chase your dreams and never let go."

My fingers moved instinctively, each note blending seamlessly with the track. The sound filled the space around me, but it was more than that—I felt it.

The vibrations from the amp pulsed through my body, shaking through my chest, surging through my arms to my hands. I could feel it in the blood flow of my fingertips. It wasn't just sound anymore—it was something alive, something tugging at my heartstrings, weaving itself into the music, moving through me like a current, binding me to it in a way that felt almost sacred.

Swampy wasn't just *singing*—she was *speaking,* telling me something I couldn't quite put into words.

That line—it wasn't just for the audience anymore. It wasn't just for the band or the critics or the label.

It was for *me.*

A reminder of everything I'd fought through, of why I was

still here, making music, pouring myself into every chord and lyric.

When the final notes faded, I let out a breath I didn't realize I'd been holding.

The room was quiet again, but no longer hollow.

Like the walls had finally heard me—and answered back.

Peace, maybe even *hope.*

I ran my hand along Swampy's neck, her strings humming faintly in the silence.

"You've got real magic in you, don't you?" I whispered, a wide, satisfied grin on my face.

I'd felt it before—many times. But right now, it was crystal clear. There was no denial.

Swampy wasn't just a *guitar.*

In her own way, she was *alive*—carrying a piece of something bigger than me.

I set her gently on the stand.

My part was done. The vocals, the guitar tracks, the raw emotion—everything was recorded, etched into the fabric of the album.

But as much as it felt like an ending, it also felt like the start of something new.

This wasn't just a *(re)collection* of songs.

It was something bigger—something I didn't quite understand yet.

Swampy's magic? *Maybe.*

Or maybe it was just me finally tearing down the barricades I'd built around my heart.

Whatever it was, it felt *right.*

And as I stepped away, I couldn't shake the feeling that the real work was only just beginning.

"Take my hand into the night.

As we dance with the stars, we can touch the sky.
Sing, wo-oh ho wo-oh, wo-oh,
Close your eyes and let it go.

Free your mind, see what comes around,
And everything's going to be all right.
Wo-oh ho oh wo-oh,
Chase your dreams and never let go."

36

ON AIR OR NOWHERE

Hovering like a thick fog, the silence settled over the studio. As the last note faded, I leaned back in my chair, arms crossed, eyes locked on the speakers as if staring hard enough might make them say something different.

I could feel everyone's eyes on me, *waiting.*

They always waited.

I didn't rush—never did. You can't rush this kind of thing.

"Well?" Ryan's voice cut through the quiet.

"Jesse, what do you think? It's solid, right?"

I didn't answer right away. Instead, I took a deep breath, letting my eyes drift across the room, over the band and the team. They felt excited, optimistic, perhaps slightly anxious. I hated moments like this.

Not because I didn't care—if anything, I cared too much. Call it perfectionist syndrome. Guilty as charged. Life sentence, no parole.

No known cure... but I keep taking the damn treatment anyway—even though it feels more like a placebo.

"Yeah, it's good," I said, finally breaking the silence.

Ryan exchanged a glance with Steve, who shrugged as if to say, he's always like this. I caught it, of course. I always caught those little looks they gave each other.

They probably thought I was a nut job. Maybe even a little unhinged. *Crazy. Obsessive.*

OCD, ADHD, OCPD—every acronym in the psychology 101 manual.

Or maybe just a mad scientist, ranting about a mythical 13th note—one you couldn't hear, only absorb—buried deep in the sound waves.

Well that's okay. I was used to it—been dealing with it my whole life.

And maybe, in a way, I deserved it. I knew I could be a pain in the ass, always pushing for more when everyone else thought we'd nailed it. But I couldn't settle for anything less than what felt *right.*

And right now, it didn't.

Ryan was about to say something—probably try to convince me that we were done, that it was good enough—when I raised a hand, cutting him off before he could start.

"Give me a minute," I muttered. I needed to sit with it a little longer, to let it sink in—and figure out what wasn't clicking.

"Look," Ryan said, trying to sound casual,

"we've got time to figure that out later. But right now, we need to focus on something else."

"Something else?" I asked, raising an eyebrow.

"Yeah. That interview I told you about—KTXS wants you live on air. It's the biggest station in Texas, and people are buzzing about your comeback. The interview's with Big Tex on his show. It's huge."

"Not a chance. We're in the middle of this. I'm not leaving the studio for some PR stunt."

Ryan didn't back down.

"*Come on Jesse, it's not just PR. People want to hear from you. This is your first major interview in years. You can talk about the album, tease about what's coming. It's good promo, and you know it.*"

"*I don't care. Just tell them to find another date. We'll do it later.*"

Ryan hesitated, then said,

"*Yeah... about that. I already booked it. It's locked in for tomorrow.*"

I shot him a glare.

"*You what?*"

"*When I brought it up last week, you said 'fine.'*"

"*Huh? I don't recall saying that. I was probably in my creative zone.*" I waved my hand dismissively.

"*You know how I get when I'm working.*"

Ryan shrugged.

"*Well, anyway, I thought it was okay. Thought we'd be pretty much done by now. Figured we could use a little break while Steve and Mike put the final touches on the mixes.*"

I rubbed my temple, feeling the frustration build.

"*Well, we're not done yet, as far as I'm concerned.*" I gestured toward the speakers.

"*And I ain't leaving until I've got it right.*"

"*I get it,*" Ryan said, keeping his voice calm.

"*But this is Big Tex's show we're talking about. His podcast is one of the most popular in the state—hell, even in the country. KTXS doesn't reschedule easily—they're booked for months, and there's even a waiting list. But Big Tex really wants you on. If we cancel now, it'll look bad. They're counting on this. We flake, we're done. No second chances.*"

I groaned, knowing he had me cornered. As much as I wanted to tell him off, he had a point. Blowing this now wasn't an option.

And yeah... maybe I do need a little break. Clear my head.

"*Fine,*" I sighed.

"*But we're heading right back after. No detours, no nonsense.*"

Steve chimed in from the console, not even looking up.

"*Don't worry, Jesse. Do what you gotta do—we've still got a few details to tweak here and there. It's only mixes in progress anyway. So once C.C. lays down her vocal parts and we swap out the old ones, it'll all fall into place.*"

I nodded, but something still gnawed at me.

Vocals, *old or new*—that wasn't what was missing.

And even if it was the final mixes, it was something else that was bothering me.

Ryan, of course, took my silence as surrender.

And with a grin and both hands lifted in mock triumph, he gave me that look—*See? Told you.*

"*Okay. Deal, Jesse. It's tomorrow, so plenty of time to prep. Quick and painless.*"

37

OUT OF THE WOODS

Waking up to Ryan's nagging had become a routine. The day started the way it always did—with him bugging me. This time, it was about the interview. I had barely finished my coffee when he brought it up again, all smiles and persistence.

"Come on, Jesse. It's KTXS. You can't turn this down."

Rubbing my temple, I was still emerging. One thought at a time, one sip at a time, one *Ryan-nag* at a time.

"Kid, we already talked about this. I said I'd do it, didn't I? No need to keep selling it."

Ryan chuckled, unfazed.

"I know, but you didn't exactly look thrilled when you agreed. Just making sure you're still on board."

I let out a sigh. He wasn't wrong. Agreeing to this didn't mean I was looking forward to it.

"Thrilled?" I grumbled.

"I'm practically jumping out of my boots."

I stared into my half-empty mug like it might offer an escape.

No such luck. No wonder Fort Knox wasn't far off.

I dragged a hand down my face.

"Alright, let's go. But you're the one behind the wheel."

Soon after, our journey began. Ryan's truck rumbled along the narrow, tree-lined road that led away from the outskirts of Texarkana. Early morning sunlight filtered through the dense canopy above, casting dappled patterns across the windshield. The air was still crisp, carrying that earthy scent you only get out here after a cool night.

In the passenger seat, I relaxed, the rhythm of the road washing over me. There wasn't much traffic this hour—just the occasional pickup or old sedan passing by in the opposite direction. The peace felt nice, giving me a moment to gather my thoughts.

"You doing alright over there?" Ryan asked, breaking the silence.

Although his tone was light, I sensed his underlying concern.

"Fine," I said, though it didn't sound all that fine to me.

I stretched my fingers until my knuckles cracked, trying to ease the restless energy that had been building since we left.

He shot me a quick glance, then grinned.

"Relax. You've got this. KTXS is big around here, and Big Tex's show? People actually listen to him. This isn't just some random gig— it's a real chance to remind folks why they liked you in the first place."

"Yeah," I muttered, shifting in my seat.

"I just don't know what they expect me to say. Feels like everything's already out there. Disappear for years, come back, try to make it again. Nothing special."

Keeping his eyes on the road, Ryan shrugged.

"Maybe. But they haven't heard it from you, not in your own words. And trust me, people want to hear it. They're rooting for you, even if you don't believe it."

I didn't answer right away, just stared out the window. The landscape was familiar—rolling fields dotted with patches of trees, the occasional herd of cattle grazing lazily near the fence line, and now and then an old barn in the distance.

It was peaceful—the kind only the countryside can offer, the kind that feels like it's always been there, waiting for you to notice it.

See, the cows had it all figured out—stand still, chew, watch the trains roll by, ignore the chaos and just go with the *flow*.

38

AU PETIT PARIS

Every tune Ryan whistled blended into the next as we rolled down the highway with the windows open. I leaned back, half-listening, half-watching the endless *Southern belle* beauty *Texas* had to offer.

Suddenly, I noticed something off.

"Wait, Kid, where are you going? The signs for Dallas are back that way," I said, sitting up straighter.

"Are you lost, or what?"

Ryan didn't seem fazed, keeping his eyes on the road and flashing me a grin.

"Nope. Not lost. I saw the highway sign for Paris. Figured we could take a little detour."

"Seriously? You've gotta be kidding me. No detours, remember?" I grumbled, glancing at the green highway sign that read:

PARIS, TEXAS – 22 MILES

"Come on, Jesse. I've never been there, and you lived there for a

while, right? Where it all started? Thought it might be fun. Plus, we can grab some lunch. Two birds, one stone." Ryan shrugged, still grinning.

I sighed, leaning back in the seat again.

"Whatever. But don't expect much. It's not exactly Paris, France."

"Yeah, but it's still Paris. How many people can say they've been to Paris, Texas, with Jesse Lawrence?" he chuckled, clearly enjoying himself.

A little while later, we pulled into town. Paris, Texas, wasn't big, but it had its charm—a main street lined with old brick buildings, a few diners, and small shops. Life here moved slower, wrapped in a stillness you could feel.

Not exactly the *City of Lights*—hell, not even la *Ville Lumière* —but it had a glow all its own.

Ryan parked the truck near the town square, and we got out, stretching our legs. As we walked down the street, something caught his eye up ahead. He stopped, squinting at the structure in the distance.

"Is that... an Eiffel Tower?" he asked, pointing.

I smirked.

"Yep. With a big red cowboy hat on top of it."

He blinked, looking at the tower, then at me, then back at the tower again—his expression caught somewhere between disbelief and amusement.

He did this a couple more times before finally saying,

"Wait, wait... is this why you wear that iconic red hat all the time?"

I couldn't help but laugh.

"Nah, Kid. Pure coincidence. But I like that theory."

We kept walking a little further, passing a few locals who gave us polite nods. Ryan glanced around, clearly taking in every detail.

"So, this is where it all started for you, huh? Must be kinda weird coming back."

"It used to be my sweet home," I said with a dry, ironic smile—more to myself than to him.

Ryan caught the reference immediately, smirking. He said nothing, but we both knew it was a callback to one of my old songs—a joke that wasn't really a joke.

"Seriously, though. You moved here first? From Paris, France, to Paris, Texas? Of all places? What happened to big dreams in big cities—New York, L.A., Atlanta, Dallas? You know, places where stuff actually happens."

Ryan gestured around at the quiet little town, shaking his head—amused and clearly still trying to make sense of it.

I shrugged, smirking.

"Well, Kid, I guess I followed my imagination a bit too much. You know, my song... 'From Paris to Texas.' I thought it'd be poetic or something."

"So, basically, you moved to the middle of nowhere because of a song?" he said, eyebrows raised, just short of calling me crazy.

"Maybe. Or maybe I figured being in a place called Paris meant I wouldn't feel too homesick," I said with a chuckle, taking a quick look at the red-hatted Eiffel Tower in the distance.

"And see—they even have an Eiffel Tower. Talk about a taste of home."

He burst out laughing.

"Right. Because a cowboy-hat-wearing Eiffel Tower screams Paris, France."

"Close enough," I said, still grinning.

He stared at the tower for a second, like he'd just seen *Elvis* riding a comet across the Texas sky.

"Man... that's wild."

We wandered farther down the street, the quiet settling in

again. Ryan took in the town, his gaze drifting over the slow pace and faded charm.

"Seriously, though. You ever think about what would've happened if you stayed?"

I paused, considering the question.

"Sometimes. But life had other plans. Met Marie, moved on, and the rest... well, you know the rest."

Ryan nodded, but didn't push further. The silence between us felt different now—not awkward, just heavy with unspoken things.

After a moment, he nudged me with his elbow, breaking the mood.

"Alright, come on. Let's grab some lunch before we hit the road."

Before long, we spotted a small diner on the corner, its faded sign reading:

AU PETIT PARIS

Promising homemade meals and coffee that probably hadn't changed in decades.

Ryan nudged me again.

"What do you say?"

I glanced at the diner, then back at him.

"Really, Ryan? Again?" I said with a grin.

"Alright, fine. I'm starving anyway."

We found a booth by the window, the place cozy with checkered tablecloths and vintage Parisian posters on the walls—*Eiffel Towers,* cafés, and street scenes, all framed in dusty wood. There were faded sketches of *Montmartre,* old prints of *Notre-Dame,* even a sun-faded shot of the *Seine* with lovers strolling along the quais. It felt like someone had tried to cram an entire postcard rack from a Paris souvenir shop into a single room—like a tiny tourist *museum exhibit.*

The mismatched chairs added to the charm, and above the counter, the crooked *"Au Petit Paris"* sign looked like it had been salvaged from a bistro back when absinthe was still legal and the *Champs-Élysées* were still actual fields.

In the corner, the jukebox played country tunes, filling the atmosphere with an oddly fitting blend of Parisian romance and cowboy grit. The whole place felt like an impossible crossroads between two worlds, where city lights met country roads and the smells of fresh-brewed coffee mingled with leather and lace, the scent of rugged charm and delicate softness.

As we finished up, Ryan relaxed into his seat, a mixed expression of amusement and satisfaction on his face.

"Well, I'd say this detour was worth it. Got to see Paris, Texas, and learned a little more about where you came from. Not bad for a lunch stop."

"Glad you're enjoying yourself," I said, tossing some cash on the table for the bill.

"Weird being back... Feels like I time-traveled or something. From one Paris to another. No DeLorean involved."

Then I brushed it off, grabbing my jacket.

"Alright, Kid. Time to move. We're on a mission. Don't want to keep Big Tex waiting."

"You got it, Frenchy. Now we're talking!" He replied with excitement.

And as we walked back to the truck, I took one last look at the red-hatted *Eiffel Tower*.

For a moment, it felt like a symbol of something—not sure what, exactly, but something that tied the past to the present. Shaking off the thought, I climbed inside, ready to hit the road again.

"Ride on, boy. Let's get back on track."

39

PIT STOP

Lost in my thoughts, I barely noticed Ryan pulling into the gas station. The tires crunched over gravel as he parked by the small convenience store. The midday sun blazed down, turning the asphalt into a shimmering mirage.

"Coffee?" Ryan asked, already unbuckling his seatbelt.

"Yeah, sounds good," I muttered, getting out and stretching my legs.

The gas station was one of those old roadside stops—sun-bleached signs, faded paint, a couple of cracked pumps. Inside, the cool blast of air conditioning was a welcome relief. It smelled like stale popcorn and windshield fluid... and something freshly brewed.

While Ryan fiddled with the coffee machine, I wandered over to the coolers. Grabbed a couple waters, a Coke... and without thinking, slid a six-pack of Buds into the basket.

Just a little insurance for later. *More fuel for my machine.*

As I headed back, I caught the tail end of a song playing

softly over the store's speakers. It sounded familiar—very familiar.

Ryan froze for a second, then turned to me with a grin.

"Hey, isn't that one of your tunes?"

Before I could answer, the song ended, and a smooth radio voice cut in.

"You're listening to KTXS, the Lone Star Radio. That was 'Frenchy and the Sweet Bandits,' and speaking of Frenchy, we've got Jesse Lawrence joining us later this afternoon on The Big Tex Show! Don't miss it."

Ryan couldn't hold back a laugh.

"Well, looks like they're already talking about you."

I gave him a look but couldn't help the small smirk that crept up.

"Guess I can't back out now, huh?"

At the register, he glanced down at the beers, the corner of his mouth twitching—but didn't say a word.

Smart kid.

The heat hit us as we stepped outside, but it wasn't the sun that burned—it was the past, catching up.

My name on the radio. Buds in the truck.

The road ahead didn't look any different, but I sure as hell *did*.

40

A GUEST AT MY OWN SHOW

Leaving—well, hopefully—our last stop behind, we were back on the road, rolling steadily down the open highway. The sun dipped low, shadows creeping across the dashboard like they were hitching a ride. Time seemed to slip by unnoticed as the miles stretched ahead.

I leaned back in my seat, though my thoughts were far from the present. The mention of the interview had stirred something—a memory I hadn't wanted to revisit.

I couldn't help but think about that one moment. The one that stayed with me long after it ended. Maybe it was the radio mention just now or the way the air felt different, but something about this drive brought it all rushing back.

It had been years ago, during the height of it all. We were in a cramped studio booth at some station, the kind with old foam walls that didn't quite keep out the outside noise—not your fancy modern soundproof barrier.

The place was cluttered—stacks of CDs and vinyls piled

next to an old-school soundboard—but it had that laid-back kind of mess only the old stations ever pulled off.

Marie sat next to me, her posture perfect, her smile practiced.

The host, a guy with slicked-back hair and a voice too loud for the small room, leaned into the mic, grinning wide.

"*So, Jesse, big hit on your hands! What's next for you and the Bandits?*" he asked, the mic catching every bit of his exaggerated excitement.

Before I could answer, Marie jumped in, her voice sweet but pointed.

"*Well, it's not just Frenchy and the Bandits, you know. We've been working on some of my material, too. Might surprise you with a duet album soon.*"

I glanced at her, caught off guard. That wasn't the plan. We hadn't even talked about it—at least, not seriously. But she said it with such confidence that the host beamed, leaning forward as if this was breaking news.

"*Wow! A duet album, huh? That's awesome!*" he said, scribbling something on his notepad like it was already set in stone.

I forced a smile, nodding along, but inside, I was reeling.

Marie had a way of steering things without asking, like she always knew better. And I let her. Every time.

What could I do? I loved her.

I wanted her to be happy. But in moments like this, it felt like my voice was being drowned out.

The rest of the interview was a blur. I answered questions mechanically, while Marie took every opportunity to steer the conversation toward herself—her songs, her future, her *plans*.

By the time it ended, I couldn't shake the feeling—I was just *a guest at my own show.*

I let out a slow breath, the past still stinging like an open wound that never healed. The road rolled on, the sun still hanging above the horizon.

Ryan looked over at me, probably catching the shift in my mood, but he said nothing. He didn't need to.

This time was supposed to be different.

This time, it was about me finding my way back—not getting dragged into someone else's story.

I straightened in my seat, chasing the thoughts away.

What's done is *done*.

But whatever comes *next*—it's mine to write.

No more guest spots.

Headliner rules.

Back to when my name was in bold at the top of the *marquee*.

41

KTXS—THE LONE STAR RADIO
WHERE TEXAS FINDS ITS VOICE

Yellow cabs started popping up as we were approaching Dallas, a sure sign the open road was giving way to city chaos. Probably heading to the airport or downtown, weaving through traffic like they owned the place.

The landscape shifted—gone were the wide stretches of flatlands; instead, the horizon filled with a maze of overpasses, highways weaving through the skyline like tangled strings of lights. The buildings grew taller, glass and steel reflecting the afternoon sun. Downtown loomed ahead, buzzing with life even at this hour—cars speeding by, horns blaring in the distance.

Ryan adjusted the radio dial, static crackling for a moment before settling on a familiar station. He seemed more relaxed now, sinking into his seat as the tension from earlier eased.

"Feel better? Told you we'd get there eventually," he said, shooting me a grin.

"Yeah, well, about time," I said.

"I'm so done being cooped up in that damn truck all day."

As we navigated through the network of freeways, the

unmistakable logo of *KTXS* came into view—bold letters atop a tall building, its broadcast tower stretching into the sky like a beacon.

"That's it," Ryan said, nodding toward the place.

"*KTXS—the Lone Star Radio. Biggest station in Dallas. Where Texas finds its voice.*"

I looked at the station, the words sinking in.

"*Lone Star Radio, huh?*" I said, a smirk tugging at the corner of my mouth.

"*Sounds fitting.*"

Ryan let out a short laugh.

"*Told you. They're good people. Just be yourself, Jesse. They're not looking for a show—they want to know you. The real you.*"

The real me? I wasn't sure who that even was anymore.

I glanced down at my hands, noticing a slight tremble. It wasn't exactly fear, it was... *anticipation.*

This was a step I hadn't planned on taking, but now that I was here, it felt inevitable—like something I needed to do, whether I was ready or not.

"*Alright, Kid,*" I said, trying to push down the mix of nerves and excitement swirling in my chest.

"*Let's get this over with.*"

Ryan turned into the parking lot and found a spot close to the entrance. He cut the engine and turned to me, his expression more serious now.

"*Just remember, Jesse, you're not doing this alone. You've got people backing you. Me, the band, everyone. This is your shot to tell your story your way.*"

I gave him a nod, appreciating the sentiment more than I could say.

Grabbing my hat from the dashboard, I stepped out of the truck—the warm Texas air hit me like a wave.

I paused, reached back in, grabbed a Bud from the floor, and cracked it open.

"Bottoms up," I muttered, and drank it half down. Just enough to stop the shaking.

Then we headed toward the building.

"Alright," I said, half to myself, half to the wind.

"Let's see what the Lone Star Radio's got for us."

And with The Kid riding shotgun, I stepped through the doors, boots heavy on polished tile—ready for whatever the hell this next showdown looked like.

42

THE BIG TEX INTERVIEW

Entering KTXS felt like riding into a saloon where nobody spilled a drop and the floors still smelled like lemon cleaner. Clean, corporate, and about as rock 'n' roll as a laminated press badge.

Not exactly the kind of grit I was used to, back in the day. Those stations reeked of cigarettes, beer, and dust-covered vinyl.

Damn world had changed.

These days, even cowboys check their *email* before a shootout.

As for the front desk, it looked more like something out of a Vegas hotel than a radio station—oversized, slick, and just waiting for someone in a headset to offer us bottled water.

I half-expected a *one-arm bandit* in the corner, blinking away like it was waiting for my last damn quarter.

From behind the desk, the receptionist greeted us with a warm smile as Ryan stepped forward and gave our names. She thanked him and checked something on her screen.

"Go ahead," she said.

"Studio A—straight down the hall."

We stepped into a short, carpeted hallway lined with framed platinum records and neatly mounted promo posters.

A few quiet steps later, we stopped in front of the studio door.

Above the frame, the red *ON AIR* sign was lit up.

Behind the glass, Big Tex was already talking—voice steady, hat tilted back as he leaned into the mic. He spotted us, gave a quick nod, and motioned us in with two fingers.

We slipped into the recording booth, careful not to make a sound. High-tech gear buzzed around us—blinking lights, meters jumping, and enough buttons to launch a *damn satellite.*

A second later, Tex reached over and cued a commercial jingle that faded in through the headphones. He stood, shook our hands, and grinned.

"Boys," he said,

"you're right on time. You're on in a few sec."

I dropped into the chair, adjusted the headphones, and took a breath.

As the station's tag faded out, Tex's voice came back—proud, loud, and pure *Texas.*

"Hi y'all, Big Tex here. You're listening to KTXS, 'The Lone Star Radio,' and today on the Big Tex Show, we've got a very special guest —someone who's been off the radar for a while but is making waves with his return. You know him as the man behind those classic hits from Frenchy and The Sweet Bandits—Jesse Lawrence, or should I say Frenchy? What do you prefer?"

I cleared my throat, leaning in toward the mic.

"Jesse's fine."

"Alright then, Jesse. Great to have you on the show."

He gave a pause, then squared up to the mic, his tone dropping like he meant business.

"*So, let's cut to it—gotta ask: why now? After all these years, what made you decide to step back into the spotlight?*"

I hesitated, fingers drumming lightly on the edge of the chair. I was running on empty.

Man, I so needed a *refuel*.

"*Well, it wasn't really planned, to be honest. Sometimes life throws things at you, and you either duck or catch 'em. I guess I decided to catch this one.*"

Big Tex laughed.

"*Fair enough. But come on, there's gotta be more to it than that. You were at the top of your game back in the day. Hits on the radio, sold-out shows... and then, poof. Gone. What happened?*"

I leaned back slightly, weighing my words. I didn't want to get into the whole story—the divorce, the burnout, the mess that followed. But I guess people deserved some kind of answer.

"*I needed time. The kind of time that lets you figure out who you are when the music stops.*"

"*And did you figure it out?*" Big Tex asked, intrigued with genuine curiosity.

"*Still working on that,*" I said, with a half smile on my face.

He chuckled, tapping the mic.

"*Aren't we all? But hey, you're here now, and from what I've heard, the new stuff's sounding great. Tell us about this new album— this comeback. What's it been like getting back in the studio, working with the Bandits again?*"

"*It's been great so far. We kicked things off with a few shows— getting back on track, finding our stance again. Reliving the past, telling war stories and cracking old jokes. The chemistry's still there... just different now.*"

"*There's a new member now—C.C.—so the dynamic has shifted, but more than that... back then, it was about chasing something— always pushing to be heard, to break through. Now... it's more about finding something. Rediscovering what made it matter in the very first place."*

"*That's deep,*" Big Tex said, his tone light but thoughtful.

"*So, what can fans expect from this new chapter of Jesse Lawrence?*"

"*Honesty,*" I said simply.

"*It's not about flashy riffs or chasing hits. It's about the music that feels real to me. If people connect with it, great. If not... well, I'm doing it because I need to.*"

"*Sounds like you've got a lot to say,*" Big Tex said, giving me a knowing look.

"*Maybe,*" I admitted.

"*But mostly, I've got a lot to play.*"

Big Tex chuckled and reached for the board.

"*Perfect cue, Jesse. How 'bout we play a little Frenchy and the Sweet Bandits and take a short break? Any favorites?*"

"*Nope,*" I just said.

Then, continuing without missing a beat, he said,

"*You're listening to KTXS—The Lone Star Radio, and this is the Big Tex Show. My guest today? Jesse 'Frenchy' Lawrence—back in the saddle and ready to ride. So let's head down memory lane, folks. Here's From Paris to Texas by Frenchy and the Sweet Bandits.*"

Back on air, after a few questions about the album...

Big Tex gave a slow nod, then looked at me like he was about to go off-script.

"*Alright, Jesse, before we wrap this up—one last question. Here's one I like to throw at the old timers: If you could go back to the start, knowing everything you know now... would you do anything differently?*"

I paused, the weight of the question settling in.

"*I don't know. Maybe I'd slow down a bit. Appreciate the ride more, instead of gunning it just to reach the finish line first.*"

"Wise words from someone who's been through it all. Thanks for stopping by, Jesse. We'll be keeping an ear out for what's next."

"Oh, and is there a name for the new album?"

"Huh? Oh, yeah. From Paris to Texas—Greatest Hits Revisited."

"I love it! That says it all. Fans are gonna eat that up."

I gave a faint smirk while slipping off the headphones.

"Thanks for having me, Big Tex."

"Anytime, Jesse," he said, already leaning back toward the mic. *"That was Jesse 'Frenchy' Lawrence on The Big Tex Show, right here on KTXS—The Lone Star Radio. Keep your dials locked, folks—this story's just getting good. And now..."*

Big Tex waved us off with a grin as he rolled into the next segment.

I stood up, stretched a little, and followed Ryan out of the booth.

Stepping outside into the late afternoon, early evening light, I felt a strange mix of relief and possibility. The past was behind me, but the path ahead was still wide open. And for the first time in a long while, I felt ready to walk it.

Ryan clicked the remote and the locks popped. I opened the passenger door, grabbed a Bud from the floorboard, and cracked it open—cold, familiar, and exactly what I needed.

"See?" Ryan said, still grinning.

"Wasn't so bad. Texas heard your voice."

I gave him a look, the corner of my mouth twitching.

"Yeah... about that."

43

THE VAULT

Truth be told, it felt good to be back at the Echo Ponds, Steve greeted us as we walked in, his eyes flicking between me and Ryan, probably wondering how things had gone. Before he could say anything, Ryan flopped down on the worn-out couch with that same smug grin he'd been wearing since we left the station.

"Well?" Steve asked, leaning against the mixing console.

"How did it go?"

I blew out a bull's breath, dropped my stuff by the door, and shook my head.

"Well, quite an adventure. Long-ass trip for twenty minutes of polite nods and a spin of From Paris to Texas—vintage version. I could've just fucking done it over the phone—and saved myself a back injury."

Ryan shrugged with that same cocky grin.

"Yeah, maybe. But those industry people? They talk. And right now, they need to see you in flesh and blood—alive and kicking. Plus... our little escape in Europe?" He winked at me.

"Priceless."

Steve raised an eyebrow, glancing between us.

"Huh... what the hell did I miss?"

"Long story," I said, waving it off.

"Yeah... figured it'd be something like that." Steve chuckled, then straightened, his expression turning more serious.

"So anyway, what's next? Ready to wrap this up?"

I ran a hand down my beard from the chin, thinking.

"Actually... not quite." I scanned the room, taking in the familiar faces.

"On the way back, I kept thinking about something."

Steve gave me a wary look.

"Here we go..."

"I'm serious," I said, folding my arms.

"We did a great job re-recording and rearranging those old tunes, no doubt. But it feels like something's still missing. I couldn't put my finger on it earlier, but now I think I get it."

Ryan leaned forward, curious.

"And?"

"This is 'Greatest Hits Revisited,'" I said slowly, trying to organize my thoughts.

"We've got the classics, sure, but nothing here feels... fresh. Like it's ours right now, not just what we were."

Steve frowned, staring at the console.

"We're working with the hits, Jesse. That's the whole point. People want nostalgia. They want the hits."

"Maybe." I tapped my fingers against the desk.

"So, okay. Nostalgia checked. But... maybe they want new hits too."

"What are you talking about, Jesse? Got anything new?"

"Not yet. But—"

"What about the vault?" said a voice, low and steady, drifting from the back of the room, cutting through the noise.

I turned, finding Billy Ray, half-sunk into the couch like he'd been there forever, hat pulled low, boots propped up, looking for all the world like a man about to tell a story of buried treasure.

Ryan shot Billy Ray a curious look.

"The vault? What's that?"

Billy Ray scratched his chin, like he was about to let Ryan in on some long-kept secret.

"A stash of forgotten tracks. Unfinished, unreleased stuff. Some gems, some junk—but all worth another listen. Who knows what might be hidden in there!"

"The vault?" Steve scoffed.

"Yeah, that black hole of half-finished tracks and 'we'll come back to it' promises. This is supposed to be a greatest hits album, not a demo dump."

Billy Ray, ever the straight shooter, drew fast.

"Who says they're demos? A hit's a hit—it just needs a little polishing. Hell, some of the biggest hits out there were B-sides no one cared about at first." Then he added, quieter but firm:

"Maybe it's time to hold onto those promises."

"Yep. Billy's got a point. There were a ton of songs we didn't finish back in the day. Some of them were damn good—just ahead of their time or didn't fit the albums we were working on." Sticks chimed in from his corner.

I covered my mouth with an L-shaped hand—thinker style, as something in Billy Ray's voice stuck with me.

"Alright, guys. You won. What do we have to lose, anyway?" I said, still not entirely convinced.

"So, let's dig up some skeletons."

Steve exhaled, turning over to his right toward the computer screen. Instead of clicking immediately, he reached into his bag, pulling out a compact hard drive.

I could tell he wasn't thrilled about the idea—but sometimes, I couldn't help being the boss and having the last say.

"The vault's not on this machine—it's all on here."

He held it up before handing it to Mike, our engineer, who plugged it into the computer and, with Steve's direction, navigated to a folder labeled:

—The Vault - Unreleased Demos—

A long list of track names flooded the screen—a mix of rough titles and cryptic placeholders, some half-finished ideas, others nearly forgotten. The past staring right back at me, *waiting.*

Billy Ray snorted, settling deeper into the couch.

"More like a trip to the attic. You sure this stuff ain't covered in dust?"

Sticks twirled a drumstick between his fingers, a leftover habit from his marching band days.

"Alright, here's my two cents," he said, cracking a small grin.

"Some dust ain't bad if it still shines underneath."

Steve pointed to a track labeled "Midnight Train to Nowhere."

"Let's start with this one."

The speakers crackled to life as the first track began to play. The drums were tight, the bass groovy, but the vocals were raw —almost hesitant.

"You remember this one, Jesse?" Steve asked, glancing over his shoulder.

I leaned back in my chair, arms crossed, just listening. The song had a pulse, a nice groove, a cool vibe... but I wasn't sold.

"Next," Steve said, not waiting for a response. Mike queued up another track, and a guitar riff burst through the monitors.

Billy Ray bobbed his head, his fingers tapping an invisible bass line.

"That's got some meat on it."

"Sure does," Sticks added, his drumsticks picking up with the beat. *"What do you think, Jesse?"*

"It's alright." I shrugged.

"Fine. Let's up the stakes." Steve smirked, crossing his arms.

The next track started—this time, it was something else entirely. A funky shuffle groove beat set the tone, with gritty *ZZ Top-style* guitars and a thick 80s bass line that grabbed you from the start.

As the track built, sharp, soulful horns sliced through, adding that *Memphis Horns* flair to the raw rock energy. It was heavy, smooth, and full of swagger, blending rock and blues in a way that made you feel it deep.

Steve straightened in his chair, his eyes focused on the computer.

"That's 'Heart on the Line.'"

I tensed slightly but kept my face straight, watching the screen as the track played.

The melody, the lyrics—they hit *right*. Tight, catchy, gritty with soul. And the track was smoking hot—rocking *hard,* shaking me to the bone.

As the song ended, the room went still.

Steve stayed focused, his expression unreadable.

"So?"

Billy Ray's voice cut through the silence, low and amused.

"Man's playing it close to the vest. I like it."

I let the silence stretch for a moment before sighing.

"It's good... but it's just a bunch of demos."

"Oh, come on, Jesse," Steve said, rolling his eyes.

"It's actually way better than I remember."

"Facts," Ryan added, throwing his hands up like a fanboy at a stadium.

"That thing's a banger. And man—Call 911—put my heart on the

line. *That's epic. If that's what's hiding in the vault, we're about to go
full Indiana Jones."*

I sighed, a bit annoyed, but still trying to be open-minded.

*"Alright, alright... I hear you, Kid. But this ain't a treasure map—
it's just a freaking vault."* I tipped my chin at the screen.

*"Okay. Go on, Steve. Keep 'em coming. And let's see what else is
buried in there."*

44

NUMBER ONE

Caught between nostalgia and frustration, we'd spent the past couple of hours sifting through fragments of the past—rough demos, half-finished ideas, and forgotten experiments. Some had potential, others were just echoes of something that never quite came together. At this point, the room felt flat—half-listening, half-bored, halfway gone. Even the speakers sounded tired of playing maybe-songs.

Steve was staring at the screen like it owed him money, then finally exhaled and rolled his shoulders.

"Alright, that's the last one. Jesse? Thoughts?"

Billy Ray drawled from the couch, hat dipped low, boots crossed, like he hadn't moved since the Alamo.

"Bet he's sittin' on fifty thoughts but won't share a single one—just diggin' through Swampy like he's panning for gold."

"Nah. Just minin', hopin' a rough diamond'll make it to the top." I smirked, still noodling.

Ryan shot up from his seat—restless, exasperated.

"Come on, Jesse. We're wasting time here. That 911 tune—'Heart on the Line'—it stuck with me. That's a killer track. It's catchy. Hit potential. Let's finish it and call it a day."

I kept noodling on Swampy for a second, then finally looked up. "Alright, alright. Steve, play the one that starts with the banjo riff again."

Steve arched an eyebrow.

"The banjo riff? You mean 'Number One?'"

"Yeah, I guess. That's it," I said, casually plucking a string.

Billy Ray chuckled, still sprawled out.

"Well, there you go, cowboy. Looks like you found it. Even the title says it all. Top of the charts—it's got 'hit' written all over it."

Sticks joined in, drumming a sharp beat on his thighs.

"Yeah, let's get this one polished. You don't even have to market it; the title does all the work!"

I rolled my eyes but couldn't stop the grin tugging at my mouth.

"Yeah, yeah. Let's play it again—see if that rough diamond's worth printin' the gold plaques."

Steve leaned forward, clicking back through the folder. The speakers crackled for a moment before the banjo riff filled the room, bright and playful, cutting through the stillness like sunlight breaking through a storm cloud.

I closed my eyes, letting the sound wrap around me like a ghost. The tune was familiar, yet distant—like catching a whiff of a scent from childhood, something you know but can't quite place.

I tapped my fingers against Swampy's body, searching for the connection. When had I written this? The chords, the phrasing —I knew them, but they felt... removed, like they belonged to someone else.

Then the lyrics dropped in—and my whole body tensed.

The words cut deep, sharper than I remembered, each line laced with something heavier than just melody.

And hearing them in Kota's voice? That only made it *worse*.

She didn't just sing them—she brought them to life, breathed something into them that made every syllable hit harder, stripping away whatever distance I thought I had.

I swallowed hard, but it did nothing to ease the sudden weight pressing against my chest. My breath hitched.

What the freaking hell?

I wasn't ready for this—didn't even see it coming. I'd been zoning out, half-listening when Steve first played it.

My throat tightened. The realization crashed over me like a wave I couldn't dodge.

The song wasn't just a *song*.

It was *him*.

It was *us*.

It was everything I'd buried, everything I swore I wouldn't let pull me under again.

But it was too late—the past wasn't creeping in; it was barreling through me.

My vision blurred.

My fingers curled around Swampy's neck, gripping tighter, like I needed something—anything—to hold onto.

But nothing could brace me against this. My eyes burned, breath catching—and just like that, the tears slipped out before I could stop them.

Shit.

I let out a slow, shaky exhale and wiped my cheek quickly, hoping no one noticed.

But the damn song just kept digging—relentless, dragging me under.

Every note, every word—one punch after another. And I was fighting hard to stay on my feet.

And just like that—*did I just get knocked out?*
'Cause I wasn't in the studio anymore.
I was *there.*

45

UNTIL I TAKE MY LAST BREATH

oneliness had a way of making even a crappy motel feel like a prison. The atmosphere was thick, and the muted light spilling through the drawn curtains barely reached the corners of the space. The table was a mess—court papers scattered among empty coffee cups and crumpled napkins with half-scribbled thoughts.

A secondhand guitar sat in the corner, one I'd picked up at a pawn shop somewhere along the way. I stared at it like it might bite, unsure if I could even pick it up without breaking apart.

But the stillness was worse, like every second was reminding me how long it had been since I'd seen my little boy.

Weeks. Or maybe *months.*

The days had turned into a blur—melted into the bottom of empty bottles and notebooks full of unfinished thoughts. Between *Good Ol' Jack*'s company and those sleepless motel nights, time stopped meaning anything.

I never stayed in one place long. Just long enough.

The constant drone of flickering neon. The hum of vending

machines. Doors slamming. TV sounds bleeding through paper-thin walls.

It was always noisy. But I felt so fucking alone.

The TV was always on, even if I never watched it—just some voices in the room trying to mask the ones in my head.

The anger I'd clung to fizzled out, leaving behind nothing but that hollow, sinking feeling.

I missed him. So fucking much.

His laugh, his little hands reaching out for me. It was a physical ache, one that wouldn't let up no matter how hard I tried to push it down.

I reached for the guitar, my fingers trembling as they wrapped around the neck. Muscle memory took over, and my hands wandered over the strings—no thought, no plan.

I was just jamming.

Just... playing. Some riffs, a bit banjo-style, over a few simple chords. *G, F, C, G.*

And then this came out.

"I didn't see it coming, when you had to go, just
     for a while..."

My voice cracked, but I kept going. The melody wrapped itself around the words like it had been waiting all this time, buried somewhere I couldn't reach until now.

"Even if we're apart, I can't bear that pain...
     Through sunshine and rain... 'Cos
     you're my..."

The chorus hit like a dam breaking. Tears came, hot and unrelenting, spilling over as the words tumbled out.

I wasn't singing—I was *pleading*.

"Number One. #1 in my heart.
Number One, on my love's chart..."

I scribbled the lyrics onto the back of a court notice, my hand shaking as I poured everything into it.

It wasn't just a song—it was some kind of *legacy.*

A way to let *Jesse Jr.* know everything I couldn't tell him now.

Or maybe not even *later...*

When the last line left my lips, the silence returned, heavier than before. I set my guitar down, my chest heaving.

I tried recording it once, some days later, with the band. Steve convinced me to lay it down as a demo, but I couldn't get through it without my voice breaking. The tape sat in a box for a while—untouched, forgotten... and somehow ended up in *the vault.*

It was too raw, too painful. The few times I played it back, it felt like tearing through scar tissue. So I buried it—like a cursed treasure, deep beneath some desert island, hoping no one would ever dig it back up.

The final line of the chorus echoed through the studio, almost a cappella:

"And until I take my last breath,
you'll always be my number one."

Billy Ray shifted in his seat, looking thoughtful.

"Man, I still don't get why we never finished that one. It's a killer tune."

I gripped Swampy's neck, my fingers curling around it instinctively—like I was holding Jesse Jr.'s tiny hand, afraid to let go.

"It was a tough time," I said, my voice quieter.

"Too painful to come back to. I had to bury it, like a treasure I couldn't touch anymore."

Steve nodded, his expression softer now.

I exhaled, stroking my beard as the thought surfaced.

"But. Wait. Hold on. Wait a second... I don't ever remember Kota singing on it. We just did the demo and never got to finish it, so..."

Steve leaned back, crossing his arms with a small smile.

"Yeah, well... that tune always stuck with me. It had something— deep, catchy. I figured it deserved a shot, so I finished up the arrangement."

He hesitated, then added,

"And had Kota come in to lay down the vocals—just in case."

He glanced at me, then at the console.

"But obviously, later on... well, there was no Frenchy and The Sweet Bandits anymore."

A beat of quiet hung in the air.

"Well, glad we didn't lose it. Safe in the vault all this time... really feels like we've been on a damn treasure hunt all day." I looked up, forcing a small grin.

Billy Ray chuckled, sitting up straighter.

"Treasure hunting, huh? Alright, Captain Frenchy! Lead the way."

Steve turned back to the console, his hands poised over the controls.

"So, what do you say, Jesse? Think it's time we finally bring it back to the surface?"

I swallowed hard, my grip tightening around Swampy. A slow smile formed—faint at first, then real.

"Well, I guess we can't leave buried treasure just lying around, can we?"

"So let's dig it up, Boys."

Billy Ray slapped his knee.

"That's the spirit. Set sail, Captain!"

46

THE PRESSURE COOKER

Echo Ponds had a way of feeling like home, even when it was just a stop along the way. Maybe it was the vintage vibe—or the cow ghosts still roaming the walls.

I was kicked back on the couch in the studio lounge, eyes half-watching some TV while Steve and C.C. were in the booth, laying down vocals. She'd arrived a few days ago, once we were finally ready for her to step in and record her parts.

New songs from the past.

That's what we'd started calling them—a mix of old hits and unfinished tracks getting a *second life.*

The place had a cozy vibe, the sort that came with musicians constantly coming and going. Somewhere down the hall, the faint strum of an acoustic guitar mixed with muffled laughter. It was the kind of noise that made it feel alive.

That's when Abby, the manager of the Echo Ponds, strolled in. She'd been a sweetheart since we got here, always making sure things ran smooth. Considering the studio was also a residency, she had her hands full, keeping the whole operation together.

"Jesse, there's someone for you on the phone."

I stretched, rubbing my face.

"Huh... let me guess. Ryan Brooks?"

"Yep. That's him. Sounded a bit agitated, by the way," she said, giving me a knowing look.

I sighed.

"Alright, thanks, Abby."

"I'll transfer the call in here," she said over her shoulder as she walked back to her office.

I leaned forward, reaching for the phone on the table next to me.

"Zup, Kid?"

Ryan's voice came through, sharp and businesslike.

"Hi Jesse. Just checking in. How's it going over there?"

I sank back into the couch, letting my head drop against the cushion.

"We're getting there. Since you had to leave, we've been polishin' those rough diamonds, blowin' off the dust, re-recordin' parts—it don't happen overnight, Kid. And turns out, I had to redo some overdubs too —stuff I didn't catch at first. You know how it is when you're tryin' to get it just right. Been a while since I've recorded anything real. C.C.'s here, already started layin' down vocals. But we're on time."

"On time? On time for what? And what kind of time—Texas time? Jesse time? Or are we talkin' Time Bandits now? Well, I got news for you—we're runnin' outta time. And we need to wrap this up by yesterday. Do you know how much this is costing, Jesse?"

I frowned, sitting up straighter.

"Relax, Kid. The label's backing us. They're not breathing down our necks."

"The label? Jesse, you don't understand," he said, his voice hardening.

"What don't I understand?"

He let out a frustrated breath, and the tension in his voice climbed.

"I'm the one financing the album, Jesse."

I froze, the words not registering at first.

"What?"

"I had to take out a loan," he said, his voice clipped, like he was trying to stay calm.

"Against my house. Nobody wanted to take a chance on you anymore. You're a 'washed-up artist'—that's what they called you."

It hit like a punch to the gut.

"What the hell are you talking about? The label—Skytown—"

"Skytown wouldn't touch you unless we financed it ourselves," Ryan snapped, his frustration boiling over.

"Rory—Rory believed in you. She told me it was because of your history together, but even she wouldn't risk their money without guarantees."

I sat there, stunned, Swampy lying forgotten beside me. The warm buzz of the lounge suddenly felt distant, like I wasn't even in the room anymore.

"Why didn't you tell me?"

"Well, because I didn't want you worrying about it," he said, softer now but still intense.

"I believed in you. I still do. And I had to make it happen, Jesse. I had no choice."

The silence hung between us, heavy and suffocating.

"I didn't know, Kid," I said finally, my voice low.

"I didn't know."

"Well... now you do," Ryan replied, his voice edged with exhaustion.

"We've got to finish this, Jesse. No more delays. No more second-guessing. Just... finish it."

I nodded, even though he couldn't see me.

"*We'll finish it, Kid,*" I said quietly.

"*I promise.*"

Ryan didn't respond right away. When he did, he was calmer.

"*Okay. I'll check in later.*"

The line went dead, leaving me staring at the phone in my hand. And all I could hear was the hiss building in my head—like a pressure cooker on the verge of blowing up.

I hung up and immediately pushed myself off the couch, heading straight for the control room. Time to check in with Steve—and deliver the news.

Well, the *bad news.*

The moment I stepped inside, the familiar noise of the studio equipment filled the air. Steve was at the console, adjusting levels, moving some faders, while C.C. sat nearby, listening back to a take. The faint sound of her vocals played through the monitors, but my mind was too clouded to focus on it.

Steve glanced up, his hands still on the board.

"*What's up? You look like you just got hit with a brick.*"

I exhaled, my shoulders tightening as I crossed my arms.

"*Ryan just called.*"

Steve's expression shifted—he knew this wasn't good.

"*And?*"

"*And... turns out, we don't have a label backing us. Ryan's been financing the whole damn thing himself.*"

Steve's hand froze over the faders.

"*Come again?*"

"*Yeah. Skytown wouldn't touch me. Rory fought for us, but even she wouldn't risk their money. So Ryan took out a loan—against his damn house.*"

I let out a humorless chuckle.

"*Apparently, I'm a 'washed-up artist'—at least that's what they're saying.*"

Steve let out a low whistle, reclining his chair.

"Holy shit..."

He shook his head, scratching the back of his neck.

"I knew things were tough, but I didn't think it was that bad."

I sighed, rubbing my temples.

"Yeah, well, it is. And now we have to finish this. No delays. No second-guessing."

C.C. finally spoke up, her brows furrowed.

"So what happens if we don't?"

I met her eyes, then looked back at Steve.

"If we don't? Ryan's screwed. And we're done."

A heavy silence settled in the room.

Steve let out a long breath, then nodded, turned back to the console.

"Alright then. Let's finish this damn thing."

47

WRAPPED IN THE BAG

Vibrations from the last note of the final mix faded into the control room, leaving behind a reflective hush—full of pride and relief. One of those rare moments that didn't ask for applause, just *respect*.

No one spoke at first—just the low hum of the monitors, and that stunned stillness you get when something finally clicks.

I leaned back in the chair, exhaling slowly.

Finally. We nailed it. It was all done. Final mixes were locked.

The album got my stamp of approval—wrapped in the bag. *Sealed.*

We'd crossed the finish line with seconds to spare—racing against the clock, chasing the pressure, and somehow sticking the landing.

"Well," I said, glancing around at the band—and Ryan, who turns out, was back in no time. Faster than the wind, and twice as dramatic, once I called him to deliver the good news.

"After a long month of blood, sweat, and way too many sleepless nights, I've got to admit... we did a damn good job."

Billy Ray let out a low whistle, stretching his legs out.

"You know what they say—pressure makes diamonds."

Steve chuckled, adjusting some knobs on the console out of habit.

"Or cracks. But yeah, I'll take diamonds."

C.C. sat cross-legged on the couch, her hands resting in her lap as she took it all in. There was a brief pause, the kind that invites reflection—then she spoke gently:

"If I may... it's been an honor revisiting these songs. Breathing new life into them, finding my place in parts that used to belong to Kota or... Marie. I just hope I did them justice."

"You did more than justice, Cassidy," I said, offering her a warm smile.

"You made them your own. That's not easy, and you nailed it. Crazy thing is... you showed up right when we needed you most. I'm real glad we found you. Call it fate, I guess."

Her cheeks flushed slightly, but she smiled back.

"Thank you, Jesse."

Swampy rested on her stand beside the console, bathed in the soft glow of the studio lights. I ran my left thumb along her neck—just a slow touch, a quick feel.

My voice dropped.

"And all this... it's because of her."

Steve looked over at the guitar, then back at me.

"Huh...Swampy?"

"Yeah." I paused, searching for the right words.

"She's more than a guitar. She's... alive. At least, that's how it feels. Like she's guiding me, transcending the music. I'm just the vector. She's the one infusing the soul, the magic, into it all."

An angel might've passed through the studio—at least that's what the old French saying goes, when it gets that quiet.

But *who knows.*

Not sure if it's true, but... sure felt like it.

Billy Ray shifted in his seat, shooting Steve a look like, *You hearing this?* C.C. blinked, her lips parting as if to say something, then thinking better of it.

Steve finally exhaled through his nose, shaking his head slightly.

"Man... I don't know if you're a genius or if you've just lost your damn mind."

Sticks scratched his head, frowning.

"So, uh... does that make Swampy, like... your girlfriend?"

Billy Ray snorted.

"Jeez, Sticks!"

"I mean... do we need to start worrying about you, Jesse?"

Steve smirked, rubbing his chin.

I rolled my eyes, letting the moment settle.

"You can joke all you want, but you guys heard it. Felt it."

Billy Ray broke into a grin.

"Alright, Captain Frenchy, whatever you say. Just don't start talking to her in public, alright?"

The room cracked up, but I kept still, my eyes drifting to Swampy, resting on her stand.

"I just hope people will hear it," I said, finally—convincing myself.

"The magic. The soul. Hope they'll feel what we've put into this album."

Steve reclined in his chair, arms crossed.

"Well, if they don't, they're deaf. This album's got everything— heart, soul, grit. It's the real deal."

I looked around at the people who'd helped make it all happen.

"Yes," I said softly.

"It really is."

Ryan, who'd been pacing in the back like a caged dog, suddenly sprang to life—like someone had tossed him a bone laced with fireworks.

"Listen, guys. This is pure fucking awesomeness. A goddamn masterpiece. Straight-up Goldies material. And I'm telling you—Rory, Skytown, all the skeptical, ignorant bastards—they're not gonna believe this."

He kept going, rambling with wide eyes and half-laughs, adrenaline buzzing through every word. Then he pointed at the speakers.

"You heard that? You saw it? Those monitors damn near caught fire. I don't know what kind of voodoo magic y'all summoned in here, but holy hell—this is true fire. Hotter than hell. This isn't just a compilation of hits—it's a fucking resurrection. From ashes to ashes."

Then, suddenly emotional, his voice cracked as tears welled up.

"Jesse. Guys... thank you. From the bottom of my heart."

He paused, shaking his head.

"You have no idea what this means to me. Thank you for this beautiful gift."

He turned toward Swampy, nodding like she was alive.

"And you? You deserve a damn statue."

I shook my head, smiling.

"Easy, Kid. Breathe. You're safe now."

I squared my shoulders and addressed the room, like a captain on deck.

"Look, I'm just glad we made it to the port. Storms and all."

I let that hang for a beat, then added:

"We did our best—like we always do. Teamwork style. I might be the captain of this ship, but without a skilled and trusted crew... I'd still be stuck at the dock."

I glanced back at Ryan, a hint of a grin.

"And whatever happens now... it was damn worth the trip."

"*Well said, Cap,*" Billy Ray said, pressing his palms together like locking something in place.

"*Spirits or not, echoes of the cow ghosts or just dumb luck... we made it, and we're damn proud of it.*"

He raised an imaginary glass, his voice steady. No jokes this time.

"*So—to Frenchy and the Sweet Bandits!*"

Steve, Sticks, C.C., and even Mike followed suit, lifting their hands in mock cheers.

"*And to Swampy!*"

"*To Swampy!*" we all shouted, as a rebel yell, wild and raw, crashing against the walls in a thunderous roar that refused to fade.

48

HOMECOMING

Even the damn truck seemed relieved as it rumbled to a stop, kicking up dust outside the ranch. I pushed the door open, stepping onto solid ground for the first time in hours. Every muscle ached, stiff from too many miles, too many days running on empty.

The engine idled, but neither of us moved right away.

Ryan had blasted the album on loop the entire ride home—hours of repeat, repeat, repeat. Nonstop playbacks, full commentary included. Praise, theories, spontaneous singalongs... hell, if I wasn't proud of the damn thing, I might've tossed him out halfway through Arizona.

And by the end, I was pretty sure the truck wanted to ditch us both.

I'd heard the songs so many times, I couldn't tell if they were brilliant or bullshit anymore. It just made me want to throw up —car sick or music sick, who the fuck knows? *Your pick.*

But Ryan? Ryan still looked like a kid who'd just seen God backstage.

I walked around to the back, grabbed my bag and Swampy from the truck bed.

As I passed his open window, Ryan finally broke the silence with a low whistle.

"Man... I know I already said it, like, a dozen times... but seriously —this is it. This is the one. It's your best work, Jesse. No contest."

I exhaled, gripping the door handle.

"Well... thanks, Kid. Appreciate it."

He nodded, eyes wide.

"Even the vault tracks, man—some of that stuff was just sitting there like buried treasure. The whole thing feels like... I dunno, like the past came back with a vengeance. But shinier. Pure gold."

I said nothing. Not right away. I wasn't sure I could.

The album had taken a toll. The mixing, the rewrites, the ghosts, the pressure... It had eaten a piece of me. And now it was finished.

And I couldn't feel a *damn thing.*

Ryan checked his watch.

"Alright, gotta go. I've got a meeting with Rory and the Skytown crew first thing tomorrow. I can't wait to play them the album and see their faces."

"Better hope they've got good taste," I said, smirking.

"If they don't, they're deaf. And I'm broke. I'll keep you posted. Later, Frenchy." He chuckled from behind the wheel.

I gave the door a quick pat and stepped back with a nod.

The truck pulled away, taillights fading into the dust as it disappeared down the road...

Leaving me standing there—alone with the night, and everything waiting for me inside.

Out here, the smell of earth and hay never changed, no matter how long I'd been gone—and it had been about a month since I'd set foot on the ranch.

Emma was already on the porch, arms crossed, watching me

like she wasn't sure if I was actually back or just passing through. Then, a small smile.

"Well, look who finally remembered where home is."

I let out a tired chuckle, brushing the dust off my jeans.

"You manage to keep the place standing without me?"

"Barely. But we survived somehow," she sighed, amused.

I climbed the steps, the wooden planks creaking beneath me, and set Swampy and my bag down near the entrance.

Emma leaned against the railing, giving me the rundown—horses stayed outta trouble, clients didn't cause any, fences held. The *usual.*

Then her eyes flicked over me, studying my face.

"You look like hell."

I rolled my shoulders, shaking off the stiffness.

"Feels about right."

Emma wasn't one for small talk. She cut right to it.

"So? How'd it go? The recordings? The album?"

I hesitated. Not because I didn't have an answer, but because I didn't know how to sum up weeks of burnout, frustration, and the ghosts that clung to every damn note.

"All done," I said finally.

Emma waited, like she knew there was more, but when I didn't offer, she just said,

"Great. I can't wait to hear it. I mean, sometime... whenever you're ready."

"Maybe," I said—sharper than I meant to, already turning for the door.

"Right now, I just need some damn rest."

Emma didn't deserve that. She'd only ever been caring. And here I was, shutting down when she was just trying to show she gave a damn.

But it wasn't her—it was all me.

The exhaustion. The drive. The sessions.

And *something else.*

Something that had been gnawing at the edges of my mind, waiting for the fatigue to sink its teeth in.

It hadn't hit me yet—not fully. But it might.

Later that night, the house was quiet. Silence draped over the ranch like a worn-out blanket—dry, heavy, and absolute.

I sat at the kitchen table, *Good Ol' Jack* keeping me company, staring at nothing. Dim starlight spilled through the window—like the vibe of a 3 a.m. recording session.

The weariness had settled deep, wrapping around my bones like a weight I couldn't shake. I should have been asleep, should have passed out the second I hit the bed.

But something wouldn't let me.

One second, my eyes were closing, sinking fast. The next, I was wide awake, pulse kicking like I'd never even laid down.

I knew this feeling. I'd felt it before—the heaviness, the emptiness, the dead stillness.

I lifted the bottle, took a sip straight from it.

Watched the amber swirl inside—slow, *hypnotic.*

Like *déjà vu.*

It wasn't here.

It was back there.

In a *studio.*

The last time I recorded an album, before my life fell apart, it was a duet.

A duet album.

A duet with her.

And just like that, I wasn't here anymore.

I was there.

Back in that *fucking room.*

49

THE DEVIL IN DISGUISE

Right here, right now—no turning back. I couldn't let that fucking feeling eat me alive anymore.

I stood in the doorway, looking at her. Marie was pregnant, belly swollen with our baby boy. The baby we were supposed to raise together.

I should have felt something—*joy,* maybe.

But all I felt was anger. And *disbelief.*

Yet somehow, here we were—having the same damn fight for the hundredth time.

"*So that's it?*" she scoffed, arms crossed over her stomach.

"*You're just gonna leave? Again.*"

I clenched my jaw.

"*Marie, we've been through this. The shows are booked. The new Bandits album is coming out. I can't just—*"

"*You can,*" she snapped.

"*You just won't.*"

I let out a bitter laugh.

"*Jeez, Marie. You think this is fun for me? You think I want to be on the road while you're pregnant?*"

"*Then don't go.*" Her tone was flat, ice-cold. Like it was that simple. Like she hadn't been in the studio with me, hadn't seen the work that went into this, hadn't watched me fight like hell to make this career last. *For us.*

"*It's not that easy,*" I said, trying to steady my breath.

"*This is for our son's future. It's what keeps the lights on, pays the bills—pays for the life you love so much. About—*"

She rolled her eyes.

"*Right. So noble. Jesse 'Frenchy' Lawrence, sacrificing it all for his family.*"

"*Are you fucking kidding me?*" My hands curled into fists at my sides.

"*I'm out there every damn time, busting my ass for us, while you sit here acting like I'm off on some goddamn vacation.*"

"*Don't twist it, Jesse.*" She tilted her head, voice syrupy-sweet.

"*I never said that.*"

I exhaled sharply. My heart was pounding now.

"*I gave you everything, Marie,*" my voice cracked, but I didn't care. "*I love you with all my heart and soul, with every fucking ounce of me.*"

I moved closer, but not too close—she was still there, just standing, as if nothing mattered.

She didn't even look at me—just stared through me like I was the problem. Didn't flinch, didn't blink. Just watched, like I was the one who messed everything up.

"*I thought you were my angel. I thought it was always going to be us—me, you, our baby boy. I thought we were building something real.*"

The words hit harder than I wanted them to, but I was already too far gone.

"*Turns out, I'd been living in a fucking lie this whole time. I was blind, Marie. Blind to the fact that you were never the one. Or even really cared."*

I paused, letting it settle, and I couldn't take my eyes off her. I should have been happy right now. There was a future ahead of us—this big, stupid duet album that the label was all in on, because I convinced them. Risked everything to make it happen.

"I risked it all for you, Marie. Gave up publishing, royalties—put it all on the line for us. The label didn't give a damn about you, but I convinced them anyway. I made them believe. Got them to back the duet album—Jesse and Marie, our album. The one we were supposed to record after the baby, when you said you'd be ready. I fought for you. And this is what I get?"

I could feel my blood boiling now, but I kept going.

"You've been using me this whole time. Playing me like a damn fool, tearing me apart whenever it suited you."

I wanted to scream. I wanted to shake her, to snap her out of whatever twisted game she was playing.

And she was pushing every damn button she knew, but I wasn't about to give her the satisfaction of losing control.

I just stood there, bracing as the truth hit me harder than any slap ever could.

"After everything I did for us... You were never what I thought. I gave you everything, and this is what you do? What kind of person does this? What kind of woman are you?"

I was on the edge, holding onto the last shred of restraint, but she was stoic—pregnant, cold, distant. Unmoved. And that cut deeper than anything else. I thought we were in this together, but she had been living in some delusional fantasy world where she didn't give a damn about me or this family.

And then it all clicked into place—the lies, the games, *the manipulation.*

Frozen, I looked at her—finally seeing her for who she really was.

A hollow feeling settled in my chest, like something had just snapped into focus. My heart pounded, and the words came out, sharp and full of rage.

"After everything, after all this time... you're the devil in disguise, Marie."

Marie didn't flinch. Instead, she looked at me with that cold, calculating expression and responded like I was the one who was out of line.

"Stop it, Jesse," she said, all smooth and condescending.

"You're exaggerating. Overreacting. It's all in your head. You're acting like a little kid."

She stepped toward me, her tone shifting to something more mocking.

"Oh, and here we go again—throwing a tantrum like a baby. You're such a drama queen, Jesse. I'm the one who's pregnant, remember? I can barely walk or move, but do you see me complaining? Do I make such a fuss?"

She crossed her arms, her face twisted with fake sympathy.

"Get over it, Jesse. We're in this together, but you need to stop acting like the world revolves around you. I'm carrying your child. I'm the one doing all the hard work. Maybe you should start acting like a man and stop whining."

Marie crept forward with snake-like grace, venom curling through her every syllable. She wasn't done yet.

"Oh, and let's not forget the groupies, Jesse," she said, her voice oozing with sarcasm.

"What about all those women at the shows? I couldn't even go with you because, you know... I'm pregnant."

Her eyes swept up with disdain, her voice dripping with contempt.

"Yeah, sure, it's totally normal for a pregnant woman to just sit at home while her partner's out doing all the fun stuff, right? I'm sure everyone gets it. I'm supposed to just rest and take it easy. But let's be

real, Jesse—don't think I didn't notice. You didn't need me there, did you? You got to hang out with the 'groupies' while I was stuck here, looking like a beached whale."

She took a step back, arms folded—passive-aggressive bite, zero empathy.

"But hey, I'm sure it was more convenient for you that way. Less distraction. More room for the fun, right?"

My chest tightened, frustration pressing in like a vice. I tried to keep my voice steady, *but the sting of her allegations was suffocating.*

"I was out there for us, Marie," I said, forcing the anger down.

"For our family. Making money for our future. It wasn't fun at all. Actually, I was fucking miserable without you there. I thought we were in this together, but it felt like you didn't even care."

I shook my head, fighting to keep the bitterness from spilling out of me.

"Yeah, I had to be out there doing it, but it wasn't easy. It was hard. But I thought it was for us—so we could have a future, a great life. I thought you'd be proud of that. I thought you'd be happy, but you weren't. You were just..."

I choked on the words, tried to catch my breath—but she cut me off with a cruel, ironic laugh.

"Yeah, right," she scoffed, that glint of cold calculation flashing like a warning.

"Sure, Jesse, all for us."

She stepped closer, savoring the moment.

"But maybe it wasn't just about that. Maybe it was about that girl from the label, huh? I remember her, you know. You told me she was cute."

She threw it at me, every syllable sharpened like a knife in a velvet glove. Dripping in bloody sarcasm.

"You two had that private conversation in her office while I was waiting outside. I'm sure it was real business, right? Nothing personal,

just professional. I bet you were just so miserable without me there, Jesse, but hey, you found a way to make it work, didn't you?"

She let the words linger, watching me, *waiting.*

"Maybe that's what you were really doing, huh? Getting a little comfort from someone else, while I sat here, all pregnant and abandoned, alone!"

She fell silent, but the accusation didn't fade. It hung in the air like poison seeping into my skin.

And that's when the realization settled.

No more smoke and mirrors. No more grandiose illusions—*Houdini's* escape-style.

The trick was revealed. The magic, *debunked.*

And like a kid finding out *Santa* isn't real... everything I thought I knew had just crumbled away.

And all I was left with—was a *lie.*

I could barely look at her anymore. My heart felt like it was being torn out of my chest.

But the words came, despite everything. And I realized—I'd been saying it to myself all along, but now I saw it clearly for what it was.

I remembered telling her once, back when I still believed in us, about the dream I had. Told her I thought she was my angel, that she was the one sent to save me.

That those eyes of hers—so bright, so blue—were like the ocean. Endless, impossible to resist. I would have sailed forever, lost in their depths, following the song of the mermaid, never questioning where she was leading me.

Angel eyes.

And with that long golden hair catching the light just right, she looked the part.

But now? Now it all made sense.

She was never my *angel.*

She was always the *devil in disguise.*

I was shocked, shook to the core, hands trembling, on the edge of a cliff. The space between us—wide as the *Grand Canyon*.

Or actually... more like a void. *Bottomless.*

And I knew, deep down, that I had been fooling myself for far too long.

But now I saw it, with absolute *clarity*.

She had never been what I thought.

She had never been who I thought *she was.*

And that was the hardest thing of all.

The pact was broken, and the devil stole my *soul.*

ACT 2B

50

GONE LIKE THE WIND

Since I got back in town, I couldn't wait to see my little boy. Whatever happened at the last show—Marie's disappearance, the ghosting—felt like just another way to make me pay for whatever I must've said or done. I didn't even know what that was, but somehow, I always ended up apologizing. I told myself I'd let her cool off, be done with her childish tantrum, and then—as always—everything would go back to normal.

Still, that night, something in me snapped. I couldn't tell who I was mad at—her, myself, the goddamn gig, the silence. I was so worked up I still can't believe I smashed my favorite guitar. Out of anger, out of rage, out of frustration—but against who, really? Against *what*?

And the worst part? I actually started to think she might be right. Maybe there *was* something *wrong* with me.

When I got home that evening, something felt off. Even the sunset looked different—washed out, like the color had drained from the world.

The house was too quiet. Too still. Hollow. Emptied of life. That gut feeling that crawls under your skin, the kind that tells you something is wrong before you even see it.

No music playing. No laughter from the living room. No soft murmur of the TV. Not even the low hum of the fridge sounded right.

Nothing.

"Marie?" I called out, tossing my keys on the counter.

No answer.

The echo of my own voice hit me first, strange and unfamiliar. Like the place didn't know me anymore.

The second clue was harder to spot. Something was missing. Like the air had shifted in my absence. The house should have seemed lived-in, warm, filled with the usual mess of life. Instead, it felt emptied. Like something had been scraped clean.

I took a few steps inside, scanning the living room.

It felt... emptier.

I couldn't put my finger on it. The room looked the same, but it didn't feel the same. Then, little by little, the details started sinking in.

The shelves—sparser.

The coat rack—bare.

The usual clutter of life—*scrubbed out.*

A cold prickle ran down my spine. This wasn't just a bad feeling. This was real.

I moved faster, my heartbeat hammering against my ribs. By the time I reached the stairs, my chest was tight. I took them two at a time.

That's when it hit me.

Lil' Jesse's bed was stripped.

His dresser drawers were hanging open—empty.

His plushes. His favorite blanket. The toy trucks he never went anywhere without.

Gone.

My anxiety surged. I turned sharply, my heart pounding as I bolted toward our bedroom. The door slammed against the wall as I shoved it open.

Marie's walk-in closet—*gutted.*

Hangers lay scattered across the floor, tangled like broken ribs. The shelves were stripped bare, the space where her suitcases should have been—*empty.*

The nightstand drawers stood half-open, a few things left behind—a hairbrush, a lone earring, a forgotten scarf draped over the bedpost like an afterthought.

She had left before. Walked out, disappeared for a night or two, just long enough to make me question everything. Make me chase her.

But this time... this time was different. The atmosphere in the house felt stripped—almost haunted. Drained, like it had been abandoned long before I even stepped inside.

This wasn't just another game. This was something else.

And now, she was really *gone.*

I stumbled back out of the room, my breath coming fast and uneven.

Then panic took over.

I tore through the house, throwing open closet doors, checking behind furniture, my voice cracking as I called out.

"Marie! Marie, where the hell are you?"

Nothing.

My pulse roared in my ears.

A break-in? A kidnapping?

I ran back down the stairs, fumbling for my phone, my fingers numb, my breathing quick and shallow.

I was about to dial 911 when—

I saw it.

A single sheet of paper, sitting on the kitchen table.

Waiting.

Watching.

Like it had been there all along, just for me to find it.

Don't look for us. This is what's best.

That was it.

A few words to erase everything.

I sank into the chair, clutching the paper, reading it again and again, as if more words might appear if I stared hard enough. This is what's best.

Best for who? *For her? For him?*

It sure as hell wasn't for me.

I grabbed my phone, dialing her number.

Straight to voicemail.

Again. And *again.*

By the fourth try, my hand was shaking so badly that I could barely hold the phone.

I sat there in the dark, replaying the fight we'd had a few days ago. Her words still rang in my ears.

"You just want control," she'd said, arms crossed, chin lifted like she was delivering a verdict.

"Admit it—you'd take him back to France if you could."

I'd laughed, a bitter, disbelieving sound.

"That's insane, Marie. I'd never take him from you. Never."

She tilted her head, studying me, calculating, like she was taking notes.

"Right. Because you're such a saint."

"Seriously, Marie? Come on. I want our little boy to have his mom and dad. I'd never do something that cruel."

I pressed my lips together and puffed out one cheek—that *"you've got to be kidding me, give me a break"* kind of face.

"Mmm." She dragged out the sound like she wasn't

convinced. Like she already knew how she wanted this story to go.

"You say that now."

"Because it's the truth."

She let out a slow breath, eyes flicking away for just a second.

A flash of something—*guilt?*

But it vanished before I could pin it down.

Then she looked at me again, full *poker face* on.

"Maybe you're not the one I should be worried about."

The mood shifted—like she'd flipped a switch, another mask locking into place.

Something about the way she said it, the way she let the words just hang there, made my stomach turn.

I stared at her.

"What's that supposed to mean?"

She didn't answer. She just held my gaze for a moment longer, then turned and walked away.

And that was it.

No screaming. No slammed doors.

But now, sitting in the dark, clutching the note she'd left behind, I realized—that had been the moment she was already *gone.*

That had been her goodbye.

She never believed me.

And she never really cared.

She'd already made up her mind, spinning her narrative like she always did.

And now, *en un coup de vent,* just like the wind.

She was, they were—

gone.

For real.

51

A FAMILY AFFAIR

O say, can you see, by the dawn's early light.

Yep. It was the Fourth of July—a warm, sunny day with not a cloud in the sky, the perfect setting for celebration. Stars and Stripes were everywhere, fluttering proudly in the breeze.

Marie's family had thrown an extravagant party at their big colonial-style mansion. The house was a masterpiece, a sprawling estate with towering columns and every detail designed to impress. The marble floors gleamed beneath the grand chandelier, which hung in the center of the grand entrance, casting a soft glow across the entire lobby. A sweeping stairwell curved up from both sides, meeting at the top floor, as if to guide you toward the heights of opulence.

On the stairwell walls, dozens of portraits lined the space, a gallery of faces that seemed to whisper the family's legacy. It looked like something out of Versailles, each frame a testament to a royal dynasty, depicting their history and heritage in vivid detail. Everything about the house was over the top—like something straight out of a Hollywood movie, with elegance dripping from every corner. Every element, every feature, every inch screamed *"grandeur."*

The party was held outside, on the vast lawn in the back of the house, which seemed to stretch for acres, almost the size of a football field. The space was adorned with festive decorations—red, white, and blue balloons floated in the air, and American flags were draped across the fences and hanging from the trees. Waiters and waitresses moved seamlessly through the crowd, offering drinks and hors d'oeuvres on silver trays. A stage stood near the back, where a local band played feel-good Americana —foot-tapping rhythms and warm harmonies drifting through the garden like the smell of barbecue and fresh-cut grass, adding to the spirit of the occasion.

It was the same kind of over-the-top opulence that had surrounded our wedding—same house, same lawn... just with more champagne and more *French flavors*.

It was the kind of event where everything felt larger than life —hundreds of people milling about, drinks flowing freely, and laughter ringing out across the perfectly manicured grounds. Somewhere among the sea of guests, little Jesse toddled around, weaving between grown-ups, chasing bubbles and giggling as the other kids ran circles around him. He was too young to understand the significance of it, but the joy on his face said it all.

For someone like me, who didn't have much family—at least none on this continent—it felt like I belonged. Like I was finally part of something bigger, something whole. They welcomed me with open arms.

Marie's parents smiled warmly as they introduced me to their friends, their voices full of pride.

Jack, her dad, was a business attorney and a partner at Pennington, Kearney & Associates, a prominent firm with deep connections in both corporate and local legal circles. He had built a lucrative, wealth-generating career representing major oil companies, cementing the firm's reputation as one of the most influential in the state of Texas.

Charlene, her mom, came from an old Southern family that prided itself on its aristocratic lineage—whether British, French, or something else, depending on the day and the amount of wine. Although it was never entirely clear whether her family still possessed the wealth that once made their name, Charlene carried herself with a certain social poise, as if she'd just stepped out of a Southern estate. She now ran a small beauty franchise —more of a passion project than a thriving business—something her husband supported to keep her happy.

Standing there among these people, with their warm welcome and open gestures, I realized something: It was the first time in a long while that I didn't feel like an outsider. We were sharing drinks, telling stories, and laughing together, and Marie's family treated me like one of their own, pulling me into their circle.

I wasn't just a guest—I was part of something real, something that felt solid and safe. At one point, a few of us—some of the Bandits, some friends, and even Marie—made our way to the stage and started jamming. Nothing formal, just a handful of songs, but the crowd loved it. The music flowed effortlessly, and for a brief moment, life was perfect. Marie and I did a duet too— her voice soft and confident, mine barely holding back how happy I felt in that moment. People clapped along, others danced. Even little Jesse was bouncing along, trying to keep rhythm, his tiny hands clapping with the beat. And I remember thinking—this was it. This was what life was supposed to feel like.

As the sun dipped lower in the sky, casting a golden glow over the gathering. I caught Marie's eye across the lawn, and she smiled at me, her face radiant in the soft light. Everything about that day felt right—like I had finally found my place, a moment full of *love* and *happiness.*

Marie's mom, Charlene, waved across the patio, her glass of cabernet catching the late afternoon sunlight.

"Maggie! So glad you could make it!" she called warmly, air-kissing a woman in a crisp linen dress.

"Let me introduce you to my daughter, Marie, and her husband, Jesse."

"Wouldn't miss it this time," Maggie replied, her tone casual yet authoritative.

Looping an arm around Marie's waist, Charlene continued,

"Marie, Jesse, this is Maggie and her husband, Bob Jenkins. Maggie and I go way back."

I extended a hand with a polite smile. Maggie shook it briskly, her attention already drifting back to Marie's mom as they exchanged pleasantries about the party. Just another guest, I thought, blending into the crowd of influential faces scattered across the lawn.

While Charlene and Maggie continued talking, I felt a tap on my shoulder. I turned to see Mr. Jenkins standing there, smiling widely and holding a glass of whiskey.

"Come on, Jesse, let's grab a drink. Charlene told me you've got some great stories from the road. You've gotta share one or two!"

I chuckled, enjoying the genuine warmth in his voice.

"Sure thing. What do you want to hear?"

"Well," Mr. Jenkins said with a wink,

"I used to be in a local band back in the day. Nothing too serious, but we had some fun. That's why I'm so curious to hear your stories. You've seen the real deal. I'm sure it's a bit different than what I remember."

I nodded, understanding.

"I'm happy to share."

As we made our way to the bar, I noticed Charlene and Marie deep in conversation with some other guests, laughing and sharing a moment of their own. I felt a flicker of pride. This was my life now. These were my people.

All around, the atmosphere was vibrant. The music played lively tunes, people shared stories, and the whole scene felt like something out of a movie—effortless, joyful, and perfectly at ease. The soft laughter from one group blended with the upbeat melodies from the band playing in the background. The clink of glasses echoed, mixing with the chatter and the sounds of a good time being had by all.

I spotted Marie's dad, Jack, a man who always looked like he was in complete control, moving from one conversation to another with confidence, greeting old friends and new acquaintances alike. His charisma was undeniable. Charlene, standing nearby, was surrounded by her circle of friends, her presence commanding attention. Yet, despite their undeniable power and influence, there was a warmth to them, a welcoming energy that made everyone feel like they were a part of something bigger, something real.

Marie leaned into me, her face glowing as she pointed out different people.

"That's Tom, the one with the wild hair. He used to play with a band that toured the West Coast a few years ago. And over there, that's Jenna. We were inseparable as kids—best friends growing up. Well, we lost touch for years; she was living abroad for a while. But we just reconnected... like no time had passed."

She beamed as she introduced me to each new face, her pride evident.

Their world had become mine. The laughter, the music, the effortless rhythm of it all—it pulled me in, not as an observer, but as someone who belonged. It didn't matter where I'd come from or how different my life had been before this. Here, I wasn't just passing through. I was home. It all felt like a historic *Independence Day* moment I wanted to hold on to forever.

As the evening came to a close, the warm glow of the party lingered in my memory. We stood in a circle, clinking glasses in a toast to the holiday, to family, to good times. Marie's aunt, Cherry Lynn, a well-known family law attorney, was there too, laughing with the rest of us, raising her glass.

"To love, to family, to never needing a lawyer!" she joked, earning a round of laughter.

I had chuckled along, feeling truly at home—like I was exactly where I was meant to be.

It had taken an ocean to cross, *miles* and *miles* around the globe, blood, sweat, and tears to make it—and pieces of myself left behind.

And *now*.

Now, I was the luckiest guy in the world, I thought—a beautiful wife, a beautiful baby boy, a wonderful new family—and I was so grateful for it. This life was everything I had dreamed of; I didn't need more.

I wanted it to last forever, to never wake up, my head lost in the clouds—never once imagining that just weeks later, that *dream* would shatter into my worst *nightmare*.

52

THE CIVIC JUGGERNAUT

The looming outline of the Tarrant County Family Law Center came into view. As I pulled into the parking structure of the Fort Worth Civic Center, I tightened my grip on the wheel. From where I sat in the truck, it looked cold and unyielding—just a structure of glass and steel stacked into a box, with none of the warmth or humanity it claimed to represent.

I parked and cut the engine but stayed where I was, gripping the wheel as my eyes traced the building ahead.

The Family Law Center stood ahead, its impersonal facade casting long shadows in the morning light. It wasn't grand or imposing, but its stark, functional design carried a weight of its own—efficient, indifferent. Above the entrance, bold metal letters announced its authority, their sharp serifed edges almost mocking. They seemed to declare this a place where lives were reduced to case numbers, where strangers who knew nothing of the people they ruled over made decisions that changed everything.

I stepped out and started toward the building, the sound of my steps against the pavement barely audible over the noise of the traffic. People streamed in and out, clutching folders and documents, their faces a mix of determination, worry, and despair. Inside, I knew the sterile halls would echo with hurried footsteps, muffled conversations, and the fluorescent lights over-head crackling and flickering like distant static.

It wasn't just a courthouse—it was a cold machine, grinding people down, spitting them out, and never looking back. And as I walked through those doors, I couldn't shake the feeling that today, I'd be no exception.

A blast of stale air hit me, a mix of industrial cleaners and the faint scent of anxiety that somehow felt oppressive. The place was alive with tangible tension: lawyers in sharp suits moving with purpose, clerks clutching stacks of papers, and people like me—hesitant, unsure, and holding onto thin hopes. Security checks were as impersonal as the building itself—tight, like an airport, but without the promise of a destination.

I emptied my pockets and walked through the metal detec-tor, met by a guard's indifferent nod.

Eric Stein, my lawyer, waited just beyond the checkpoint. He wasn't the most experienced attorney—he looked like he was in his late twenties, younger than I'd expected when we first met just a few days ago. I'd found him at the first firm I called—the only attorney they had available—scrambling to respond to the injunction that had arrived so suddenly, leaving me with almost no time to act.

Still, there was something about his honest demeanor that convinced me to hire him. Not that I really had much choice, anyway.

"Good morning, Jesse," he said, his expression measured.

"Ready?"

"Do I have a choice?" I replied, tugging at the collar of my suit.

It felt stiff, unfamiliar. The last time I wore one was five years ago—on my wedding day, a day that now felt like a lifetime ago.

All of a sudden, someone walked up to me.

"Mr. Lawrence?"

"Yes," I answered, instinctively. Before I could even process what was happening, an envelope was shoved into my hands.

"You've been served," they said, their tone flat and indifferent, before turning and walking away.

I stood there, frozen, the envelope gripped in my hand like a live wire. My lawyer, equally stunned, didn't say a word at first.

Then, breaking the silence, he said,

"Divorce papers, my guess. That's the law. You can't get to trial without being served first."

And with a sigh, he added,

"Restraining orders—classic move. Standard divorce tactic these days."

Of course. Nothing here was ever about making things right —only making them *official.*

I stared at the envelope. Shocked.

It was legal. Clinical. Lethal. *Final.*

So *that's* what she meant by:

Don't look for us. This is what's best.

Cold words, etched like epitaphs.
And her will was just some fucking paperwork—
no tear, no tremble,
just ink and cruelty pressed to the page.
And with it, she buried *us.*

Today wasn't a family reunion, like I might've stupidly hoped. No.

It was a damn *love's funeral.*

As Eric exhaled sharply, adjusting his tie, the sound snapped me out of it—dragging me back from that headstone in my mind, back into another kind of cold. Fluorescent now.

"Alright Jesse, let's get to it. Just stick with me, follow my lead, and don't react to anything you hear unless I tell you to—like we rehearsed the other day at the office. Got it?"

"Got it," I muttered, though the words felt hollow. I was already bracing for the worst.

He didn't look particularly confident, but then again, neither was I.

We rode the elevator up a few floors, my stomach sinking with each passing second. A chime rang out, and the doors slid open to a long corridor lined with courtrooms—some with their doors slightly ajar, where lawyers murmured in hushed tones with their clients, trying to hammer out last-minute deals. In smaller rooms, tense negotiations played out, voices low but urgent.

A few people paced the hallway, their hands shoved deep in their pockets, their faces etched with worry. Some clung to their documents like life preservers, others just clenched their fists. A woman sat on one of the stiff wooden benches, dabbing her eyes with a crumpled tissue, staring blankly ahead like she was already mourning whatever verdict awaited her.

Eric barely glanced around. He just kept walking, his pace steady, focused. Then, without breaking stride, he nodded toward a door at the end of the hall.

As we entered the courtroom, they were already there— Marie and her team, fully assembled.

One of them—maybe her lead counsel—was up near the front, laughing with the officers, the bailiff... maybe even the clerk, as if they were old friends. That voice carried, calm and confident, like someone used to owning the room.

And somehow, it sounded... *familiar.*

Assistants bustled around, carrying boxes stacked so high

they could barely see over them. They looked like they were setting up *camp*.

A slow, sinking feeling crept into my gut.

"Just stay calm," Eric murmured.

Easy for him to say. He wasn't the one fighting for his *son*.

53

MASTER OF CEREMONY

History meant nothing in this room.

Or did it? *Ever?* Or maybe just the illusion of it.

Marie was already seated at the table. Then the woman who'd been chatting near the front turned... and took the seat beside her.

That's when it hit me—her attorney was the *Cherry Lynn.*

Her *aunt.*

My breath caught in my throat as I stared at Cherry. Just a month ago, at the Fourth of July barbecue, she and I were clinking glasses, laughing like family. Now, she was seated across from me, flanked by Marie and a small army of paralegals and assistants.

Boxes of documents were stacked high in front of them, their labels crisp and clean, as though Cherry had been preparing for this moment for months. Meanwhile, I'd only just been served —walking into this fight blind, *unarmed.*

This wasn't just a case. It was an *ambush.*

A well-prepared, carefully planned, *full-on attack.*

Even from her seat, Cherry Lynn kept chatting and tossing out small jokes, but I could still hear her laughter from earlier—easy, confident, echoing off the walls like this place had always been her *playground*—and she was the commander-in-chief on a battleground.

I gritted my teeth and shot Eric a sharp look—a mix of disbelief, anger, and something closer to stunned *betrayal*.

"*Seriously?*" I muttered under my breath, my lips barely moving.

Eric didn't even look up, just flipped a page.

"*Yeah, well...*"

His voice was low, distracted, like he'd seen it a hundred times before—and had more important things to deal with.

The courtroom was smaller than I expected, almost claustrophobic. It wasn't the grand, dramatic hall you'd see in movies. Instead, it was plain and cramped, with rows of benches that looked like they hadn't been replaced since the 70s. At the far end, the judge's bench loomed, flanked by flags that seemed to droop under the weight of expectation.

As the tension rose, thick and suffocating, the courtroom felt less and less like a place of justice—and more and more like a *trap*.

Marie didn't glance at me. She'd mastered the art of ignoring me, her head held high, focusing entirely on her aunt's whispered instructions.

Eric leaned in.

"*Don't let it get to you. They're playing the intimidation game.*"

"*Seems to be working,*" I said, my stomach tightening.

"*All rise.*"

The bailiff's voice cracked across the room like a whip, chairs scraping, papers rustling, heels clicking against the floor as everyone stood.

From the side door, the judge entered, her presence

commanding despite her small frame. She walked to the bench, adjusted a few papers, then took her seat. And with a swift motion, she grabbed the gavel and slammed it down, breaking the charged silence.

"This court is now in session."

For a moment, I barely registered her. My eyes skimmed over the placard on her desk:

Judge M.C. Jenkins.

Just another official in a room full of strangers.

That's when my stomach dropped. My breath caught as recognition hit me like a punch to the chest.

Maggie?

No fucking way.

That same Fourth of July, at the Penningtons' party a month ago—that's where I met her for the first time. Her husband had waved me over, eager to hear stories from the road. She'd laughed along, asking questions, listening like she genuinely cared. She made me feel welcome, like I was part of their circle.

And now, here she was, perched above it all, presiding over my case, watching from her high seat like a vulture circling its promised next meal.

Her gaze swept the room, keen and instinctive, like a predator catching the scent of blood, before landing on me.

Neutral face. A beat too long.

She knew exactly who I was. No doubt about it.

And I? I wasn't a player—I was the greatest pawn in a game I didn't even know I'd entered.

Eric shifted closer, his voice low.

"Jesse? What's wrong?"

I couldn't answer. My jaw tightened, and I looked away, gripping the edge of the table. *How the hell is this happening?*

She knows me. She knows Marie.

This has to be a conflict of *interest.*

It felt like the oxygen had been sucked out, the space squeezing tighter and tighter until I realized I was locked inside a cage.

The trap was now in place—fully set—and already closing in, sealing my *fate.*

When the judge—*Maggie*—finally spoke, her voice was steady, but I could hear the slightest edge of familiarity.

"This court will now hear the case of Pennington versus Lawrence."

I stayed put, stunned. Just weeks ago, these people were part of my world—*my family*—laughing, sharing stories, drinking beers.

Now, they felt like strangers.

Familiar strangers, but strangers all the same.

If this was justice, it felt like I'd already lost.

Lost the war before the first shot was even *fired.*

54

LOST IN TRANSLATION

Everyone was sitting there, waiting for the battle to start. Finally, Judge Jenkins pushed her glasses up and turned to the bailiff, who bent down to whisper something. She nodded and cleared her throat.

"We're still waiting for the court-appointed translator. I've been informed they're caught in traffic... in a taxi," she said, her tone measured but with a hint of frustration.

I blinked and leaned toward my lawyer.

"What translator?"

Eric gave me a sideways glance, lowering his tone.

"They insisted on one because of your dual citizenship. Potential language barriers."

"But I don't need one," I said, my stomach tightening.

"Standard procedure—well, at least in this court, I guess," he replied.

"Yeah, right. Well, I don't buy it," I muttered, eyeing the judge.

"More like procedural overkill."

Before Eric could respond, the judge's voice cut through again.

"We'll wait for a few more minutes to allow the translator to arrive. In the meantime, please remain seated and prepared to proceed promptly."

I sank back in my chair, the rope coiling, the gallows set.

A translator? For me? It didn't make any sense.

The absurdity of it all was enough to make my blood boil, but I kept my mouth shut. For now. No point in spitting dust before the noose was even tied.

Somewhere in the back of my mind, I couldn't shake the feeling that this wasn't just a misunderstanding. It felt deliberate —another way to tilt the scales against me. Like a sheriff picking the jury from his own poker table.

And now we were all stuck, waiting for someone to show up in a cab.

As if on cue, Judge Jenkins looked toward the door as it creaked open, her expression neutral but her tapping fingers betraying her impatience.

The translator showed up at last, after what felt like an eternity. The wait had dragged on far beyond a few minutes—long enough for the tension to settle over the courtroom like a thick fog. When they finally tottered in, it felt anticlimactic, almost surreal.

A tiny, frail elderly woman, her gray hair pinned up in a way that screamed she'd been plucked straight out of a knitting circle. Her movements were slow and cautious, as though every step required careful thought.

The bailiff helped her into the translator's seat, but to my surprise, that seat was right next to me. She lowered herself down slowly, letting out a quiet sigh of relief as she adjusted her glasses.

I stiffened, suddenly hyperaware of her presence. I could feel the faint rustle of her papers and even hear her shallow breaths. Her proximity made the ridiculousness of the situation even harder to ignore.

I peeked at my lawyer, hoping for some kind of reassurance, but he was absorbed in his notes, lost in his own thoughts— oblivious to the circus unfolding around us.

Great. *I was on my fucking own.*

Just a warm body in the middle of a firing line, with nowhere to *hide.*

Then Judge Jenkins cleared her throat, her tone firm, but even.

"All right, everyone's here now. Let's resume the session."

55

COMMEDIA DELL'ARTE

Dressed for war, Marie's lawyer—or should I say, her *aunt*—Cherry Lynn, stood, buttoning her pristine blazer like she was accepting an award. Her tone was warm yet calculated, her words laced with calm menace.

"Your Honor, my client is requesting to remain the sole holder of the child's passport. She has serious concerns regarding Mr. Lawrence's intentions."

She began pacing, her heels clicking softly on the floor, each step deliberate and commanding. She moved like she owned the room, her presence drawing all attention.

"He holds dual citizenship in the United States and France. He's expressed, on multiple occasions, a desire to return to France—and still holds non-refundable plane tickets for an international trip to Paris scheduled next month. Originally purchased as a so-called 'family vacation.' These remain active, raising serious concerns about unauthorized relocation or even abduction. Your Honor, there is a significant risk he could flee with the child."

"That's absurd!" the words burst out of me before I could stop them.

The judge's eyes snapped to me, sharp and unyielding.

"Mr. Lawrence," her voice was like a whip crack.

"You'll have your turn." addressing Eric, she added,

"Counsel, refrain your client, please."

I dropped back into my chair, heat rising in my chest. Eric shot me a warning glance, shaking his head ever so slightly.

"This isn't speculation," she continued, *her tone dripping with fake concern. "My client genuinely fears that Mr. Lawrence could act on these impulses—taking their son away permanently."*

"Does your client have proof of these tickets?" Judge Jenkins asked, raising an eyebrow.

Cherry Lynn didn't even blink. She turned slightly, gesturing to one of her assistant.

Her assistant—more paralegal than secretary—moved with polished efficiency, stepping forward to hand the judge a neatly labeled folder.

"Yes, Your Honor. We've submitted copies of the itinerary and purchase receipt under Exhibit A."

Seriously? They used the fucking tickets. The ones I held onto like a fool. Not to run—but to remember. To believe. To dream that maybe... somehow, we'd go to France together like we planned. And now? They're 'evidence.' A family vacation turned into a motive for kidnapping. That's what it had come to. Every gesture of love turned into ammunition. You can't make this shit up.

I fought the urge to react as Eric gave my sleeve a subtle tug, his silent plea for restraint. How could I stay quiet when every word she spoke was a cynical, distorted version of the *truth?*

Cherry Lynn paused for a moment, her statement hanging in the air, before casting a brief, knowing smile at the judge. My stomach churned.

This wasn't a fair fight—it was a performance. And I was the *outsider.*

I sat there like an extra on my own movie set, watching them rewrite the script in real time—line by line, frame by frame.

Judge Jenkins reclined slightly, her face impassive as she surveyed the stack of boxes on Cherry Lynn's table.

"Ms. Johnson," she quipped, a bit amused,

"how many trees did we kill for this case?"

A ripple of chuckles spread through the courtroom. Cherry Lynn's demure smile barely masked her smugness.

"Just enough to ensure the truth, Your Honor."

I clenched my fists under the table, the laughter grating against my frayed nerves. The game had already begun, and I felt like I was losing before I even had a chance to play.

The formalities dragged on until Cherry Lynn finally addressed the judge.

"Your Honor, I'd like to call Ms. Pennington to the stand."

Acknowledging the request, the judge said,

"Ms. Pennington, please proceed to the stand."

Marie rose gracefully, smoothing her skirt with a calculated poise that screamed perfection. As she walked toward the bench, her eyes briefly brushed over me before settling on Maggie, Judge Jenkins. It was so brief, it was almost like she wanted me to see her, but not for long enough to matter.

Her long blonde hair was styled perfectly, every strand in place. Her outfit was deliberately chosen to strike that impossible balance between professional and approachable.

She wasn't just Marie anymore—she was the picture of the struggling, devoted *mother.*

I watched as she transformed before me. Her stance was perfect, her expression vulnerable. She wasn't the woman I'd married, or even the one I'd fought with. She had become someone else entirely, an ideal archetype—the brave mother, the perfect wife, the wounded *victim,* the selfless caretaker. A role built to withstand the *truth.*

Once seated, she adjusted her posture and smoothed her skirt again, as if the action itself might steady her nerves.

"Ms. Pennington," her lawyer began, her voice steady and reassuring,

"can you describe your concerns about Mr. Lawrence's parenting?"

Marie nodded slightly, her hands clasped tightly in her lap. Her voice trembled, soft but clear.

"I... I just want what's best for our son. Jesse... he's a musician. His career keeps him away for long periods. When he's home, he... well, he struggles to maintain stability."

A flush of anger surged through me, burning under my skin. *Stability?* What did that even mean?

"Could you elaborate on what you mean by stability?" Cherry Lynn prompted, her tone gentle but suggestive.

Marie's eyes welled up with tears, perfectly timed. She paused, her lips trembling just enough to seem genuine.

"There were times when he... he'd disappear into his studio for hours, sometimes days. And... there were nights when he came home smelling of alcohol. I... I was left to hold everything together."

Her words felt like punches to the chest, each one calculated and pointed. I wanted to stand up, to shout that it wasn't true— or at least not the way she was saying it. Yes, I spent hours in the studio, but I was working, creating, providing. And the way she talked about me drinking? It wasn't like I came home falling-down *drunk.*

Eric eased a hand toward my arm, brushing it just enough to remind me to stay calm. But how could I, when the woman on the stand was twisting pieces of my life into a story I barely recognized?

Cherry Lynn turned back to the judge, her voice calm and composed.

"Your Honor, we'd like to submit Exhibit B: a series of photos taken over the past six months, documenting Mr. Lawrence's behavior."

A paralegal handed one neatly stacked pile of glossy prints to the judge and another to Eric.

Eric began flipping through them, and as the photos passed from his hands to mine, I caught glimpses—me in the studio, focused on my guitar; me at a gig, laughing with a drink in hand; me leaning against my truck, exhaustion on my face.

Each one felt like a moment stolen out of context and turned into a weapon.

Cherry Lynn continued, her voice unwavering.

"These photos show a pattern of behavior that raises serious concerns about Mr. Lawrence's ability to provide a stable environment for his son."

My stomach churned again as I watched the judge linger on a photo of me at a bar, the flash catching the drink in my hand like a spotlight.

The room held its breath like a firing squad—guns loaded, *execution-style,* aim ready, just waiting for the command.

I could feel Eric shift beside me.

"It's just photos," he whispered, leaning slightly toward me.

"Stay calm."

Stay calm?

I wanted to shout that this wasn't the truth, that these pictures were cherry-picked moments twisted into lies. One photo stood out—the one taken from upstairs. It showed me sitting beside the stroller, a glass of beer in hand, while my son slept peacefully.

I could still see Marie and her mom standing on the patio above me. They'd gone wine tasting and asked if I wanted to come. But getting the stroller up there was too much trouble, so I stayed below, content to let my son rest.

I remember asking Marie why she took that picture, and she

just shrugged it off—*"Oh, just to show you."* I hadn't driven that day; Marie had, so a single beer hardly mattered.

Yet here it was, held up as evidence, completely out of context.

Meanwhile, on the stand, Marie was playing her part to perfection. She sniffled softly, pulling a tissue from somewhere and dabbing at her eyes with the practiced ease of someone who'd rehearsed every movement.

"I've tried everything to make this work," she said, her voice cracking just enough to sound genuine.

"But Jesse... he's never here. His career is his priority, not his family."

Her words came slowly, measured, each one perfectly placed to twist the knife.

She paused for effect, the courtroom frozen, suspended on her words as her tears fell in rhythm with her testimony.

"I just want what's best for my son. And a young child being raised in a toxic environment? That's not best. I need to protect him... and myself. That's why I left—with our son, and without warning. I was scared. Scared he'd find us. So I had to hide. And now, I just hope the court will protect us."

My jaw tightened, my teeth grinding together as her tirade reverberated like a line from a tragedy. *Protect him? From what?*

Cherry Lynn didn't miss a beat, cutting through the tension.

"That's what a caring and concerned mother does."

She turned slightly toward the judge.

"So, Marie, you've mentioned that several times—while Mr. Lawrence was intoxicated..."

"Objection, Your Honor," Eric interjected sharply, rising from his seat.

"Leading."

The judge raised a hand.

"Sustained. Continue, Ms. Lynn, but keep it neutral."

Cherry Lynn adjusted her posture and pressed on without hesitation.

"So, you said that while Mr. Lawrence was having a few drinks, he was often agitated and yelling at you. Did Jesse ever hit you?"

I held my breath, short and shallow. Like a scathing accusation, waiting for its verdict. What is this *masquerade?*

I thought, my mind reeling. The question itself was designed to plant a seed of doubt, no matter the answer.

Marie hesitated for a moment, her face a perfect mask of uncertainty. Then, finally, she spoke, her voice soft but clear.

"No, he didn't."

Relief barely had time to settle before the French translator, seated beside me, leaned in and murmured her version of the response.

"Oui, il m'a frappé."

Yes, he hit me.

The words sent a jolt through my entire body. My head snapped toward her, disbelief and panic flooding my senses.

What the fuck did she just say?

Did I hear that right?

Her whisper had already felt like gibberish before, a jumbled mess that barely resembled proper French.

But now, *this?* This wasn't a mistake—it was *sabotage.*

"N'importe quoi!"

I said, barely under my breath, the words slipping out as I tried to stay composed. It was complete nonsense—absurd, surreal, and impossible to fight against, like something straight out of a *Kafka novel.*

I locked my hands together tightly under the table, trying to keep my composure. My focus was splintering—between the courtroom's gravity, Marie's theatrics, and this so-called translator whispering lies into my ear.

It wasn't just distracting—it was dangerous. If this woman

could flip something as simple as *"No, he didn't,"* what the hell would she say when it was my turn on the stand?

The realization hit me like a gut punch. If I testified in French with her translating, I might as well be signing my own *death sentence.*

Marie dabbed at her eyes again, her gaze lowering in what must have seemed to everyone else like vulnerability and victimization. To me, it was theater—her final act in a charade designed to bury me alive.

And as if that wasn't enough, the translator's twisted words, half *charabia,* echoed in my ear, making it harder to stay grounded. My head was spinning, the courtroom blurring into the backdrop of this *grotesque play.* This whole thing was so fucked up it felt like *satire*—except no one was laughing.

Marie's masterpiece performance was nothing short of an audition for the role of a lifetime. She shifted seamlessly from one mask to another, each more convincing than the last. One moment, her face was etched with sorrow, her lips trembling as if she were carrying the weight of the world. The next, her tears vanished like they'd never existed, replaced by a calm, measured focus as she delivered her lines with chilling precision. It was as if she'd rehearsed this a hundred times in front of a mirror, each act polished to perfection. She played the grieving mother, the abandoned and neglected wife, and the unshakable protector in quick succession, her transitions so smooth they were almost imperceptible.

The courtroom became her stage, and everyone in the room —judge, clerks, and even the bailiff—her captive audience.

To them, it was *sincerity.*

To me, un vrai spectacle *macabre*—a baroque theatrical farce in pure *Italian style,* where she wore a new mask with every word, every glance.

And the worst part? They were all buying it.

Every single one, front row seats to the *farce of a lifetime.*

Signore e signori... La Commedia dell'Arte.

56

FROM ROMANIA WITH (NO) LOVE

E ric sat stone-faced as Marie's testimony concluded, but my blood was boiling. Then, Judge Jenkins turned to the counsels.

"Do either of you have anything to add?"

When neither side spoke, she adjusted her glasses and continued,

"Let's break for lunch. We'll resume the afternoon session in one hour."

I barely heard the shuffle of chairs or the murmurs of the courtroom dispersing as everyone prepared to leave. My thoughts were racing, my frustration building with each passing second.

As soon as we were in the hallway, I grabbed Eric by the arm and pulled him aside.

"What the hell is going on with this translator?" I hissed, my voice low but urgent.

He shot me a sharp look, clearly not thrilled with my sudden outburst.

"What do you mean?"

"She's screwing up the translation," I said, lowering my volume.

"She's saying the opposite of what's being said."

Eric sighed, rubbing his temple.

"Well, it's too late. She's been sworn in and assigned to your case. Unless we can prove she's unqualified, we're stuck with her."

I leaned in closer.

"Look, I can't testify in French with her translating. It'll be like signing my own death sentence! When Marie said I didn't hit her, that woman, always in my ears, whispered to me in French, 'Oui, il m'a frappé,'—'Yes, he hit me.' What the hell is that? This is insane! She's not a native speaker—I'm telling you."

"Alright then... if you can prove it, we might have a shot," Eric said, pressing his lips together.

"Okay," I said, my pulse pounding.

"Let me talk to her—I'll prove it."

I spotted her near the end of the hallway, thumbing through a small notepad.

My hands were clammy as I approached, but I forced a polite tone.

"Hi there. I just wanted to say thank you for your help today. It must be stressful."

She glanced up, offering a brief smile.

"Oh, not at all."

"Right. Of course." I hesitated, trying to sound casual. Now time to test this.

Switching smoothly to French, I asked,

"Dites-moi, j'ai noté que vous aviez un accent... Vous n'êtes pas Française, hein? Vous venez d'où ?"

(Tell me, I noticed you have an accent... You're not French, are you? Where are you from?)

Her smile faltered just slightly. For a second, she seemed to process my words, her eyes flickering with hesitation. Then, as if flipping a switch, her face lit up.

"Oh—uh..." She blinked before answering in English.

"No! I'm from Romania."

I stared at her, stunned.

"Romania?"

She nodded, still smiling, like it was the most normal thing in the world.

"Yes."

I barely managed to keep my cool before spinning around and heading back to Eric.

"She's Romanian. Not French! We can't keep her. I told you something was off—she's not even fluent, and definitely not a native speaker."

"Alright, that might work. Let's give it a shot," he simply said.

57

ON THE GRILL

Voices hushed as everyone gathered back in the courtroom after lunch break. The tension in the air was palpable, like menacing thunder waiting to strike. The translator had already taken her seat beside me, shuffling her papers with a slowness that set my nerves on edge.

With a sharp rap of the gavel signaling the court was back in motion, Judge Jenkins resumed the afternoon session.

Eric stood, his tone measured as he addressed her.

"Your Honor, my client has expressed concerns about the translator. She's not a native French speaker, and we're worried this could lead to inaccuracies in his testimony."

The judge raised an eyebrow, her expression sharp and unimpressed.

"Mr. Stein, this court goes to great lengths to ensure fairness and access for all participants. The translator is court-appointed, and she's here as part of our standard procedure."

Eric pressed on, his voice calm but firm.

"I understand that, Your Honor, but Mr. Lawrence is fluent in

English and would prefer to testify in English to avoid any potential misunderstandings."

Judge Jenkins settled deeper into her seat, her lips pressing into a thin line.

"Are you questioning this court's process, Counsel?" she said, carrying an edge of irritation.

"This woman," she gestured toward the translator,

"has spent her day here to ensure this trial runs smoothly. She's already had trouble getting here, and I won't have her efforts dismissed lightly."

I felt the weight of the room crushing down on me as the judge continued.

"However," she added after a beat,

"your client is free to testify in English if you so choose. That's his right. But the translator will remain here for the duration, just in case she's needed."

Turning to the translator, she softened her tone slightly.

"Ma'am, you can stay. Thank you for your service and your time today."

She gave a small nod, her smile barely there, her movements slow with weariness.

Eric sat back down, leaning toward me.

"Well, that's the best we're going to get," he said quietly.

I clenched my jaw, frustration simmering just below the surface. The Romanian translator was staying. Her *charabia* was staying. And I was left bracing for the inevitable chaos her presence might bring.

When I finally took the stand, the air seemed heavier, colder. The murmur of voices in the room dulled as I settled into the chair, my hands gripping the edges of the wooden armrests. Eric's advice echoed in my head: *Stay calm. Tell the truth.*

I shot a look at Maggie—the judge—her face as silent as a

stone tomb, and then at Marie. She avoided my eyes entirely, her gaze fixed on some invisible point in the distance.

"I love my son... so much," I began, my voice shaking slightly.

"Everything I do is for him. I've never—not once—thought of taking him away from his mother. I just want to be there for him, to be a great dad. And I believe he deserves to be raised by both his parents."

Cherry Lynn stood slowly, her heels clicking on the floor as she approached. She leaned on the podium, her tone sharp but controlled, a predatory gleam sparking to life.

"Mr. Lawrence, isn't it true that you've expressed a desire to return to France?"

I hesitated, knowing where this was going.

"I... yes, I've talked about it. But not to take my son away."

"Talked about it?" Her words dripped with mockery.

"Mr. Lawrence, have you or have you not told people—multiple people, in fact—that you miss your family in France and wish to move back?"

"Yes," I admitted, heat rising in my cheeks.

"But that has nothing to do with my son—"

"Isn't it true," she cut me off, her voice rising slightly,

"that your dual citizenship and ties to France create a significant risk of flight?"

"No, that's not true! I would never—"

"Answer the question with a yes or no, Mr. Lawrence," she snapped.

I swallowed hard, my throat tightening.

"No."

Cherry Lynn's eyes narrowed.

"And isn't it true that your career as a musician often takes you away from home for extended periods of time?"

"Yes, but—"

"And during those periods, who takes care of your son?"

"His mother," I said through gritted teeth, like it burned leaving my mouth.

"The same mother who decided to fly to Phuket for her birthday—with someone she barely knew—when our son was just thirteen months old. I had to cancel shows to take care of him. She was gone for a week. No calls. No texts. Not even a 'How's he doing?' for three days."

I glanced toward Marie's table, my voice rising.

"And when she finally showed signs of life? It wasn't a check-in. It was beach photos. Poolside mojitos. Sunset selfies. All smiles. Like she didn't have a baby on the other side of the world—or a husband trying to keep everything together—just out there having the time of her life."

I leaned back slightly, gripping the edge of the witness stand, trying to steady my breath.

"That's not a mother putting her child first. That's someone putting herself first. Every time."

"Objection, Your Honor—irrelevant, and clearly an attempt to paint the mother in a negative light," Cherry Lynn snapped.

"Sustained," Judge Jenkins said firmly.

"Mr. Lawrence, you are to answer the questions asked, not offer commentary."

I gave a slow nod, swallowing back everything else I wanted to say.

But the silence that followed said enough.

Eric rose immediately, his voice steady and assertive.

"Your Honor, with the court's permission, I'd like to introduce text message records and related exhibits that corroborate my client's statements. These messages clearly show communication—or the lack thereof—during that trip, as well as the strain it placed on Mr. Lawrence's ability to maintain professional obligations while caring for their son."

The judge didn't blink. Just another procedural step in a show trial that had already picked its villain.

"Very well," she said.

"Submit your exhibits."

The next two hours blurred into a mess of examination and cross-examination.

Same *accusations,* twisted different ways.

Same defenses, falling on *deaf ears.*

Eric had done his best. Calm, collected, bringing up facts, evidence, logic.

"No further questions, Your Honor," he'd said, stepping back like a man who knew none of it was going to matter.

I exhaled, slumping slightly as the pressure of her interrogation bore down on me. Every word I spoke felt like another step deeper into a doomed trap.

The judge shifted her attention to Marie's lawyer.

"Counsel?"

Cherry Lynn stood slowly, smirking as if she'd just scored the winning goal.

"No further questions, Your Honor," she said, her voice dripping with satisfaction.

Judge Jenkins checked her notes, her expression as blank as ever.

"Mr. Lawrence, you may step down and return to your seat."

I pushed myself up from the stand, my legs shaky, my chest tight.

Tears pricked at the corners of my eyes, but I held them back, refusing to break down here.

As I walked past Marie's table, I caught her gaze for the first time that day. She quickly looked away, as though the sight of me was too much to bear—or too *inconvenient.*

By then, none of it mattered.

It was all bullshit. This whole performance.

This circus. This translator. This court.

Nothing I said would've changed a damn thing.

It was all fucking *useless.*

I could've testified in French or Martian, for all I cared—
with that Romanian translator turning every word against me—

Like playing some rigged *Russian roulette.*

Every chamber loaded.

Every bullet ready.

On the grill.

Fucked to lose.

THE VERDICT

Inside the courtroom, the silence had never felt heavier. Even the distant hum of the air conditioning seemed to fade as everyone settled back into their seats. My heartbeat pounded in my ears, relentless and deafening, as Judge Jenkins adjusted the stack of papers in front of her, each movement unhurried, dragging the moment out with excruciating patience. Every second stretched, thickening with unspoken tension.

She scanned toward both tables, her tone formal but neutral.

"Counsels, are you ready to submit, or do you have anything further to add?"

Cherry Lynn stood first, her posture as crisp as her tailored blazer.

"Submitting, Your Honor."

Eric rose next, adjusting his tie and nodding once.

"Submitting as well, Your Honor."

I caught his expression—measured, but something flickered in his eyes—concern, maybe doubt. Beside me, the translator sat still, barely reacting, as if she weren't even part of the moment. Physically present, yet lost in her own world of half-mumbled gibberish, like she was translating for herself more than anyone else. Her presence had been an irritant all day, a constant reminder of how surreal and tilted this whole process had felt.

Judge Jenkins finally looked up, stoic and cold.

"After reviewing all testimony and evidence presented in this case, the court has reached a decision."

I was clinging to the last liane of hope I had left. My stomach knotted, every muscle in my body tense with dread.

"The primary consideration in custody cases is the welfare and stability of the child," she continued, her tone professional but detached.

"It is clear to this court that both parents deeply care for their son. However, the evidence suggests that the current arrangement does not provide the consistency and stability that the child needs at this time."

I held my breath, waiting for the inevitable.

"The court awards sole physical custody to Ms. Pennington, with Mr. Lawrence granted supervised visitation until such time as the court determines it is appropriate to reassess."

The ruling slammed into me like a sledgehammer.

Supervised visitation. Like I was some kind of danger to my own son.

The label stung, branding me with a shame I didn't deserve.

Beside me, Eric leaned in, whispering,

"Stay calm, Jesse. We can appeal this."

I barely heard him. My gaze locked on Marie, who was wiping at imaginary tears with a tissue, her face a picture of quiet relief. It was the same tissue she'd been using all day, a prop she wielded like an actress in a long-running drama. Her expression shifted as she glanced at me—calm, practiced, almost triumphant—before she looked away, her eyes fixed on Cherry Lynn.

Judge Jenkins pressed on.

"Furthermore, the court recognizes concerns regarding Mr. Lawrence's demanding career and potential ties abroad. While there is no conclusive evidence to suggest a flight risk, these factors cannot be ignored. The supervised visitation is intended to allow Mr. Lawrence to demonstrate consistency and reliability in his parenting role."

Consistency and reliability. Those words twisted in my gut like a dull blade. I'd done everything I could to be there for my son, but it wasn't enough—not for *them*.

The memory of the Fourth of July party flashed in my mind —Maggie, the judge, laughing with Marie's family, Cherry Lynn pouring her another drink.

They hadn't seemed like acquaintances that day.

They'd been close, like old friends.

How was this fair? How was this justice?

Maggie—or rather, Judge Jenkins now—cleared her throat slightly before continuing.

"As for financial matters, including spousal support and asset division, these issues will be addressed at a later date once discovery and necessary filings are complete. Today's ruling pertains solely to custody, and the matters presented in this hearing."

Judge Jenkins shut her folder, the decision sealed.

"This concludes the matter of Pennington versus Lawrence. Court is adjourned."

A sharp crack of the gavel echoed through the room, final and unforgiving. Quiet tension exploded into motion—lawyers, assistants, and clerks packing up, chairs scraping against the floor, murmurs rising. I stayed frozen in my seat, staring at the judge's bench as the weight of the verdict settled over me like a lead blanket.

Eric placed a hand on my shoulder.

"We'll fight this, Jesse. It's not over."

It felt over. It felt like they'd taken the one thing that mattered most and locked it behind a wall I couldn't climb.

Marie rose from her seat, her minions by her side. They gathered their things with a practiced ease, their movements brisk and precise. Cherry Lynn bent slightly toward Marie, murmuring something, her lips curving into a subtle smirk as they made their way toward the exit. Marie didn't look back. *Not once.*

The translator pushed back her chair, moving as if she had all the time in the world. The absurdity of her presence struck me again, her whispers of *charabia* echoing faintly in my mind. I wanted to scream, to demand answers, but the courtroom's indifference swallowed me whole.

I gripped the edge of the table, my knuckles white, my breath shallow. The shuffle of papers, the scrape of chairs, the muted hum of voices—it all blurred together, a dull roar that faded into the background.

I sat there, motionless, the world moving around me as though I wasn't even there.

I wasn't a husband anymore. Or a family member. Or a friend.

And worst of all—I wasn't a *father* anymore.

My identity had been gutted—filed away in folders, argued over like property, reduced to fragments of forms and a judge's tone.

My name was just ink on a page now. Not a man. Just a case number, stripped of meaning.

A ghost in my own life. A stranger in my own story.

A number, free to walk—but under supervision.

Welcome to the fucking Village.

59

IS IT LEGAL?

Lightning had struck, and I was the only tree left burning. Waves of sunrays shimmered off the asphalt parking lot, dancing across the pavement, reflecting the strong late afternoon light. I leaned against my truck, arms crossed, staring at the Family Law Center's looming facade. It felt even colder now than it had that morning, even in the Texas heat.

Eric adjusted his tie, loosening it slightly as he joined me. He had that lawyer face on—calm, measured, unshakable. It only made my frustration boil harder.

"*I know, Jesse,*" he started, his tone almost apologetic.

"*It's not fair. And we will try to fight back.*"

I shook my head, my fists clenching at my sides.

"*But look at it, Eric! It was a masquerade, the whole damn thing! How can this even be legal? That judge—connections everywhere, a damn Fourth of July barbecue! Does that sound fair to you? You want to call that justice? I call it bullshit.*"

Eric sighed, loosening his tie a little more, the tension in his posture evident.

"I understand your frustration, Jesse. Believe me, I do. But unless there's solid evidence of direct conflict or bias—something we can prove—it's not illegal. Unfair, absolutely. But legal? Unfortunately, yes."

I turned away, my jaw tightening as I stared at the shimmering pavement.

"So they just get away with it? Cherry Lynn laughing it up like it's her personal circus, Marie pulling off that performance like she's up for an Oscar, and that judge—hell, she didn't even hide it."

He placed a hand on my shoulder, firm but not dismissive.

"Look, connections happen. It's not right, but it's part of the system. That's why we appeal. That's why we don't give up."

I exhaled sharply, the fight draining out of me for the moment.

"It just feels like they've already erased me, like I'm not even part of his life anymore."

Eric's face softened.

"You are part of his life, Jesse. Don't let today make you believe otherwise. This is a setback, not the end of the road. We'll regroup, strategize, and figure out the next steps. But you have to hold on, for him."

I nodded, swallowing hard past the tightness in my throat.

"Yeah."

"For him."

Eric gave my arm a reassuring squeeze before stepping back.

"Take a breath, Jesse. You've been through hell today. Go home, get some rest. We'll start fresh tomorrow. Hang in there."

I watched him walk away, expressionless, his suit jacket slung over one shoulder, his words lingering like the faint promise of a storm that might one day pass.

For now, I climbed into my truck, the heat inside stifling. The

Family Law Center loomed in my rearview mirror as I pulled out of the lot, the knot sinking from my chest to my stomach, cinching tighter with every mile—a visceral pain, deep and unrelenting, like it was pulling me apart from the inside.

It was like watching my own biopic on the big screen—*Groundhog Day style*—except every loop ended in the same damn nightmare.

A month ago, I had stood in that backyard, surrounded by warmth, by family, by the people who made me believe I belonged. They had hugged me, toasted with me, laughed with me. They had called me one of their own.

And *now?* Fucking cold as ice—with their money, their power, their firm, their connections—they had *erased me.*

They had turned me into a fucking criminal.

A criminal without a crime.

It was a masquerade. A perfect *illusion.*

Straight out of a textbook case of character assassination—framed in silk, tried in court, and dressed up as justice.

And I had fallen for it.

And now, I was paying the price for believing it was *fucking real.*

60

GOOD OL' JACK

I was driving back home, the city slipping past me in streaks of motion—streetlights, buildings, all bleeding together like a half-finished painting. My mind was racing, but my body felt heavy—like every mile I put between myself and that courthouse weighed a hundred pounds. The verdict played on a loop in my head, each word hitting harder than the last.

The streets were quiet, but my thoughts weren't. My knuckles whitened against the steering wheel, the urge to scream clawing at my throat. But instead of screaming, I just drove. *Aimless.*

That's when I saw it—the glow of a neon sign cutting through the dark.

LIQUOR DEPOT

Its flickering light painted the gravel parking lot in a pale, uneasy blue.

I didn't plan to stop. Didn't even realize I'd pulled in until the truck came to a halt, the engine rattling to a stop. I stared at the storefront for a moment, my fingers drumming against the wheel. Then, like some invisible force was pulling me, I stepped out and headed inside.

A bell over the door jangled, sharp and shrill, cutting through the suffocating stillness of the store. It smelled like stale beer and dust, and the fluorescent lights overhead buzzed faintly, blending into the low drone rattling in my skull.

I walked the aisles slowly, my eyes scanning rows of bottles. Tequila. Rum. Vodka. None of it felt right. Then my gaze landed on it—a squat, square bottle with bold black and white lettering.

Jack Daniel's.

It wasn't special. It wasn't complicated. It was just there. And right now, that would do. I never even liked whiskey that much —but tonight, beer wasn't going to cut it.

So *Jack Daniel's?*

Yep. That sounded like *rock 'n' roll.* Like *rebellion.* Like sharing a drink with a buddy after getting your ass kicked by life.

I grabbed it off the shelf, the cool glass pressing into my palm, made my way to the counter, and set the bottle down.

The clerk barely glanced at me, his attention fixed on a small TV playing an old Western. He hesitated for a second, then, without looking away from the screen, muttered,

"Anything else?"

I didn't say a word. Just handed him some cash.

He rang it up without another glance, the register's ding piercing the silence. I waited for the change out of habit more than anything, then walked back to the truck.

I climbed into the truck, dropped the brown paper bag onto the passenger seat, and just sat there for a moment. The paper crinkled under its own weight, slumped against the worn leather. It didn't need a label for me to know what was inside.

But still, I reached over, peeled it open, and let the black-and-white lettering stare back at me. Like it was daring me to cross a line.

The courthouse. The verdict. The emotional wreckage of it all still loomed in the back of my mind, clinging like smoke that wouldn't clear.

I twisted off the cap and took a swig, the burn of the whiskey sharp and unforgiving. It wasn't the kind of fire that hurt—it was the kind that numbed, dulling the edges of everything I couldn't bear to think about.

The world outside the truck window felt distant, like it wasn't mine anymore. I tipped the bottle back again, the whiskey pooling in my stomach like lead.

"Guess it's just you and me now," I muttered, the words slipping out before I could stop them.

Of course, the bottle didn't answer. Didn't need to.

I started the truck, the engine groaning as I pulled out of the lot. The liquor store disappeared in the rearview mirror, swallowed by the night.

A few turns. A couple of stop signs. And then I was home.

As I pulled into the driveway, the house looked like a prison cell—an empty shell, a shadow of what it used to be. It didn't feel like home anymore—just walls and a roof holding memories that hurt too damn much.

I walked through the door, the silence hitting me like a freight train. Every sound I made felt too loud, too intrusive. My boots echoed on the hardwood as I wandered aimlessly, unsure of what I was even looking for.

Eventually, I found myself standing in the doorway of my son's bedroom. The emptiness of it hit harder than the courtroom ever could. His bed was neatly made, his shelves lined with toys he hadn't played with in weeks. It felt like a museum exhibit—a shrine to a life that was slipping through my fingers.

I sank to my knees, the ache in my chest too much to bear. The tears came fast and heavy, hot against my face.

"I'm sorry," I whispered, my voice cracking.

"I'm so damn sorry, Little Jesse."

I don't know how long I stayed there. When I finally pulled myself up, the room felt colder, emptier. Like it was waiting to be forgotten.

Back in the living room, I grabbed the whiskey and didn't bother with a glass. The burn in my throat was sharp, like someone pressing a knife against my skin—but it was nothing compared to the pain buried deep in my heart. I drank until the world started to blur, the edges of reality softening just enough to make it bearable.

I slumped into the couch, the bottle resting on my lap.

"Well," I mumbled, the words slurring,

"this house ain't totally empty."

I raised it in a mock toast, the liquid sloshing inside.

"There's Jack, keeping me company. And he's great at it. A born entertainer."

I laughed—a bitter, hollow sound that echoed in the dark.

"Yep, Good Ol' Jack. A hell of a storyteller."

I tipped the bottle back again, savoring the warmth as it spread through me.

The surrounding silence was deafening, but I didn't care anymore. At least Jack wasn't asking me questions, wasn't judging me, wasn't *leaving me.*

And as the room spun, the comfort ran low and the numbness caught up. I let myself fall deeper into the void, knowing that tonight, *Good Ol' Jack* was the only friend I had left.

Well, more like the only one I had *left.*

61

WILD CARDS AND SMOKING GUNS

S itting in the old leather office chair in front of my mixing desk, I slumped forward, staring at the mess around me.

The room felt like a graveyard—not just for music, but for everything I'd lost.

My home studio had been my refuge once, the space where I could create, dream, and forget the world outside. Now, it was a tomb, filled with ghosts of what could've been. My guitar leaned against my leg, but it wasn't pulling me back this time. No spark. No salvation. Just dead weight.

I grabbed the crumpled piece of paper off the console, the one I'd scribbled on during one of my sleepless nights. My eyes skimmed the words I barely remembered writing:

"I had to run, I had to hide in order to survive..."

Survive. The word stuck in my throat like a jagged stone. That's all I'd been doing for days—*surviving.* But what was the point?

The visits with my son had started becoming less and less frequent. There was always an excuse.

Someone was sick.

Plans had to be postponed.

"Something came up."

At first, I fought it, desperate to hold onto every moment I could get. But the excuses piled up, and I felt myself slipping, falling deeper into a darkness I couldn't claw my way out of.

I tried to keep it together, for him, but the divorce had gutted me. It had left me with nothing—no resources, no strength, no courage. I was drowning, and they knew it. They saw how broken I'd become, and they used it against me. Every step of the way, they worked to erase me from the surface of the earth, like I'd never *existed.*

My heart tightened as I thought of my little boy, *Jesse Jr.*

His laugh, the way he'd wrap his tiny hands around my finger, holding on like he never wanted to let go.

Now he was gone—stolen by a system that didn't care, and a woman who played the game better than anyone.

A master manipulator.

A strategist. A praying mantis. Queen of the bluff. Draped in grief, dealing lies like Texas Hold'em—I was under a spell, like a voodoo puppet. I went all in, with all my heart—blind, naive, in love. And when she flipped her cards, it was all smoke—but she walked off with the pot and left me sitting in the ashes.

My gaze fell back to the sheet in my hand. The chorus stared back at me:

> "Your love was a big ol' lie...
> just playing me all this time.
> It was all wild cards and smoking guns."

I clenched my fist around the paper, the anger rising like a wave. My life had turned into some twisted game, and I'd lost everything that mattered.

Eventually, I stopped fighting. The noise, the chaos, the constant reminders of everything I'd lost—I couldn't take it anymore. So I left. I moved far away from it all, thinking that maybe the distance would bring peace.

But it didn't. It only made the silence *louder*.

I stopped caring about anything—my career, my music, even my son. It was eating me alive from the inside, gnawing away at what little was left of me.

I ripped that stupid piece of paper apart and threw the scraps across the room. The guitar slipped from my leg and hit the floor with a heavy thump. I didn't pick it up. It didn't matter anymore.

I paced the floor, the walls pressing in on me. This wasn't a studio anymore. It was a prison, a cage. I ran a hand through my hair, my eyes darting to the door.

The thought had been circling my mind for weeks, but now it felt real.

Final.

Marie had taken everything. My career. My band. My home. Legally, it was hers now. It didn't take long before I had nowhere left to stand. And *Sebastian?* The one I thought I could rely on? The one I trusted? *My brother?* He played both sides like a wild card, never showing his hand until the game was already won— and making damn sure he never came up short. He didn't lift a fucking finger. Just stood back and let it happen—watched me lose everything like it was just another bad hand.

But the worst of it?

She took my *son.*

She'd cut all ties, shut down every line of communication. The next thing I knew, she was remarried. Hell, I'd heard she was planning the wedding before the ink on our divorce papers was even dry. She'd already found her next target—a new prey, fresh and unsuspecting. *And I was the cheater?*

And my boy? My Little Jesse?

He was gone. Just... *gone.*

I needed to leave. Not just the studio, not just the house. I needed to disappear.

No more calls. No more emails. No more music. No more *Jesse*, no more *"Frenchy"*, no more *"Mr. Lawrence".*

I couldn't bear the pity in people's eyes, the whispers of *"What happened to Jesse?"*

And I couldn't bear to see my son growing up in photos, a stranger to me.

So, I grabbed my keys and shoved them into my pocket, glancing one last time at the guitar lying face down on the floor. I wasn't taking it with me.

I didn't know where I was going, but it didn't matter. All I knew was that I couldn't stay.

"This game?" I said to myself as I closed the door behind me.

"It wasn't about heart, and I never had the spades. It was just wild cards and smoking guns."

62

A BROKEN FENCE AND A PORCH

I'd been driving west for weeks, burning through what little money I had left on motels and gas station dinners, searching for somewhere to disappear. Somewhere that didn't remind me of courtrooms, lawyers, or what I'd lost.

Maybe I'd head to New Mexico or Arizona—somewhere with wide skies and endless expanses, where I could vanish and forget what had been chasing me.

France?

Hell, I'd left that behind years ago, and it felt like a lifetime ago now.

No, something was telling me to stay. And this time, I *would*.

I kept going, letting the miles swallow me whole.

And while heading toward the Rio Grande, something caught my eye, somewhere past Marfa, in the Chihuahuan Desert.

I eased off the gas, pulling the truck to a stop beside a weather-beaten post. A faded wooden sign was nailed to it, barely holding on.

FOR SALE: FIXER-UPPER RANCH. AFFORDABLE.

Below it, a phone number, the paint nearly flaking off.

Fixer-upper, I thought, smirking bitterly.

That's about where I'm at.

The ranch stretched out before me, a patchwork of over-grown fields and rusty barbed wire fences that sagged like they'd given up years ago. The barn, if you could call it that, leaned heavily to one side, its roof patched with mismatched tin sheets. The house wasn't much better—small, weathered, and clearly untouched in years. But the land was vast, stretching out to meet the horizon, where the sun dipped low, painting the sky in bruised oranges and purples.

I stepped out of the truck, dirt kicking up around my boots, and leaned against the door. The silence wrapped around me, thick and heavy, broken only by the faint rustle of dry grass in the breeze.

No traffic. No shouting. No noise pollution. Just an inde-scribable feeling of bliss and *peacefulness.*

I ran a hand over my face, the exhaustion of the past few months catching up with me. My whole life had been gutted, every piece ripped out and left in ruins. This ranch looked like it'd been through the same.

Before I could second-guess myself, a voice called out.

"Help you with something?"

I turned to see an older man walking toward me from the house, a cowboy hat perched on his head and a skeptical look in his eye. His jeans were worn, his boots scuffed, and his wrinkles ran deep, like the cracked earth of the desert—etched by time and an arid journey he still carried every day, never flinching, never quitting.

"I saw the sign," I said, gesturing toward the post.

"The ranch for sale?"

He nodded, eyeing me up and down.

"That's right. You looking to buy, or just sightseeing?"

I almost laughed. *Sightseeing?* No. *Running,* maybe. *Hiding, probably.*

"Depends," I said.

"How much are you asking?"

He shrugged.

"Depends on how handy you are. She's a good piece of land, but she needs work. Roof's leakin'. Fences are shot. Couple of critters still hangin' around, but I haven't kept up with the place in years."

I made a vague gesture, not bothering to tell him I didn't have the first clue about ranching. I wasn't looking for perfection. I wasn't even looking for good. I was looking for anywhere but where I'd come from. Just a retreat for a renegade. No rules. No past. No map. Off the grid and out of reach.

"How bad's the roof?" I asked, mostly to stall for time.

"Bad," he said flatly.

"But I'll cut you a deal."

He crossed his arms, waiting for me to make the first move. My gut told me to turn around and drive, keep moving until I hit a dead end. But something about that place—its quiet, its brokenness—felt like it matched me.

And man, that porch. Big, solid, stretching wide like it had stories to tell. When I was a kid, I used to dream about a house with a porch like that—somewhere I could sit with a beer, a guitar, and a damn good old-school rocking chair. Let the world do whatever the hell it wanted while I just sat there, watching the dust settle. Stupid, maybe. But right then, it didn't seem so stupid anymore.

"How much of a deal?" I asked, finally.

"Not enough to get rich off you, son." He smirked.

"Let's just say you'd have enough left over for a hammer and some nails."

He then pulled a crumpled piece of paper from his back jean pocket, snatched the pen tucked behind his ear, scribbled a number, and handed it to me.

No formality. No handshake. Just a number on a torn scrap that could change *everything.*

I stared at the figure, my mind racing, chewing the inside of my cheek, thinking about the little money I had left. Hell, selling my guitar collection and the last of my savings had given me just enough to scrape by after paying the lawyers. What he was asking was less than I'd expected, but it was still more than I should spend.

I glanced back at the truck. The last rays of sunlight caught the windshield, glaring back at me like a sign. My fingers tightened on the doorframe, itching for an answer—to make sense of this mess the only way I knew how.

The man must've seen the hesitation in my eyes.

"Look," he said, his tone softer now.

"I ain't gonna sell you a dream," he continued.

"This place is rough. It ain't pretty, and it sure as hell ain't easy. But if you're looking for quiet... well, you won't find much quieter."

I let out a slow breath, staring out at the open land.

Empty, rough, forgotten—but still standing.

"No neighbors?" I asked, half-joking.

The man huffed a small laugh.

"Only if you count coyotes and tumbleweeds."

I rubbed my chin with my left hand. I shouldn't be considering this. But I couldn't help myself.

It felt right—so right. And man, that porch.

"Why are you selling it, anyway?" I asked.

"Ain't got it in me no more," he said, shrugging with a blank and distant look.

"I paid my dues, and now the place deserves someone who can put in the work and keep it alive."

"*Yeah. I hear you. Alright. So, how much down?*" I then asked.

The man tilted his hat back, looking at me.

"*Enough to prove you ain't gonna vanish by next week. Rest, we can work out later.*"

I swallowed hard. This was reckless.

Hell, maybe even a *mistake.*

But at least it was mine.

This time.

"*Deal then. I'll take it,*" I said before I could talk myself out of it.

63

THAT LITTLE LITTLE SONG

November had come and gone, slipping through my fingers like the last leaves of fall. *Thanksgiving* hadn't been that long ago—just a few weeks, maybe. The day I found *Swampy*.

I hadn't been thinking about holidays then. Just about surviving—same as always, just dragging one foot in front of the other.

But now, the holiday season was there, in the back of my mind, stirring up things best left alone. This time of year when families got together, when people went home, celebrating love and life. This time of year when children's laughter filled the air, their joy spilling out as they tore through wrapping paper, eyes wide with that spark of pure amazement.

And today, for whatever reason, it wouldn't let go.

Low in the sky, the sun was streaking the horizon with bands of orange and gold. I was sitting on the porch, and Swampy was resting against the railing beside me, *untouched.*

Everything was silent, the air thick with heat and dust, hanging like a smoke cloud that refused to move.

Like an anvil, it was all pressing down on me—my son, my family, my career.

Marie had taken it all. I had tried to fight, but in the end, they won. They didn't just take him—they cancelled me, like I'd never existed.

Elbows digging into my knees, staring out at the horizon, I leaned forward. My rocking chair creaked behind me—a soft, lonely sound, echoing everything I was trying to leave behind.

The quiet that once felt like peace didn't anymore. Now, it was oppressive—a slap-in-the-face reminder of how fucking *miserable* and lonely I was.

I hadn't seen my boy in years.

How old was he now?

A teenager? A young adult?

Twenty-something?

What did he look like? How had he grown?

Maybe he was married. Maybe he even had *kids.*

And what does he do?

Was he still the same little boy I'd been forced to let go of, or had time already turned him into someone I wouldn't even recognize?

I missed him so much—the way he used to say *"Papa,"* the love and trust in his eyes when we played together, the bond we had had from the very first day he was born.

I didn't even know if he still remembered me. Maybe I was just a dream, something faded and forgotten, buried deep in his subconscious.

I felt the tears coming, big ones running down my face. That pain... I had felt it before. I had been there. A fucking *broken heart.*

Would I ever see you again, *mon amour?*

But no matter what happened or will happen, Jr.,

je t'aime et t'aimerai du plus profond de mon cœur et de toute mon âme. À jamais. For ever.

The moment was swallowing me, thick and overwhelming, like I was drowning in it. And then, without thinking, I reached for Swampy, the strings cool and familiar under my fingertips. I wasn't planning to play—just to feel something. Anything. But then my hands moved, like they had a mind of their own.

Then something *shifted*.

Cowboy chords. *D, G, A, Bm*. Nothing fancy, just the kind of changes you could play with your eyes closed. The kind that felt like home.

"Wait... what is that? Sounds familiar."

The chords stuck, like a puzzle begging to be solved. I kept playing, trying to pin it down. My hands knew before I did, and as the pieces clicked into place, the melody hit me like a freight train.

> "And that little little song that I sing for you..."

The words tumbled out, raw and instinctive. It wasn't just a melody anymore—it was a *memory*.

I was back in Jr.'s room, sitting on the edge of his crib. He couldn't have been more than one, his tiny hand reaching out for the strings. I laughed, pulling the guitar back just before he could grab them, and kept singing:

> "It's the only way I know how to say those things
>   to you.
> It's the melody that speaks what words can't do."

He giggled, his laugh as pure as anything I had ever heard.

His little fingers brushed the strings, trying to join in, and I sang the final line:

> "In every note that I play,
> I'm just saying... I love you."

For an instant, the world was still. Just me, my little boy, and a song I had poured my heart into.

Back on the porch, the image was fading, but the ache lingered. My hands were resting on Swampy, her wood smooth and warm, grounding me in the here and now.

"That was you, wasn't it?" I murmured, letting my touch glide over her body.

"You always know how to remind me."

The air felt heavier, like the guitar was listening, holding onto something I wasn't ready to name.

I shook my head and laughed softly.

"Damn," I said, my throat tight.

"I haven't played that in years."

I strummed the chords again, letting the notes loop—not to solve it this time, but just to feel it.

The song wasn't just for *him*.

It was for anyone I had ever loved but couldn't find the words for.

For everyone who never found them to express their *love*.

And maybe, in some way, it was for me too.

> "And that little little song that I sing for you
> Is the only way I know to say those things to you.
> It's the melody that speaks what words can't do,
> In every note that I play,
> I'm just saying, I love you."

64

BAITING THE STUBBORN COWBOY

Texas time, some days, moved so damn slow out here. Just me, the porch, and a beer in my hand. I rocked back, feeling the wood groan beneath me.

The afternoon sun hung low, stretching long shadows across the porch. The heat had settled in, thick and steady, but the air still held a trace of coolness from the morning. I'd spent most of the day feeding the horses, mending tack in the barn, patching a few loose boards in the stable, and oiling the saddles—the scent of hay and dust still clinging to me. Now, finally, a moment to breathe. Perfect time to take a break.

Peaceful. Predictable. Just how I like it.

"*Jesse!*"

Emma's voice carried on the breeze before I even saw her, the kind that always had a hint of laughter in it. I grumbled under my breath.

Uh-oh. Here we go.

Sounds like my break is over. Whatever she's up to, I already know I'm not gonna like it.

She rounded the corner of the house, a wide-brimmed hat shading her face, a mischievous grin plastered on her lips.

"What are you doing out here? Hiding?"

"Not hiding," I said, tipping the bottle in her direction.

"Just taking a break. What can I do for you?"

She didn't answer right away, just leaned against the railing with her hands on her hips, surveying me like I was a stubborn colt.

"I've got a plan," she said finally, drawing the words out like she was offering me gold.

"A plan, huh? Should I be worried?" I said, side-eyeing her.

"Nope." She popped the *"p"* and flashed a bright smile.

"I'm taking you to the fair tomorrow."

I barked a laugh, shaking my head.

"The fair? You're kidding."

"Do I look like I'm kidding?" She crossed her arms, her tone challenging.

"It's once a year. You can handle that much, can't you?" She gave me a look.

"Come on, it'll be fun. You've been holed up in that studio for weeks, and since you got back, it's not like you really cleared your mind. I mean—you still haven't even played me anything from the album. Look, we could use a break. A real one. At least I know I could. And you? I'm sure it'll help you get out of your head for a bit." She shrugged, throwing in the final punch.

"And I'd really like to go anyway."

"Fun," I repeated flatly.

"Emma, in case you haven't noticed, fun and I aren't exactly on speaking terms these days."

"That's why you need this! You can't just sit here on this porch forever, staring at your guitar like it's gonna start talking back."

I pointed the bottle at her.

"Woo woo, easy. You disrespect her again, she might just play out of tune. Swampy's got a temper."

Emma rolled her eyes, but didn't miss a beat.

"Fine. You and Swampy can come. I'm sure the two of you could use a change of scenery."

Wait, *what?* She wants me to go *where?* A *fair?*

I took a long swig of my beer, mulling over the idea. The fair. Crowds, noise, overpriced food. Definitely not my scene.

The thought bounced around my head again, louder this time.

"Don't you have someone else to drag along? You know, someone who actually likes... fairs?"

"Nope." She grinned, leaning closer.

"You're my guy."

I narrowed my eyes at her, but she didn't flinch.

"What's in it for me?"

"Fresh air, fried food, and watching me outshoot you at the game stalls," she said smugly.

"Oh, and there's line dancing. I'm dragging you into that too."

"What? Now I know you're trying to kill me," I groaned.

Emma laughed, the sound warm and full of life.

"Stop being so dramatic, Jesse. Come on, it's just one day."

I sighed, setting my Bud down on the table beside me. She'd been running the ranch for over a month while I was holed up in the studio, lost in the album. Keeping things running, making sure the horses were fed, the fences didn't collapse—hell, making sure I didn't collapse.

She'd been here, day in and day out, helping me get my shit together—and not once had she complained.

Not about the work, not about the mess, not even about me.

That *part?* That was the *weirdest thing.*

I glanced at her, standing there, arms crossed, waiting. She had a way of looking at me that made it hard to say no, even when I wanted to.

I knew damn well she wasn't asking for much, and after everything, I owed her this one.

I exhaled through my nose, shaking my head.

"All right, fine. But don't expect me to dance."

Emma grinned like she'd already won.

"We'll see about that." Then she tilted her hat back, eyes glinting. *"First thing in the morning. Don't even think about sneaking off before I come knocking."*

She turned, stepping off the porch.

"I gotta wrap up a few things, but I'll be here at sunrise. So don't even try pulling a disappearing act. And yes—I already made sure the horses'll be fine."

I watched her walk away, her laughter trailing behind her like a damn victory song.

The fair, *huh?*

Non, *merci.*

But guess I better buckle up for a wild ride.

Please.

Lord have mercy—on me.

65

A FAIR GAME

Heading into the parking lot, it already looked like a dust bowl when we got there. Trucks and trailers were packed in tight under the mid-morning sun. I stepped out of the cab and tugged my hat lower to block the glare, squinting at the commotion beyond the gates.

It looked like half the county had turned out for this thing. *Great.*

Emma, on the other hand, was already bouncing with excitement, adjusting her hat and straightening her plaid shirt like she was about to take the stage.

"Isn't it perfect?" she said, spinning around to face me, her smile brighter than the sun overhead.

I gritted my teeth and let out a low grunt, jamming my hands into my pockets. The air was thick with the smell of fried food, kettle corn, kicked-up grit, and livestock—a cocktail of scents that reminded me why I avoided places like this.

Hell, I wasn't even supposed to be *here.*

I'd been dead asleep when the blanket got yanked clean off me.

"What the—?" I groaned, reaching blindly to pull it back, but it was gone.

"Rise and shine, cowboy! Fair day."

Emma's voice rang out way too damn cheerful for the hour.

I cracked one eye open, just enough to catch her standing there at the foot of my bed, arms crossed, looking way too pleased with herself.

I made a noise somewhere between a growl and a death rattle, turning over and dragging the pillow over my face.

Emma tsked.

"Uh-uh, don't even try it. You agreed yesterday. I should've made you sign something."

"Well, ain't the fair gonna be there all week?" I tried, grasping at the lamest excuse I could find.

The pillow disappeared a second later.

"Sure, but I know you—you'll come up with a reason to skip it every single day if I don't get you there now."

I sighed, rubbing my face.

"Emma, the sun just came up."

"Exactly. Morning. And the fair's already started," she shot back. *"Today's the only day we don't have much going on. Tomorrow we've got clients coming, and after that—who knows? You'll find some excuse, and then—poof—it's over."*

She had a point. A damn annoying one. I squinted up at her.

"I hate how much sense that makes."

She grinned, tossing my boots onto the bed.

"That's why I'm in charge."

I let my head fall back onto the mattress.

"You're relentless, you know that?"

"Yep." She clapped her hands together.

"Now get up. I'm not above dragging you."

I grumbled a curse that didn't even make sense, but I swung my legs over the side of the bed anyway.

No point in fighting it. She won *again.*

And here we were, standing in the middle of a parking lot hotter than hell, the fair stretching out ahead like some kind of neon-colored trap.

"Oh, come on." Emma grabbed my arm and started dragging me toward the entrance.

"Don't be such a grump."

I dragged my boots like a man headed for the gallows.

She glanced back at me with a smirk.

"Look at you, cowboy. Maybe you shouldn't have left your girlfriend at home."

"Yeah, whatever," I muttered, shoving my hands deep into my pockets as we moved forward.

The fairgrounds were a living postcard of cowboy clichés. There were banners strung between wooden posts, swaying in the breeze. Booths lined the dusty paths, offering everything from leather belts to hand-carved horseshoes. The distant twang of a country band playing near the rodeo arena mixed with the laughter of kids chasing each other through the crowd. It was chaos, but the good kind—the kind that brought back memories of simpler times. Well... when you're in a good *mood.*

Emma tugged me toward a booth selling cowboy hats and boots.

"See? This is what you've been missing. Doesn't it feel like home?"

"If home came with overpriced funnel cakes and screaming kids, sure," I snorted.

She elbowed me lightly, her grin never wavering.

"You're impossible."

As we walked, Emma waved at a family she seemed to know, exchanging quick pleasantries before dragging me further into the chaos. The deeper we went, the louder and busier it got—

kids running past with cotton candy, couples arm-in-arm near the mechanical bull, ranchers showing off their prize livestock.

Then she pointed toward the arena, her excitement obvious.

"Let's check out the riders!"

I hesitated, looking for an excuse.

"Don't we have all day for this?"

She gave me a look that could've melted iron.

"You're not backing out already, are you?"

"Fine," I sighed, letting her pull me along.

"But if I see one more booth selling cowboy-themed shot glasses—or God forbid, Texas snow globes—I'm out."

As we got closer, a gust of wind kicked up dust, carrying the faint smell of barbecue and hay. I caught Emma sneaking a glance at me, a smile tugging at her lips.

"What?" I asked, scowling.

"You're not fooling anyone," she said.

"I can tell you're starting to like it."

I shook my head, biting back a grin.

"Don't get ahead of yourself, Emma."

But the truth was, I could feel her energy working its way into me, like the sun warming cold soil.

This wasn't my scene, but watching her light up like that—it was hard not to get caught up in it, even just a *little.*

66

RODEO TANGO

E mma and I had barely stepped into the arena when her eyes lit up like a kid on Christmas morning. It was packed—rows of wooden bleachers full of people waving hats and cheering as a cowboy wrestled a steer to the ground in a cloud of dust. The announcer's voice thundered from the speakers, calling out the next rider, riding the wave like a rodeo star himself. And like a stampede rolling in, the crowd surged—restless, rowdy, ready.

Emma tugged on my arm.

"This is the best part of the fair. Look at that—pure skill, Jesse."

I glanced around, then back at her.

"You mean pure madness. Who in their right mind gets on a freakin' bucking bull for fun?"

"Come on, don't tell me you've never tried it," she said, rolling her eyes.

"Nope. And I plan to keep it that way."

Emma shook her head, laughing.

"Well, you're missing out."

She leaned on the rail, her face glowing with excitement as another reckless fool burst out of the chute. The bull bucked and spun like it was possessed, the poor guy holding on for dear life while the crowd roared.

I found myself watching Emma more than the show—the way her eyes followed every move and how she clapped along with everyone else when the buzzer sounded.

"You're really into this, huh?"

"Of course I am!" she said, turning to me with a wide smile.

"It's a real test of guts and skill. You can't fake this."

"Guess that rules me out," I said, earning a playful shove.

After the last rider finished, Emma grabbed my hand.

"Come on, let's check out the games. I want to see if you're as bad at shooting as you claim."

"I never said I was bad," I replied, letting her drag me toward the game stalls.

"I just said I haven't done it in a while."

"That's what they all say," she teased, her voice sing-song.

"But when the pressure's on..."

The shooting booth was decked out with tin cans, little paper targets, and a row of BB guns. Spotting us as we approached, the guy running it tipped his hat at Emma.

"Step right up, Ma'am. Think you can outshoot your boyfriend here?"

Emma's cheeks flushed, but she didn't correct him.

"We'll see," she said, grabbing one of the guns.

"Jesse, you're up first."

I sighed, taking a rifle and squinting at the targets. It felt awkward in my hands, and my aim was off at first, but I managed to hit the first tin can on the second shot. Then the next one fell. By the end, I'd cleared about half the targets.

Emma applauded, half-impressed, half-teasing.

"Not bad for an old-timer."

"Well, let's see what you've got," I said, stepping back.

She took her turn, her tongue peeking out in concentration. She missed the first shot, but after a few tries, she found her rhythm, knocking down more cans than I expected. By the time she was done, I had to admit she'd beaten me.

"Okay, fine," I said, holding up my hands.

"You win."

"Damn right, I do," she said with a triumphant grin.

"So, what's next?" I asked, half-expecting her to throw me into a dunk tank or something.

We wandered to a roping game, where contestants had to lasso a fake calf. Emma didn't hesitate, seizing the rope and stepping into the circle. Her first attempt missed completely, the loop landing in a heap at her feet.

"Careful now," I said, smirking.

"Don't embarrass yourself."

"Oh, shush," she fired back, trying again.

On the second attempt, she managed to loop it around the calf's horns, throwing her hands up in victory.

"See? Easy."

"Yeah, sure," I said, grabbing the lasso.

"Step aside, cowgirl. Let me show you how a real cowboy gets it done."

I took my time swinging the lasso a few times before letting it fly. It landed perfectly on the first try, earning me a surprised look from Emma.

"Beginner's luck, huh?" she said, humoring me like a toddler with a toy lasso.

"Skill," I corrected.

"Something you can't fake, remember?"

She laughed, shaking her head.

"All right, John Wayne. Let's find something else before you get too smug."

As we made our way through the crowd, I realized I was smiling more than I had in months. Emma had a way of pulling me out of my shell, making the noise and chaos feel less overwhelming.

And for the first time in a long while, I didn't mind the *distraction*.

67

MAMA SUE'S BBQ

Damn, that barbecue smell hit hard—sweet, smoky, and impossible to ignore. My stomach growled, loud enough for Emma to hear. She looked at me, smiling.

"Sounds like someone needs some food. Lucky for you, I know the best spot."

I followed her through the maze of stalls until we reached a little barbecue shack with a hand-painted sign reading:

MAMA SUE'S BBQ

The line was long, but Emma seemed unfazed.

"Trust me, it's worth the wait."

I crossed my arms, glancing at the menu. Pulled pork, brisket, ribs—every Southern staple you could think of. My eyes drifted to a smaller sign hanging under the main one, its letters drawn in a cheerful, curling script:

Southern Comfort. Like Mama's Hug.

"'Like Mama's Hug,' huh?" I said, raising an eyebrow.

"That's a bold claim."

Emma turned to me, grinning.

"You'll see. It's the real deal."

"You've been here before?" I asked.

"Pretty much every year," she replied, tilting her hat back.

"It's tradition. They've got the best brisket this side of the Rio Grande."

I rolled my eyes, but couldn't hide a small smirk.

"Let's hope Mama's lives up to it."

Emma let out a short laugh, the kind that said she knew something I didn't.

"Oh, it will."

When we finally reached the front, Emma ordered for both of us, flashing me a look that dared me to complain. A few minutes later, we had a tray piled high with brisket sandwiches, cornbread, and baked beans. She led the way to a picnic table under a big oak tree, plopping down with a satisfied sigh.

"See? Told you it was worth it," she said, unwrapping her sandwich like the verdict was already in.

I picked up mine and took a bite, and damn if she wasn't right. The meat practically melted in my mouth, smoky and perfectly seasoned.

I nodded, reluctantly impressed.

"All right, I'll give you this one."

She beamed, content, as we dug in. For a moment, we just ate. The sounds of the fairgrounds carried in the background. Kids were laughing, a band was playing somewhere in the distance, and the faint squeal of the Ferris wheel rose above it all.

"So," Emma said, breaking the silence.

"What was your favorite fair memory growing up?"

I paused mid-bite, the question catching me off guard.

"*Fair memory?*"

"*Yeah,*" she said, her eyes curious but kind.

"*Everyone's got one. Come on, don't tell me you never went to a fair as a kid.*"

I leaned back, wiping my hands on a napkin.

"*Not really. My mom wasn't big on fairs, and my dad... well, he wasn't around much. I guess the closest thing was the carnival they'd set up in town every summer. But I didn't go for the rides or the games. I went for the music.*"

Emma tilted her head.

"*The music?*"

"*Yeah, they'd have local bands play in the evenings. I remember this one time—I must've been twelve or thirteen—there was this old blues guitarist. Played a beat-up Strat like his life depended on it. I sat there the whole night, just watching him.*"

Her expression softened.

"*That's where it started, huh? Your love for music.*"

"*Guess so,*" I said, shrugging.

"*Didn't have much else to hold on to back then.*"

Emma studied me for a moment, her sandwich forgotten.

"*You know, you don't give yourself enough credit.*"

"*For what?*"

"*For surviving,*" she said simply.

"*You've been through hell, Jesse. Most people would've given up, but you didn't. You're still here.*"

That caught me by surprise.

How the hell does she know? At least that *much*.

Still, I tried to look away, focusing on some trees.

"*Doesn't feel like surviving most days.*"

She reached across the table, resting her hand on mine.

"*It's more than that. You're fighting. And that matters.*"

I swallowed hard, the lump in my throat making it difficult to respond.

"You've got a way of making things sound simpler than they are."

She smiled, her grip firm but gentle.

"Maybe they are. You just don't see it yet."

Something stirred—like a crack in the wall I'd built around myself. And I realized Emma had a way of seeing the world that I couldn't ignore, no matter how hard I tried.

"Thanks," I said finally, my voice quieter than I intended.

She squeezed my hand, then pulled back, her usual grin returning.

"Don't get all sentimental on me now, French boy. Finish your sandwich."

I laughed, shaking my head.

"Yes, Ma'am."

68

MOVIN' BOOTS

Ever had *BBQ* that good before. Emma was right—it lived up to the hype. Lunch had barely settled before the sound hit me—the rhythmic stomp of boots and the twang of guitars echoing across the fairgrounds. Emma perked up at the first few notes, her eyes lighting up like she'd been waiting for this moment.

Before I could say a word, she grabbed my wrist and pulled me toward the dance floor—a large open space bordered by string lights and hay bales. A sea of people was already there, moving in perfect unison, their boots scuffing against the dusty ground.

I stopped at the edge of the floor, arms crossed.

"You've got to be kidding me."

Emma turned to me, her eyes sparkling with excitement.

"What? This is the best part of the fair!"

"Wait—I thought the rodeo was the best part?" I said, deadpan.

"Well... second best. But this is my favorite best fun part. Come on." She grinned.

"*I already told you, I don't dance,*" I said, my voice firm. "*Remember?*"

She smirked, grabbing my hand.

"*And I told you we'll see about that.*"

Before I could protest, she was dragging me onto the floor, weaving us into the lineup of dancers. The rhythm was lively and upbeat, the kind you couldn't ignore even if you wanted to. I stood stiff as a board, watching everyone around me step, spin, and clap like they came out of the womb wearing *cowboy boots.*

Emma nudged me, leaning close.

"*Relax, Jesse. It's just a little line dancing. You don't have to be Fred Astaire.*"

"*I'm pretty sure Fred Astaire would be laughing his ass off right now,*" I muttered, but my feet started moving anyway, mimicking the steps as best I could.

As the last notes ended, dancers clapped and cheered, shifting back into place for the next round.

Emma turned to me, beaming.

"*See? That wasn't so bad.*"

"*All right, there. I danced. Can we go?*" I exhaled, already stepping back.

But before I could make my escape, the next song kicked in, and Emma let out a little squeal of delight.

"*Oh my God, it's 'Movin' Boots!' That's my jam!*"

"*Your jam?*" I asked, half-laughing.

"*Didn't take you for a line dance anthem kind of gal.*"

She twirled in place, her hat tipping slightly as she spun, the hem of her sundress catching the movement.

"*Shows what you know.*"

I let out a quiet huff of laughter, shaking my head.

"*Yeah? Well, I wrote this one.*"

She paused mid-step, blinking at me.

"*Wait—seriously?*"

"Yep."

She tilted her head, considering it for half a second, then shrugged.

"Huh. Never paid attention to who did it, but it's always been my go-to line dance song."

I scoffed, taking in the sea of cowboy hats moving in sync.

"Figures."

I couldn't help but smile at her. She looked so damn happy, her energy contagious as she moved with the music, the light fabric of her dress swaying with every step. I stumbled through a few moves, trying to keep up, but my boots felt heavier than usual, like they didn't belong to me.

"Come on, Jesse," she said, lacing her fingers with mine, pulling me into the rhythm.

"Just follow me."

Her grip was firm but reassuring, and somehow, it worked. My feet found the beat, and I stopped overthinking every move. For a few minutes, I forgot about the crowd, the noise, and the fact that I was completely out of my element.

As the tune built up, Emma leaned in closer, her voice low enough that only I could hear.

"You're not half bad, you know."

I glanced at her, the corners of my mouth twitching.

"Nice try, Emma."

"Okay, maybe not half bad. But you're getting there." She laughed, her eyes shining.

The next spin came too fast, and I almost tripped, catching myself just in time. She steadied me, her hands on my arms as she looked up at me, her smile softening.

"See? That wasn't so hard."

For a moment, everything else faded—the music, the voices, the fair. It was just us, standing there, her warm touch grounding me and her face lit up like she was the only star in a dark sky.

I cleared my throat, stepping back slightly.

"Another win for you, huh, Emma? Happy now?"

She let out a soft laugh, brushing a stray hair from her face.

"I stopped keeping score a while ago. But yeah... maybe still a little," she said, her grin returning as the tune ended and the crowd erupted in cheers.

As we walked off the dance floor, I caught myself looking at her again, my mind drifting. I thought about all the work she'd done since she first showed up at the ranch, how Ryan had introduced her as *"a friend who could help,"* and how I'd been skeptical at first.

She wasn't just passing through—she threw herself into everything: repairing stalls, mucking out, dealing with clients, tending to the horses—whatever needed doing.

Things I hadn't been around to do, Emma handled like it was *second nature.*

But it wasn't just the work. She brought something else—*life.*

The ranch hadn't felt alive in years, not since... well, not since everything fell apart. And now, thanks to her, the place didn't feel so empty anymore. Neither did I, though I wasn't ready to admit that, not even to myself.

She'd patched up more than broken fences. She'd started to patch me up too—piece by stubborn piece, without even trying.

"Thanks," I said, the word slipping out before I could stop it.

"For what?" she asked, tilting her head.

"For dragging me out here," I said, my voice quieter.

"And for everything else. The ranch. Me. All of it."

Emma's smile softened, her hand brushing mine as we walked.

"That's what I'm here for, cowboy."

69

A CLOUD ON A SUNNY DAY

The fair wasn't my idea. If Emma hadn't talked me into it, I'd still be on the porch with a cold beer and nothing but the sound of the wind for company. But now, standing in the middle of the chaos, I had to admit—it wasn't as bad as I thought.

Emma was smiling from ear to ear, balancing a basket of kettle corn in one hand and a giant lemonade in the other.

"See? Told you this wouldn't kill you," she teased, pressing the basket into my hands before I could protest.

I shook my head but couldn't keep the corner of my mouth from twitching.

"Don't get ahead of yourself. I'm just here to keep you out of trouble."

"Sure you are." Emma smirked.

She nodded toward a big open-air stage, where a set designed to look like an old Western town stood against the fairground lights.

"Come on. The shootout show's about to start. Let's grab some seats before it fills up."

I sighed but followed her anyway.

We found a spot on the creaky old stands just as the show kicked off. A group of men in dusters and cowboy hats burst onto the scene, guns blazing—blanks, obviously, but loud enough to make a few kids in the front row jump. The *sheriff* swaggered out of the mock saloon, looking like he'd done this gig one too many times, while the outlaws hollered and took cover behind wooden barrels.

Emma, of course, was eating it up, leaning forward with wide eyes as one of the stuntmen took a flying leap off a balcony, crashing through a stack of crates. I crossed my arms, watching as they choreographed a full-on saloon brawl, complete with fake punches, shattered bottles, and an outlaw getting kicked clean through a set of swinging doors.

For a while, it was almost... *fun.*

When the stunt show ended, Emma dragged me back to the game stalls. She made it her mission to hit every one we hadn't tried yet—from the ring toss to the balloon pop—and somehow, she kept winning. By the end of it, I was stuck holding a ridiculous stuffed bull under my arm like some kind of prize mule.

"Told you I'd win," she said, her laughter ringing out as we wandered through the fairgrounds, weaving between the crowds and booth-lined paths.

Funny how life works sometimes. I'd fought tooth and nail not to come here, and yet, in the middle of all this noise and chaos, something cracked open. A feeling I hadn't let myself have in too damn long. Something close to joy. The kind that makes you forget everything else for a little while.

But deep down, I knew better.

Storms don't wait for *blue skies.*

That's when I heard a voice that cut through the noise like a blade.

"Jesse! Jesse, is that you?"

I turned, and there he was, grinning like a wolf in a chicken coop, all dressed in black like a crow delivering bad news. His tailored shirt and polished shoes looked out of place in the dust and frenzy of the fair, but the gleam in his eye was exactly as I remembered it—sharp, calculating, and just a little too familiar.

I froze for a second. He hadn't aged much since the last time I saw him, back when my life was unraveling. Back when he'd been one of the few I thought I could rely on. One I could trust.

He was like the brother I never had. Back then, he was my *manager.*

The flash hit me uninvited, sudden and intense. I saw him in his tux, arm slung around my shoulder at the reception, laughing as if we'd conquered the *world.*

"You're the lucky one, Jess. I mean, look at her—Marie's a knock-out, man. Don't screw this up."

Lucky. Yeah, *right.*

I blinked, and the man in front of me brought me back to the present—the best man by my side at the altar, the one who once led me toward *heaven,* now the same man who'd walked out on me when everything came crashing down to *hell.*

I let out a slow breath, shaking my head.

"Well, look at that, Sebastian. Even in hell, the devil still finds you."

"Jesse, is that any way to greet an old friend?" he said, phony as ever.

His grin widened, and he spread his arms like we were old war buddies meeting on neutral ground.

"Didn't think I'd run into you at a place like this. Thought you'd vanished off the face of the earth."

"*Not quite.*" I shifted the ridiculous stuffed bull I was carrying, jaw set like stone.

"*So tell me, are you lost? Out here, they don't serve champagne. Or maybe you just smelled blood, scouting for the vultures.*"

He chuckled, a sound that was just a little too smooth.

"*Yeah, well... life's full of surprises, isn't it? So, how's the music business treating you these days?*"

"*Just a hobby now—*" I said, my tone clipped.

"*I walked away from that fucking circus. Got too dangerous. Knife throwers missed on purpose, lions broke loose, and no one could be trusted—not even the ringmaster.*"

His eyes flicked to the stuffed bull, and his smirk deepened.

"*Well, I see you're keeping busy. Always thought you were the rock star type, not the carnival prize collector.*"

The jab hit harder than I cared to admit. My grip tightened on the plush toy, the cheap fabric scratching against my palm. Heat crept up my neck, but I forced myself to stay still.

"*What do you want, Sebastian?*"

"*Want? Come on, Jess, can't a guy just say hello to an old friend?*"

The word friend twisted something in my gut. *Friend.* That's what he used to call himself, back when he promised he'd have my back no matter what. Just like he used to call me Jess—like we were brothers, like I wasn't just another rung on his damn ladder. Instead, he'd used me—my name, my connections, my vulnerability—to climb his way up.

"*You were never good at just saying hello,*" I said, my voice low.

"*Cut the crap. What's this about?*"

He didn't flinch, a mask as unreadable as ever. That same poker face that fooled me once. Never again.

I was already bracing for whatever game he was about to play when Emma appeared by my side, her expression cautious.

"*Everything okay?*" she asked softly, her eyes darting between me and him.

Sebastian's smirk didn't falter. He extended a hand toward her, slick as oil.

"Gray. Sebastian Gray,"—he said, delivering it like a line straight out of a *James Bond* movie.

Yep. Spy for sure. Double digits for a *double agent.*

Emma hesitated, her gaze flicking to me before she shook his hand.

"Emma."

"A pleasure," Sebastian said with a slight bow, like he was at a gala instead of a dusty fairground. He turned back to me, his smile cold enough to cut glass.

Then, just before he walked away, he leaned in slightly— close enough that Emma couldn't hear.

"I see you still have good taste," he said with a wink.

"Good to see you still alive and kicking, Jesse. Not everyone thought you would."

Yeah, he's still got skills—just the wrong kind. The words sliced close, sharp like the knives he always throws—aiming at his partner, not the board. But I didn't give him the satisfaction of a reaction.

I just watched as he disappeared into the crowd as quickly as he'd appeared, leaving a bitter taste in my mouth.

Emma touched my arm lightly.

"Who was that?"

"No one," I said, though the weight in my chest told a different story.

"Just a ghost from the past."

Emma hadn't moved, still fixed on the direction Sebastian had gone, her brow furrowed.

"I don't know him, and I just met him, but... there's something fishy about him."

I let out a humorless laugh, shaking my head.

"You don't know the half of it."

Her hand stayed on my arm, a steadying presence. The fair buzzed around us—laughter, music, the shuffle of boots on dirt —but it all felt muted now, like the sun had slipped behind a *cloud.*

Freaking crows. I never liked crows.

As we say in French, *oiseaux de malheur.*

Bad omen, I'm telling you.

Bringing *a cloud on a sunny day.*

70

NOT BAD AFTER ALL

As the fair slowed to an easy sway, the heat of the day gave way to a cooler dusk. Overhead, the sky stretched in a blend of deep indigo and fading ember, the last traces of sunlight smudging the horizon like the final strokes of a dying fire. String lights flickered to life along the stalls, their soft glow casting a warm ambiance over the grounds. The laughter of children had softened into the background, replaced by the low murmur of conversations and the occasional twang of a distant guitar.

Emma and I sat on a bench off to the side, away from the bustle, her boots resting on the bottom rung, mine planted firmly in the dirt. Between us, a half-empty tray of funnel cake sat forgotten, the powdered sugar catching the last of the light.

"Hey. What's up, cowboy? You've gone all quiet on me," Emma said, breaking the silence.

I leaned back, letting my hat tilt forward to shield my face.

"Just taking it all in."

She didn't push, but I could feel her look on me, steady and curious.

"*Was it really that bad?*" she asked after a moment.

I lifted my hat just enough to glance at her.

"*What?*"

"*The day,*" she said, smirking.

"*You've been acting like I dragged you through hell, but I caught you smiling at least twice.*"

"*Twice, huh?*" I said, my lips twitching.

"*Must've been the brisket.*"

Emma rolled her eyes, but the warmth in her laughter was undeniable. She looked out at the fairgrounds, her expression softening.

"*You know, days like this are good for the soul. A little chaos, a little fun... reminds you that life's not all bad.*"

I nodded, though my thoughts were elsewhere. Sebastian Gray's grin lingered in my mind, sharp and smug, a ghost from a chapter I thought I'd closed. Seeing him had stirred up feelings I wasn't ready to face, a mix of anger, regret, and something darker that settled like smoke in my lungs.

"*Not all bad,*" I echoed, my voice quieter.

Emma settled back beside me, tipping her head as she studied the stars beginning to peek through the darkening sky.

"*Who was he?*" she asked softly.

"*Who?*"

"*That guy we ran into earlier,*" she said, her tone cautious.

"*The one who... put that cloud over your sunny day.*"

I let out a low chuckle, though there was no humor in it.

"*Just someone I used to know. Someone I thought I could trust.*"

"*And now?*" she asked, glancing at me.

"*Now I know better,*" I said simply.

She didn't press further, her gaze returning to the sky.

"Funny how people like that show up when you least expect it. Like they know just when to kick you when you're starting to stand."

She was right. She was *damn right.*

I reached for the tray of funnel cake, breaking off a piece and popping it into my mouth, more to fill the silence than anything. The sweetness felt out of place, a stark contrast to the bitterness I couldn't quite shake.

"You have a way of making sense of things, you know that?" I said finally.

"Already told you—that's what I'm here for, cowboy," she said, smiling as the corners of her lips quirked up.

Around us, the lights held steady as the fair wound down. Vendors packed up their wares, the crowd thinning as families and couples drifted toward the exits. The Ferris wheel turned slower now, its glow softening against the deepening night.

"Ready to head out?" Emma asked, standing and brushing off her dress.

"Yeah," I said, rising to my feet. But as I looked over my shoulder, something in me hesitated, like leaving this moment behind would mean stepping back into the heaviness I'd managed to forget for a while.

Dammit—she was right *again.*

Indeed, it had helped me get out of my head for a few hours.

And as if reading my mind, Emma touched my arm lightly.

"Hey," she said, her voice softer now.

"It was a good day. Don't let him ruin that."

I met her eyes, deep with sincerity.

"Yeah," I said, my voice firmer this time.

"It was."

We walked toward the truck in comfortable silence, the crunch of gravel under our steps the only sound.

As we left it all behind and the dark began to creep in,

I had to admit—*it wasn't bad after all.*

71

JUST LIKE THAT

I t had been a couple of days since the fair, but it was still on my mind.

The sunlight streaming through the window woke me up, pulling me out of a restless sleep.

I stretched, groaning as my body reminded me of the miles walked, the dust kicked up, and maybe even the dancing.

The fair had been... good. Better than I wanted to admit. I couldn't remember the last time I let my guard down—it had been years, maybe even a lifetime ago. I'd even had some *fun.*

Emma had a certain aura about her. Something warm, calm, caring—almost *angel-like,* yet playful. Like she could breathe life into the dead and have them dancing before they even knew they'd risen.

And for a little while, I let myself believe that *maybe—*

The thought trailed off as I pushed out of bed and headed toward the kitchen. I was still tangled in the memories—her laugh during the rodeo, the way her hair caught the light as she spun on the dance floor, wild and free. The way she'd looked at me—not just at me, but into me—as if she were reading me like a book I hadn't even finished writing.

Her hand, warm when she took mine—steady, reassuring, unafraid. The quiet understanding in her eyes when she steadied me, like she knew I needed grounding before I even realized it myself.

Like *maybe*—

I shook the thought off and reached for the coffee pot, but the feeling lingered, something I couldn't quite name. Something I wasn't ready to name.

But was there even a *name?*

I froze mid-step. Emma was standing by the front door, suitcase in hand.

"*What the hell is going on?*" I asked, my voice rough from sleep.

"*You're leaving?*"

She spun around, startled.

"*Jesse—I didn't want to wake you. I left a note on the table.*"

"*A note?*"

My chest tightened as I glanced toward the table, where a folded piece of paper sat waiting.

"*What's going on? Why are you leaving?*"

Emma hesitated, her grip tightening on the handle of her suitcase.

"*I have to go. There's... something urgent. Family business I need to take care of.*"

"*Family business?*" I stepped closer, my voice rising despite myself.

"*Emma, what are you talking about? What happened?*"

"*I can't explain right now.*" She shook her head, her eyes darting to the door.

"*I'll call you, okay? I'll keep you posted.*"

"*But—*" The words caught in my throat.

"After everything, after—"

"I'm sorry," she said, cutting me off, her voice soft but firm.

"I have to go, Jesse. Goodbye."

She opened the door and walked outside before I could stop her, leaving me standing there, barefoot and stunned. The wheels of her suitcase rattled over the gravel, each scrape sharp against the silence. And then—just like that—she was *gone.*

I didn't move, for what seemed like forever, staring at the open door. My heart sat heavy, my mind spinning. Like I'd just stepped into the road without looking, and a semi clipped me before I even saw it coming. The note on the table caught my eye, but I couldn't bring myself to read it.

I'd let myself believe, for just a moment, that things could be different. That maybe, for once, I wouldn't be left behind. Or maybe I'd fucked it up without realizing it.

Either way, fate had other plans. It always *did.*

I sank into a chair, the emptiness pressing down on me, familiar and unforgiving. The fair, the laughter, the brief flickers of hope—they felt like a cruel joke *now.*

And once again, I was the *punchline.*

72

WHEN QUIET BECOMES LONELY

THE RIGHT THING

L ike a bad song on repeat, the days dragged on after Emma suddenly left. Longer than they should have. The ranch felt hollow again, like it had before she came crashing into my life. I tried to keep busy—fixing fences, cleaning out the barn, even tinkering with Swampy—but it wasn't the same. It felt like the silence clung to me, like an iron collar chained to the wall—every time I reached for something more, it yanked me back and choked the fight out of me.

I spoke to her briefly a few times, but the calls were rushed, her voice distant. She was always in a hurry, always brushing off my questions with that same vague, *"I'll call you soon."*

It wasn't enough. I started to worry—about her, about what might've happened, and about whether she'd ever *come back.*

I missed her, plain and simple. And I hated admitting it, even to myself.

I stood on the porch that evening, beer in hand, watching the sun sink behind the hills. I thought about how much she'd done since she'd been here—how she'd breathed life back into the ranch and, in some ways, into me.

She didn't just help with the chores; she took over everything, even while I was gone. She made things lighter, easier. Hell, she even got me to line dance, for God's sake. I chuckled bitterly at the thought, the sound dying as quickly as it came.

Would she ever come back? I couldn't help but wonder.

Did I do something wrong?

Did I push her away without realizing it?

I could've asked Ryan for her number the last time he called to check in, keeping me posted on the album and the business, but I didn't. Part of me wanted to, though. Part of me wanted to hear her voice again, even if it was just to make sure she was okay.

But would Emma even want to hear from me?

Was I just clinging to the past, hoping to rewrite what was already lost?

I let it all sit with me, because maybe, in some messed-up way, I deserved it.

Maybe it's just how things are for me. Maybe some people aren't meant to stick around.

And she had her life to live. And maybe... maybe that was the problem. I couldn't let myself need anyone anymore. It always ended the same way—people left, and I was right back where I started, holding onto nothing but a memory of something I couldn't have again.

That I wasn't doomed to repeat the same cycle of loneliness. I thought Emma might be the change I needed. Maybe I was expecting too much, too soon. Maybe I dreamed that story, tricked my mind into believing something that was never there. Maybe she was just passing through, like a sign from the universe—meant to appear, not to stay.

But what is the message?

That night, the porch felt colder than ever. Or it was just me. I stayed there long after the stars had come out, a bottle of Good Ol' Jack in hand. The darkness wasn't just around me—it was inside, curling up in my chest like a *parasite.*

I told myself I was fine, that I liked being alone. Pretended I preferred it that way. A recluse by choice. Hiding in the desert like a wounded coyote—too proud to howl, too broken to move. Let them call it solitude—hell, I called it that too. But I knew better. It was just hibernation with a heartbeat. But deep down, I knew I was *lying.*

I wanted her back here, sitting beside me, teasing me about something stupid, making me feel alive. But all I had now were my own thoughts.

I tipped the bottle back, hoping for oblivion, but found none. Instead, the demons of the past came crawling back—slow, cruel, and patient—just to torment me all over again.

That's when I started talking to Swampy. Not playing—just rambling. Like she was the only damn thing that might listen.

"She said I had to do the right thing.

The right thing, huh?

What the hell's the right thing?

I did the fucking right thing, didn't I?

I left. I walked away. I gave her space.

That's the right thing, right?

But no—no, no, no. It's never enough.

Never the right right thing.

It's gotta be her version of fucking right.

Her version of truth.

I stayed quiet. That was the right thing.

I didn't fucking fight. That was the fucking right thing.

I let her go. That was the right thing, right?

And still... I'm the fucking asshole."

So tell me, Swampy—you got the right answers in those strings?

'Cause I'm fresh out."

I chuckled, dry as the desert wind.

"Yeah. I know. Full De Niro rant. Fucking pathetic."

Funny thing is, I don't even know who I was talking about anymore.

Marie? Emma?

Maybe it didn't matter.

'Cos maybe that was the *real fucking right thing*.

And then I realized—the quiet that was my home, the one I'd welcomed, the one I thought I knew... had *changed*.

That's *when quiet becomes lonely*—it cuts deeper than you ever expect.

73

TIME TO SAY GOODBYE

Sitting on the porch, it felt colder tonight. Or maybe it was just me.

I was slumped in my chair, rocking back and forth, a bottle of Good Ol' Jack balanced on my knee. This time, it didn't feel like company anymore. It was different. He was running dry of *stories.*

The stars were out, scattered across the black sky. But they had nothing to say. They never did.

I took a long swig, letting the burn settle in my throat. It was supposed to help—it always did. But tonight, it didn't.

There was no escape, no softening of the edges. The tightness clawed at my ribs, relentless—like a blade sinking deeper with every breath. I stared at Jack in disbelief, almost angry at it for failing me.

"Figures," I muttered, setting it down on the table.

"Can't even count on you anymore."

The night stretched wide and empty. Emma was gone, and I

wasn't surprised. Maybe I should have been, but deep down, I always knew nothing good *lasted.*

Now it was back to just me, Ol' Jack, this damn porch... and the shotgun leaning against the wall.

My attention drifted—almost without thinking—to it. It had been there forever, part of the furniture. But tonight, it felt... different.

I looked away and reached for Jack instead.

I closed my eyes.

"How the hell did it come to this?" I whispered to no one.

And then it all came back.

Marie's face. Her smile—the one that made me believe, the one that turned out to be a lie. The manipulation, the gaslighting, the slow unraveling of everything I thought was real. The way she took everything we built and burned it to the ground, watching the flames like they meant nothing.

The band, gone. The music, gone. The life I'd spent my whole damn existence building—*gone.*

But nothing cut deeper than him.

My son.

I still remember the day he was born. I should've cried, but I didn't. I just stood there, staring, knowing my life had just split in two—before him and after him.

I remember his tiny fingers curling around mine, the way his whole body relaxed when I held him, like he already knew I'd keep him safe. I remember the weight of him asleep against me, the warmth of his breath.

And now?

Now, there's nothing. No small hand reaching for mine. No laughter echoing through the house. No bedtime stories, no whispered goodnights. Just an empty space where a *father* should be.

Because she took him.

Ripped him away, turned me into nothing more than a shadow, a name on a birth certificate.

And the worst part?

He doesn't even know me anymore.

My chest tightened as I shook my head, gripping the arms of the chair.

"When did I lose control?" I asked the stars, my voice cracking.

But they didn't answer. They just stared back, watching me unravel.

It wasn't supposed to be like this. I had it all once—a family, a career, a future. And now I was here, drinking alone on this porch, wondering if I'd even make it to morning.

Everything came rushing back, hitting hard—like a bull charging with no way to stop it. Marie. The fights. The betrayal. Every wrong turn I had made along the way. And Emma— Emma, who I thought might save me from myself. She was gone, *too.*

The bottle felt heavier in my hand.

Why keep fighting it?

The thought was sharp, clear, and terrifying in its simplicity. Why keep dragging myself through this? The pain was unbearable, suffocating, and I was so goddamn tired of carrying it.

I glanced between the bottle and the *shotgun.*

"Maybe it's time," I whispered, exhausted from an encore that refused to be the last.

Time to say goodbye.

The words hung there, echoing in the stillness. I closed my eyes, the weight of them pressing down on me like a boulder. For a moment, I felt like I was standing on the edge of something I couldn't come back from.

But then, his face flashed in my mind.

My little boy. Little Jesse.

His bright eyes, his laughter. The way he used to call me

Papa like I was his whole world. My heart was about to explode, like a damn grenade with the pin already pulled, and tears spilled down my face, hot and bitter.

I hadn't seen him in years. Didn't even know if he remembered me. But I remembered. I remembered every laugh, every time his tiny hand reached for mine. I remembered promising him I'd always be there.

And I failed. *God, I failed him.*

But the thought of never seeing him again, of giving up on even the faintest chance of holding him just once more—it was worse than the pain.

I wiped my face with a trembling hand, glancing at Jack. He wasn't going to save me. He never really did.

My gaze flickered back to the shotgun, then to Jack.

The tears kept falling as I whispered,

"No. Not tonight... I can't."

The wind picked up, carrying a faint hum from Swampy. It was probably just the breeze vibrating the strings, but it sounded like something more.

I glanced at the guitar, its silhouette blurred by my tears.

I didn't pick her up.

But she was there.

Waiting.

And so was the *shotgun.*

I couldn't bear the pain anymore.

It was time to close the curtain—*the show is over.*

The end of a never-ending farewell tour.

Maybe it was *time to say goodbye.*

Au revoir. Adieu.

74

MESSAGE IN A BOTTLE

More often than not, Earl, the mailman, stops by every other day, taking his duties seriously to make sure everyone out here gets their mail, no matter how far off the beaten path they live. In a place like this, where neighbors are few and far between, Earl isn't just delivering envelopes—he's delivering a familiar face, a quick word, a reminder that the world hasn't completely forgotten you. But today, he came early.

"*Hi, Earl. How're you doin'?*" I asked, stepping out onto the porch.

"*Hi, Jesse. Same ol', same ol'. Just pretty chilly today,*" Earl replied, rubbing his arms and shivering slightly. His breath puffed out in little clouds—a drop in temperature that crept in overnight.

Seriously, these days, the weather's all over the place—unpredictable. Cold snaps in May, heat waves in February. Global warming, they say. *Who knows anymore?*

"*Yeah, I hear you. Not much happening 'round here, though, so I guess it fits the mood.*" I shrugged, pulling my jacket tighter.

"*So, what you got for me?*"

"*Not much—the usual. Bunch of junk,*" he said, flipping through the small stack of envelopes in his hand.

"*And bills,*" I added with a smirk.

"*Always bills,*" Earl chuckled, shaking his head. He handed me the stack.

"*Oh, wait, actually I almost forgot—there's a package for you. Here you go.*"

He reached into his mailbag and pulled out a large bubble envelope, the kind with that soft crinkling sound when you press it.

I took the package, turning it over in my hands.

"*Thanks, Earl.*"

"*You have a good day now, Jesse,*" Earl said, shifting his strap higher on his shoulder.

"*Gotta go—busy day ahead. Take care.*"

"*Alright, Earl. Take care—and, as I'd say back home, bon courage!*"

I said it out of habit, but maybe he could really use a little courage out there today.

Earl tipped his hat with a grin, then headed down the path to his truck, boots crunching on the frost-kissed ground.

I walked back inside, the chill following me for a moment before I shut the door. The envelope was cold against my hands, its return label catching my eye.

Skytown Records.

"*Jeez, finally,*" I muttered.

"*Took them long enough to send a few promo CDs.*"

I ripped it open, pulling out the shrink-wrapped cases. But tucked in with them was something unexpected—a small, brown envelope with my name scrawled across it. No return address, no explanation.

I set it aside, then grabbed a CD and turned the case over in my hands, staring at the cover like it might tell me something I didn't already know. The packaging was fancy—glossy, heavy stock, with a booklet so thick it was damn near a book itself.

I snapped open the case, flipping through the pages. Thick paper, full-color photos, and every single lyric printed inside, like a tribute to everything I'd ever written. Skytown had spared no expense. They wanted this to look important.

Page after page, old photos stared back at me—shots from the early days, backstage moments, live performances, press shoots. A whole history, frozen in time. The rise, the fall.

Frenchy and The Sweet Bandits, in all its glory and chaos— captured like a story with no clear ending.

It should've been nostalgic. Instead, it brought back a flood of mixed feelings, a reminder of everything gained and everything lost.

Talking about *nostalgia*... the vinyls were still on the way.

I knew they took longer to press, but Ryan said the label had rushed out the CDs first. Holding it now, I wasn't sure what I had expected to feel.

Ryan's words came back to me, clear as day—

"Skytown is very pleased with the record. They're going to push it hard, Jesse. Full radio promotion, marketing, everything. They think it's your best work yet—there's a lot of excitement around it. They believe there are several potential hits."

I had snorted, shaking my head.

"Yeah, well, it's called 'Greatest Hits Revisited', so I'd hope there's a couple in there."

Ryan had just laughed, brushing past my sarcasm.

"No, I mean it. The new versions sound fresh. And those unre-

leased tracks? They think those could really hit, too. This isn't just some rehash—people are excited."

I'd just replied, *"Okay,"* back then, letting the words roll off me. Now, holding the damn thing in my hands, I still didn't know how to feel.

Satisfaction? *Pride? Relief?*

None of it came. Just an empty space, like the thrill had been drained out before it even hit.

I let out a slow breath, setting the CD case aside. It was done. The album was real, out in the world, carrying pieces of me with it. But somehow, it still felt distant—like a story I wasn't fully part of anymore.

That's when my eyes landed back on the brown envelope. I had almost forgotten about it, sitting there on the table, unassuming but out of place.

At first, I figured it was just a mistake—maybe someone at the office threw it in with the shipment. But when I tore it open, the contents made me freeze.

Inside the envelope was a handwritten letter, folded neatly, and a single Polaroid. I turned the photo in my hands.

On the bottom, scrawled in the same looping script, were the words:

"You made me believe in magic. Thank you."

Curious, I grabbed my glasses from the counter—damn things were becoming more necessary these days—and sat down at the kitchen table.

I set the Polaroid aside for a moment and took the paper.

75

DEAR MR. LAWRENCE

Opening the letter, the handwriting was the same as on the photo—neat, like someone who took their time, but just uneven enough to betray how much it mattered. And it reads:

Dear Mr. Lawrence,
You don't know me, but I've carried your music with me for most of my life. My name is Cole Stapleton, and I'm the kid in the photo. That guitar I'm holding was a gift from my dad—not long after we saw you play live at The Red River Festival in New Orleans. He told me it was the closest thing to magic he'd ever seen—watching you on stage with that guitar, like the two of you were made for each other. He called it pure soul.
I wanted to write this letter not just for myself, but for him. You see, my dad believed in music the way some people believe in miracles. And that day, watching you

bring those songs to life, he believed in you, too. He told me later that you gave him hope when he needed it most. And you gave me something, too. I didn't know it at the time, but that moment changed my life. Your music became a lifeline—a reminder that even when things felt impossible, there was still something worth holding onto.

I never pursued music. I found a different path, but the lessons stayed with me. The drive, the passion, the belief that anything is possible if you give it everything you've got. There were times in my life when I thought I couldn't keep going, when everything felt too heavy, but I'd remember that day and how you made the impossible seem real. You gave me the strength to keep going.

I've had some success—more than I could have dreamed of, honestly—and I owe a part of that to you. I just wish my dad could see how far I've come. He'd be proud, I think. And if he were here, I know he'd want me to send this letter to you. It's not just my message—it's his, too. So, this is my message in a bottle, sent in the hope that it finds its way to you.

Thank you—for the music, for the inspiration, and for being a part of a memory that will always mean the world to me. And thank you for reminding me, even without knowing it, that life is always worth fighting for.

With gratitude,

Cole Stapleton

76

NOT BY A LONG SHOT

Not until I finished the letter did I realize warm tears were running down my cheeks. I hadn't even noticed at first—too caught up in the words, the weight of what they meant.

I set the letter down gently, my fingers lingering on the paper for a moment before I reached for the Polaroid. Something about it tugged at me, like it held answers to questions I hadn't even thought to ask.

Drawn to it, I studied the photo more closely this time around. The picture was faded, its colors softened by time, but the details were still clear enough.

A *kid*—maybe ten years old—stood front and center, grinning wide as he held a guitar that looked way too big for him. The strap hung awkwardly over his shoulder, like it hadn't been adjusted right, but the pride in his face was unmistakable.

Beside him, a man stood with one arm draped around the boy's shoulders. His other hand rested lightly on the guitar's neck, steadying it, like he was teaching the kid how to hold it just right. They were both smiling, the kind of genuine smiles that came from somewhere deep, like the occasion itself was worth capturing forever.

It didn't take much to guess who the man was. He looked like he could've been the boy's dad—a father sharing a piece of himself with his son.

I stared at the photo for a long time, lost in thought. And then something grabbed my attention. I leaned in closer, my breath catching.

"I'll be damned," I whispered.

"It can't be."

I looked closer at the guitar in the picture. It was shiny, new, but there was something unmistakable about it. The body shape, the grain of the wood, the faint residue of a paint color that wasn't there anymore.

"It looks like a swamp ash Tele," I said aloud, my voice shaky.

"It's clean, almost new, but that paint... I remember those faint traces of color when I found it. The marks were in the same exact spots. Could it be...?"

I set the Polaroid down slowly, the weight of it settling in my chest. If it was what I thought it was, then this guitar had a story —one that started long before me.

I sat there, staring at the photo and the note, the words replaying in my mind. You made me believe in *magic*.

It hit me all at once—what this letter truly meant. My music, my journey, my struggles, every inspiration—they had never just belonged to me. What I had almost let slip away had the power to mean everything to someone else.

This wasn't just a thank-you letter from a fan. It was a lifeline. A reminder that what we leave behind, even unknowingly, can ripple out and change lives in ways we never see.

I glanced at Swampy, lying on the couch where I'd left her, her battered body gleaming faintly in the light. She was more than a guitar—she was a vessel, a storyteller. And as long as I kept playing, those stories would keep reaching people, keep finding the ones who needed them most.

I thought of Little Jesse—his laugh, his tiny hands gripping the strings when he was just a few months old. If this letter could find its way to me, then maybe there was still a chance.

A chance to keep *going.*

To make my music matter. To find my way back to him.

I wiped my face, set the photo gently on the table, and stood up. There was still work to do.

I wasn't done.

Not by a long shot.

77

DO YOU BELIEVE IN GHOSTS?

As I jolted awake, my neck screamed in protest. The empty bottle of Good Ol' Jack rattled against the table as I stirred, the sound too sharp in the morning stillness. My head pounded, my mouth dry, the stale taste of whiskey coating my tongue. Maybe that letter gave me a little glimpse of hope—but it didn't last. The demons came back louder, crueler. Especially with Emma gone. I wasn't just hurting. I was *haunted.*

How long had I been out here?

The last thing I remembered was drinking, the night stretching on, blurring at the edges. At some point, I must've passed out right here in this damn chair. Morning hit hard—sun burning my eyes, too bright, too unforgiving. A thick hush suspended in the air, like the universe had pressed pause, leaving me stuck in its leftovers.

Even the birds seemed to have taken the morning off.

Swampy caught my eye, still leaning against the wall, like she'd waited through the night with me. The rising sun hit its surface just right, making the wood look almost alive. For a second, it seemed to shimmer, like heat rising off the desert sand.

I blinked hard and rubbed my eyes, like I could wipe the illusion away.

Still drunk. *Gotta be.*

But then I heard it—a faint hum. Low, steady, barely more than a whisper, but unmistakable. It wasn't coming from the trees or the wind. It wasn't even coming from the porch. It was coming from Swampy.

I froze, staring at the guitar like she might bite me. The sound deepened—not much, just enough to make the hair on my arms stand up. My gut twisted.

"What the hell?" I muttered, glancing around. Nothing moved.

The ranch was as still as I'd ever seen it.

I didn't want to touch her. Hell, I wanted to leave her there and go back inside, lock the door, and pretend I hadn't heard a damn thing. But something pulled at me, a nagging voice in the back of my mind that I couldn't shake.

My hand moved on its own, reaching for *Swampy.*

The moment my fingers touched her neck, the sound stopped. A heavy, absolute silence descended; it felt as if the world itself was breathless. I felt a sudden tightening in my throat, and I almost let go. But I didn't. Instead, I pulled Swampy into my lap, my hands trembling as they settled on the strings.

I didn't think. I just played. The first chord that rang out was sharp, cutting through the stillness like a knife. A minor chord. Dark. Haunting. It felt... right. I didn't know where it came from, but it was mine, and it was real.

The notes came slowly at first, dragging themselves out of me like they'd been buried deep and were finally clawing their way to the surface. The melody wasn't a song. It wasn't anything

I'd ever played before. It was raw, jagged, full of every ounce of pain I'd been carrying.

My vision blurred, the horizon wavering like a mirage creeping in with the rising heat.

A dry whisper threaded through the bushes, stirring the tumbleweeds along the fence line. The wooden planks beneath me creaked, as if something unseen had passed over them. Shadows stretched out long and thin across the side of the house, twisting in ways they shouldn't. My breath hitched as I saw them ripple, like water disturbed by a stone. At first, I thought it was just the light playing tricks on me. But then I saw them—vague silhouettes, shapeless and shifting, moving like *ghosts*. One by one, they began to morph—blurring, then sharpening—until they became something else.

Memories. Hallucinations. Maybe something *worse.*

Marie's face appeared first, as emotionless as the day she walked out the door—empty, unreadable, the mask she always shifted to fit the moment. Then my little boy—his voice, bright and full of life, his blond hair shining in the sun, a memory slipping through my grasp. The band—Steve, Billy Ray, Sticks and Kota—staring at me with those hollow eyes that screamed betrayal. I stopped playing, my hands frozen on the strings.

That's when I saw it.

A figure stepped forward from the shadows, darker than the rest. Its eyes glowed faintly, pinpoints of light in the void. It didn't speak. It didn't need to. Its stare locked onto me, pressing down like a silent verdict. It pointed at me, an accusation as loud as any scream, and my heart pounded so hard it hurt.

The longer it stood there, the more the shadows seemed to ripple, as if the figure's presence disturbed the very air around it. The hum returned, low and pulsing, and for a moment, it felt like the guitar in my hands was vibrating with its rhythm. My fingers clenched tighter around the neck, as if holding Swampy closer might keep whatever this was from breaking through.

And then, like a whisper carried on a breeze, a thought pushed its way into my mind: You were never supposed to *destroy it.*

The words weren't mine. They didn't come from the shadows or the figure staring at me. But they settled in my chest like a stone. My breath caught, and before I could make sense of it, an image flashed through my mind—the old woman's weathered hands placing my first real guitar in mine. Not a hand-me-down or some cheap beginner's model, but the first guitar that felt too perfect, too rare—almost sacred. Like something you don't just own—you *protect.*

"This one's special. You'll see," she said, her voice warm, certain.

It crashed over me like a flood, overwhelming and disorienting all at once. I saw myself—young, eager, holding that guitar like it was the key to something bigger. And I remembered the end—the way it splintered beneath my hands that night, the night she never showed. I'd smashed it to pieces, angry, broken, lost.

I shook my head, hard. The flashback dissolved, leaving me staring at Swampy. It couldn't be. That guitar had been shattered, its pieces scattered to the wind. But for a fleeting moment, I swore I could feel it—its spirit, its weight—woven into the strings beneath my fingers.

"What do you want?" I finally managed to choke out, the words barely audible over the pounding of my heart.

The figure didn't answer. It just stared, unblinking, before dissolving back into the shadows.

The porch was still. Quiet. Empty. But the question lingered, heavier than Swampy in my lap.

"What the hell was that?" My voice was hoarse, unsteady.

"Some kind of ghost?" I swallowed hard, exhaling slowly.

"What did he want?"

I ran my fingers along the worn edges of Swampy, brows furrowed in disbelief.

"And you, Swampy?" The words barely left my lips.

"Do you believe in ghosts?"

Swampy didn't answer. She just sat there, unmoved, like she always had. I strummed a single chord, letting it ring out into the empty morning air.

For the first time in days, the sound didn't feel hollow.

It felt... *alive.*

Not healed, not whole, but enough to remind me that I was still here.

Still *breathing.*

Maybe that was enough.

Or maybe... ghosts don't let go that *easy.*

78

SOME (KINDA) GOOD NEWS

Most afternoons felt quieter, and the house emptier without Emma around. I hadn't heard from her, and every time the phone rang, a part of me wondered if it might be her with some news. Even with the downtime, my mind didn't feel any lighter. Finishing the album hadn't given me the relief I thought it would. If anything, it left me feeling more unsure about what came next.

So when the phone rang on the table, I couldn't help but think it might be Emma. I reached for the receiver and picked up.

"Emma?"

"Jesse, it's Rory."

Of course it wasn't her.

"Oh... hey, Rory. What's up?"

"Jesse! Glad I caught you. Listen, I've been trying to reach Ryan for a few days now, but no luck. Have you heard from him?"

"No, haven't heard from him either," I said, frowning.

"You know The Kid—always busy doing this or that. He's prob-ably caught up in something."

"Yeah, maybe," she said, though there was a hint of concern in her voice.

"Just thought I'd check. Anyway, I've got some good news—great news, actually."

"Oh? Really?"

"Yes. And you're gonna love this—one of the tracks from the album is making waves. KTXS put it in heavy rotation a few days ago, and now other stations are picking it up—state by state, all across the country. It's catching fire, and people are loving it!"

For a moment, I didn't know what to say. I should've felt excited, but something about the news caught me off guard.

"That's... great."

"And that's not all," Rory continued.

"There's already talk about putting together a national tour. Nothing set in stone yet, but some big promoters are very interested."

"A tour," I echoed, letting the word hang in the air.

We'd done a few shows with the *new* Bandits, sure, but they were just warm-ups—rehearsals to get ready for the recordings.

But a full tour?

The idea of getting back out there should've lit a spark in me, but all it did was stir up old doubts. Was I ready to live that life again? To throw myself back into it, knowing exactly where the road led last time.

"I know it's a lot to take in," Rory said, sensing my hesitation.

"But think about it, okay? This could be the start of something really big."

"Yeah—yeah, I'll think about it."

"Good. And let me know if you hear from Ryan, okay?"

"Will do."

We hung up, and I set my phone down, staring at it for a moment. The room was quiet again, but my mind wasn't. Rory's words played over and over in my head. This could be the start of something really big.

It should've felt like good news. It was *good news.*

But all I could think about was whether I was ready for it— or if I ever would be.

And Ryan... *where the hell was he?*

79

THE TRUTH IN A NAME

I was out by the barn, knee-deep in chores I'd been putting off for too long. Ever since Emma left, I'd let things slide more than I should've. I'd gotten used to her handling things, delegating, keeping me from falling too far behind. Now, with the sun burning overhead, I was finally trying to catch up —fixing fences, cleaning stalls, tackling the dozen little things I kept pushing off.

I didn't hear Ryan's car pull up.

"Jesse!"

I turned, wiping the sweat from my forehead, and saw him striding toward me. No warning. No call ahead. Just showing up out of the blue, like always.

My grip tightened around the hammer—an old habit—but as soon as I saw it was him, I exhaled, tossed it onto the workbench, and crossed my arms.

"Where the hell have you been, Kid? Rory's been trying to get a hold of you. She had some good news."

Ryan barely reacted.

"I haven't talked to her." His voice was clipped, distracted.

"Maybe you should," I said, picking the hammer back up.

"She said the album's getting traction. One of the songs is blowing up—"

"Jesse," he cut me off, stepping closer.

"I need to talk to you. Like, right now!"

"Huh? What's this about, Kid?" I frowned.

Ryan hesitated, glancing toward his car, then back at me. He wasn't his usual cocky, smart-ass self. He looked... *unsettled.*

"It's important," he said.

"I can't explain it out here. Can we go inside?"

I sighed, eyeing at the half-finished fence post, at the mess of tools scattered around.

"Kid, now's really not a good time. I got a million things to do—"

"I don't care," he snapped. His tone wasn't angry, but there was a gravity to it that made me pause.

"This can't wait."

Something about the way he said it sent a chill up my spine.

I studied him for a second. He looked like hell—like he hadn't slept in days. His hands were clenched into fists at his sides.

Without another word, I wiped my hands on my jeans and nodded toward the house.

"Alright," I said, giving in.

"Let's go."

Inside, I grabbed a couple of beers from the fridge, set them on the table, and dropped into my seat. Ryan didn't reach for his. Instead, he stood for a moment, like he was working up to something, then finally pulled out a chair and sat down.

Then, he exhaled sharply, like he was ripping off a *Band-Aid.*

"My mom's dead," he said. Just like that. Bam. Blunt. No hesitation. Just the raw, brutal truth.

"What?"

I blinked. The words barely registered at first.

Ryan didn't slow down.

"It happened months ago. A car crash. Her and her husband. No survivors."

He let out a dry chuckle, though there wasn't any humor in it.

"Guess you didn't hear about it."

I stared at him, trying to piece together why the hell he was telling me this. His mom? *What did this have to do with me?*

"I—" I started, but he cut me off.

"Don't." He waved a hand, brushing off whatever I was about to say.

"Spare me the 'I'm sorry for your loss' speech." He leaned back, rubbing his face, looking exhausted in a way that went beyond lack of sleep.

"Truth is, I don't even know how I feel about it. I spent my whole life trying to prove something to her, and now she's just... gone."

The weight in his voice hit me, but I still didn't understand. Why the hell was he telling me this?

After a moment, he sighed.

"I inherited the house, but I couldn't go through her things for weeks—months, actually. Every time I tried, it just... felt like too much."

I nodded slowly, still trying to catch up.

"And then finally, I decided to do it. To start clearing things out, to try and move on."

He shifted, reaching down for something, and when he straightened, he was holding something.

"And then I found this."

He pulled it from a bag I hadn't even noticed, setting it on the table between us. His fingers lingered on the lid before he pulled away.

A small wooden box.

It was worn with age, the faded letters spelling *Paris* alongside a painted *Eiffel Tower*.

My eyes lingered on it for a second, something about it tugging at me. But I didn't reach for it. Didn't dare.

"I found this in her closet," he said, his voice low and steady.

"It was hidden, shoved under a pile of old clothes. I wasn't looking for anything, but... I don't know. Something about it felt like it was meant for me to find."

I stayed silent, my stomach tightening.

"So, I opened it," he continued, his tone sharpening.

"And there were some pictures inside. Her. You. And me. Together." He looked up at me, his eyes narrowing.

"We looked like a family. A real family. I must've been one, maybe two—you're holding me, she's next to you, smiling like it was all perfect. Like some happy little family."

He paused, chasing his thoughts.

"See, I don't remember any of it. I grew up thinking someone else was my real dad. Could've been a stranger holding me in those photos. So why keep them?"

His words hit hard. *Now what??*

My mind scrambled to keep up, but I didn't interrupt.

"There was this newspaper clipping, too," he said. *"Some article about a wedding. 'French uprising music star ties the knot.' There you were, with her. All smiles. Like you were some goddamn celebrity or something."* He shook his head, letting out a bitter laugh.

I looked down at the clipping.

And then I saw her.

Marie?

Is Ryan's mom?

My breath hitched, my grip tightening on the paper. My mind barely had time to process before Ryan reached into the box and pulled out a folded document.

"And then..." His voice cracked. He set it down in front of me.

"This."

I hesitated, my gut twisting as I looked down.

A birth certificate.

Older, slightly yellowed at the edges, but clear as day. My eyes scanned the lines, and then I saw it—the name that made my breath catch.

Jesse Michael Ryan Lawrence, Jr.

My fingers curled against the table. My name. My *blood.*

I barely had time to process before Ryan reached into his jacket and slapped another piece of paper down beside it.

"And then there's this." His voice was sharp now, cutting through the room like a blade.

A paternity test.

"My mom must've had it done. It's got her name, your name, my name... everything. 99.99% probability."

He let out a short, bitter laugh.

"Guess there wasn't much doubt."

I stared at the papers, my breath heavy in my chest. My mind scrambled, grasping for something—anything—to hold onto. And then like pieces of a puzzle finally locking into place, it jumped at me—the hard truth of an enigma I'd been circling for years.

Ryan is my little boy. My little *Jesse Jr.*

I tried to keep my emotions in check, but my throat was tight, my pulse hammering in my ears. My vision blurred for a second as I forced myself to focus on the words in front of me.

Jesse Michael Ryan Lawrence, Jr.

Michael Ryan... Ryan...

My stomach twisted. I never made the connection. Why the hell would I? Brooks might be his stepfather's name. With her family's influence, she could've had his birth certificate amended, changed his legal last name when she remarried—made it so I never existed on paper. But Ryan—she kept that. She took my son, erased me from his life, and still left a piece of me hidden in plain sight.

I swallowed hard, my voice barely above a whisper.

"Mais quelle salope..."

I forced myself to look up.

"Was your step-dad's last name Brooks?" The words felt heavy, like I was barely able to push them out.

Ryan frowned, clearly not expecting the question.

"Yeah... why?"

I exhaled sharply.

"Well, your mom could've had your birth certificate changed. With her family's pull, she might've had a brand-new one made."

Ryan let out a short, bitter laugh.

"Yeah, well, the real question here is—why didn't you ever come for me?" His voice was sharp, cutting through the air like a knife.

I felt the jab, but I didn't look away.

"She made sure I couldn't. She told the court I was a flight risk, said I'd take you to France. She called me an alcoholic, that I was toxic, and with her family's law firm backing her... I didn't stand a chance. Fighting cost me everything. The fees, the lawyers... she left me with nothing."

Ryan's face was unreadable, but I could see the way he shifted in his seat, tension rising in his shoulders.

"I fell into a deep depression," I admitted, my voice barely above a whisper.

"I stopped making music. I let my career fall apart. I lost... everything." I leaned back, letting the words hang in the air.

"She didn't just take you away from me, Ryan. She took everything I was. And I didn't know how to fight my way back."

He didn't say anything right away. He just sat there, staring at the papers, fingers curled against the table like he was trying to anchor himself. His jaw clenched, his breath slow but measured, like he was keeping something in check.

The conversation stretched on, maybe a couple of hours or more. I told him everything—about Marie leaving, about the court battles, how I fought for him until there was nothing left to fight with. I laid it all out, every last piece of it, the parts I never talked about, the things I tried to bury.

And Ryan listened. He didn't interrupt, didn't push. He just sat there, stoic, absorbing it all.

And then, just like that, he got up. Wordless. No second look.

His chair scraped against the floor, the sound sharp. *Final.*

He straightened his jacket, his eyes were blank, detached— like we hadn't just ripped open the past and let it bleed out between us.

"Well then, goodbye, Mr. Lawrence. We'll be in touch."

I opened my mouth, but nothing came out.

Speechless. *Frozen.*

Mr. Lawrence.

Like I was nothing. A formality. A transaction. Just another name on a contract—not the father he had just found.

And then he was *gone.*

The door clicked shut behind him, leaving nothing but silence.

It shattered me, breaking my heart into a million pieces.

That night, I really needed Good Ol' Jack to keep me company, drowning my pain and sorrow in an ocean of whiskey and regret.

And the tears... Jeez, the tears. Pouring like someone forgot to turn off the damn faucet. Mixing with booze, irony, and rage.

Ryan is my little Jesse. My *son.*

And Marie? Well, turns out she beat me to the grave.

Of course she did. Always had to get the last word, *right?*

I thought I'd feel something—anger, sorrow, maybe some twisted sense of justice. But all I felt was... *empty.*

She'd been dead to me for years already. This was just the universe filing the paperwork.

Still, dead or not, she was Ryan's mom. My son's mother. And that should mean something, even if all it meant to me was a cautionary tale in a cheap dress.

I raised my bottle, a bitter toast to the *queen of smoke and mirrors.*

"Here's to you, Marie," I said, half amused, half troubled.

"Even six feet under, you're still pulling the damn strings."

Because, in the end, Marie—Marie, from *outre-tombe,* funding my comeback without ever meaning to.

How's that for poetic justice?

Ryan's anger—I understand it. Hell, I *feel* it.

It's a total fucking mess. Complete *chaos.*

All those lies. After ruining my life, she went and ruined her own son's.

I remember staring at the birth certificate, the paper trembling in my hands.

Jesse Michael Ryan Lawrence, Jr.

The whole fucking *truth was in a name.*

ACT 3

80

A PRODIGAL HABIT

It was dim inside the house, the light filtering through the windows, casting long streaks across the floor—a reminder of how the afternoon was slipping by. I was at the fridge, grabbing a few more beers, moving slow after the night before, when the sound of tires crunching on gravel barely registered. It was the kind of noise that could've easily slipped by, drowned out by the fog in my head. The weight of the last twenty-four hours pressing down on me like a damn anvil.

I straightened, blinking as I moved toward the window. The glare off the dirt road hit hard, making me squint. It took a second for my eyes to adjust, for my brain to catch up.

Ryan. His *words*. The truth I never saw coming.

Jesse Jr.—my little boy.

I'd barely done a damn thing all day. Woke up late—or whatever you could call waking up when you barely slept—dragged myself through the motions, halfheartedly fixing the cooler outside, but mostly just sitting around, staring at nothing, drinking just enough to take the edge off.

The cooler had run dry, so I'd come inside to grab enough to restock it. My head was thick with everything that happened—Ryan, the truth, the damn birth certificate.

Then, the crunch of gravel again. A car slowing to a stop. I frowned, blinking myself back to the present.

Starting to be a damn habit—people showing up unannounced.

I reached for my beer, then hesitated. Maybe it was Ryan, coming back to finish what he started. Maybe he had more to say. Maybe he wanted to twist the knife a little deeper.

My hand twitched toward the shotgun by the door—just instinct. Muscle memory. A reflex burned in over time.

I moved toward the window, my chest tightening.

But then I saw the car.

Not Ryan's.

Emma.

She cut the engine, sat there for a second. Then the door swung open, and there she was—like she hadn't been gone for weeks, like she hadn't left at all.

She stepped out, stretching slightly, then moved toward the trunk. A moment later, she pulled out a suitcase, slinging it casually at her side, like this was just another day.

I paused, staring for a second longer than I should have, trying to make sense of the moment. The way she always seemed to drift in and out, appearing exactly when I needed her —even when I didn't know it myself.

I opened the door just as she reached the porch.

"*Emma,*" I said, my voice rough.

"*You're back.*"

"*Told you I'd be back.*" She gave me that soft, knowing smile and brushed past me into the house like she'd never left.

I turned, following her inside. The air felt different, charged with something I couldn't put my finger on. My head was still spinning from yesterday—from Ryan, from the past clawing its way to the surface. And now this.

The questions tumbled out before I could stop them.

"What happened? Are you okay? You didn't say much when we talked."

She waved a hand, dropping her suitcase to the floor with a dull thud.

"Everything's fine now. I had to take care of some family business, but it's all good. Back to normal."

"Family business," I echoed, frowning.

"Emma, I thought—"

"I know what you thought," she cut in gently, turning to face me. *"But Jesse, I'm here now. That's all that matters, right?"*

I studied her, searching for something beneath her words. She stood there like nothing had changed, like she hadn't just walked out and left me to drown in my own past—only to return and stitch it all back together with nothing more than her presence.

"I thought maybe you weren't coming back," I admitted quietly.

Her expression softened, and she stepped closer.

"Why would you think that?"

I let out a dry chuckle, shaking my head.

"I don't know. I thought maybe I'd done something wrong. Or that... you'd had enough of this place. Of me."

Without a word, she moved closer and wrapped her arms around me, drawing me into a hug—warm, certain, and comforting.

I stood there for a second, caught off guard. Then I let myself breathe.

She eased back just enough to meet my eyes and gave me a big smile.

"Jesse," she said, her voice steady, unwavering.

"*I know you worry. But I'm here now—just like I always am when you need me.*"

Her words settled over me, something lifting off my heart even as a dozen more questions filled the space. I nodded slowly, swallowing hard.

"*Well, it's good to have you back.*"

"*It's good to be back,*" she said, her grin returning.

"*Now, where's that guitar of yours? I bet Swampy's missed me too.*"

And just like that, the ranch felt alive again. Like she'd never left. Like some things—*some people*—just have a way of showing up exactly when they're meant to.

A prodigal habit.

81

THE PAINTING

Funny how easily Emma moved around, like she belonged here all along—settling in without a word. No explanations, no questions. Just here. Meant to be.

And, I let it be.

What else was I gonna do?

To occupy my mind, I just kept going through the motions—putting stuff away, cleaning up a bit, doing whatever I could to avoid thinking.

After a little while, she stepped out of the house—maybe to grab something from the car, or just to get a minute to herself. When she came back in, a large, carefully wrapped package tucked under her arm, her expression was unreadable but carried a hint of something... *different.*

I watched her, my curiosity getting the better of me.

"What is this? Is that what I think it is?" I asked, raising an eyebrow at the bundle.

She set it down gently on the table and started unwrapping it.

"*Depends on what you think it is,*" she said, a small smile
playing on her lips.

I leaned in as she carefully peeled back the layers of protec-
tive cloth, each fold revealing more of what lay beneath. First,
the edge of an old, ornate frame—dark wood, worn with time
but still elegant. Then, bit by bit, the image inside came into
view.

A painting.

A woman in a flowing white dress. Her long, dark hair
cascaded down her shoulders, framing a face that was both
serene and unsettling. Her posture held something I couldn't
quite place—like she knew something the rest of us didn't. The
background was a swirl of muted colors, soft but deliberate,
giving it an *ethereal,* dreamlike quality.

I exhaled slowly, my chest tight.

"*Where the hell did you find this?*"

"*This,*" Emma said, stepping back to admire it,

"*has been in my family for generations. It's... well, kind of an heir-
loom. I guess it's my turn to take care of it now.*"

"*A painting, huh?*" I said, scratching my head.

"*Not what I expected you to come back with.*"

"*I didn't think so either, but... it's important. To my family,
anyway.*" She chuckled softly.

I studied the painting for a moment, my eyes lingering on
the woman's face.

"*She looks a little like you.*"

Emma shook her head, her smile faint but unwavering.

"*You think so? No, not at all. No one even knows who she was.
Maybe an ancestor, or maybe just... the girl next door.*"

Her words hung in the air, but something about it tugged at
my memory. I couldn't put my finger on it, but it felt bizarre—yet
familiar, in a way that sent a strange chill down my spine.

"*Where are you going to hang it?*" I asked, trying to shake off the feeling.

"*I haven't decided yet. Somewhere it won't get too much sunlight, I guess. It's old—fragile.*"

As she carried it toward her room, I sat back, the image of the woman burned into my mind.

Why does this feel like something I've seen *before?*

It hit me later that night, maybe with a little help from Ol' Jack, as I lay awake staring at the ceiling. The memory rose unbidden, clear as day. Thirty-something years ago. The old woman's house.

I sat there, waiting for her to return. At some point, she'd come back with her husband's guitar, but for now, the room was dimly lit, the faint smell of lavender and something musty drifting in the air. To pass the time, I'd started scanning my surroundings, taking in the odd collection of antiques and knickknacks scattered around.

And then my eyes had fallen on it—a large painting mounted on the wall. The same painting Emma had brought back.

The woman in the white dress. The long dark hair. The calm, kind expression that radiated something I couldn't describe.

Peace? Kindness? Purity?

I didn't think much of it back then—it was just a painting on the wall of a stranger's house. But something about it had stuck with me, like it had imprinted itself on my subconscious.

Maybe it was the way she looked—almost *divine,* pure, like a guardian protecting the world with quiet *wisdom.*

Or maybe it was because, even back then, I felt like I was in the presence of something... *more.*

I'd stared at it for what felt like hours, unable to look away.

The image had struck me as something more than just pastels and paint on a canvas.

There was nuance in the brushstrokes—shifts in color, rose, purple, light, and shadow so delicate and caring, they made the figure feel like she might step out of the frame and speak.

It felt alive, almost *sacred*—like an unseen force hovering in the room, watching over everything.

Like an angel.

82

THE BOOZE OR THE BLUES

Yet, even with Emma back, offering her quiet and well-needed support, I was still drinking. Maybe even more. Still trying to digest Ryan's revelation. He was—is—my little boy. That truth hadn't fully settled, and neither had the question of what came next—if there even was a *next*.

I wanted to tell Emma about Ryan—to spill everything—hoping it might make me feel lighter. But I hadn't found the moment. Or maybe I just hadn't found the *courage*.

As the screen door creaked open, I heard her step onto the porch before she said anything. Emma's got that way about her —quiet, deliberate, like she's trying not to wake a sleeping bear. Whatever was hanging between us softened a little as she stood there, waiting for me to look at her.

But I didn't.

"You know, Jesse, the drinking feeds the depression," she said. Her words were soft, but they hit like a hammer.

I let out a dry laugh, sharp and bitter, like the whiskey burning its way down.

"*Oh yeah? And the depression feeds the drinking! Round and round we go.*" I waved the bottle in the air, like it was the punchline to some *cosmic joke.*

"*It's not funny,*" she said, stepping closer, her voice steady.

"*Sure it is,*" I said, smirking, still not looking at her.

"*It's like one of the greatest questions in the universe, right? What came first—the booze or the blues? Hell if I know.*"

Emma didn't laugh. She never did when I needed her to. Instead, she sat down beside me, close enough that I could feel the tension of her silence, thick and palpable. That patience of hers—God, it made my chaos feel bigger somehow.

"*You're better than this, Jesse,*" she said, her voice softer now.

Better? Sure. I took a swig, then paused.

"*What'd you think, Ol' Jack?*" I muttered, giving it a little tilt, as if waiting for it to answer.

"*It's killing you. You know that, don't you?*" she said after a long pause.

I didn't answer. *What was there to say?*

She wasn't wrong.

Yeah, I know. That's the point, isn't it? And so what?

The silence stretched out between us, her words hanging there like smoke in the air. I wanted to laugh again, to brush it off, but even that felt like too much effort.

I stared out at the dark horizon, swirling the whiskey in the bottle like it held answers. It didn't.

"*And so what?*" I said again, softer this time, almost to myself.

"*There are people who rely on you, Jesse,*" Emma said, her voice calm but warm.

"*People who count on you. Care about you.*"

I let out a snort, shaking my head.

"*Fans? Please. They're just waiting to see if I'll crash and burn for good. The Bandits? They've moved on. And friends, family? Hell, Emma, who's left?*"

She didn't flinch.

"*Ryan,*" she said simply.

"*A few of the guys who still ask about you every time they see me. And... me.*"

That last one landed harder than I expected. *Me.* She said it like it was obvious, like it shouldn't need explaining.

I turned to look at her then, really look at her, and the way her eyes caught mine made my heart beat faster. She didn't break the stare, didn't look away.

"*I'm not exactly the kind of guy you should be rooting for, Emma,*" I said, my voice low, almost a whisper.

"*Well, too bad,*" she said, her lips quirking into the faintest smile.

"*I guess I'm just stubborn like that.*"

Her words struck deeper than I wanted to admit, but I didn't have a response. I took another swig of the whiskey instead, though it didn't taste as sharp anymore. The burn was fading, leaving me with something tougher to swallow.

I stood up then, bottle in hand, and raised it to the sky like I was toasting the stars—or maybe daring them to answer.

Feeling the cold desert breeze on my face, I shouted it out like a lone wolf in the darkness.

"*The booze or the blues!*" I said, letting the howl cut through the silent night.

83

ON BORROWED TIME

O h my god, *what had I done?* I didn't even know what time it was—late morning, judging by the faint light filtering through the curtains. Was the bottle in my hand half-empty? Or was it half-full?

I couldn't tell anymore. My head swam every time I moved, and my stomach churned like it was ready to revolt. The air smelled stale, sharp—whiskey and something else I couldn't quite place. A wave of heat crawled over my skin, followed by a shiver that had nothing to do with the morning cold.

As the bottle slipped from my hand, crashing onto the floor with a sharp bang, I didn't care. I couldn't even sit up. My breathing was shallow, my chest heaving with each strained inhale. For a second, I wondered if this was it. If I'd finally pushed my luck too far.

Then I heard her.

"Jesse? Jesse!"

Emma's voice cut through the fog, urgent and panicked. Her footsteps echoed in the quiet as she rushed into the room.

"*Oh, my God. What the hell is going on?*"

I tried to answer, but my tongue felt like sandpaper, and the words got stuck somewhere in my throat. All that came out was a groan.

Emma was next to me in an instant, crouching down and brushing the damp hair off my forehead. Her fingers were cool against my burning skin.

"*You're burning up,*" she murmured, her eyes scanning the room.

Her gaze landed on the bottle I'd just dropped, then drifted to the beer cans and empties scattered across the floor. One was tipped over, dripping onto the rug like a clock counting down.

"*Damn it, Jesse. Is this—have you been drinking all night?*"

I tried to form a phrase, to explain, but all that came out was a slurred,

"*'M fine.*"

Even to me, it sounded hollow. My throat felt raw, my voice like gravel.

"*Fine? You look like hell.*" She pushed my hair back again, her hand resting there for a beat before she pulled away. Her expression hardened.

"*Come on, get up. I'm bringing you to the hospital.*"

"*No,*" I tried to argue, but the word barely escaped my lips. She wasn't listening anyway.

"*Don't do this to me, Jesse,*" she growled, looping my arm around her shoulders. I didn't have the strength to fight her off even if I'd wanted to. The room tilted violently as she hauled me to my feet, and I thought for a moment I might pass out.

My knees buckled, and Emma staggered under the weight.

"*You're not dying on my watch,*" she snapped, her tone firm with determination.

"*Stay with me, Jesse!*"

But I couldn't. My legs gave out completely, and the last thing

I remembered was her voice calling my name, frantic and scared.

Everything went *dark*.

When I came to, the car was moving. Ice-cold leather pressed against my back, and the sudden shift in temperature sent a fresh wave of nausea rolling through me. The engine's low rumble vibrated through my body, amplifying the pounding in my head. My mouth was dry as bone, like I hadn't had a drop of water in days.

"Emma..." I croaked, barely able to form the word.

"Where are we...?"

She shot me a quick glance, her knuckles white against the steering wheel.

"Closest ER's over an hour away. Just hold on, Jesse."

An hour? The words rattled in my foggy brain, but I couldn't process them. The ache in my rib, the throbbing in my skull—it all felt bigger than me, like the distance itself.

"Stay with me," she said again, her voice tight but steady.

"Don't pass out on me."

"Not gonna..." My words slurred together, barely audible. My lungs felt squeezed, every breath shallow and labored. I could feel the sweat sticking to the back of my neck, cold now, like my body was playing some cruel joke.

She kept glancing at me as she drove, her grip tight on the wheel. The lights from the road blurred past, streaking like comets, and I let my head loll to the side.

"Emma," I murmured, my voice barely above a whisper.

"Don't talk," she said, her eyes darting between me and the road. *"Just hold on. We're almost there."*

The ER was all fluorescent lights and sterile chill that bit at my skin. I was vaguely aware of someone shouting medical jargon, of hands tugging at my clothes and hooking me up to machines. A nurse leaned in close, frowning.

"How much has he had to drink?" she asked, not looking at me.

Emma hesitated and looked away, like she could still see the ocean of alcohol flowing across the floor, rippling in her mind.

"Too much," she said quietly, her voice thick with something I couldn't place.

Guilt? Worry? I couldn't tell.

I wanted to speak up, to tell them they were wrong, but my mouth felt dry and useless. The effort to move was too much, so I just lay there, letting them poke and prod like I wasn't even in my own body anymore.

Eventually, the chaos settled. Voices blurred together, machines beeped, and footsteps echoed, but it all felt distant, like I was sinking underwater. I couldn't move, couldn't speak—just existed in the space between consciousness and the void. Then, through the haze, something real anchored me.

Emma. Her hand, steady and warm, wrapped around mine.

"Don't leave," I whispered, barely audible.

"Please, Emma... don't leave me."

Her fingers curled tighter around mine, like she could feel the words in her bones.

"I'm here, Jesse. I'm not going anywhere." Her voice was soft, steady, like the melody of a lullaby.

"You'll be fine. Just hang in there."

I swallowed hard, my throat burning. Was it the fever, the booze, a poisonous delirium—*all of it?*

Or maybe I just felt like this was my very last chance. But the truth clawed its way up before I could stop it.

"Ryan?"

Emma's brow creased.

"Huh? Ryan what?"

I took a slow, shaky breath. The ER room spun around me, the ceiling too bright, too white.

"Ryan..." My voice cracked.

"He's my son."

She didn't react, didn't flinch. Just stared at me for a long moment, her grip never loosening.

"I know," she said, giving a small nod, like she'd known all along.

I exhaled, my body sinking deeper into the bed, my hand still wrapped in hers. For the first time in a long time, I felt something close to relief. Not enough to take the pain away, but enough to breathe.

I couldn't speak. Couldn't even say thank you. I just lay there, staring at the ceiling, feeling the weight of her comforting touch on mine—the only thing rooting me to this earth.

The exhaustion pulled me under before I could say anything else.

* * *

When I woke up, the doctor was standing at the foot of the bed, clipboard in hand. His face was equal parts relief and disappointment.

"It's not alcohol poisoning," he said, looking at Emma.

"Just a severe flu—high fever, dehydration. He'll need rest, plenty of fluids, and to take it easy for a few days."

He sighed, flipping through his notes.

"But with a fever that high and dehydration that bad, it could've gone south fast. Lucky you brought him in."

Emma let out a shaky laugh, one hand still resting lightly on my arm.

"Lucky for him," she muttered, almost to herself.

"But," the doctor continued,

"the drinking is catching up to him. You're playing with fire, Mr. Lawrence."

"I'll keep that in mind," I rasped, my sarcasm weaker than I

wanted it to be. I glanced at Emma. She wasn't smiling anymore
—just staring at me, her eyes full of something I couldn't name.

"*Well,*" I said after a long silence, trying to lighten the mood,
"*guess I dodged another bullet.*"

Emma's gaze didn't waver.

"*How many more bullets do you think you've got left, Jesse?*"

Damn. That hurt. Her words hit like a punch to the gut,
leaving me breathless. I looked away, focusing on whatever I
could get a grip on in the room, unable to answer, letting the
silence fill the space between us.

Well, good thing is, at least I wasn't *dead...yet.*

Maybe just living on *borrowed time.*

84

THE RECKONING

Under extreme stress—and a bit of IV juice—I didn't know how much time had passed since we got back. The haze of fever and exhaustion blurred everything together—fragments of car rides, distant voices, the cold bite of an IV needle. But the worst had passed. The meds were kicking in, dulling the sharp edges of everything, though my body still ached like I'd been run over twice.

But I wasn't alone.

Emma sat beside me—quiet, but present. Her hand rested lightly on mine, fingers warm against my cold skin. She hadn't said much since we walked through the door, but she didn't need to. Her presence was enough—steady, unwavering, reassuring, like a lifeline I hadn't realized I needed until now.

I shifted slightly, wincing as the deep soreness flared up again. Emma noticed, of course. She always noticed.

"Easy," she said softly, her voice calm but firm.

"You don't need to push yourself right now."

"I'm fine," I muttered, though the rasp in my tone betrayed

me. It was an automatic response, a reflex I couldn't seem to control, even when it was obvious I wasn't fine.

Emma didn't argue. She just gave me that look—the one that said she knew better but wasn't going to push it. Not yet, anyway.

A long pause settled between us, thick with things left unsaid. I could feel her watching me, not with judgment, but with something else.

Concern, maybe. Or was it something deeper?

I didn't know. And honestly, I wasn't sure I wanted to.

"You don't have to stay," I said after a while, my voice quieter now. The thought felt wrong even as it left my mouth. Maybe I didn't want her to leave. Maybe I just didn't know how to ask her to stay.

"I'm staying," she replied without hesitation.

No argument, no drama—*just fact.*

I closed my eyes for a moment, letting her words wrap around me, soothing like a lullaby. There was something in her voice—appeasing, soft, almost nursing—that made it comforting, like it wasn't even a question. Like she'd already made up her mind and nothing I said was going to change that.

"You always do that." I exhaled, finally looking at her.

"Do what?"

"Stick around. Even when you shouldn't."

She tilted her head a bit, a faint smile tugging at the corners of her lips.

"Someone has to. You're not exactly good at taking care of yourself, you know."

I huffed a stifled laugh, though it came out more like a cough.

"Guess that makes you the world's most patient babysitter."

Emma didn't laugh. Instead, she squeezed my hand gently.

"No, Jesse. I'm just someone who cares. Maybe it's time you let someone do that."

I didn't know how to respond to that. Not anymore. Last time I did, it cost me more than I could afford. Since then, I built up my armor, and after a while, it just felt easier to keep it on. Instead, I let my gaze drift to the guitar case propped up against the corner of the room. Swampy. She should have felt like an anchor—something solid, something to hold onto. And for a while, she had been. A crutch, helping me learn how to walk again. A tether, keeping me steady as I found my footing. But now, even Swampy felt distant, like a part of me I couldn't quite reach—like I was unmoored all over again.

Emma noticed where I was looking, her expression softening.

"It's still there, you know. You just have to find it again."

"Find what?" I asked, my voice sharper than I intended.

"The magic? The part of me that made it all worth it? Because right now, it feels like it's gone."

"It's not gone," she said firmly.

"It's just buried under everything else. You've been through a lot, Jesse. But you're still here. And that means there's still something left to fight for."

I wanted to argue, to tell her she didn't understand. But the truth was, she did. Probably better than I did.

"You really believe that?" I asked after a moment, my tone softer now, almost unsure.

She nodded, her eyes steady on mine.

"I wouldn't be here if I didn't."

For a long moment, neither of us said anything. We just sat there, while I was still processing, still trying to make sense of what she meant. I didn't know what to believe, or if I'd ever be ready to believe her.

But why not give it a try? She'd nearly saved my life. Maybe it was time I started trusting her, for *real.*

"Alright," I finally said.

"I'll try."

Emma's smile was small but genuine, and for once, I didn't feel like I was standing on my own.

At least, not just with a guitar and a bottle of whiskey as my sole company—but with an actual human being. One who truly cared about me.

So maybe I wasn't anymore.

Or maybe I didn't have to be.

The journey had felt never-ending, but maybe, at the end of the tunnel, there was more than just light.

Maybe the destination was...

something called...

Redemption.

85

BACK ON THE BUS

Rolling down the highway, the hum of the bus engine blended with the chatter and laughter bouncing around the cabin. Sticks was tapping a random beat on the armrest, his drumsticks nowhere in sight for once, but his restless energy was still in full swing. Billy Ray leaned back, eyes half-closed, a lazy grin plastered on his face as he threw out half-hearted jokes at Steve, who was flipping through a worn-out notepad, probably running through the setlist again.

The vibe was loose, familiar—but I didn't feel any of it.

I sat near the back, Swampy resting in her case against the window beside me. The road blurred past outside, nothing but shadows and streaks of headlights. Across from me, Ryan sat, his face closed off, the usual spark of confidence dulled by something else.

Since the revelations, we hadn't really talked. Not in any real way, at least. Sure, we'd exchanged words—necessary stuff about the tour, logistics, the band—but nothing that actually meant something. And now, here we were, stuck in the same space for hours, maybe days. The silence between us felt more awkward than it should've.

"So," Ryan started, breaking the uneasy quiet.

"This is what it was like? Rolling around the country in one of these?"

I smirked, shaking my head.

"Kid, I've spent more nights in these buses than I can count. It ain't the Ritz, but it gets the job done."

I glanced at him, wondering how much of this he was really taking in. Ryan had tagged along for the first leg of the tour— not because he had to, but because he wanted to make sure everything started off right. He wasn't going to stick around for all the shows. Eventually, he'd head back to his world, back to whatever deals and calls waited for him.

'Cos yeah—that tour, that big comeback tour, finally happened after all. The album had taken off—way much more than I ever saw coming, and I'll admit, it knocked me sideways. Ryan, Rory, everyone was right—a damn fucking hit record. We went gold, platinum, diamond for all I know. There was momentum, pressure, and a hell of a lot of calls pushing for it. But in the end, it was Emma who convinced me I'd be fine—that I could handle it, that the road still had something to give me. And maybe she was right. After a few rehearsals, it all started to click again. So we hit the road. And leaving the ranch this time didn't feel like abandonment. Emma had already done a damn good job keeping it afloat before, but now... it felt like her home too. Maybe even more than *mine*.

"More or less, Kid. The scenery doesn't change much—just the people," I finally replied.

He sat up straighter, his hands loosely clasped.

"And the people back then?"

I turned to look at him, half-expecting some kind of dig, but his expression was earnest. He actually wanted to know. Like he was trying—in a weird, hesitant way. Maybe not to understand, not yet, but to find some kind of footing between us.

A start. *Something.*

I sighed, leaning back in my seat.

"Different crowd. Different time. We were young, hungry, stupid. Thought we had it all figured out," I said, my voice trailing off at the end. Some things were better left unsaid—at least for now.

Ryan didn't push. He just nodded, letting the silence settle again.

From up front, Sticks called out, cutting in.

"Hey, anyone want to bet how long before we hit traffic?"

Billy Ray chuckled, not bothering to open his eyes.

"Sticks, man, you're the only one who finds traffic exciting."

The bus filled with easy laughter, and for a second, it felt normal—like the old days. But as soon as the laughter faded, that weight crept back in.

Ryan shifted in his seat, looking at me.

"Did you ever... regret how things went down with Kota? With the band... with everything?"

The question hit harder than I wanted to admit. I straightened up, tension knotting in my shoulders.

I let out a slow breath.

"You really don't pull punches, do you, Kid?"

Ryan raised a hand, defensive but calm.

"I'm not trying to start anything. Just... curious. You guys were tight, right? Back then."

Before I could respond, Steve's voice cut through from a few seats ahead.

"Hey, let's not get into that now."

His tone was calm, steady—the way he always handled things when tensions ran high.

Ryan backed off, settling back into his seat.

"Alright. Just asking."

I didn't say anything. I didn't know what to say. The mention of Kota stirred up too much—regret, guilt, anger. And I knew Ryan wasn't just asking about her. He was testing the waters, seeing if I'd actually talk about it—about Marie, about the choices I made, and the real reasons it all fell apart.

But now wasn't the time for that.

Still, I got it. He was upset, still trying to process everything. No rush. Just like the road ahead, he'd get there when he got there. And when he did, I'd be here to welcome him.

As the night wore on, the bus quieted down. Sticks had finally stopped drumming on everything, and Billy Ray was half-asleep. Steve had his headphones on, lost in whatever music he was using to prep for the next show.

I grabbed Swampy and pulled her onto my lap, my fingers moving over the strings, just messing around. The familiar sound filled the space, a soft melody that didn't need an audience.

Ryan sat across from me, watching silently before speaking.

"That's... cool. What's that you're playing?"

"Nothing," I said, barely glancing up.

"Just messing around."

He hesitated, then moved closer.

"Think you could show me a few chords?"

I paused, my hand hovering over the fretboard. I didn't expect that. He'd never shown any interest in learning before—not that I knew of, anyway.

"Well, Kid, you used to come in my studio and bang the strings like a rock star—barely out of diapers," I said, half-smiling.

Ryan let out a small laugh, the tension easing just a little.

"Yeah, sure," I said after a beat, shifting Swampy slightly so he could see.

"Come here."

Ryan moved to sit beside me, and I placed the guitar in his

hands. It felt strange—teaching him something like this. But as I guided his fingers on the neck, the distance between us softened. A strange sensation rose in my chest, like my heart was refueling with joy.

The joy of a father who had lost his son, but found him *again*.

Weeks, months, years—just numbers. Time flies, but *love? Blood?*

That stays. *Forever.*

"You're pressing too hard," I said, adjusting his grip.

"Relax your wrist. Let the strings breathe."

Ryan exhaled through his nose, shaking his head with a crooked smile.

"Easier said than done."

86

ONE CHORD AT A TIME

E motions crept in, some from the past—uninvited, but *welcome.* Watching him fumble with the strings, it felt like yesterday.

It was one of those relaxed afternoons at home—a rare break between tours, when life slowed down just enough to let me breathe. My little boy was barely two, a tiny whirlwind of curiosity and wonder. The studio had always been my sanctuary —amps humming, polished wood under my fingertips, and the scent of patchouli incense drifting through the air, wrapping the room in a peaceful haze.

It was my lil' *zen gateway*—an open invitation to create.

The floor was a tangle of vintage pedals and cables, a mess only I could navigate. A few guitars stood on their stands, always within reach, waiting for the next spark.

I was sitting on the worn leather couch, fiddling with my Tele, trying to work out a riff that had been circling my head all morning. The door creaked open, and there he was—Junior, little Jesse, with his messy blond curls and wide, curious eyes, peeking into the room like he was stepping into a world both strange and fascinating, unsure if he truly belonged.

"Hey, buddy," I said, setting my guitar down beside me.

"What are you up to?"

He didn't answer—not with words, anyway. He toddled in, his little feet making soft thuds on the hardwood floor. His eyes were locked on the guitars, a mix of excitement and curiosity lighting up his face. I watched as he approached one of the stands, his tiny hands reaching out, fingers barely brushing the strings. He glanced back at me, as if seeking permission.

"Go ahead," I encouraged, smiling.

"Give it a try."

With a grin that could brighten the whole room, he wrapped his hands around the neck of the guitar, barely able to reach, and gave the strings a hearty bang. The resulting sound was more noise than music, a discordant jumble of tones, but to him, it was magic. He laughed, that pure, unfiltered laugh only kids have—the kind that makes you forget everything for a moment.

He banged the strings again, harder this time, the guitar wobbling slightly on the stand. I instinctively reached out to steady it, but I didn't stop him. Instead, I leaned back and watched, letting him explore.

"You like that, huh?" I said, chuckling.

He didn't react, too engrossed in his new discovery—my little rock star, hammering away like he was headlining the biggest stage in the world. For the next few minutes, he went from one guitar to the next, strumming wildly, creating his own chaotic symphony. And I let him. It wasn't about music; it was about curiosity, about that first spark of something new.

Watching him, I felt a pang of something I couldn't quite name—hope, maybe, or the quiet wish that someday he'd want to learn for real.

Eventually, he grew tired of his impromptu concert and waddled over to me, climbing onto the couch with the clumsy determination only toddlers have. He curled up against me, his head resting on my arm.

"Did you have fun?" I asked, brushing a curl from his forehead.

He nodded, his eyes already drooping with sleep. I sat there, holding him, the quiet settling back into the room. I didn't play any more that day. There was something about that moment that felt complete, like it didn't need anything else.

That was the last time he touched a guitar.

Or so I thought.

A sharp twang snapped me back to the present.

"Damn, how do you do that?" Ryan muttered, frustration clear in his voice as he struggled to make a clean sound.

"Easy, Kid. Baby steps."

"Easy for you." He banged on Swampy—just like he used to back then.

Same hands—just bigger now, older, and carrying the weight of the years we'd lost.

"Well, as we say—walk, don't run, Kid. You just gotta keep at it. Like learning how to walk."

The night stretched on, the road lulling the rest of the bus to sleep while Ryan kept at it, stubborn as ever.

And finally, I said, with hope in my voice,

"You'll get there, Kid. You'll get there. It just takes time."

Ryan exhaled, adjusting his posture.

"And if I fall?"

I met his eyes, steady.

"Then you get back up and do it again."

And here we were. In this tour bus. In the middle of nowhere. With no tension, no pressure—just a *father and son,* trying to find their way back.

Trying to build a new *home.*
Brick by brick.
Side by side.
One chord at a time.

87

OFF THE RECORD

As you know, the road doesn't wait. One day you're flat on your back in a hospital bed, wondering if you'll ever get up again. The next, you're back on a bus, rolling toward another city, another crowd, pretending you've got it all together. But pretending only gets you so far. And now, here I was, backstage, staring down another show, another night of trying to be the guy they expected.

Backstage—the green room—wasn't much. Just a few worn-out couches, a stack of water bottles, and a snack tray that had seen better days. The air was thick with the smell of sweat, stale coffee, and whatever cheap air freshener the venue had half-heartedly sprayed to cover it all up. Another stop in a blur of cities, faces, and shows that all started to blend together.

Most of the band had scattered after soundcheck—Steve probably buried in sheet music somewhere, Billy Ray out back smoking, and Sticks... well, who knew where he'd wandered off to—hopefully out of trouble. That left me and Ryan sitting in a corner, both nursing bottles of water.

Mine, well... might be filled with beer.

While it wasn't exactly quiet—techs were still tweaking levels, fine-tuning the drums, and moving gear—the silence between us lingered. Not awkward anymore. Not uncomfortable. Not easy. Just there, waiting for one of us to break it.

After everything—the revelations, my trip to the ER, the rehearsals, and the tour kicking off—it felt like we were circling something neither of us knew how to say.

Ryan broke the silence first, his voice low.

"You ever get tired of it?"

I glanced at him, one eyebrow raised.

"Tired of what?"

"This." He gestured vaguely around us.

"The constant moving, the shows, being... on."

I took a sip, weighing his question for a moment.

"Yeah. All the time."

I set the bottle down, tapping my fingers against my knee.

"But it's what I do. What I've always done. And I have to admit, it took me a minute to get back at it, after all those years off the road. But you know how it is, Kid—you never forget how to ride."

Ryan nodded slowly, turning that over in his head.

"Still... I didn't think you'd actually do it."

"Yeah, well... neither did I," I snorted.

He smirked.

"So what changed?"

I exhaled, rolling the beer between my hands.

"Guess I got tired of arguing with you, Kid."

"That easy, huh?" he said, chuckling.

"Nah. Just figured if I was gonna get dragged back into this circus, might as well be on my own damn terms," I shrugged.

I leaned back, my fingers idly tracing the edge of the bottle.

"And maybe... finding Swampy pulled me back—slowly, but

tighter and tighter—like a lasso roping in a wild horse. Back from my solitude. Back to the music. Back to who I really was."

He studied me for a second, and in a very Ryan way, he smirked.

"And here I thought you were some cowboy philosopher out on that ranch."

"Yeah, well, turns out cows don't clap."

That got a real laugh out of him—short, but genuine. I couldn't help but think that *sarcasm* might just run in the *family.*

But still, I could tell he wasn't done yet. He rubbed the back of his neck, a nervous habit I'd started to notice.

"But seriously, I don't know. This whole thing. You, the band, the tour—it's not what I expected."

I gave him a doubtful look.

"What did you expect?"

Ryan looked down, his eyes drifting toward the floor.

"I don't know. Something more... polished, maybe. Less... human."

That caught me off guard.

"Huh... Less human?"

He hesitated, then exhaled sharply, like he was wrestling with something.

"I guess... growing up, my mom talked about you. A lot. The shows, the music, how she used to be on stage with you. She made it sound legendary—like you were larger than life. So, yeah, I listened to the albums, dug up old videos. To me, you weren't just some musician. You were the guy on the album covers. The legend people talked about. Like a real-life superhero."

He gave a short laugh, almost to himself.

"Maybe, unconsciously, I wanted my dad—the one who raised me —to be more like you. Or maybe she wanted me to see you that way. Maybe it was guilt. Or regret. Or just another way to keep you in her story." He lifted his hands, palms upward in a helpless shrug.

"Who knows... Anyway..."

He paused, searching for the right words, his jaw tightening.

"But now..." He exhaled.

"Now, you're just a guy. A normal guy. A guy who gets tired, screws up, and drinks too much."

I let out a slow breath, feeling that one land.

"So what? You saying I'm a disappointment?"

Ryan shifted, his shoulders stiff.

"No." His voice was quieter now.

"Just... different."

I let that sit for a moment, the weight of it settling in.

"Never meet your hero, I guess," he said with a small, dry chuckle.

I sighed, shaking my head.

"Yeah, well, legends are just people who got stuck in a fairy tale."

I raised my drink in a mock toast and nodded toward the cooler.

"Come on, Kid. Grab a beer and let's enjoy the fun while it lasts."

He hesitated, then smirked as he grabbed a bottle.

"Off the record?"

I clinked mine against his.

"Off the record."

The door opened, and Sticks strolled in, twirling a drumstick in one hand and holding a bag of chips in the other.

"Hey, you two having a heart-to-heart?" he teased, grinning wide.

"Something like that," Ryan said, giving him a flat look.

Sticks plopped down in the nearest chair, tossing a chip into his mouth.

"Well, don't get too sentimental. We got a show to kill."

I rolled my eyes, but I couldn't help the small smile tugging at my lips. Maybe Ryan was right—maybe we weren't polished, or perfect, or anything close to larger than life.

But we were here, doing what we love, with the people we love.

And yeah, sometimes, we mess up, we screw up. Miss a note, sing out of tune. But isn't that *life?*

Nothing's perfect. No one's *perfect.*

But we try, and try again, pouring ourselves into it with everything we've got.

And yes, *off the record,*
we're all human, after all.

88

CEDAR GROVE STADIUM

Daunting, like the echo of the last chord ringing out through the empty expanse of the *Cedar Grove Stadium.*

We had just finished the soundcheck, but Swampy still vibrated as if we had a full house. I took a step toward the edge of the stage, scanning the rows of vacant seats that would soon be packed with bodies and voices, ready for the night ahead.

We'd been on the road for weeks now, crisscrossing the country in a whirlwind of music and miles. Dates kept getting added. Every venue packed to the rafters.

It wasn't just a tour—it was a *phenomenon,* fueled by word of mouth that seemed to grow louder with every city we played.

From New York to Nashville, Chicago to Austin, Los Angeles to Denver—hell, you name it, from east to west, state after state —the response had been overwhelming. People showed up in droves, filling theaters, arenas, even outdoor festivals. It was more than just a comeback—it felt like we were reclaiming something we'd all thought was lost.

The energy from the audience was like nothing I'd felt in years. They didn't just sing along; they lived every note, every word. From the slow ballads to the foot-stomping grooves, they were right there with us, cheering, clapping, crying.

Cedar Grove was the next stop, and tonight was already sold out, just like the rest. The stadium sat on the outskirts of St. Louis, tucked near a grove of trees that gave it a strangely tranquil vibe for such a big venue. The kind of place that felt intimate, even with thousands of seats stretching far and wide.

It wasn't sleek or flashy, but it had a timelessness to it—brickwork facades and steel arches that told you it had seen its fair share of legends. The retractable roof hung open above us, revealing a sky that was starting to darken, heavy clouds gathering in the distance. The crew kept one wary eye on the forecast, talking about the possibility of rain.

Being back with the Sweet Bandits, it felt good—no, it felt *right*. Steve was still at the keys, his hands dancing across them like the years hadn't touched him. Billy Ray held it down on bass, as steady and unflappable as ever. Sticks was a machine on the drums, his energy giving the band a tight, relentless rhythm.

And the new girl, C.C., on guitar and vocals, was finding her groove. She wasn't Kota—no one could play or sing like Kota. Kota was unique, irreplaceable—a genuine soul—but she had something else. Her voice carried grit and a polished rawness, powerful and full of heart. She pushed me—not just in playing, but in presence—forcing me to step up and meet her *fire*.

I lowered myself onto the stage, letting my legs dangle over the side. Swampy glowed softly in the dim light, her wood smooth and familiar under my hands. My fingers wandered across the strings, the sound blending with the rising whisper of the wind.

I glanced around the empty stadium, taking it all in. The air was charged, like the storm brewing on the horizon was waiting for its cue. The wind carried the humid smell of rain, mingling with the scent of fresh-cut grass and something else—*anticipation,* maybe.

I looked down at Swampy, the light catching her curves as if she had a life of her own. A cool breeze tugged at my shirt, sending a slight shiver through my entire body. And before I knew it, my thoughts drifted to Kota.

I sighed, running a hand along Swampy's neck.

"I still feel bad about what I did to her. She didn't deserve that. Not one bit. And I hate myself for it. It was fucking unfair, so fucking unfair!"

The thing about regrets. They lurk in the dark, waiting for the right moment to sneak back in—torturing you until you make peace with them.

89

LA VOIX DE SON MAÎTRE—HIS MASTER'S VOICE

The green room was still buzzing with the leftover energy of the show. Empty beer bottles clinked as someone cleaned up, and bursts of laughter spilled in from the hallway. I leaned back against the couch, letting the adrenaline settle. My fingers tapped a beat on my knee, still riding the high.

"That was incredible," I said, grinning.

"The crowd tonight—did you see them? They were on fire! I mean, this tour's been great, but tonight? Tonight was something else."

Marie stood by the mirror, wiping at her makeup like she was scrubbing away more than foundation. Her reflection was a mask, no trace of the excitement I felt.

"Yeah," she said, her tone flat.

"I saw it all." She turned, and the look in her eyes wasn't what I expected. It was sharp, accusatory.

"Especially the way you were looking at Dakota."

"What?" I blinked, the adrenaline crashing in an instant.

"What are you talking about?"

Marie dropped the cloth onto the counter and crossed her arms.

"Don't act like you don't know. The smiles. The little winks. The way she was all over you out there—getting closer and closer."

I shook my head, laughing nervously.

"Marie, come on. We were all smiling. It was a great show. Everyone was having fun—Kota included."

"Yeah, right. Fun," she snapped, her voice dripping with sarcasm.

"Sure, Jesse. Fun. That's what you think it was. But I saw what was really happening. You're so blind sometimes, it's almost embarrassing."

I frowned, my stomach twisting.

"What's that supposed to mean?"

She stepped closer, her arms still crossed tight.

"It means I'm a woman, Jesse. I see things you don't. And what I saw was Dakota playing her little game—smiling at you, giving you those looks, like I wasn't even there."

"Marie, seriously—"

"No, seriously, Jesse," she cut me off, her frustration rising with every word.

"You think I'm imagining this? That I don't know when another woman is trying to make a move? God, you're so clueless sometimes it's pathetic."

"Clueless? Marie, what the hell are you even talking about?" My voice was louder now, matching hers without meaning to.

She threw up her hands like I'd just confirmed everything she was saying.

"Of course you don't get it! You never do! Dakota's in love with you, Jesse. 'Sticks' told me himself. She said I'm in her way and that she'll do anything to get rid of me. Anything!"

"That's insane," I said, staring at her, stunned.

"Is it?" She arched an eyebrow, whispering like she was sharing a secret defense.

"You think you know her, but you don't. She's been waiting, Jesse. Watching. Just waiting for the right moment—for you to slip up—so she can take everything."

I ran a hand through my hair, trying to make sense of what she was saying.

"Marie, this is crazy. Kota's been nothing but professional—"

"Professional?" She shot back, eyes narrowing.

"You call flirting with you on stage professional? Smiling at you like that? Winking? Rubbing up against you? Do you see her doing that with the rest of the band? Wake up, Jesse! She's playing you. And don't pretend you didn't like it—it sure didn't seem to bother you."

"Marie, it's just stage moves. We're performing. No big deal," I scoffed.

"Plus, I didn't see her wink at me the way you—"

"You didn't see it? My ass!" she snapped.

"God, Jesse, you're so naïve it's disgusting. Or maybe you're just not that innocent—it's disgusting. She's been undermining me for weeks, stepping on my toes, pushing me aside, and you just stand there like it's nothing. Do you even care about me? About us?"

"Of course I do," I said, my voice breaking under the weight of her accusations.

"Then prove it," she said. She was calmer now, like she'd flipped a switch.

But the determination and coldness in her eyes was chilling.

"Fire her. Right now. Get her out of this band before she tears everything apart."

I took a step back, the words hitting me like a punch.

"Marie, you can't be serious—"

"Oh, I'm very serious." Her arms crossed again.

"I'm tired, Jesse. Tired of being disrespected. Tired of being treated

like I don't matter. So here's how it's going to be: either you fire her, or I'm gone. And if I walk out that door, you'll never see me again."

I froze. My throat tightened as the stage high collapsed into an excruciating downfall.

"Marie," I started, but nothing else would come out.

"Choose," she said, sounding like an angel, but couldn't hide the flames of triumph.

I didn't even realize how long I'd been standing there, frozen, until Marie's voice cut through the haze.

"Well?" she said, impatient, tapping her fingers against her elbow.

"What are you waiting for, Jesse?"

I was speechless, almost dizzy. My head spun, like the withdrawal was in full force. It felt like she'd planted a knife in my heart.

Bleeding. Bleeding over something I knew was wrong, *unfair.* And yet, I stood there, motionless—just a *puppet,* waiting for her to pull the strings.

The door creaked open, and Kota stepped inside, her guitar in hand.

"Hey, great show!" she said, still buzzing.

Then she caught our faces and hesitated.

"Huh... everything's okay here?"

Marie didn't even look at her. She just stared at me, like she was using some unseen force, daring me to make my move.

"Kota," I said, my voice cracking. I cleared my throat, tried again.

"Look, uh... we need to talk."

She blinked, a bit confused.

"Huh... okay."

I glanced at Marie, then back at Kota. My palms were slick with sweat.

"It's... huh... it's not working out anymore," I said, the words tumbling out like broken glass.

"We think...I mean, I think it's best if you... step away from the band."

Kota looked stunned, caught between shock and disbelief.

"Excuse me? What?"

"It's just—there's been tension," I stammered, hating how it sounded even as I said it.

"And I think... maybe it's better for everyone if we part ways now before things get worse."

"Tension?" she repeated, surprised.

"What tension? Jesse, what the hell are you talking about?"

I caught the flicker of Marie's smirk at the edge of my sight. I couldn't look at her. I couldn't look at Kota either.

"It's not personal," I said weakly, fully aware of how shallow it sounded.

"You're incredibly talented, Kota. You'll... you'll be fine. It's just... you know, creative divergences. That's all."

Her laugh was sharp, bitter.

"Not personal? Are you kidding me? After everything we've worked on? After all we've shared? After I put my whole heart into this band and the music? Your music! Fully committed, always there for you, the guys. Like musketeers. One for all, all for one. Remember? And it's not personal?"

I tried to respond, but she held up a hand to stop me.

"No, don't. I know what this is."

She looked at Marie for a second, then back at me.

Like she saw the truth. The real truth. *Crystal clear*—like a reflection in an enchanted mirror that only reveals cruel honesty.

"You're so blind, Jesse. You really don't see it, do you?"

I opened my mouth, but no words came.

She stepped closer, aiming gently, but her arrow went

straight to the heart of the target, precise and cutting right through it—like she was some kind of *Robin Hood.*

"*As upset as I am right now, I feel more for you than for me. I'll have you in my prayers, Jesse. She's got you completely brainwashed. She owns you. She's the master, you're the slave.*"

My stomach twisted as her words sank in. Kota shook her head, grabbed her stuff, and slung her guitar gigbag over her shoulder.

She threw the final punch, though I was already K.O., standing.

"*Good luck, Jesse. You're going to need it.*"

She turned and walked out, the door clicking shut behind her. The room became a tomb—like someone had just drawn their last breath.

Marie let out a long, exaggerated sigh.

"*Good job,*" she said, her voice smooth and condescending, like she was praising a dog, patting me on the back.

Then, in a grandiose gesture, she gave me a kiss—like a *reward*—spun on her heel, and exited like royalty, leaving me there, alone, waiting for my orders and my next *treat.*

Just like that old commercial—the dog sitting in front of the gramophone, listening, obedient.

The French tagline said it all:

La Voix de Son Maître—His Master's Voice.

And I was the *dog.*

90

BEHIND THE CURTAIN

Hiding. Yep. That night, right before going on stage, I was nowhere to be found. I was hiding like a damn *coward!* My heart was pounding so hard it felt like it might break through my chest. My hands were clammy, and every breath I tried to take barely filled my lungs. The flashback and the scene from this afternoon still resonated in my head, spinning like a broken record.

"Good job," she said—and it triggered everything else.

"You're such a loser."

"You're not good enough."

"You're stupid."

All the gaslighting. All the mental abuse for years. I felt like I had some sort of trauma—*PTSD* for sure—still trying to recover from such a toxic and manipulative evil mind—somehow called a *narcissist.*

I clutched Swampy, trying to steady my breathing, but it wasn't working. The walls felt like they were closing in, and the buzz of the crowd on the other side of the backdrop only made it worse. Right now, I was hiding backstage, paralyzed by stage fright, feeling unworthy of this successful comeback and the overwhelming love from the fans.

Lost in my thoughts, I suddenly heard someone yell,

"I found him!" It was C.C.—the new girl replacing Kota.

I never really got over that. It was so unfair to fire her. I should've stood up to Marie. I shouldn't have let her use me to do her dirty work.

Where was my *dignity?* My *integrity?* My *core values?*

I hated myself for what I'd done. That wasn't me. And Kota... she had always been so devoted, loyal, respectful, and talented. She never did anything wrong. A genuine sweetheart. But maybe that's exactly why Marie didn't like her. Jealousy. Insecurities. She had turned me into some kind of puppet.

Then I heard C.C.'s voice again, closer this time.

"Jesse, are you okay? Everyone is looking for you, the fans are waiting, and we're running late."

I tried to speak, but the words caught in my throat. I was so tense, my breath shallow.

I wasn't sure I could do it—I wasn't sure I could face them.

C.C. stepped forward, concerned. She didn't rush me. She just stood there for a moment, like she understood exactly what I was feeling. Then, without a word, she reached out and took my hand—like a lost little kid needing a guide—and squeezed it gently.

"Jesse, you've been through hell and back, and somehow, you're still here. You didn't come this far to let fear win now." Her tone softened as she took a step closer.

"You're the reason I'm here. You're the reason I chased my dreams in music... in life. And you're the reason so many of us believe that anything is possible."

I glanced up, my breath still shallow, heart racing. She wasn't just saying it—she meant it.

"You, the Bandits, Ryan, the fans, friends—we're all a big family, Jesse. We're here because of you. We're here to celebrate our love for the music, for you, and for each other. Nobody's expecting perfection. They just want you."

She smiled—her eyes steady and calm.

"We're here to support you, and we've got your back. Always."

Before I could say anything, she gently pulled me forward, leading me out of my hiding spot. I didn't resist. It felt like she was grounding me, keeping me from slipping back into that dark place.

As we approached the rest of the band, C.C. called out, drawing their attention,

"Alright, Jesse's fine! Let's break a leg!"

The stage manager yelled over the noise, and waved us forward.

"Okay, hurry up, guys! They've been waiting long enough—you hear them? Now, showtime!"

As the crowd roared louder, suddenly I was there, standing just behind the curtain. I took one last shaky breath, feeling the weight lift just a little.

It was time—to be *live* and *alive.*

91

NOT JUST A WASHED-UP COWBOY

I finally had a moment to rest—at least for a few hours. The hotel room was quiet, a rare pause in the whirlwind of the tour. It had been a long day on the road, another stop in a journey that had blurred into a mess of cities and states. Traveling for weeks, I wasn't even sure where we were anymore—it got confusing sometimes, the way places blended together.

The tour had been incredible—tiring, but full of surprises. The response from the fans, both old and new, had been overwhelming, with each venue filling up more than the last. Having Ryan on the bus sometimes had helped too, in ways I didn't expect. Slowly, we were building something—something real. *A second chance.* A new bond. And Swampy... she was at the heart of it all.

And right before I was about to call Emma to check on her and the ranch, the phone rang.

Its old-fashioned chime cut through the stillness. I frowned, startled. Nobody called the hotel unless it was important.

I picked it up, and before I could even say hello, Ryan's voice came through, half-amused, half-annoyed.

"Hey, Jesse! Glad I caught you in the room. But jeez, not having a cell phone—like it's the '60s or something—really doesn't help, man. Took me forever to track you down. Anyway, just checking on my favorite washed-up cowboy."

"I'm fine, thanks." I leaned back against the headboard, already bracing for whatever whirlwind he was about to throw at me.

"So what else, Kid? I was about to call Emma and crash."

"Are you sitting down?"

His voice practically buzzing with excitement.

"Yeah, why?"

"You're not gonna believe this," he said, barely pausing for breath.

"I just got off the phone with Rory at Skytown. And she's over the moon—like, screaming into the phone. She said you got nominated twice at the Goldies, 'From Paris to Texas' is nominated for Best Album of the Year. And—wait for it—your song 'Number One' is up for Best Song of the Year."

I sat up straight, the words hitting me like a thunderclap.

"What?"

"You heard me." Ryan's laugh was light, almost giddy.

"Two big nominations. Rory wanted to call you herself, but I told her I wanted to be the one to break the news."

Wow. I was speechless. I'd never been nominated before, not even at the height of The Bandits' *success*. But this—damn—it felt like they were finally acknowledging my music, our work. Songs that had always been there but never got the attention they truly deserved, at least not from the industry.

"Holy shit, I don't even know what to say."

"You don't have to say anything," Ryan replied.

"You earned this, Jesse—all those years, all those songs... people are finally seeing it again."

A lump caught in my throat, but I swallowed it down.

"Well," I said, trying to keep my cool, *"guess I'll have to dust off the old suit, huh?"*

Ryan let out a spontaneous laugh.

"You better. And I'm not letting you skip this one."

I stretched out on the bed, staring at the ceiling, the weariness of the day settling deep in my bones.

"I won't. And thanks, Kid. For everything!"

"Always, Papa."

Wait, *what?* Just as I realized what he'd said, the line cut off.

I lay there, exhausted—physically and mentally—trying to process it all. My mind was racing, thoughts tumbling over each other at full speed. *Wow.* Two nominations at the *Golden Awards.* After everything—after all the losses, the wasted years, the doubts, the resignation, the sacrifices—this wasn't just another trophy. It was recognition. The pinnacle of success in the music world.

I guess I was finally where I was always meant to be.

And not just a *washed-up cowboy.*

I couldn't wait to tell Emma, but that would have to wait until morning. Right now, my body was calling for a reset—a good night's sleep and full recovery.

I glanced over at Swampy's case across the room and shook my head, a smile tugging at the corner of my mouth.

"Guess you're still pulling strings, huh?"

92

A NIGHT TO REMEMBER

S tepping out of the makeup room, Emma and I left the door swinging shut behind us. I'd asked her to join me for these last few iconic dates—first, the legendary *Blue Ridge Hall* in Nashville, tonight here at *Rockwood Canyon,* which was being broadcast live on *Heartland TV,* and finally, the *Desert Coach Festival.* She'd managed to find someone trustworthy to watch the ranch for a week, freeing her to be part of this journey. Having her by my side felt comforting, even if I hadn't fully admitted it yet. At least to her.

I'd never been a fan of all the prepping and polishing, but tonight was televised and, apparently, it came with the territory. The rest of the Bandits were already getting ready on stage, probably tuning up or shaking off their nerves. Emma had stayed with me through it, keeping me calm—or at least trying to—as the makeup artist fussed and brushed, ensuring I looked camera-ready.

As we walked down the narrow hallway toward the waiting

area, the backstage was pulsing with precise, military-like efficiency. Operators maneuvered cameras, sound techs adjusted microphones, and stagehands guided acts on and off stage with split-second timing. The space was tight, filled with focused faces and quick, controlled movements, creating an environment that felt less chaotic and more like a carefully choreographed operation.

Around us, the venue's atmosphere seeped through the walls, the audience's anticipation building steadily as we approached. The precise, tightly orchestrated backstage activity made it tough to concentrate, but I forced myself to stay focused on the stage ahead, tuning out the distractions. It wasn't easy, but I kept my eyes straight ahead—until a voice cut through the commotion and stopped us.

"Jesse?"

I turned toward the sound, a woman standing a few feet away, smiling warmly.

"Just wanted to wish you good luck for the show. I saw you were on the roster."

"Thanks," I said instinctively, not fully registering her face. Emma stood beside me, watching the exchange curiously. Then something clicked in my head. My eyes narrowed slightly, and I tilted my head.

"Wait... Kota?"

She laughed and nodded.

"Yeah, it's me."

I blinked, stunned for a moment.

"Wow. Kota, I... I almost didn't recognize you."

It took a second to sink in. Dakota Jones, standing right here looking like she hadn't aged a day. She still had that effortless elegance, the kind of classy Southern belle beauty that turned heads wherever she went and could light up any room she walked into.

"Well, it's been a while," she said with a big grin.

"Anyway, I didn't want to keep you—I just wanted to say hi and wish you luck."

"No, no, wait. Don't go," I said quickly, the shock wearing off.

And just like that, we were face-to-face, the years between us disappearing. Before I could think too much, I found myself saying,

"Kota look, what happened back then... I just want to say, I'm..."

I hesitated, the words catching in my throat.

"Sorry?" she said, finishing my sentence.

"Yeah, sorry," I replied, relieved and awkward, all at once.

"Truly."

"That's okay, Jesse. I forgave you years ago," she said with a calm smile.

"I know it wasn't the 'real' you. We tried to warn you about her, but you couldn't listen." She shrugged, her tone more understanding than accusatory.

"Turned out to be a blessing for me, though. Being kicked out of the band pushed me to find my own voice and career. Honestly, I'd like to thank you for that. I've been able to achieve my dreams—and then some."

I blinked, speechless for a moment.

"Well... that's great, Kota. I'm really happy for you."

"And by the way," she added, her grin turning mischievous,

"that new girl—she's a keeper, Jesse. Don't screw it up this time."

She winked.

"Okay?"

I froze. *New girl?* Was she talking about *C.C.?* Or *Emma?*

"She's really talented, and she's got a great voice," Kota clarified.

Ah, okay. *C.C.* That makes sense.

"Well, I'm glad you think so," I said.

"Hey, why don't you join us for the last tune? Jam like old times— the guys would love to see you, and the fans would go crazy."

Her eyebrows lifted in surprise.

"Yeah, sure. Why not? That'd be cool."

"Awesome," I said, feeling both excited and relieved.

"We'll figure something out."

"Sounds good," she said, waving as she walked off.

"See you out there."

Standing at the side of the stage, Swampy in my hands, I was waiting for my cue. The Bandits were set—locked in, focused, waiting for the downbeat. Ready to rock.

The show's host stepped up to the mic, his voice booming.

"Thank you, Nashville! What a fabulous audience we have tonight here at Blue Ridge Hall—and we're live on Heartland TV!"

He paused as the crowd erupted.

"Now, coming to you from Paris, Texas—or maybe Texas via Paris, France—Goldie Award-nominated, the legendary Frenchy— and the Sweet Bandits!"

The hall roared to life, applause echoing everywhere.

That was my cue...

And as we were still playing—an hour or so into the show— it was finally about time. The moment I'd waited for so long: a reunion, a chance to make peace with the past.

"Y'all, tonight is very special—something I thought would never happen again," I said, sensing the cameras zooming in, capturing every word, every expression. The murmurs of curiosity quickly turned to cheers as I continued.

"We've got a little surprise for you. It's gonna take us all on a trip down memory lane."

I stepped back, gesturing toward the wings.

"Ladies and gentlemen, the one and only, the original Sweet Bandit herself... Miss Dakota Jones!"

The audience went wild, shouting, whistling, and clapping as Kota walked onto the stage, her guitar slung over her shoulder. I glanced back at the guys—Steve's jaw was practically on the floor, Sticks looked like someone had just been hit by a brick, and Billy Ray stood frozen, wide-eyed, like he'd just seen a *ghost.*

Then, grinning wide, I said,

"Alright, boys, let's give 'em a night to remember."

DESERT COACH FESTIVAL

Beneath the scorching sun, the desert stretched out endlessly, a sea of gold and burnt orange. Indian Wells shimmered in the distance, a mirage of palm trees and white-washed resorts nestled against the rugged San Jacinto Mountains. The air smelled of dust and heat, tinged with the faint sweetness of blooming cacti. It was the kind of place that made you feel small, a speck in the vast, timeless expanse of the desert.

Sprawling across miles, the Desert Coach Festival grounds formed a labyrinth of stages, tents, and bustling crowds. Tens of thousands of fans swarmed the festival, their voices blending into a constant roar that echoed across the valley. The energy was electric—a living, breathing pulse that thrummed through the air.

Backstage, it was another world entirely—a chaotic mix of artists, managers, and crew moving with purpose, yet somehow managing to stay cool under the scorching sun. I spotted familiar faces here and there, nodding in recognition as I passed.

It had been a long time since I'd walked through an event like this, and the memories hit me in waves.

"Frenchy!"

A booming voice pulled me out of my thoughts. I turned to see an old friend—*Jackson Blake,* the country-rock star who had been a fixture on the charts for decades. His signature cowboy hat and leather vest were unmistakable, and his grin was as wide as the open plains.

"Jackson," I said, shaking his hand firmly.

"It's been a while."

"Too long," he said, clapping me on the shoulder.

"Man, it's great to see you back in the saddle. I've been following the buzz—your album's fantastic. And congrats on the Goldies nominations. Damn well deserved, ol' pal."

"Thanks, man." I said, a smile tugging at my lips.

"It's been a hell of a journey."

He nodded, his expression warm.

"You've earned it, Frenchy. Break a leg out there—I'll be watching."

Before I could respond, someone called his name from across the backstage area. Jackson waved quickly, gave me an apologetic wink, and hurried off.

"Appreciate it," I said anyway, watching him vanish into the rush-hour-like swirl of people moving in every direction.

Then I took a moment to soak it all in. The weight of the past few years felt lighter here, surrounded by the familiar vibe and the promise of music. Taking a deep breath, I stepped onto the stage.

From there, the crowd looked like a living ocean, shifting and swaying as the sun dipped low, painting the sky in hues of pink and purple. The Bandits were already in position, ready to roll, their instruments gleaming under the stage lights. I adjusted Swampy's strap and walked to the mic, the roar of the crowd washing over me like a tidal wave.

"Desert Coach!"

I yelled into the mic, my voice echoing across the massive audience.

"Looks like you're on fire tonight—the heat is on!"

I laughed, pausing briefly to take it all in—the applause energizing every nerve in my body. Sticks counted us in.

Showtime!

The set flew by in a blur of lights, rhythm, and sound, each song building effortlessly into the next. The audience stayed right with us, dancing, cheering, singing every word. I lost myself completely, letting Swampy take the lead, connected deeply with the band, and reveling in the overwhelming joy of performing again. Before I knew it, we'd reached the end of the show.

I wiped the sweat from my forehead, my shirt drenched, and took a quick drink of water from the side of the stage.

Meanwhile, the crowd kept chanting, louder and louder:

"Frenchy! Frenchy! Frenchy!"

Grinning, I walked back to center stage and grabbed the mic.

"Well, this is it—our last stop on the tour. You've been incredible, every single one of you. Thank you so much."

I glanced at the Bandits, sharing a nod and a smile, then turned back toward the sea of faces.

"But we've got one more. This one's for everyone who's been with us through thick and thin. You've made this song what it is—and now it's even nominated at the Goldies. So, from the bottom of our hearts, here's to you—because you're our 'Number One.'"

The opening chords rang out, clear and resonant, cutting through the desert air like a call to arms. As I played, I felt something different—like Swampy was feeding off the desert's energy.

The sound was crisp, almost too perfect, each note carrying farther than it should, resonating beyond the crowd and into the vast emptiness of the open sky. The crowd erupted, their voices rising in unison as the melody took hold. It was magic—the kind of moment that reminded me why I'd started playing in the first place.

As the song built, twilight settled in, stars flickering softly above us. Swampy came alive in my hands, each note weaving effortlessly through the band's groove.

By the final chorus, the massive audience had joined in, singing along, blending into one powerful choir—a communion of souls that echoed far beyond the festival, reaching into the endless night.

When the last note faded, I stepped back to the mic, the applause crashing over us like thunder. I tipped my hat, my chest heaving as I caught my breath.

"Thank you, Desert Coach. You've been unforgettable. We love you. Goodnight!"

The Bandits and I stood together, basking in the moment as the stage lights dimmed. It wasn't just another show—it was a triumph, a reminder that even after everything, music still had the power to heal, to connect, to bring us home.

As we packed up backstage, I caught Emma's eye. She smiled, giving me a small nod, a silent acknowledgment—like we'd just shared something sacred. I nodded back, feeling the significance of it all. Emma wasn't usually one for life on the road, but this was different. The Desert Coach Festival, a huge event way beyond just music, felt like a *pilgrimage*. People came from all around the country, even the world, to be part of it. And having her here meant so much to me.

The tour was over, but the journey *wasn't*.

Next stop—Los Angeles, and the *Goldies*. But first, *home*.

Home to regroup, breathe, and recover. It had been a long

tour, and I needed time to find my footing before stepping into the bright lights of what was coming next.

94

RISING TO THE TOP

Relief washed over me as I stepped onto the land, finally home. After weeks of crowds, noise, and endless miles, the stillness felt almost unreal—a deep calm that wrapped itself around you, sinking into your bones. Warm Texas air drifted lazily over the ranch, carrying familiar scents—dust, mesquite, sagebrush. On the horizon, the sun slipped lower, painting the landscape in shades of amber and rust.

Emma had joined me for the last couple of tour dates, steady and reassuring as always. But right now, I needed room to breathe. Time to clear my head. It had been way too long since *Buck* and I had taken off alone.

I saddled him slowly near the old corral, beneath the broad shadow of the cottonwood tree, my hands working by instinct, leather and buckles sliding into place as I felt Buck's restless energy beneath my fingers. He nudged me impatiently, as if to say, It's about time. I swung into the saddle, feeling every tired muscle protest, then gradually relax as we settled into an easy rhythm.

Soon, the only sound was the steady drumbeat of Buck's hooves on packed earth, blending with whispers of wind through dry brush. A hawk called from somewhere far off, its cry slicing through the silence like a distant memory. Moments later, we were heading into the open desert.

Out here, there was nothing but me, Buck, and a thousand tangled thoughts.

The tour had been unreal. Packed houses every night, the album kept breaking sales records, whispers of awards. Old fans had returned, new ones discovered me for the first time—it was everything I'd stopped believing could happen again. It's all great.

No—it's *incredible*. And I'm *grateful*.

Yet underneath the triumph was an unease—a suspicion I couldn't shake: that Swampy was the source of it all, her mysterious power.

That *je ne sais quoi*—that magic she carries. I don't just play her—she plays me. Every time I touch her, it's like she's leading, and I'm just along for the ride.

The way she seemed to take control, guiding my fingers, my music. Was it even me they *loved*?

Or was it *her*?

And what about *me*?

Then there was Ryan. I was thrilled to have my boy back in my life. *Thrilled.*

A true gift, but twenty-something years don't just disappear with a handshake and a few good times. And no matter what I do, I can't go back and relive those moments. They're gone. I'd missed everything—his triumphs, failures, loves and losses. His entire childhood had slipped by without me. That was a wound no quick reunion could heal. And that's a hard truth to live with.

And Emma... Emma... always there, never demanding, giving endlessly.

Why was she here?

What kept her beside me?

What does she see in me?

Sure, I felt something—an attraction, a connection—but after so long alone, imagining anything more felt impossible. Well, the company is great—but the toll is pricey. And man, I'd tried it before—damn, I tried—but it ended pretty badly. No more money left in the heart bank... hell, I didn't spend it all—I got fucking robbed.

Now it's too late for me to have the kind of family I dreamed of. The one I thought I'd build. That vision had slipped away— just a mirage in the desert.

Or maybe I'm just too old for all of it.

Come on...

I've seen the rise, the fall... and now, I'm rising to the top again.

So why now?

Why?

Why can't I just enjoy what's *here*?

What's right in front of me?

95

THE GOLDEN AWARDS CEREMONY

At last, here we were, right in front of *The Paramount Theater,* home of the *Golden Awards,* on *Hollywood Boulevard*—the end of a long journey, or maybe just a new beginning. Either way, it had been a hell of a ride.

It was one of those *California* nights, when the stars above seemed to bow to those below. *Avenue of the Stars* shimmered nearby, a reminder of the dreams this city was built on, and high above, the iconic Hollywood sign stood proudly atop the hills— a *cinematic* backdrop to it all. A moment when enchantments felt tangible, the atmosphere charged with possibility—a night where anything could happen.

The evening was warm and calm, as if the universe itself had decided to pause for an instant. It had been sunny all day, and while the calendar said January, you wouldn't know it here in *Los Angeles.* Winter in California wasn't like winter anywhere else—well, usually. There was a quiet energy in the air, an anticipation that seemed to mirror my own.

Turns out, I didn't have much time to recharge and regroup

after the tour—just a few weeks before already gearing up for this big event.

Funny to think it all started over a year ago though—Thanksgiving, me, Buck, a hangover, and an old beat-up guitar half-buried in a swamp.

But this past *Thanksgiving?* First one in years I didn't spend alone. Emma and Ryan were there. Swampy too, of course. That table felt a little less empty this time.

We all arrived together at the ceremony—my first time at something like this. The red carpet, camera flashes, celebrities everywhere, a sea of glamorous people dressed to the nines—it was overwhelming in a way I hadn't expected. Voices shouted my name, reporters called questions, and flashes burst from every direction, making me blink. Adrenaline surged through me, mixing with disbelief. I tried to soak it all in—the laughter, the murmurs of anticipation, the chatter of a hundred overlapping conversations. It felt surreal, standing among legends, faces I'd seen only on TV or magazine covers.

But soon enough, we were inside, finding our seats. There we were, all in the same row: Ryan, Emma, Rory, and the Bandits.

My family. My *people.*

I'd been nominated twice—*Best Album of the Year and Best Song of the Year.* To even hear my name among the other nominees felt surreal. It was the kind of recognition I'd long stopped dreaming about, but here I was, back in the game. And not just back—I was in the running. It was almost too much to take in.

The ceremony moved quickly, or maybe it just felt that way. My mind kept drifting, thinking about everything it had taken to get here. The late nights in the studio. The fights, the doubts. The sheer grind of trying to put my life—and my music—back together. And now, here I was, waiting for them to call my name... or *not.*

As the evening moved along, each award brought its share of cheers, applause, and a few tearful speeches. I clapped politely when others won, but my hands were cold and my heart was racing. Nervous energy I used to feel before stepping on stage had settled into my chest, heavy and relentless. Ryan leaned over at one point, nudging me with his elbow.

"Relax, Jesse," he whispered with a smirk.

"You're not gonna die tonight."

I smiled weakly, but inside, I wasn't so sure. Winning or losing didn't feel like the real weight on my shoulders. It was just being here—being back after everything.

Finally, the moment came. One of the guest presenters leaned toward the microphone from behind the podium, holding an envelope that might as well have been the keys to a new life.

"The nominees for Song of the Year are..."

A voice-over rolled through the theater as names and titles flashed onscreen, along with a few brief live shots and promo stills for each nominee.

"'Number One,' by Frenchy and The Sweet Bandits!"

It was called along with the others. I barely heard the titles or the applause. My pulse thudded in my ears, drowning everything out. And then—

He broke the seal and opened the envelope.

"And the winner is..."

The guest host paused for what felt like an eternity.

"'Number One,' Frenchy and The Sweet Bandits!"

And then boom. The room erupted, but all I could hear was a loud whooshing in my head, like the air had been sucked out of the place. Ryan slapped me on the back, and Emma reached over to squeeze my arm. Rory was already on her feet, cheering louder than anyone else. I stood, legs shaky, and made my way to the stage.

As the stage lights flared overhead, I stepped into their glow and, for a moment, forgot what I was supposed to say. I took the award in my hands, its weight unfamiliar but satisfying.

"I... uh... wow."

The crowd chuckled, and I exhaled, finding my footing.

"Thank you. Thank you so much—this is... just... wow... uh, incredible. Surreal. Anyway, uh... good evening, y'all. It's such an honor to be here with you tonight. Uh, sorry—I'm still shocked. Never thought that would ever happen. So, um... okay, where do I start? You can tell I didn't prepare anything."

A few chuckles rippled through the audience—I guess they could tell I was winging it.

"Alright, so... here we go. I'd like to thank...

Everyone who believed in me—even when I didn't believe in myself.

Rory and everyone at Skytown—thank you for fighting for this album like it was your own.

To my band—past and present—Steve, Billy Ray, Danny, Kota, and C.C.... thank you for carrying the music with me, through every storm. Bandits for life.

Also thank you—

To Emma... for being my angel, my grounding force.

To Swampy... the soul of it all. For making my music alive.

And to my son, Ryan... for believing in me, even when I wasn't there to believe in him. This moment... this song... this one is very special. It's all because of you. And this... is for you too.

Love you, son. Love you all."

I glanced down at the award, swallowing hard, trying to keep it together.

"Oh—and one more thing. An old wise man once told me... Sometimes the treasures we thought we lost forever may resurface—unexpected—like they were never really gone. And time don't matter, 'cos like rivers to the sea, they always find their way back home, where

they belong. So... never lose hope. And keep the faith. 'Cos you're my number one."

That got a hell of an applause—loud, warm, thunderous. I guess they liked the old cowboy philosopher.

I let it wash over me for a second, then scanned the audience and found my row. Ryan was grinning ear to ear. Emma's eyes shimmered, and even Rory, usually all business and toughness, looked like she might get emotional. I stepped off the stage to more applause, my heart pounding like I'd just run a *marathon*.

Back at my seat, I barely had time to process the win before, a few minutes later, the next announcement came.

"And now, the moment you've all been waiting for... Here's the nominees for best Album of the Year."

Another list of names. Another blur of words. Our album. Our band. *Could it happen twice?*

Winning once felt impossible. Winning twice? That was unreal.

As the on-screen presentation ended, the host stepped forward, wireless mic in hand and a wide, excited grin on his face.

"And now, to present the most anticipated award of the night," he said, pausing just long enough to build suspense,

"Ladies and gentlemen, please welcome to the stage a true American icon—country-rock legend Jackson Blake!"

The crowd roared as Jackson Blake, all swagger and showmanship, strolled onto the stage, his signature cowboy hat catching the lights.

Approaching the podium mic, Jackson tipped his hat and grinned, holding the golden envelope in one hand with a little theatrical flair.

"Alright, y'all," he said, voice full of gravel and pride with that Southern drawl,

"this one means a hell of a lot to folks like me. It's a labor of love

and pain, full of life stories—raw and polished. This is the artist's crown jewel."

From front to back, the entire room held its breath.

"So, the Album of the Year goes to..."

He cracked the seal, slid the card out, and with a slow smile forming, announced:

"'From Paris to Texas,' by Frenchy and the Sweet Bandits!"

This time, I almost didn't move. Ryan had to push me to my feet. The applause hit like a California quake—louder, sharper, shaking me to my core, or maybe it was just my head spinning.

Winning once felt impossible. Winning *twice?* That was unreal.

I turned, motioning for the Bandits to join me—but nothing.

Time seemed to stall for a second, like the noise swallowed my gesture whole.

In the middle of the frenzy—people cheering, congratulating me, rushing me toward the stage—I caught Steve and Billy Ray's eyes. Just a quick look and a nod—like they were saying, *"This is your moment, Frenchy. Just go."*

And so I did.

I climbed the steps to the stage again, the award heavier this time—not in weight, but in meaning.

As I stood there, stunned, Jackson stepped forward, handed me the Goldie, and clapped me on the shoulder.

"Much deserved, brother."

I nodded, still in disbelief.

"Thanks, Jackson."

Back at the podium, I was trying to make sense of it all.

"Well, well. Wow. Two in one night...huh? Damn, man...If you told me this would happen, I'd have laughed and figured you were either stuck in the desert too long with no water—or hit the bar too hard thinking 'open' meant drink it dry."

That got a bigger laugh than I expected. Might throw a little stand-up routine on the next tour.

"*Well, gonna try to be short this time. Looking back, these past few months have been some of the wildest of my life. It all started on a Thanksgiving Day—with a guitar named Swampy. This album was a second chance. A new beginning. A shot at redemption. Full of scars, and doubts. A hell of a journey.*

But somehow... here we are. And I'm so very grateful. Like Jackson said, this labor of love and pain wasn't just about me—it was a team effort. So once again, from the bottom of my heart, thank you to everyone I mentioned earlier. This one's yours as much as it is mine. Thank you all, for believing in an old washed-up cowboy. And hey... if you're out there wondering if it's too late... it's not. Thank you."

As we were ushered to the side of the stage, the main host's voice rang out.

"*And now, let's take a little trip down memory lane.*"

The lights dimmed, and a hush settled over the room. Then, the massive screens above the stage flickered to life, rolling a montage of *Frenchy and The Sweet Bandits*—old tour footage, behind-the-scenes clips, sold-out shows from the past and present. Moments frozen in time, stitched together like a road map of everything that had led to this night. The *rise*. The *fall*. And now—the *rebirth*.

As the lights came back on and the screen faded to black, the host beamed as he returned to the center of the stage, announcing—

"*Well, we've heard from Frenchy twice tonight. So I think it's time we hear him with the Bandits and let the music do the talking. Ladies and gentlemen, please give it up for Frenchy and The Sweet Bandits.*"

96

THE CALLING

V for *victory,* or maybe a peace sign, my hands shot up as the applause erupted while I was stepping back. A tech handed me Swampy, gleaming under the stage lights, cutting through the haze. She was so damn beautiful tonight, like an old book you can't judge by the cover—worn, but full of stories waiting to be told, or *secrets* to be discovered.

The Bandits were already in position, waiting for me—and for Sticks to count us in. But something stirred inside me, something I couldn't quite explain.

We were supposed to play *Number One.* That unfinished song we'd thrown on the album as a bonus had blown up beyond expectation—hell, it had even just won *Song of the Year.* The show had arranged a gospel choir to back us up. Every potential winner had rehearsed a song leading up to the awards, just in case. Everything was mapped out, down to the second.

But as I stood there, guitar in hand, I couldn't shake the feeling. A weird, insistent pull. A voice in my head saying, Not this time.

Not this song.

And just like that, I turned to the band.

"We're doing 'Ride or Die.'"

Steve froze, eyes wide.

"What? Jesse, we can't—"

I cut him off.

"That's it, guys. 'Ride or Die.'"

No more second-guessing. No more playing by someone else's script.

Without waiting for a response, I slung Swampy across my shoulder, stepping forward as the spotlight blazed down. The roar of the crowd swelled around me, but all I could hear was my heartbeat, loud and steady.

I walked to the mic, gripping it tight.

"Alright, y'all," I said, as the room quieted.

"It's been a hell of a night... and one hell of a ride to get here. So, no more talkin'. This song says it all."

I took in the faces before me, letting the weight of the moment settle in.

"It's called 'Ride or Die.'"

Silence settled over the venue, thick with expectation. The choir stood in perfect formation, their bright robes catching the light. They were ready, just like we'd rehearsed, their arrangement perfectly tailored for *Number One*.

But now, they were shifting uneasily, exchanging uncertain glances. The choir leader looked surprised, eyes darting toward the wings—either at the producer or the event's music director —lost, searching for some kind of explanation. Behind me, I could feel the weight of their stares, their frantic *What the fuck is he doing?* energy practically radiating off them.

Steve gave me a hesitant shrug, his expression a mix of confusion and trust. The Bandits were with me—but just barely. I took a breath, steadying myself, and nodded to him.

No turning back *now.*

Finally, Sticks counted us in, his drum fill rolling in like distant thunder—bold, driving, inevitable.

The intro was big and powerful, yet carried a haunting groove. The start of a soulful road trip, en route to its destination. The band was locked in, and Swampy took the wheel, guiding us through notes and chords, filling the room with something almost mystical.

And just like that, the music and I were *one.*

Bare for everyone to see. *Ride or Die*—the story of my *life.*

Because sometimes, you don't get to choose the moment.

It chooses you.

And tonight, it was the right *calling*—at the right *time.*

> *"I hit the road with nothing but my dreams,*
> *Leaving behind a life that tore at the seams.*
> *I've been knocked down,*
> *but I won't stay on the ground—*
> *I'll keep on moving, until my purpose is found.*
> *I'll make it through the twists and turns,*
> *It's my lesson to learn.*
> *I'm a lone rider, on a dusty road,*
> *With nothing but my guitar and a heavy load.*
> *I won't stop 'til I feel alive,*
> *I'm gonna find my way home.*
> *I'll keep on going and seek the truth,*
> *I'll gamble my life—it's a win or lose.*
> *No matter how hard I try,*
> *It's a ride or die.*
> *I'm on my way, on a mission to survive,*
> *I don't know where I'm going,*
> *but I know where I've been.*
> *In the land of stories, where the tales are told,*

Lies the place where I've buried my own gold.
I'll face the wind and the pouring rain,
I'll take the hits and the pain.
I'm a lone rider, on a dusty road,
With nothing but my guitar and a heavy load.
I won't stop 'til I feel alive,
I'm gonna find my way home.
I'll keep on going and seek the truth,
I'll gamble my life—it's a win or lose.
No matter how hard I try,
It's a ride or die.
Across the plains, I found a sign, a guiding star
A buried name, left in the sand,
To get me through the gates of hell.
No turning back, I'm ready for the final stand
I'll keep on fighting until my soul is saved.
The fire still burns, but I remain,
It is my fate to earn.
I'm a lone rider, on a dusty road,
With nothing but my guitar and a heavy load.
I won't stop 'til I feel alive,
I'm gonna find my way home.
I'll keep on going and seek the truth,
I'll gamble my life—it's a win or lose.
No matter how hard I try,
It's a ride or die."

97

THE GRAND FINALE: SWAMPY'S LEGEND

Over the moon, I was—or maybe outer space, who knows where? As we were about to put an end to the song, I was riding so high I felt transported, like I'd stepped out of my own skin. It was like I wasn't even there anymore—just floating somewhere above the stage, watching it all unfold. I wasn't in control of my fingers, my hands. Swampy took over, pulling me deep into some kind of out-of-body trance. The wood was breathing, alive—like some ancient spirit had crawled out of the swamp and into the strings. Pulling the strings, turning me into a puppet again, losing control—but this time, it felt right.

Like that piece of moss-covered swamp ash wasn't just wood —it was alive. *Possessed. Breathing. Hungry.*

The band slid into a vamp, holding down the groove like an anchor, and I just let go. Soloing and improvising over it, shredding, tearing into licks, bends and runs I'd never played before —like the music was writing itself right there in the moment. It wasn't just a solo—it was a confession, a scream, a prayer, all wrapped in six strings. I played like my life depended on it, because maybe it did. It was *ride or die.*

The notes came faster, sharper, dirtier, like something breaking free after years locked in a cage. I didn't want to let it end—like if I stopped, the spell would shatter and I'd crash back to earth. The Bandits chased me, matching every twist and turn, like they knew this wasn't just music anymore. This was *exorcism.*

And then came the last lyrics of the chorus, like a final breath:

> "No matter how hard I try,
> It's a ride or die."

That was the cue. The Bandits slammed the last chord, and it hung there—buzzing in the air like smoke after a gunfight. My fingers trembled on Swampy's neck, sweat soaking my back, my pulse hammering so hard I thought it might knock me over.

And again, the applause hit like a damn wave, crashing over the stage, rolling through me, filling every empty corner I'd carried for years. They were standing—all of them—clapping, shouting, whistling.

I bowed, swallowing back everything that wanted to break loose inside me, and raised Swampy high in the air like a trophy.

The *real award.*

I had no idea how long I stood there, soaking it in, but eventually, I forced my feet to move. Backstage was a total blur—hands slapping my back, faces grinning at me like I'd just pulled off some impossible miracle, someone shoving a cold bottle of water into my hand. I couldn't even process the noise, but through all of it, two faces cut through the madness.

Ryan. Emma.

They were waiting just past the curtain—smiling, proud, grounded. Real.

I pushed through the crowd toward them, Swampy still tight in my grip. I held her up, brandishing her like some medieval sword. My voice was shot from the singing, but that didn't stop me.

"See? I told you guys," I said, holding Swampy up between us.

"This guitar's my Excalibur—fucking pure magic," I said, laughing, overwhelmed by the moment.

"It's my damn soul, a gift from above. It fucking saved me... it's Swampy."

Ryan kept clapping, his smile proud but knowing, like he'd been waiting for me to say that. But Emma stepped forward, soft and calm the way only she could be.

She placed her hand on my arm, grounding me the same way she did the first day she showed up at the ranch. Her touch was soft, but her eyes—damn, they held me in place like chains.

Then she leaned in, kissed my cheek, and said,

"Jesse, don't you see? It's not Swampy that's magic—it's you. It's your soul. It's been there all along. You just... forgot how to hear it."

I shook my head, took a step back, gripping Swampy like a damn life raft.

"No. That's bullshit, Emma. You weren't there. You didn't see what I was like without her. I was empty. I couldn't play a damn note—couldn't even pick up a guitar."

Before Emma could say another word, a slow, familiar drawl cut through the noise.

Billy Ray.

"She's right, Captain."

I turned, and there he was—leaning against the wall, arms crossed, hat tipped just enough to show his eyes.

"Ain't my place to preach, but Emma's got it. Swampy's special, no

doubt—but it ain't her soul that's been pourin' through them strings. That's all you, brother."

He took a step closer, slow and steady, like he was closing in on a *spooked horse.*

"*My granddaddy used to say—ain't no treasure worth a damn if you forget who buried it. And ain't no map gonna find your way home if you don't remember who drew it.*"

He glanced at Swampy, then back at me.

"*That old girl's just the shovel, Captain. You? You're the one who buried the gold in the first place.*"

Billy Ray's words hung in the air, but my mind was already running.

That old woman back in that tiny village in France, pressing her husband's guitar into my hands like it was some kind of torch being passed.

That Polaroid—the one that kid, Cole Stapleton, sent me months later, showing Swampy—or a hell of a twin—in his daddy's hands long before I ever found her—and that letter, calling me magic. *Calling us magic.*

Thanksgiving—the day I found her, half-buried in that swamp, a thin veil of mist rolling across the desert floor—like the earth itself was trying to hide her.

All of it—every piece—made me believe she was something more. Some kind of talisman. A bridge between my past and a past I didn't even know existed.

But none of those guitars made me who I was.

I brought the music to them—not the other way around.

Emma was *right.* It's just a tool—and a tool doesn't make the craftsman. The hammer don't make the blacksmith. The pen don't make the poet.

Deep down, I knew that all along. I just needed something to hold onto—some story to help me find the strength to reconnect with my first love, my only true *passion.*

Maybe that's why it took me so damn long to see the truth.

Maybe the only thing Swampy ever really did... was make me face *myself.*

I stared down at Swampy—weathered, scarred, carrying all my ghosts—and for the first time, I didn't see magic. No spells. No miracles. Just wood and wire. A damn good guitar — but not the reason I was still standing.

I looked at Emma—really looked at her—and the truth of it all hit me square in the chest.

"Maybe you're right," I whispered.

"Maybe it wasn't Swampy that saved me. She just... pointed me back to myself."

Emma smiled—and for the first time, I felt the shift. I smiled too.

She came closer, eyes locked on mine, and for a second, I thought she was gonna say something—something deep, something wise, something Emma. But she didn't.

She just kissed me. No warning. No asking. Just us—all the words we never said, all the nights she sat next to me when I was too broken to talk, all the times she held my arm a second longer than needed — all of it poured into that *kiss.*

When we finally pulled apart, I grinned, scratched my jaw, and said,

"Took you long enough, Angel."

Emma just laughed and gave me another kiss. No more words, no smart remarks—she was the *messenger,* delivering me the *good news.*

The noise of the backstage chaos faded around us, the echoes of the night still buzzing through all my muscles and bones. I glanced down at Swampy one last time, running a thumb over the worn swamp-ash wood, feeling every scar, every mile.

Yep, I've been through hell and back. Trapped in a maze where I thought *death* was the only escape.

'Cos see, in this other book?

It's called *The Devil Named Marie.*

And he didn't wear horns—just a big smile in public... and a knife behind your back.

In hell, I was left in limbo, on the battleground of psychological warfare. And when he and his demons thought I was dead, I somehow found—deep inside me—the courage and strength to survive.

Like a fucking cockroach after a *nuclear blast.*

And whoever you call them, they try to rewrite your story—and the hardest part is remembering it was yours to begin with.

The nonstop gaslighting. The mindfuck games. The brainwashing. The isolation. The *abuse.*

The manipulation by master psychological predators.

It can kill you. Literally *kill you*—one way or another.

And after all this, if you survive in this fucking blind and senseless modern society?

You don't get a fucking medal.

Nope.

You don't even get the recognition of being the true victim.

No, your only reward is to live with the trauma. The pain. The scars and the fears.

For the rest of your life—just hoping for the best.

But if you're reading this? You're still here. So don't let them write your ending.

And yeah, my journey really did feel never-ending—but somehow, like the *fucking cockroach,* I found the way. Swampy guiding me and Emma, welcoming me to the *final destination.*

A sacred place.

A place called *Redemption.*

I let out a breath I didn't know I was holding, shaking my head with a half-smile.

And half-talking to myself, I said,

"Damn. Guess the devil didn't steal my soul after all."

EPILOGUE

The pen rested in my hand, the last sentence still fresh on the page.

This is how it happened.

I leaned back in my chair, the notebook open on the desk in front of me. Outside, the ranch was alive with the sounds of a new kind of life—the laughter of Ryan's kids, the sweet hum of Emma singing to the horses, and the steady breeze carrying a hint of sagebrush.

Oh, and yep—you heard that right. I'm officially old now. Now it's *Grandpa Jesse.*

Turns out, not long after the Goldies, there was another ceremony—a little chapel a few miles away.

Ryan married his high school sweetheart.

And here we were—*Thanksgiving again.*

The same day I once rode out, bitter and lost, and stumbled upon Swampy in that impossible swamp. A day that started as just another reminder of everything I'd lost, and somehow became the day I started to find my way back.

In the end, I found my son, my soul, a renewed love, and success. And I was saved by an angel—one from a painting.

A hell of a trip... but worth every damn minute.

I also learned that sometimes the truth is hidden in plain sight, just waiting to be revealed. We just have to pay closer attention.

My gaze drifted to Swampy, resting on her stand beside me. I ran a hand over her worn body, tracing the grooves time had etched into the wood.

I still wonder how she ended up there, out of nowhere. What her story really was.

For a long time, it haunted me.

I tried to track down Cole Stapleton—the kid who seemed to be Swampy's first owner—hoping for answers. But no luck.

Maybe some mysteries aren't meant to be solved.

Or maybe... they're just waiting for the right time.

But Swampy's tale...well, like all the best legends, leaves room for wonder. They unleash our wild imaginations and remind us that the real magic comes from within.

And still, there's so much of my life I haven't told yet.

See, music has 12 notes in the tempered system—but maybe the 13th note is the key to unlocking those secrets.

Ryan's voice broke through my thoughts, calling from the porch, his kids tumbling around his legs, yelling something about pie.

"Hurry up, Papa! We're starving!"

I used to flinch every time he called me that.

Now? I wouldn't trade it for the *world*.

Standing there, I stretched as the sunlight warmed the room, and glanced back at my notebook.

This is my story. My road back to myself.

A chapter has been closed, and a new one has started.

As I stepped outside, I caught the laughter of my new family.

Emma waved from the barn, and Ryan's youngest was trying to wrangle a runaway chicken like it was the final round of a toddler rodeo.

Life moves on.

And somehow, I did too.

And yep, as we say—*shit happens.*

Call it fate, bad luck, or just the price of living.

But let me quote the Bandits on this:

> *"It's an American story, but made in France—*
> *The Seine's bittersweet, forever in my veins.*
> *I've packed my bags, said 'Au Revoir,' can't you see?*
> *Well, there it is, that's right: 'Oui, c'est la vie.'"*

FROM PARIS TO TEXAS:

SONGS FROM A GUITAR NAMED SWAMPY

Each song is a chapter of its own—capturing the emotions, memories, and moments that shaped the lives of *Frenchy and the Sweet Bandits*.
Presented in alphabetical order for easy reference, let these lyrics take you deeper into Jesse's journey.

All lyrics written by Emmanuel "U-Nam" Abiteboul

© 2024 Emmanuel "U-Nam" Abiteboul

Published by Music by Skytown Publishing (BMI), a division of Swampy Tales Entertainment

Used by permission of Music by Skytown Publishing

Baby's Got It Fo' Sure

I just woke up, someone's knocking at my door.
I got no sleep, thinking of you all night.
You just surprised me, bringing love and more—
No doubt, my baby's got it fo' sure.

You grab my hand, picking me up off the floor,
Taking me out to feel the sunshine.
You gave me all your heart, filled mine with joy—
There's no doubt, baby's got it fo' sure.

I just woke up, someone's knocking at my door.
I got no sleep, thinking of you all night.
You just surprised me, bringing love and more—
No doubt, my baby's got it fo' sure.

You grab my hand, picking me up off the floor,
Taking me out to feel the sunshine.
You gave me all your heart, filled mine with joy—
There's no doubt, baby's got it fo' sure.

From Paris to Texas

I left my heart in Paris, the city of romance.
Now I'm on a journey,
Taking chances with every glance.
Cali calls my name, land of dreams and fame—
With my trusty guitar, I'm staking my claim.

Cruising down the highways, new conquests ahead—
From the City of Lights to the Wild Wild West.
I'll pen my rhymes, flow with grace and finesse;
In this American trek, I'll find my address.

Tried my luck in Vegas, roamed from coast to coast.
I've been on the road, trying to find my zip code.
From Miami's beaches to Chicago's pride—
In every state,
I've been welcomed with arms open wide.

The Big Apple's hustle, New Orleans' charm.
Hotlanta, baby—oh, what a ride!
North, East, South, West—
Y'all made my heart truly blessed.
Yet, that lil' movie town is my Southern belle.

Woo ooh ho
Such a long way to go.
From Paris to Texas, yeah—
From Paris to Texas,
An urban cowboy with a rebel soul.

Woo ooh ho
I found my new home.

Sweet home, Paris, Texas, yeah—
Home sweet home, from Paris, France to Paris, Texas.

Well, I saddle up my Chevy, kick it into gear—
Heading to Music City, ridin' without fear.
With my boots on the pedals and my hat on tight,
I'm a rebel with a cause, gonna own this right.

Rollin' down the highway, dirt on the track—
I'm a firecracker spark, there's no turnin' back.
Got the spirit of a renegade, a heart of a steed;
In this concrete rodeo, I'm planted like a seed.

A modern-day cowboy, I'm wild and free.
I'll be rockin' these streets with a country decree.
From the neon lights to the starry sky,
I'm the urban legend—watch me fly high.

It's an American story, but made in France—
The Seine's bittersweet, forever in my veins.
I've packed my bags, said "Au revoir," can't you see?
Well, there it is, that's right: "Oui, c'est la vie."

Woo ooh ho
Such a long way to go.
From Paris to Texas, yeah—
From Paris to Texas,
An urban cowboy with a rebel soul.

Woo ooh ho
I found my new home.
Sweet home, Paris, Texas, yeah—
Home sweet home, from Paris, France to Paris, Texas.

Heart on the Line

In the still of the night, all by my lonesome,
Eagerly awaiting, like a heart back home.
Shadows sway, secrets in the air—
A story unfolds, a connection we share.

Now tell me, don't you feel the rush?
A fire so fine, is it more than a sign?

Call 911, keeping eyes on the prize.
In a whirl of thoughts, my heart's on the line.
In the mess of time, where our paths align,
Racing against the clock, with my heart on the line.
Woh-oh-oh, with my heart on the line.

Nowhere to run when love takes the lead.
In the twists of time, hand in hand we'll heed.
Trying to resist, it's like stopping rain
In the path of a storm, a wild terrain.

Can't deny it when fate shows us the sign.
Come on, let's uncover what's in store,
yours and mine.

Call 911, keeping eyes on the prize.
In a whirl of thoughts, my heart's on the line.
In the mess of time, where our paths align,
Racing against the clock, with my heart on the line.
Woh-oh-oh, with my heart on the line.
Woh-oh-oh, put my heart on the line.

Don't you see? It's like a hit and run—
Adrenaline's high, life's saver, love's begun.

So...
Call 911, keeping eyes on the prize.
In a whirl of thoughts, my heart's on the line.
In the mess of time, where our paths align,
Racing against the clock, with my heart on the line.

Call 911, keeping eyes on the prize.
In a whirl of thoughts, my heart's on the line.
In the mess of time, where our paths align,
Racing against the clock, with my heart on the line.

Woh-oh-oh, with my heart on the line.
Woh-oh-oh, put my heart on the line.
...with my heart on the line,
...put my heart on the line.

Husbands and Wives

It starts with a promise, simple and pure,
To love and to honor, to always endure.
Through seasons of joy, through trials we face,
We find in each other our safest place.

It's not just words; it's more than a line,
It's the strength we share, it's yours and mine.

Husbands and wives, a seal for life,
A vow we make to stand the test of time.
For better or worse, having each other's back,
Together we walk, until death do us part.

In sickness and health, in darkness and light,
We stand as one through the longest night.
A bond that's unbroken, through all we've known,
A love that we build, a family, a home.

We'll weather the years, with grace and pride,
With faith in our hearts, and love as our guide.
When silver and gold replace youth's fire,
We'll hold to the promise, to never tire.

Husbands and wives, a seal for life,
A vow we make to stand the test of time.
For better or worse, having each other's back,
Together we walk, until death do us part.

And here I stand, for all to see,

With trembling hands and a bended knee.
For all we are, for all we'll be—

Will you marry me?

Little Little Song

I might get tough, a little rough on the edges,
But that don't mean I won't break any wedges.
I've been through some things, I've seen some hard
times,
But I'll stand tall, I'd never lose my mind.

I might come off as a little bit wild,
But that's just my spirit, just my inner child.
As the rhythms take control, I can feel it deep inside—
Let me take you on a lifetime ride.

And that little little song that I sing for you
Is the only way I know to say those things to you.
It's the melody that speaks what words can't do,
In every note that I play, I'm just saying, "I love you."

I know I'm not perfect, but I'll always try
To be the one you need, to be your shining light.
I'll be your rock, your shelter, your safe haven too.
I'll be always there for you, no matter what you do.

I'll pour my heart out, in every line.
I'll sing it proud, I will sing it loud.
And I hope this tune stays with you for all time,
So you can feel my love when I'm not around.

And that little little song that I sing for you
Is the only way I know to say those things to you.
It's the melody that speaks what words can't do,
In every note that I play, I'm just saying, "I love you."

And that little little song that I sing for you
Is the only way I know to say those things to you.
It's the melody that speaks what words can't do,
In every note that I play, I'm just saying, "I love you."

And that little little song that I sing for you
Is the only way I know to say those things to you.
It's the melody that speaks what words can't do,
In every note that I play, I'm just saying, "I love you."

And that little little song that I sing for you
Is the only way I know to say those things to you.
It's the melody that speaks what words can't do,
In every note that I play, I'm just saying, "I love you."

I'm just saying, "I love you."

Never Let Go

Hey y'all, are you feeling?
Come on, boys and gals!
Let's get this party started,
Shake it down, bring it home.

Got a dream in my pocket,
Set to fly high like a rocket, never coming down.
You are not alone—
It's about time to prove them wrong.

No matter who you are, no matter where you're from,
Big city, little town,
You can shine bright in the crowd.

Take my hand into the night.
As we dance with the stars, we can touch the sky.
Sing, wo-oh ho wo-oh, wo-oh,
Close your eyes and let it go.

Free your mind, see what comes around,
And everything's going to be all right.
Wo-oh ho oh wo-oh,
Chase your dreams and never let go.

Can you feel it coming?
Let's celebrate tonight.
Let the music take you—
It's right there, take it home.

Keep on dancing with every move,

Break the chains, let loose and groove.
As we're going strong,
Let's sing our victory song.

No matter who you are, no matter where you're from,
Big city, little town,
You can shine bright in the crowd.

Take my hand into the night.
As we dance with the stars, we can touch the sky.
Sing, wo-oh ho wo-oh, wo-oh,
Close your eyes and let it go.

Free your mind, see what comes around,
And everything's going to be all right.
Wo-oh ho oh wo-oh,
Chase your dreams and never let go.

Close your eyes and let it go-oh-oh.
Chase your dreams and never let go.

Side to side, step in time,
Join the line and free your mind.
Clap your hands, stomp your feet, can you feel it?
Close your eyes and let it go.

Step in sync, in perfect rhyme,
Join the beat—it's your time to shine.
Raise your hands, touch the stars, you can reach it!
Chase your dreams and never let go.

Take my hand into the night.
As we dance with the stars, we can touch the sky.

Sing, wo-oh ho wo-oh, wo-oh,
Close your eyes and let it go.

Free your mind, see what comes around,
And everything's going to be all right.
Wo-oh ho oh wo-oh,
Chase your dreams and never let go.

Close your eyes and let it go.
Close your eyes and let it go-oh-oh.
Chase your dreams and never let go.

Carry on, sing along,
Take my hand, don't dance alone.
Count to three, and get ready—can you feel it?
Close your eyes and let it go.

Sing it loud, sing it proud,
Spin around, round and round.
Sky's the limit—just go for it!
Chase your dreams and never let go.

Step by step, build it up,
From nine to five, working hard.
Pushing through, break it up—you can reach it!
Close your eyes and let it go.

Hold on tight, don't let it slip,
Power up and feel the grip.
Feel the magic, let it flow—can you feel it?
Chase your dreams and never let go.

Number One (You're My)

I didn't see it coming,
when you had to go just for a while.
I felt something was wrong as I kissed you goodbye.
You didn't say why, but I saw it in your eyes—
Your heart was silently crying, crying deep inside.

That night, you were away, I cried all alone,
And I promised it won't happen again someday.
Even if we're apart, I can't bear that pain,
Through sunshine and rain, 'cos you're my...

(Number one)
#1 in my heart.
(Number one)
On my love's chart, it goes straight to the top.
(Number one)
There's no other way 'cos you're second to none.
And until I take my last breath,
you'll always be my number one,
Number one.

From the first time I met you, love took hold so deep—
Unconditional and rare, a bond spiritual, it seems.
Your innocence and kindness,
your positive life's embrace,
We grew and evolved together, each at our own pace.

We built tons of memories, sharing every little smile,
And on this trip by your side, we are going for miles.

(Number one)
#1 in my heart.
(Number one)
On my love's chart, it goes straight to the top.
(Number one)
There's no other way 'cos you're second to none.
And until I take my last breath,
you'll always be my number one.

(One)
(One)
Number one.
(One)
(Number one)
(One)
(One)
And until I take my last breath,
you'll always be my number one.

I vowed to never let you down.
Through sacrifices, I will fight.
We might be separated again,
but nothing to worry this time,
As we'll be looking forward to hold each other tight.

You're with me every second of the day.
You're my star, headliner, my number one.

(Number one)
#1 from the start.
(Number one)
There's no stopping it, it will stay at the top.

(Number one)
You're my pride, my joy, you're the only one.
And until I take my last breath,
you'll always be my number one.

(Number one)
#1 in my chart.
(Number one)
A love's ascension that peaks at the top.
(Number one)
You're my moon, my stars, you're my morning sun.
And until I take my last breath, you'll always be my
number one.

(Number one)
#1 in my heart.
(Number one)
On my love's chart, it goes straight to the top.
(Number one)
There's no other way 'cos you're second to none.
And until I take my last breath,
you'll always be my number one.

(Woh-oh)
(Woh-oh)
(Woh-oh)
Number one.
(Woh-oh)
(Woh-oh)
(One...)
(Woh-oh)
(Woh-oh)

(Woh-oh)
You'll always be my number one.
Number one.
You'll always be my number one.

Ride or Die

I hit the road with nothing but my dreams,
Leaving behind a life that tore at the seams.
I've been knocked down,
but I won't stay on the ground—
I'll keep on moving, until my purpose is found.

I'll make it through the twists and turns,
It's my lesson to learn.

I'm a lone rider, on a dusty road,
With nothing but my guitar and a heavy load.
I won't stop 'til I feel alive,
I'm gonna find my way home.
I'll keep on going and seek the truth,
I'll gamble my life—it's a win or lose.
No matter how hard I try,
It's a ride or die.

I'm on my way, on a mission to survive,
I don't know where I'm going,
but I know where I've been.
In the land of stories, where the tales are told,
Lies the place where I've buried my own gold.

I'll face the wind and the pouring rain,
I'll take the hits and the pain.

I'm a lone rider, on a dusty road,
With nothing but my guitar and a heavy load.
I won't stop 'til I feel alive,

I'm gonna find my way home.
I'll keep on going and seek the truth,
I'll gamble my life—it's a win or lose.
No matter how hard I try,
It's a ride or die.

Across the plains, I found a sign, a guiding star
A buried name, left in the sand,
To get me through the gates of hell.
No turning back, I'm ready for the final stand
I'll keep on fighting until my soul is saved.
The fire still burns, but I remain,
It is my fate to earn.

I'm a lone rider, on a dusty road,
With nothing but my guitar and a heavy load.
I won't stop 'til I feel alive,
I'm gonna find my way home.
I'll keep on going and seek the truth,
I'll gamble my life—it's a win or lose.
No matter how hard I try,
It's a ride or die.

Wild Cards + Smoking Guns

I thought I found my home
When you left me all alone.
It was just wild cards and smoking guns.
Your love was a big ol' lie,
Just playing me all this time.
It was all wild cards and smoking guns.

Once upon a time, I moved to the West,
My bag full of dreams of happiness and success.
My past was hunting me down,
I had to leave my old town,
Following the gold rush, searching for a new crush.

I found you so quickly, never been so lucky.
Felt like I finally beat the one-armed bandit.
I thought you were so sweet,
that you were the one for me,
But turned out to be really the good, the bad,
and the ugly!

I thought I found my home
When you left me all alone.
It was just wild cards and smoking guns.
Your love was a big ol' lie,
Just playing me all this time.
It was all wild cards and smoking guns.

Even with an ace up my sleeve,
There was no way to win.
Wild cards and smoking guns.

I heard the bells ringing, calling for my wedding—
In fact, a love funeral, right there in the making.
"Forever 'til I die," you said you'll have my back,
'Til one day, out of the blue, I was under attack.

I had to run, I had to hide in order to survive.
I had to keep on fighting to save my life and stay alive,
To save my life and stay alive...

I thought I found my home
When you left me all alone.
It was just wild cards and smoking guns.
Your love was a big ol' lie,
Just playing me all this time.
It was all wild cards and smoking guns.

Wild cards and smoking guns...
Wild cards and smoking guns...
Even with an ace up my sleeve,
There was no way to win.
Wild cards and smoking guns...

Dive Deeper Into the Experience

You've just finished the story—but the experience doesn't have to end here.

Now's the time to bring the lyrics to life.
Put music behind the words—and experience the songs the way Jesse did: raw, real, and full of soul.

This book was always meant to be more than just words on a page. In fact, the songs came first. The album **From Paris to Texas: Songs from A Guitar Named Swampy— An Original Soundtrack** was written and recorded before the book was even started.
Those melodies carried the weight of the story before a single word was written—emotions turned into music, scenes translated into sound.

Written and performed by **U-Nam + The Sweet Bandits** (the real-life band behind the name **Frenchy and The Sweet Bandits**) — blending country storytelling with rock, blues, and soul, each track gave voice to Jesse's journey—his struggles, his soul, his redemption.
This is where the music and the story become one.

Listen to the Music

Scan the QR code on the next page to access a dedicated page with all the links to stream the songs—whether they're already released or coming soon.
This page will always guide you to the music released under **U-Nam and the Sweet Bandits**.

Or simply search:
"U-Nam + The Sweet Bandits" on your favorite streaming platform.

Or visit:
www.u-nam.com/a-guitar-named-swampy

A Note from the Author

In the book, the band is called **Frenchy and The Sweet Bandits.** In real life, the music is released under **U-Nam + The Sweet Bandits.**
Two names. One experience. One story. One soul.

NOTE FROM THE AUTHOR

My success, my failures, my life—it was all meant to write this
book.
And just as maybe Swampy found Jesse... maybe this book
found me.

*"Sometimes the truth is hidden in plain sight; we just need to pay
closer attention. Not all secrets are buried—some are right in front of
us. But tell me... did you really read everything?"*

A quiet nod to Maurice Leblanc—who reminded us that the
most beautiful tricks are the ones you never see coming.

ABOUT THE AUTHOR

Born in Paris, France, in 1970, Emmanuel "U-Nam" Abiteboul has lived a life that reads like a novel—chasing his musical dreams across the Atlantic, moving to California in 2008, where he now holds dual citizenship. A Billboard #1 chart-topping artist, multi-platinum producer, multi-instrumentalist, designer, and now author, U-Nam's career has spanned continents, decades, and genres. Through it all, U-Nam has always believed that music and storytelling are two sides of the same coin.

Having worked with legends like Barry White, Kool & The Gang, George Benson, George Duke, and Marcus Miller — and with a career shaped by constant reinvention, multiple #1 best-seller albums, 9 Billboard-charting singles, Grammy considerations, and years spent touring the globe — U-Nam has built a reputation as a true musical force. His signature sound, blending funk, soul, jazz, and raw passion, earned him global recognition and a dedicated following.

Now, with his debut novel, *A Guitar Named Swampy,* U-Nam brings a lifetime of experiences to the page, turning his storytelling talents from music to words. Weaving his own journey into a powerful tale of music, loss, and redemption, the book also comes with an original soundtrack—performed by U-Nam + The Sweet Bandits—featuring the very songs from the story itself. Blending Country, Pop, Southern Rock, Blues, and R&B, the soundtrack is made up mostly of vocal tracks, bringing Jesse "Frenchy" Lawrence's world to life the way only music can.

When he's not creating, U-Nam can be found cheering for Paris Saint-Germain, or watching Spaghetti Westerns — especially the work of Sergio Leone, which inspired his lifelong love for the Wild West. He is also a proud father of two sons.

For more, visit: www.u-nam.com

MORE FROM U-NAM

Spanning over 20 years of music, here's a selective discography of **U-Nam**'s solo albums — the sound and stories that shaped his unique journey.

Selective Discography (Solo Albums Only)

- *The Past Builds the Future*
- *Back from the 80s*
- *Unanimity*
- *Weekend in LA - A Tribute to George Benson*
- *C'est Le Funk*
- *Surface Level*
- *The Essential Collection*
- *Future Love*
- *Sunshine of Mine*

Available on all major digital and streaming platforms.
For more info, visit: www.u-nam.com

The Story Isn't Over...

Jesse's legacy—and Ryan's journey—are just beginning.

"The most important things aren't the ones we chase after. Distractions make us deaf and blind to what truly matters. But some secrets refuse to be ignored. Not all Swamp's secrets have been unlocked—but the 13th note might be the key."

The 13th Note: A Guitar Named Swampy – The Sequel

Scan the QR code below to check for updates, previews, and exclusive content.
Who knows? You might unlock a secret before anyone else.

Coming Soon...

Or visit:
www.u-nam.com/the-13th-note

ABOUT THIS EDITION

Published by **Swampy Tales Publishing**

A division of **Swampy Tales Entertainment**

First Edition: 2025

© 2025 **Emmanuel "U-Nam" Abiteboul & Swampy Tales Publishing**

For any inquiries regarding **U-Nam, The Sweet Bandits,** or **Swampy Tales Publishing,** please contact:

contact@skytownrecords.com

For more information, visit:

www.swampytales.com

Printed in the United States of America

Swampy Tales